Perris, California

Perris, California

A NOVEL

RACHEL STARK

PENGUIN PRESS

NEW YORK

2024

PENGUIN PRESS
An imprint of Penguin Random House LLC
penguinrandomhouse.com

LIBRARY OF CONGRESS CATALOGING-IN-PUBLICATION DATA
Names: Stark, Rachel, 1985- author.
Title: Perris, California : a novel / Rachel Stark.
Description: New York : Penguin Press, 2024.
Identifiers: LCCN 2023035359 (print) | LCCN 2023035360 (ebook) |
ISBN 9780593656204 (hardcover) | ISBN 9780593656211 (ebook)
Subjects: LCGFT: Novels.
Classification: LCC PS3619.T37377 P47 2024 (print) |
LCC PS3619.T37377 (ebook) | DDC 813/.6—dc23/eng/20231102
LC record available at https://lccn.loc.gov/2023035359
LC ebook record available at https://lccn.loc.gov/2023035360

Printed in the United States of America
1 3 5 7 9 10 8 6 4 2

Designed by Amanda Dewey

For all the women who have supported,
encouraged, and mothered me

Perris, California

1992

Angie

It was sometime in the middle of the night when Angie woke to a sharp pain in her chest. She put a hand there. She was waiting to see if it would pass when she heard a tapping on her bedroom window. She moved her hand from her chest and shook Buck's shoulder. The tapping got louder. "Buck," Angie whispered. "Buck, wake up."

There was the sound of something snapping underfoot outside, and Buck was on his feet. He picked up the flashlight on his nightstand and took his rifle out from under the bed. He and Angie went to the window. He had the light and rifle in hand and ready when he gave the nod to Angie, signaling her to pull back the curtain.

Tessa, Henry's girl, was standing there squinting into the light. The side of her face was blown out so bad that the skin was pulled taut across the bridge of her nose and the eye on that side was shiny-wet and pinched shut.

"Jesus," Angie breathed. She and Buck ran outside to her. The poor thing was leaning up against the house to keep from falling over. She didn't have shoes on, and her feet were torn up and bleeding. She was bent and holding one arm in close with the other. Buck stayed froze to the earth a yard away from the girl while Angie walked to her. Tessa was taking in quick, shallow breaths. Her open eye was big and showing all its white. Angie had seen that same look once before in her neighbor's colt when it was pinned down and straining against four grown men; its leg was broken in three places after a bad jump, and there wasn't no coming back from that. Angie walked up to Tessa slow and steady like she'd done with the horse before she put a bullet between its eyes.

"Easy, baby," she said. Tessa let a sharp exhale out her nose. "It's alright now, honey. You're alright." She looked busted up even worse up close. Worse than any of her boys or Buck had ever been after any schoolyard scrap or bar fight. Angie didn't let her face show the sick she was starting to feel. "Honey, would it be alright if I have Buck carry you inside so I can help you?"

Tessa made no move or change in expression. Angie slowly reached her hand out and touched the side of Tessa's face that wasn't broke. "No one's gonna hurt you here. You're safe now. I promise."

Tessa gave a small nod, and Buck came over. When he lifted Tessa, she let out something between a groan and a gurgle. "Easy with her, Buck," Angie said.

She had Buck lay her down on the sofa at an angle so the girl would be propped up enough for Angie to get a good look at her. "Where you hurting most, honey?" Angie said. Tessa didn't speak.

2

Maybe with the side of her face like that, she couldn't. "I'm gonna look you over a bit, okay? That way I can help." Angie got down on her knees and closer to the girl. Tessa had her right arm tucked in like a bent wing. It was hanging separate and heavy from her shoulder joint, the way overcooked meat hangs off a bone. With the way she was breathing shallow and the way they had found her leaning outside, Angie guessed there might be a couple cracked ribs beneath the dislocated shoulder. She wasn't gonna move her now to check. The girl was hurting bad enough already.

Angie continued looking her over, placing gentle hands on the girl's body as she went. Her eyes stopped when they hit the pee blooming on the sofa cushion between Tessa's legs. Tessa's wide, flat stare finally broke when Angie looked up and met her eye after seeing that she'd wet her pants. Tessa's lip turned out, and she started a noiseless cry. Angie got up off her knees quick to sweep her mother's quilt off the family hope chest and wrap it around Tessa before Buck could see what the girl had started crying for. She gently hugged Tessa to her.

"You're okay now," she whispered near Tessa's ear. She felt the girl shaking then. She spoke over her shoulder. "Buck, honey, go get us a big bag of ice and a dish towel, wet with cool water. Bring those pills for your back and something to wash them down with." Buck nodded. "Be quick, honey, and don't you let Henry come near that door, not yet. Understand?"

Angie let Henry in after she'd helped the girl into her softest sweat suit. She cleaned up the girl's face as best she could. She and Henry would take Tessa to the emergency room as soon as the pills kicked in and the girl felt ready to be moved again. She left Henry in the room with Tessa and stood outside the door talking in hushed tones with Buck.

"I think you better go pay Wayne a visit and collect Tessa's things. She's going to be staying with us from now on." Buck nodded. "She wants some leather purse from under her bed awful bad. Don't leave there without it."

Buck went to wake their two oldest boys, Gordy and Benny, to bring them along. When he came back downstairs, Angie gave him what little information she'd been able to pull from the girl. She kept secret the parts Tessa had made her swear to leave between just them.

"And, Buck, it may be the case we already have a dead body on our hands over there. You do what needs doing, but I think it best if we don't make it two."

Buck

Wayne's place was a two-mile straight shot from their ranch as the crow flew, but with the way the dirt roads took them, it was usually about a fifteen-minute drive. That night, Buck got him and his boys there in seven. Thinking about what Angie had told him made his foot heavy.

Buck pounded on the door until he could hear someone coming and then pounded some more.

"Wait a goddamn second," Buck heard Wayne say from inside as he undid the dead bolt. Soon as Wayne opened the door, Buck gave him a solid blow to the stomach, and Wayne crumpled to the ground. After a ten-second count, Wayne sucked in a deep breath and rolled to his side in a fetal position. "What in the hell you do that for?" he said, coughing.

Buck had known Wayne's sorry ass for most of his life. They were both born and raised in Perris. They'd gone to grade school together. Wayne had been a smart and weasely little fuck back then too. He was a drunk now, and he got by in life by cheating or leeching off good people. Buck knew the only reason Wayne had let Tessa stick around after her mama split was for the government check he received on account of her being there. Buck hadn't imagined things were great for Tessa living there with Wayne and his dipshit boy, but he didn't think the son of a bitch had it in him to allow the girl to be beat halfway to death like that. Wayne's son had done it this time around, Angie had said, but Wayne had let it happen, and the way Angie had heard it, Wayne had taken a liking

5

to roughing Tessa up in the years since her mama left. Tessa had just never told no one about it. Wayne was smart enough not to get himself caught by taking it too far, the way his son had. Buck wished Tessa would have come to him before she had to get it so bad. He'd've put an end to things sooner.

"Where's Tessa's room?" Buck said.

"What the fuck you care?" Wayne pushed himself up to sit with his back against the entryway wall.

"You're talking like a man who's tired of having his teeth, Wayne." Buck turned to Benny and Gordy behind him. "Pick him up," he said. Benny and Gordy lifted Wayne's short and solid body up from the floor and held him under his armpits. One on each side. Buck gave him another hard punch to the gut. Wayne tried to crumple again, but Buck's boys, who were strong, grown men now, kept him up. Buck stepped on Wayne's bare foot and ground the heel of his boot into the bones there. He grabbed Wayne's collar and jerked him in close. "Where's her things?"

Wayne let out a groan. Buck stepped off his foot and let him go. Wayne took in a deep breath and shook his head. "Second door on the left. Take her shit. I don't care. You're doing me a favor," he said. A sick, sour, wet cloud of Wayne's beer breath stuck to Buck's face like a hot morning fog.

Buck didn't like Wayne's face being so close to his. He didn't like spending time in Wayne's dirty-ass house neither. He wanted to leave, and Wayne was drawing things out. Buck was trying to keep things from getting too rough. He was trying to show some restraint and set an example for his boys, but he'd had just about as much as he could stand of Wayne's bullshit, and images of that poor girl's busted face kept flashing in his mind. If he didn't teach Wayne a lesson now, he wasn't sure Wayne'd ever get what was coming to him. The world didn't seem to work that way. Assholes like Wayne got off scot-free all the time. The way Buck saw it, he had an obligation. He turned to his boys.

"Get them duffel bags out the truck and get her things. Be quick," Buck said. His boys stood still, knowing that their father had him a temper and that it had gotten the best of him and ended with trouble on more than one occasion. Buck's need to keep others in line had wound him up in jail twice now, and his boys had suffered for it.

"I ain't going to do nothing stupid. Get," Buck said. Benny let go. He went over to the other side of Wayne, where Gordy was still holding him, and pulled his brother away by the elbow. Wayne jerked his arm free and tried to straighten himself up. The boys went for the truck.

Buck started to undo the buttons at his wrists. He folded the sleeves of his flannel back in clean, straight lines. Wayne lifted his chin after hiking up his pants and smoothing out the front of his shirt. His face jumped alert like his bowels had just let loose.

"Now hold on a second," Wayne said. "What did that dumb bitch tell you? She's a liar, you know. Just like her whore of a mother." Buck grabbed him by the thick, coarse hair on top of his head and began to drag him toward the back door. Wayne reached up for the hand at his head and held there while he tried to get his feet under him, but Buck was moving too fast. He opened the back slider and threw Wayne down the steps so that he went tumbling over himself onto the dirt porch.

"Get up," Buck said.

"Now come on," Wayne said. "I done right by that girl giving her a roof over her head all these years. She ain't even blood, and I done that."

7

"I ain't going to ask you again. On your feet. Show me some of that tough guy stuff you got. Or do you save that just for little girls?"

"She must've told you some real lies to have you out here in the middle of the night like this, Buck. I'm telling you. I ain't done nothing out of line. Never."

"She didn't have to tell me nothing, Wayne. Her broked-up face was enough for me to make the trip. Truth is, I'm glad to have an excuse. I been wanting to pay your sorry ass a visit for a while now." Wayne opened his mouth to speak again, and Buck began to let him have it. He'd hardly touched Wayne before he was on the ground again.

"Up," Buck said.

"Wait, wait." Wayne was on all fours in the dirt trying to crawl away.

"Up, goddammit. I'm gonna teach you a lesson good, so you don't forget." Wayne continued to try and scramble away. "It'll be worse for you on the ground. I can guarantee you that. Get up on your feet like a man." Wayne acted like he hadn't heard him and continued his pathetic crawl. It lit Buck up something fierce.

"Suit yourself." Buck took three quick paces and kicked Wayne in the ribs. Wayne dropped flat on his stomach. Buck reached down for his shoulder and flipped him over on his back so he could get to him better. Buck grabbed ahold of his collar and lifted him enough to throw three hard punches to his face. Wayne was feebly grasping at Buck's arms when Buck gave him a headbutt that sent Wayne's neck dropping back limp. Buck felt a hand on his shoulder.

"Dad," Benny said, "I think he's had enough." Buck nodded. He let Wayne fall to the dirt and sat back on his heels to catch his breath. Gordy went to check on Wayne.

"Get your sorry-ass hands off me," Wayne said. He batted Gordy away but made no move to stand up. Buck knew he was fine. Wayne had probably caught ass-whuppings worse than this plenty of times before. Guys like Wayne, low-life cheats, learned early on how to take a punch. It come with their line of work.

"You had that coming for a long time now, Wayne. You be grateful I got my boys here keeping me from giving you what you deserve. You thank your fuckin' lucky stars." Buck stood up. "I'm alright," he said to his boys, who had moved to stand beside him. "I said I'm alright." Buck shrugged Benny's hand off his shoulder. "I ain't going to do no more. You got her things? The purse?" They nodded. "Good." Buck sighed. He put his hands on his hips and spat on the ground.

"You have until sunup to get your miserable ass out of the state. If I were you, I'd stop feeling sorry for myself and start packing. Ain't no talking your way out of this one." Buck and his boys took a few steps toward the door before Buck turned back.

"Your son had an accident in the hayloft of the barn on Wilkinson's old property. I hear he ain't doing so good. I'd look into it if I were you. And, Wayne, if he's still breathing when you get to him, he ain't welcome in this valley no more neither.

ONE

1999

Tessa

Tessa knocked on the Garrisons' trailer door, hiked Ruby up on her hip, and watched the clouds of steam coming out of her mouth. Luke bent the blinds in the window by the door with two big fingers. He met her eyes and gave a nod before he let the blinds go, called for Carly, and opened the door.

"Get in quick so the cold don't follow you," he said. Tessa stepped inside and slid Ruby off her hip to the floor. Ruby started to run for the calico cat curled up on the couch across the room. Tessa caught her by the hood of her jacket and tugged her boots off. Luke went back to the kitchen. "Carly," he hollered again.

"I'm right here," she said, folding back the collapsible door that separated their room from the rest of the place. Carly brushed her wispy blond hair back into a ponytail. "Hey, sugar," she said. She leaned in and pressed her lips against Tessa's cheekbone. "Preston back at school today, then?"

"Well, I figured if he was feeling good enough to come wake me at the crack of dawn to ask for pancakes, he was fit for school. He has just a bit of a runny nose left is all."

Luke came in from the kitchen with his thermos and lunch box. "You girls behave," he said. He swatted Carly on the ass, then bent to give her a kiss.

"Bring home coffee filters. We're nearly out," she called after him. Luke gave a thumbs-up over his shoulder and shut the door behind him. The roar of his truck followed a moment after.

"How many kids you have coming today?" Tessa said.

"Just the one. Trudy called this morning to ask if I could watch her boy for a few hours while she and her brother head out to Hesperia to see about getting work at the poultry plant."

"That's a drive. Hardly worth the check after paying for gas, isn't it?"

"Something is better than nothing."

Tessa clicked her tongue and shook her head. "It's a lucky thing Luke and Henry manage to keep steady work."

Carly nodded. "Ain't that the truth," she said. They both went quiet. Then Carly clapped her hands. "Enough of that. Take your coat off there, girl. Let's see that little belly of yours." Tessa flushed a little. She still sometimes forgot she was pregnant or, rather, put it out of mind so much that when someone reminded her of the fact, it would catch her off guard. A wave of guilt sloshed around in the small space of her stomach that felt like it was still just hers. She gave a weak smile and undid her coat. "Come on," Carly said. Tessa pulled her coat open and off and stood in her sweater. Her seven-month-full belly had started to pop out a few weeks back. "Oh God, isn't that so cute," Carly said and placed a gentle hand on her. "Another baby." She sighed and stared down at the bump her hand was still resting on. Her smile trembled, and her eyes welled up.

"Oh, Carly, I'm sorry."

"Don't you be sorry." She wiped at her cheeks and smiled. "I'm happy for you."

"What about seeing that doctor you looked up?"

"Luke won't hear of it. He says if it happens, it happens. If not, just the two of us is enough. He never had his heart set on kids like I did. He's happy the way things are. Not like your Henry, who's wanting to make enough to have his own baseball team." Carly nudged Tessa's elbow and let out a fragile laugh. Tessa forced another smile.

"I'd be happy with just one. We were married at least two years before you and Hen. Wasn't it? And we were eligible to be making babies awhile before that." Carly went quiet and fidgeted with the hem at the bottom edge of her shirt. Tessa reached over and took ahold of Carly's hand. Carly held the grasp tight for a moment. Then she sniffed and let go. "Thank you, honey," she said. "I have some of that spiced tea. You want a cup?"

"Sounds like heaven."

"Well, okay. Some tea, then." Carly slapped her thighs and made for the kitchen.

Tessa went over to where Ruby was sitting on the floor. She was petting the cat and talking to herself like she sometimes would when she was playing. She was using a gravelly voice for what Tessa guessed was the bad-guy part in the story she was spinning. She was petting that cat awful hard.

"Gentle," Tessa said. She lifted Ruby's hand off the cat, and Ruby pulled away from her.

"Stop it, Mama," she said and went back to stroking the cat.

"Okay, just softer."

Carly set two mugs on the coffee table. She patted the couch cushion beside her. "Now, tell me everything. Like how come it's going on a month since you last come to visit and I haven't had the good fortune to catch you in town neither."

"You know how time can get away from you. Between the kids and Henry and Henry's mama, I hardly have a minute to think. She tried to guilt me for coming over here today as it is. I had to promise we'd have Sunday dinner at her house for the next month just to borrow the truck." Tessa looked over to where Ruby was sitting to make sure she wasn't paying attention and lowered her voice. "God, I feel like I can hardly take a full breath living in that tiny trailer on her property."

"You and Henry having any luck looking for a place?"

"Nope. Every place we gone to see, Henry says ain't big enough. He says that when we move, he wants it to be to a place where we have room to grow. We've been stepping over each other and the kids in that trailer for going on six years, but he's in no rush and thinks I shouldn't be neither. He thinks it's a gift having his mama so close to help. Meanwhile, I can't so much as let out a fart without Angie coming over and knocking on my door to tell me how I could've made it smell sweeter."

Carly snorted and choked on the tea she was sipping. She set the cup down and coughed until she was laughing hard. She pushed Tessa and leaned back into the couch, wiping tears from the corners of her eyes. "Stop it," she said.

"I mean it," Tessa said. "I can't do anything without her knowing about it. You know, she found out about me being pregnant this time before I even had the chance to tell Henry, before I even had a chance to confirm it for myself. She told Henry she hadn't noticed me buying my cottons the last couple times we drove in for groceries."

"No," Carly said. Her mouth was hanging open now.

"Yes. She's a meddler and a control freak, and I can't wait to be in a position where we don't have to depend on her so much. She's just as baby hungry as Henry. You'd think she'd be content with the four she made on her own. It's no wonder Benny and Gordy moved away." Tessa stopped. She turned to Carly. "I'm sorry to be complaining and running my mouth about babies like that."

"Honey, that woman can be a terror," Carly said. "She means well, but Lord knows I couldn't put up with it. It's a blessing Luke's mama lives all the way over in Beaumont. Don't never tell him I said that. He *looooves* his mama just as much as Henry loves his. We live in the land of mama's boys here."

"Sure seems that way," Tessa said.

"Listen, me and Luke will keep on keeping our eyes and ears open for a place for you and Henry. You just hang in there." She patted Tessa's knee. "Something will turn up."

Tessa's front pants pocket started vibrating and lighting up. She stood, pulled her flip phone out, and opened it. She recognized the number. "Shit." After giving a few short replies, she said, "I'll be there as soon as I can."

"The sooner, the better," the school secretary said.

"I understand that. Thank you." Tessa closed the phone.

"What was that all about?" Carly said.

"Well, things just keep getting better, don't they?"

"What?"

Tessa sighed. "They found lice on Preston's head."

Carly stood up and backed away. "Oh Lord, that stuff catches like wildfire. You sure you and Ruby don't have it?"

"Well, I don't think so."

"Your head been itchin'?"

"No. Why are you acting like I brung the plague with me? They're just some tiny white bugs," Tessa said.

"I know that, but those bugs are bad for business. I can't have the children I'm watching leave here with lice. I'll lose what little business I've managed to drum up."

"I hadn't thought of that. I guess we better go." Tessa stood and went over to where her and Ruby's stuff was piled on the chair.

"Well, shit. Shit, shit. I wanted to have the day with you. Now the only thing I've got to look forward to is that Miller boy coming by. Last time I watched him, he couldn't keep his finger out of his nose. I found little green boogers wiped on the arm of our recliner," Carly said. Tessa laughed. "I'm not kidding you. There was a whole mess of them stuck to the armrest. He must have run to that chair every chance I wasn't looking."

"Better keep an eye on him this time, then," Tessa said.

"Guess so," Carly said. Tessa looked up from sliding a beanie onto Ruby's head to see Carly making a weepy face.

"We'll come back to visit next week for sure," Tessa said.

"I just miss you, is all." Carly could be tenderhearted. She'd cry most of the times Tessa left, regardless of the amount of time Tessa'd spent there. "And it's lonely here, you know? Luke gets to hang out with the boys at work all day while I'm stuck here cleaning boogers off the furniture and talking to myself." Carly dropped her chin to her chest and crossed her arms. Tessa hugged her close and let Carly lean on her shoulder.

"I'll be fine." Carly pulled away. She dabbed at her face with the sleeve of her shirt. "You two get going, and take your bugs with you."

Tessa sat with the truck running to warm the engine. Ruby was content for the moment playing with her dolls in the booster seat behind Tessa in the truck's extended cab. When the engine was warm enough, Tessa gave a short honk of the horn and pulled away. She'd go to the drugstore before picking Preston up. If she stalled long enough, Preston would get his free school lunch. He'd be okay waiting that long.

She turned into the Thrifty's parking lot and maneuvered her way around potholes to a parking spot close to the entrance. Inside, she made her way to the first-aid aisle and started looking for the medicated shampoo. After checking there, she searched the aisles on either side. She gave up searching for the shampoo on her own somewhere in the jock-itch section. She was looking for someone in a red vest to ask for help when she heard a voice behind her.

"Tessa?" She spun around. The shock felt like someone had poured an ice bucket over her head. She sucked in a breath and felt her skin go damp and cold.

"Mel" is all she could get out.

"I thought that was you." Mel had a big, warm grin on her face. Her eyes pinched shut and nearly disappeared with her huge smile, the way they used to, and the same dimples made divots in her cheeks, just beyond the corners of her mouth.

Tessa heard Ruby say something, and then she felt her trying to pull her hand away. It was enough to bring Tessa out of her momentary daze. She held Ruby's hand tighter. "I heard you were away at school," she said.

"I was. I got a degree and certificate." Mel pointed to the badge pinned to her vest that read FRIENDLY PHARMACIST TECHNICIAN. "Turns out this is where I could find work, and it's good to be close to home with Doreen getting older."

Tessa nodded. "That's something, getting your degree and all." Her mouth was dry, and her words felt clumsy, like they were sticking to her tongue. She tried to swallow, but she was coming up short on saliva. "Your mama must be so proud."

"Oh, Doreen is." Mel laughed. "Everyone within earshot knows just how proud she is, and I'm sure they're all tired of hearing about it." She was talking so easily, like their running into each other right then was no big thing. Tessa was thinking about Mel getting a degree and about how she looked the same—maybe a bit more grown up but just as pretty—when she realized Mel had stopped talking and was waiting on a response.

"They're all glad to hear about it, I'm sure. And glad to have you back." Tessa reached out her hand and lightly tapped Mel's forearm.

"Maybe," Mel said.

Tessa suddenly felt aware of how she must look to Mel right then. The tired she wore on her face. She hadn't washed her hair in more than a week on account of the cold weather and the water heater giving out. She sure had changed. She tucked her hair behind her ears and fidgeted with her beanie, pulling it a little lower over her forehead in hopes of covering some of the wear of the past few years.

"And who is this?" Mel said.

"Ruby, say hi to my friend." Ruby stopped yanking on Tessa's hand and went shy. She moved behind her mama's legs.

"Hi, Ruby," Mel said.

"She's bashful only when I don't want her to be."

Mel nodded. "I was that way growing up too." She looked down at the squeaking wheel on a shopping cart as a customer pushed it past them. Then she lifted her chin and met Tessa's eyes. "So, you and Henry, then?"

"Yeah. We got married summer after high school."

"Another one coming?"

Tessa felt her face flush and hoped it wasn't showing none. She put a hand on her belly. "Yeah, and I have another one a couple years older than this one too." Tessa nodded in Ruby's direction.

"You've been busy."

"Seems like it, don't it?" They spent a long pause looking at each other. Tessa tried to read Mel but couldn't.

"Well, anything I can help you find?"

"Uh, yeah, as a matter of fact. My oldest, Preston, picked up lice. I'm looking for a shampoo to get rid of them."

"Motherhood." Mel laughed.

"Tell me about it. Wait, you're not a— Do you have children?"

"Me? No, I'm not a mother." Tessa sensed an edge in her voice. Mel bent down and stood back up with the box she'd grabbed. "This is the one you want."

"Thanks." Tessa took the box of lice shampoo and waited to see if there would be more conversation. When it seemed there wouldn't be, she spoke up. "Well, we better get going."

"I should get back to it here," Mel said.

Tessa was stumbling around in her head over conflicting feelings of wanting to keep the conversation going and needing it to end. She shook the box and said, "Thanks for this."

"Anytime," Mel said. She gave a wave, then turned and walked back down the fluorescent-lit aisle.

"It was good to see you," Tessa called after her. Mel turned. She stood there a second. Then she flashed Tessa that smile of hers and continued on her way. Tessa tried to stem the electric current buzzing through her. She was so distracted by the feeling she let Ruby sneak a Ring Pop onto the conveyor belt at the register.

"Pick out a treat for your brother too," she said. "He'll need a little something sweet."

Ruby clapped her hands together and bounced in front of the candy display. She tossed an Abba-Zaba bar, Preston's favorite, so that it landed next to the Ring Pop and then sparkled up at her mama. Tessa put her hand on Ruby's head and couldn't help but feel some of that sparkle too.

1989

Tessa

Mel was Tessa's first and only real friend she ever had in high school. Neither of them fit in very well there—Tessa because she wore her stepbrother's hand-me-downs and was bony and severely quiet, Mel because she had transferred from another school and gotten herself suspended her first week at Perris High for punching a guy in the throat so hard it crushed his windpipe and the paramedics had to be called. Tessa had thought it served the guy right. He had come up behind Mel and goosed her when she was bending down to grab her backpack. She turned around and clunked him right in the throat like it was nothing. He dropped down to the ground, flopped around like a fish, and started making this hoarse gasping sound, like he was trying to breathe through a clogged-up straw. In response, Mel casually swung her backpack over her shoulder, stepped around his thrashing body, and went on her way.

The first year of high school without Mel there had been painful. Tessa was tall and lanky for her age. While all the other girls seemed to be getting curves, Tessa stayed flat as a board, front and back. It was just as well to her; she liked the invisibility her plainness offered. It was that way with the boys—at least for a while, anyway. The girls saw her just fine. They didn't like how she kept to herself. They took her for thinking she was better than them on account of her minding her own business.

The second week of sophomore year, Mel transferred to Perris

High, and life got a lot better for Tessa. She had noticed Mel right away. The classes weren't so big, and Mel had stood out in the way she seemed to radiate an energy of being pissed off at the world. Mel took the bus to Perris High. Tessa had seen her getting off at the C Street stop and figured she must have come from somewhere closer to town, where there were paved roads and street signals and places you could get to easily. Tessa came from farther. She lived out in the sticks, where people were more spread out. There were a couple ranches that did okay out there. The rest of the land was spotted by small homes and trailers. She had to take two different buses and walk some in order to get to school every day. Past the sticks, even farther out, was the middle of nowheres, which was mostly known for brush fires and meth labs and the kinds of people who kept to themselves and didn't want others coming near their property.

Seeing Mel in class that first day, Tessa couldn't understand why she'd gone through the trouble of changing schools. Wherever it was she'd come from had to have been better than their dump of a school.

They first spoke later that day. Mel was assigned the PE locker next to Tessa's. They undressed and dressed in silence. It probably would have gone on that way for a long time had Sandy Nelson not walked by to harass Tessa. Sandy lived in town and thought her shit didn't stink because her family had a little money and could afford to buy her new clothes and other wastes of cash, like the big, stupid-looking neon-green plastic earrings she was wearing that day.

"Look at the granny panties Tessa's got on," Sandy hollered to the group of girls primping in the adjoining bathroom mirror. Tessa reached for her gym sweatpants and tried to slip into them before the others could come, but they caught the hook meant for hanging book bags and clothes inside the locker, and she wasn't fast enough unhooking them. She pulled the pants on as swiftly as she could, but the other girls saw the droopy, elastic-shot cotton underwear before she managed to get her sweats up.

They had been her mother's underwear. Amber Jean had left them behind when she took off years before. Several pairs of underwear, a worn leather purse, a long jean skirt, a teal cotton shirt, and a white blouse—that was all her mother had left behind when she went. Tessa had grown out of all the girls' clothing she had from when she was young and her mama was still around to take her shopping. Wayne, her stepfather, never let her buy any replacements, not even from the Goodwill. He'd say she was an ungrateful bitch when she'd ask for clothes or anything else. He said she ought to be happy with the roof over her head and the castoffs her stepbrother had grew out of. He said she was lucky he let her stick around. Tessa knew luck didn't have nothing to do with it. Her mama had made Wayne sign legal guardianship papers when they married, and because of that he received a check every month that kept his sorry ass afloat.

The girls went on standing there and laughing and joking about the underwear as Tessa zipped up her bag and shoved it inside her locker. "Did you see all the bruises she's got on her legs?" Sandy said. "Are you sick or something? She must have a disease." She made a disgusted face. Tessa saw Mel straighten up from bending to reach into her locker.

"What do you have against this girl?" Mel said. Sandy shot a look at her like she'd just realized she was standing there.

"Look at that. It can speak." Sandy turned her head to laugh with the girls behind her. She didn't see Mel coming.

In a movement so quick it was barely perceivable, Mel threaded her fingers up the back of Sandy's head. She took hold of her hair and yanked her head down hard and fast to the bench in between the lockers so that she was pressing one of Sandy's rosy cheeks into its wooden surface.

"I can do a lot more than speak," Mel said. One of the girls ran to get their PE teacher. The others stood frozen in fear. Mel put a hand over Sandy's mouth to stop her from screaming. She bent and whispered something inaudible in Sandy's ear and let her lips hover there for a moment. Then she lifted her mouth away so the others could hear. "We hunky-dory, then?" Sandy nodded eagerly against the bench. Mel looked hard at the other girls circled around them. Wide-eyed, they nodded too. Mel gave a final jerk of Sandy's hair before letting her go. She patted Sandy on her shoulder and turned back to her locker to finish dressing. Mrs. Clark ran in from around the corner.

"What's going on here?" she asked. Mel continued dressing, but Sandy was stock-still where she stood. "Hello, people," Mrs. Clark said. "Yoo-hoo!" She waved her hand in front of Sandy.

Sandy blinked her eyes a few times. "Nothing," she said.

"Tina here tells me—"

"We were just playing," Sandy said. It was plain to see that Mrs. Clark didn't believe her but even plainer to see that she didn't care.

"Well, quit it, and get your asses out on the field, or I'll sign you all up for Saturday school," Mrs. Clark said. The girls scattered. Tessa leaned into the locker behind her. The cool metal pressed against her skin.

"What did you whisper?" Tessa said.

Mel flashed a big smile. "You don't have to worry about her or any of those girls bothering you anymore." She tugged on her lock to make sure it was closed, then walked away.

1999

Tessa

Tessa's heart sank when she walked into the elementary school office and saw what the two children had been pointing and giggling at from outside the office window. Preston, her boy, was sitting by himself with a plastic bag taped over his head in a chair in the little waiting area for all to see. He was swinging his legs and staring down at his folded hands. He lifted his chin when her and Ruby come in. The plastic bag atop his head wafted above him with the movement. The school secretary didn't acknowledge their arrival. Instead, she tapped the nail of her pointer finger against the mouse and stared at the screen in front of her. Tessa went to Preston.

He winced when she peeled back the tape on his forehead. "I'm sorry, baby." She swept the bag off his head and dropped it on the ground. "How long they been making you wait out here with this bag on your head?" Preston didn't respond. His eyes brimmed with tears. She hugged him to her and kissed the top of his head. "Hey, Pres, Ruby got a treat for you at the store. Didn't you, Ruby?" There was an imprint of snot on her sweater when Preston pulled his head away from her stomach. Ruby nodded, grinned, pulled the Abba-Zaba from of her back pocket, and held it out so her Ring Pop could be admired. Preston wiped his nose on his sleeve and took the bar from her. "You two go sit where I can see you."

Tessa stood in front of the reception desk. The woman behind it

25

still had not taken her attention from the screen. "Excuse me," Tessa said.

"Yes," the woman answered, barely glancing at Tessa. Tessa felt heat bubbling up from a deep reservoir within her.

"It's Ruth Ann, right?" Tessa said. She recognized Ruth from school days. She was the younger, pudgy-faced sibling of one of Tessa's classmates.

"It is," Ruth said and went back to her screen, as if that settled things.

Tessa leaned in close. "What in the hell is wrong with you?" This caught Ruth's attention. Her eyes grew large, and her mouth opened. "I'm just asking because I can't understand why someone with their full mental capacity would leave a child sitting out in front where everyone can see him with a plastic bag taped to his goddamn head. I can't understand why a person would want a six-year-old to feel shamed like that. You'd have to be a certified moron or an evil bitch to do something like that."

The woman pursed her lips. "You can't talk to me that way."

"The words are coming out just fine. And I'll tell you what else, Ruth Ann. You're real lucky I believe in setting a good example for my children. Otherwise, I'd climb over this desk and teach you a lesson. I'd start by ripping off those nasty press-on nails you got on one at a time. Next, I'd see about wiping that snooty look you got right off your face." Tessa stared hard at her and let the words land. Then she leaned away, gathered some composure, and walked over to where her children were sitting.

Just before they got to the door, the secretary called after her: "I'm reporting you, you hear? And the principal said not to bring him back until he's got a doctor's note that says he's bug-free."

Tessa spun around, pointed a finger at her, and gave a crazy-eyed look that made Ruth Ann sit down and hush up quick.

Angie was out watering her geraniums when they pulled onto the property's dirt driveway. She dropped the hose, waved, and started for them. Tessa had just set the emergency brake when Angie arrived at her window, beaming. Tessa said a silent affirmation and asked God for strength, then opened the driver's-side door. Angie barely moved enough for her to squeeze out.

"What are you all doing home so early?" Angie said.

"Hi, Angie," Tessa said. She opened the cab's door and started to undo Ruby's booster seat.

"Preston's got bugs on his head," Ruby announced as Tessa lifted her out of the truck. Preston scrunched up his face and gave Ruby a pinch on the arm that sent her yelling and chasing after him.

Angie grabbed ahold of Preston's shirt so he couldn't get away. "Now what's going on here?" she said. "Don't go pinching your little sister like that. You know better."

"Ruby," Tessa called, "get back over here." Ruby sulked back over to her mama led by her stuck-out bottom lip. "He pinched me," she said, holding out her arm to show a little pink mark on her bicep. Tessa rubbed it and hoisted Ruby into her arms. "You'll be okay."

Tessa turned back to see the look on Angie's face. The look she'd grown accustomed to. The look that both accused and pitied her. "What's this all about?" Angie asked.

"Preston picked up lice at school," Tessa said. Angie's eyebrows rose. "I bought some shampoo for it. We're heading in to sort things out now." Tessa extended her hand for Preston to grab ahold of it.

"You can't use that shampoo on his head. It's poison." Preston looked up at Tessa, alarm on his face.

"It's poison for the bugs. It's fine for the kid," Tessa said.

"No, no, no. None of that junk. Not on my grandchild's head. I have a jar full of mayonnaise in the fridge. I'll goop that on his head, and in a couple hours, all the lice will have been smothered. We'll pick the eggs out with a comb. Your hair will be nice and soft after." Angie bent and affectionately pinched Preston's cheek. Then she turned back to Tessa. "I'll have to clean the beddings and check yours and Ruby's heads, and Henry's head when he gets home too. We'll have this little problem solved before dinner. You get in there and strip the beds, and take anything you all have been wearing on your heads and put them in trash bags for me to wash and dry extra hot at the house. I'll be back with the mayonnaise in a jiff." She was scooting away back to her place before Tessa could reply. Both children looked at their mother.

"Well, you heard her. Let's get to it."

Three hours later, Preston was pushing a toy car around on the floor with a jar's worth of Hellmann's mayo spread on his head like cake frosting. The process had delighted Ruby. Tessa had to keep pulling her hand away from Preston's head to keep her fingers out of it. Ruby had eventually lost interest and was settled now, content with her crayons and coloring book at the fold-down kitchen table. Angie had taken the bags of bedding and the truck back up to her place a while ago.

Tessa sighed with the relief of feeling like she could take a moment for herself. She walked to her bed and flopped down on her back. Then, not feeling like she had enough space, she pushed up onto her side and pulled the curtain that divided the bed from the rest of the trailer shut. She lay back down and closed her eyes to rest.

She thought of Mel. What a thing it was to see her after all this time. How strange to think of the two of them back then, now. It hadn't been that long since high school, really, but she was a whole different person now, or she had a whole different life, at least. It was hard to know if there was much of a difference between the two. She guessed you had to be a different person if you had a different life.

She felt her pulse grow strong up in her neck, the way it would when she lay on her back. She rolled to her side, and the throb went away. She reached for the remote control on the bed and curled around her belly. Sure enough, Joel Osteen was giving a sermon. He had himself worked up preaching about the power of prayer and intention. Tessa didn't believe in God or the devil or any of it, but she liked the idea of being able to change things with thoughts and prayers. Because it was the only channel they got and because he always seemed to be on it, Tessa had become very familiar with the doctrine of the power of prayer and intention. It hadn't done her much good so far, but it kept her mind occupied when she needed the distraction.

She clicked the television off mid-sermon when she heard Henry's truck out front. The kids heard it too. They rushed him when he came in the front door. Tessa stayed put and swallowed a laugh when Henry asked, "What've you got on your head there, bud?" She heard the kitchen sink running and imagined Henry was rinsing mayo off himself as best he could.

"Where's your mother?" he asked after turning off the faucet.

"She's laying in bed," Ruby said.

"Laying in bed?!" Henry said in his teasing voice. He pulled back the curtain. "What's Mom laying in bed for?"

Tessa lifted her head, rolled her eyes over her shoulder at him, and flopped her head back down. Henry unbuttoned his shirt and threw it on the pile of dirty clothes in the corner, then lay down behind her. He hugged her in close. She could feel his warm breath on her neck and smell the stink of the day's work on his skin.

"Did you know our son has a head full of mayonnaise?"

"That was your mother's idea. I wanted to use the shampoo."

"Oh, I know it was. Me, Gordy, Nate, and Benny all got lice the same time. The house smelled like a sandwich shop for a week. It worked, though."

"Great. Your mama wants you to head up to her place after you wash up so she can inspect your scalp. Me and Ruby already had the honor."

"I know. She called on my way home."

"Of course she did."

"She wants us up there for dinner."

"I'm not hungry."

"Come on, you gotta eat, Tess. Keep that little belly of yours growing." He patted her outer thigh and hopped up. Moments later, she heard the shower running and Henry yelping in the cold water.

She didn't go up to dinner with them. Henry had relented when she'd said she was tired and needed a break. She stayed and ate sliced bologna and buttered toast instead. After dinner, she peeled off her clothes and got into the shower. The cold water shocked her skin. When she felt she could bear it, she held her head under the spray. She shut the water off to soap up with the good-smelling bodywash and shampoo she kept hidden from Henry and the kids. She worked the soapy washcloth from her feet up her legs. When she got to her tummy, she paused and let the cloth rest stretched out and smoothed against her skin there. She put a hand on either side of her belly and looked down at the mound between them. "How we doing in there, buddy?" she said in a soft voice.

Tessa felt shy and remorseful when she spoke to her baby now. She knew it remembered what she'd asked of it in the first couple of months. She knew it had heard all her prayers and affirmation work during that time too. She hadn't wanted anything bad to happen. She had just wanted this baby's spirit and its few formed cells to travel to the belly of some other mama who was wanting and deserving of it. She had just wanted to get her period before Henry caught wind of its absence and got excited. She was sorry now for making the baby feel unwanted and felt it judging her from within.

After she got out of the shower, she put on just underwear and a tank top. Feeling a little hungry again, she opened the cupboard and pulled out some old saltine crackers and a jar of peanut butter. She walked around the trailer spreading peanut butter on top of the crackers as she ate them. She left a trail of stale crumbs behind her. She had to set the snack down momentarily so she could lift her bed and pull a crate full of books and papers out from under it. She dug around until she found an old cigar box full of folded paper. She sat on the floor next to the crate and sifted through the box of notes and old movie ticket stubs. There was a stack of photos from a throwaway camera she'd saved up for and bought specially for their sophomore-year field trip to the Old Perris Train Station. She flipped through the pictures until she found one of Mel putting bunny ears on the flustered-looking docent beside her. Tessa studied the picture for a while before she packed everything back up and closed the storage space.

Later that night, after the kids were asleep, Tessa and Henry climbed into bed.

"You feeling better?" Henry asked.

"Yes."

"Good," he said. He nestled in closer to her. "Your hair smells like flowers."

"Thank you," she said. Tessa was on the verge of sleep when Henry sighed and spoke up again.

"I know something's bothering you, Tess," he said. "Is it Mama? She can be a lot to take. I could talk to her. I could ask her to give you some space. Ask her to—"

"No. She's fine. I'm fine. Really. I just needed a night to myself." Tessa paused. She saw an opening. Her skin tingled, and her head buzzed with the thought.

"I didn't get to visit with Carly very much today. I had to leave just after getting there to pick up Pres. You think you could convince your mama to watch Ruby and lend me the truck another day this week or next so I can go see her?"

"I could do that," he said.

1990

Tessa

Tessa and Mel were up in the branches of the big eucalyptus tree on Mel's mama's property. Her mama's place was the last in a string of spaced-out houses with dirt yards, chain-link fences, and loud barking dogs. It backed up to a big swath of wide-open land that Tessa and Mel spent most of their free time exploring.

It was spring break, and the rolling hills and meadows were covered with tall, wild, lush grass. It had been an unusually wet winter, and the soil responded to the sun like it had been holding its breath for years. Green as far as the eye could see, so thick it gave your legs a workout to walk through. The dollops of big white clouds off on the horizon made Tessa hungry for Cool Whip.

"Come on, get up," Mel said. "Let's go."

"What?" Tessa was lying belly down on a thick branch so that her legs and arms dangled parallel to one another. She felt peaceful and didn't want to move none. Mel was already hanging from the first branch up from the ground. Her boots made a dull thud when they hit the earth.

"I've got an idea," Mel said.

"Oh, Mel, can't we just—"

But it was useless. Mel was already marching in that determined way of hers when she had one of her "ideas." She was headed toward the garage.

"Brother," Tessa murmured as she negotiated branches on her

climb down. "Wait up!" she called but knew it was she who would have to adjust her speed. Mel was prying up the corner of her mama's old, wooden, bolted-shut garage door. It budged a bit, giving a gap of about a foot and a half.

"Crawl in there," she said.

"Are you crazy? I'm not crawling in there. There's got to be loads of black widows and God knows what else inside there."

"Don't be a baby, Tess. Once you're in, put all your weight against the corner, and I'll climb through after."

"Christ, Mel, come on."

"Hurry up—my arms are about to give."

"This is as stupid as it gets," Tessa grumbled as she got on her belly and army-crawled in through the small opening. Mel let go, and the bit of light coming through the small space disappeared. Everything went dark.

"Now me," Mel said from the other side of the door. Tessa squatted, braced her feet, and put all her weight into her shoulder that pressed against the door. It gave some, and soon she saw Mel scrambling in on her elbows. Once all of her had made it in, Tess let go. There was a creak of the springs and whoosh of air.

"Dark in here, huh?" Mel said. Tessa rolled her eyes, not that Mel could see them. "You're going to have to press up against that door to give me some light so I can look around." Tessa knew it was pointless to argue or try and get some idea about what the hell they were doing. She'd taken the bait, and now she depended on Mel to get her out. She braced her feet again and pushed. Tessa could see outlines of boxes and other unidentifiable junk. It was packed in there. Down by her ankle was the corner of a metal bed frame. Mel climbed and sidestepped until Tess couldn't see her anymore. The dark, dusty air was pierced with intermittent grunts and swear words.

"Shitfire," Mel said. Her voice came from somewhere toward the back of the garage.

"You okay?" Mel didn't answer and kept at whatever she was doing. "Watch for spiders, Mel." Tessa's arms were burning, and her left calf was starting to cramp up. She was about to call out again when she heard Mel scrambling over what was maybe an old air-conditioning unit. She had a large disklike object in her hand.

"Got it," she said. Mel was next to her face now, breathing hard.

"Well, slide it under there, whatever it is, and get out already." Mel did as Tessa said.

"Now you," Mel called from the other side. Tessa slid under the door, she scraped her shoulder against the splintering wood on her way out.

"Christ alive." Tessa unzipped her hoodie and pulled off her pants to shake them out. "I feel like there's spiders crawling all over me. What the hell did we do that for?" She turned to see Mel beaming while holding up a cheap plastic sled. It was hot pink and about the shape and size of a large trash-can lid.

"You're kidding me."

Mel snuck into her mama's kitchen and came out with a tub of Crisco. A half hour later, they were standing at the edge of a steep grassy bank with the greased-up plastic sled. "Do you trust me?" Mel said.

"No, but that's beside the point now, ain't it? It's not going to move like you think it will in this grass, Mel. Otherwise, other people would've thought of it by now. We wasted a whole afternoon, and I scraped my arm pretty good on that goddamn door." Mel didn't seem to hear her, or at least she didn't show that she did. She was looking for the right spot.

"Here," she said. "See? Goes pretty steady. It will be smooth down that way. The velocity of the slope is just right." Tessa didn't look to where she was pointing, nor did she acknowledge the nonsensical comment. It never ceased to amaze Tessa how Mel would suddenly become an expert in whatever topic happened to surface. Mel set the disk down where she wanted it.

"The heavier person is supposed to go in back," Mel said.

"You mean me in front? Ha! Ain't happening. I go behind or not at all."

"Well, fine. I guess I don't weigh much more than you, but the laws of physics—" Mel stopped when she looked up and saw that Tessa had her jaw set.

"Alright, alright. Easy. We'll do it your way," Mel said. Mel held the disk in place, and Tessa sat. She looked down the slope. The hill seemed to go on forever. It ended way down in the ravine, where a small creek would run come spring in the rare years they got a season of decent rain. Tessa was reassured when she felt her weight sink down in the grass. No way it was sliding. Not with all the growth to keep them from moving. Mel stomped down the grass directly in front of the disk.

"Ready?" she said.

"Ready to get this over with." Tessa looked back to see the disappointment on Mel's face. She softened. "Alright, Mel. Let's give it a try." This seemed to perk Mel up.

"Okay." Mel squatted down and sat in front, between Tessa's legs. She was careful to dig her heels in to keep them from moving. Mel held on to the sled, and Tessa held Mel around the waist. "Here we go." Mel pushed off and lifted her legs and they sat still. She used her heels and legs to try and scooch them forward. They moved inches with every scooch. Tessa couldn't hold it in and started laughing.

"We are flying," Tessa said, cracking herself up some more.

"It's going to take a second to get going," Mel said. Tessa could hear the irritation in her voice but had lost the ability to contain herself.

"Roger that," Tessa said in hysterics. "Ready for blastoff."

Mel kept up her ridiculous scooting, and the sled started to move slowly. Tessa was wiping at her tear-filled eyes when the disk started to go. The momentum took a little while to catch, but when it did, they went. Shocked by the wind in her face and the sudden motion, Tessa went silent and held tight around Mel's waist. Mel shouted in triumph. "I told you, Tess! I told you!" The brief moment of elation was followed by sobering fear.

"Shit!" Tessa screamed. They were barreling down the hill fast and building speed. Mel tried to dig her heels into the grass, but the ground kept kicking them up. Mel gripped the disk tighter, leaned into Tessa, and dug her heels into the grass again with all she had. Her boots caught traction this time and gave some slowing resistance. A moment later, Mel's right ankle turned out and folded back at a stomach-churning angle. Mel made a sound halfway between a whimper and a wail. Tessa had no time to respond. The disk slammed into a boulder hiding in the grass, and she was airborne. She didn't know when she'd lost her grip on Mel. She was hurtling solo through the air, ass over head. Then she landed on her back with a heavy thunk. Her rib cage bounced out of her chest on impact, and the back of her head slammed the grassy earth. The wind and sense were knocked clean out of her. With a deep breath, she rolled over onto her stomach. Was she alive? Yes. Was she hurt? She couldn't feel any major pain. There was an intense flush of adrenaline coursing through her body and a throbbing in her head. And Mel? Tessa pushed up on her shaky arms and knees to a tabletop position. A wave of nausea hit, and she puked in the grass between her hands. "Mel?!" she called out. "Mel?!"

"Awww, shit," Mel groaned from somewhere nearby. Tessa wasn't able to stand, so she crawled in the direction of Mel's voice. When she made it over to her, Mel was lying on her back. Her lip was busted open pretty good, and she'd lost a boot somewhere.

"You okay?"

"Think so. My ankle's wrecked for sure, though." Mel put her forearm across her face to shield her eyes from the sun. "Your breath smells like barf."

Tessa flopped down on her back next to Mel. "Fucking A," she said.

Later—after Tessa had helped Mel crawl up the hill and after Mel's mama had yelled at them for being so stupid, after the trip to the ER, where they took X-rays and wrapped up Mel's ankle—Mel and Tessa, bruised and scratched up all over, sat on the porch swing on Mel's patio drinking ice tea Mel's mama had brought them.

"Dumber than doornails, the both of you," she had said, shaking her head as she handed them their glasses.

Mel's mama had gone back inside and left them on their own. They were quiet and exhausted. Mel's foot was propped up on a chair. Her swollen bottom lip stood out in her silhouette against the setting sun. Tessa stopped the gentle rocking her foot made against the floor. She reached for Mel's hand. When she took it, Mel turned to her. Before Tessa could think about what she was doing, she leaned in and kissed her. She tasted the salt of Mel's blood on her lips.

"What'd you do that for?" Mel said after Tessa pulled away.

"I'm sorry." Tessa felt sick to her stomach, like she was going to spew again. What had come over her? She made to stand up, but Mel put a firm hand on her leg to stop her.

"Dumber than doornails," Mel said. She tucked the piece of hair that had come loose from Tessa's ponytail behind her ear and smiled. "You and me both."

TWO

1999

Tessa

Tessa pulled into the Thrifty's parking lot around ten. She had survived two of Ruby's meltdowns, found the missing piece to Preston's Transformer, and answered the barrage of nosy questions Angie had for her when she dropped the kids off that morning. She had done all of it with a nervous excitement that kept a determined pep in her step. Ruby had seemed confused by the sweet, worry-free smile Tessa held throughout her morning tantrum. Tessa gently stepped over Ruby's writhing body, arms and legs flailing on the kitchen floor, and continued to make breakfast. She hummed a pleasing melody to herself over Ruby's yelling. When she had the cream of wheat almost ready, she turned her attention to Ruby, who had wound herself up so much that her face was a deep red and her hair was stuck to the snot smeared on her cheek.

"You'll have a Ring Pop this afternoon if you stop that nonsense and get yourself cleaned up and dressed and ready by the time break-fast is on the table. You act like an angel for me the rest of the morning and I'll make sure it's grape flavor, like you like." Tessa could feel Preston's eyes on her then. She swiveled to face him before he could complain about the disparity. "And I'll have an Abba-Zaba for you, Pres, because you're mama's sweet boy and you done such a good job getting ready this morning." Preston beamed at her and began to set the table. "Oh, look at that. Breakfast is almost ready, and Preston's almost got the table set. I hope you can earn yourself a Ring Pop, Ruby. I sure hope it."

Tessa smoothed her bangs down on her forehead, let out a big breath, and walked into Thrifty's with all the casualness she could muster. There was a short, squat, plain-looking man running the pharmacy counter. No sign of Mel. After taking three circles of the store, she went for the candy aisle. She grabbed Preston's candy bar and sifted through the cardboard box of Ring Pops. There wasn't a single grape-flavored pop. "Christ," Tessa whispered, imagining the hell she'd have to pay for the broken promise.

Thinking of the high-pitched grief she'd be given and the bargaining she was going to have to do to end it, she grabbed two strawberry flavors and a lime Pixy Stix to pull from her back pocket when the time came.

After the candy and three more laps, Tessa began to feel the weight of her foolishness. What, exactly, had she been expecting anyhow? When an employee started tailing her, suspicious of her behavior, Tessa supposed, she gave up, paid for the candy, and left.

Tessa got into Angie's truck and decided to sit there for a bit. She caught a glimpse of herself in the rearview mirror and wiped at the mascara she had put on that morning. "You look nice," Henry had said when he saw her getting ready in the mirror.

She felt her eyes wanting to water up and clenched her jaw. "Stupid," she said. "Stupid, stupid." She bent and rested her head against the wheel.

Tessa jumped a minute later at the sound of a knock on her window. Mel was peering in with her hand held like a visor over her eyebrows to block the sun's glare. She had a concerned look on her face. Tessa reached for the knob and cranked the window down.

"You okay?" Mel said.

"Yeah."

"What are you doing out here?"

"Just taking a break."

"Well, you need anything from inside?"

"No."

"You been here long?"

"A bit, I guess."

Mel looked down and kicked at the pavement with her boot. "I'm headed in now. I could ask to take my lunch early. In a couple hours, if you're still in the area, we could get something to eat?"

Tessa shook her head. "I've got to pick up the kids not too long from now."

Mel nodded and looked toward the building. She squinted into the sunlight reflecting off another car's windshield. "I work earlier tomorrow. Maybe you could come this time then?"

"I won't have the truck."

Mel chewed on her cheek a moment. "Shit. Well, alright. Sit tight a minute here. I'll be right back." Tessa nodded. "And Tess . . ." Mel looked at her with a seriousness.

"Yes?" Tessa said.

"You've got some black stuff up on your forehead." Mel smiled, tapped the side of the truck, and jogged toward the double doors. "Be right back," she called over her shoulder.

"Damn you," Tessa whispered. She licked her pointer finger and tried to scrub the mascara off her forehead. "How the hell'd it get up there anyway?" she muttered to herself. Five minutes later, Mel came trotting out and hopped into the passenger seat of the truck.

"Got time for coffee and pancakes down the street. Sound good?"

"Sounds alright with me." Tessa turned the engine over and pulled out of the parking lot. "How'd you manage to get free?"

"The pharmacist owes me. I pretend not to notice the fudging he does with the refills sometimes. A pill or two short here and there. That sort of thing." Mel nodded her chin toward the candy on the dashboard. "For the kids?"

"Yeah."

"That why you came here today?" Mel said. There was a self-satisfied smirk growing across her face.

"Yup," Tessa said

"Hmm," Mel said. She let the obvious falsehood of Tessa's response linger for a moment before she continued. "Where's the little one today?"

"With Angie."

"That Henry's mama?"

"Yup."

"How's that?"

"How's what?" Tessa said.

"Big-family living. All you together like that. Dropping the kids off with Grandma for the day." Mel leaned forward, pulled the sun visor down, then settled back into her seat. She looked at

Tessa. "Dropping the kids off to sit in the drugstore parking lot with your head against the wheel. How's that going?"

"What's that supposed to mean?"

"What *does* it mean, Tess?"

Tessa felt heat growing around her collar. "Look, you want to get some pancakes and coffee or not? I didn't plan on you interrogating me when I said yes to breakfast."

"Let's get some pancakes, Tess," Mel said. Tessa turned on the radio, and they listened to the static from a local station for the block-and-a-half ride to Denny's.

I'll take a side of pancakes, extra butter, extra syrup, and decaf coffee with four creamers," Tessa said and handed her menu to the waitress.

"I'll have the same, except for the extras, and I'll take my coffee regular and black," Mel said.

The waitress clicked her pen and slipped her notepad into her apron. "I'll be right back with that coffee."

"How long have you been back?" Tessa asked.

"Three months," Mel said. Tessa leaned into the plastic cushion behind her and marveled at how casually Mel had just said that.

"Interesting," she finally said, sharp and insincere.

"Oh yeah? What's interesting about it?" Mel said.

The waitress returned from the coffee stand a couple booths away. She set their coffees down and pulled two creamers from her apron. "Two more, please," Tessa said and tapped the table with two fingers. The woman nodded, then took two more out and put them on the table.

Tessa peeled back the foil tops and emptied the creamers into her coffee one after another. She took her time as she stacked the empty creamers and placed them on the edge of the table. She cleared her throat.

"What's interesting about it?" Tessa shook her head and put a shit-eating grin on her face. She stirred her coffee three times and then carefully set her spoon down on the napkin beside her plate. She placed her folded hands on the table. "Oh, I don't know, Mel. I guess I just wondered about you over the years. After all, I never heard a peep from you. Not a call. Not a note. Not a goddamn messenger pigeon. Not a word after that shit show at your mama's place." Mel made to speak, but Tessa raised her hand to stop her. "And then you show up out of the blue and make me feel dumber than shit when I run into you after all this time. You acted all cool—like I was some nobody. Like I was someone you hardly ever even knew."

"Can I speak now?" Mel said.

"Sure," Tessa said.

"Doreen sent me away back then. I didn't have a choice."

"You could've wrote. You know, it took me a month to work up the courage to go by your place and check in on you. Your mama spoke to me through the screen door like I was trash. She said she figured if you'd wanted me to know where you was, you'd've told me."

"Well, you had your answer, then, didn't you?"

"Stop it, Mel. Goddammit. Why are you acting this way? Huh?" Tessa's eyes started to blur against her will. It was the goddamn hormones. "I didn't mean for us to get caught. I didn't want your mama to send you away. In any case, it seems like it done you some good. You're a college graduate with a degree and a career and everything." Tessa pressed her palms into the table and leaned forward. "Jesus, Mel, I'm happy for you. I just thought you might give a damn how I've been doing, but I guess I don't know you now. I don't seem to know you at all." Tessa began to scooch her way out of the booth, her belly brushing against the table.

"Tessa"—Mel wadded her napkin and threw it down—"come on, wait a second, alright?"

"I ain't waiting, and I ain't leaving neither. I'm pregnant, in case you forgot, and have to pee every other goddamn minute. I'm going to use the facilities. When I get back, there better be pancakes on the table and a goddamn good explanation from you. Because, Mel, I've waited long enough, and you owe me at least that." Tessa continued her undignified scoot until she got to the end of the bench and stood to speed walk to the bathroom.

She gathered herself in the bathroom mirror. She had a mind to sneak out the back and leave Mel's sorry ass there waiting. After all, that's what Mel had done to her. And the animosity Mel had toward her?! Where the hell did she get off talking to her like that? If it weren't for the thought of warm pancakes and melted butter, maybe she would have left. As it was, she was hungry as hell. She'd leave Mel to foot the bill. At least she'd do that. After all, she was some big shot now with a degree, or at least she acted like she was. But Tessa knew better. She saw that Mel was the same smart-mouthed pain in the ass she'd always been. Tessa pulled herself together. She blew her nose and straightened the front of her skirt. She'd been generous and hopeful about the encounter. She could see now that was a mistake. She was coming out of the bathroom and back to the table as a tough, take-no-bullshit bitch. She was a tough bitch with a couple buttered pancakes waiting.

The waitress got to the table the same time Tessa did. *Perfect*, Tessa thought. She slid into her seat and looked at the plate the girl had just set down in front of her. There was one sad dollop of butter in the center of the top pancake. Tessa stuck her fork in to lift the stack. No sign of any extra butter.

"Oh, for Chrissake," she said and dropped her fork so that it clattered on the table. The waitress, who had just set Mel's plate down, jerked her head in Tessa's direction. "Now does that look like extra butter to you?" Tessa said, lifting her eyebrows and pointing to the dollop. It was shrinking in size due to the heat, and it started to slink toward the edge of her pancake, as if it were buckling under the scrutiny. The girl shook her head.

"No, ma'am."

"Well?" Tessa said. The girl just stood there. "Stop staring and go grab some more before my cakes get too cold to melt it." The waitress left and came zooming back a moment later with the extra butter. She set down a small bowl heaped full of it and zoomed away.

Tessa felt Mel's eyes on her, and yes, she'd overreacted a bit there, but whatever. She didn't care. Tessa took a scoop of the side of butter and slabbed it between her pancakes. She poured the two sides of syrup—at least the girl had brought those—over the entire surface area of the cakes. She took up her knife and fork and cut into the stack. She sliced off a big hunk and put the whole thing in her mouth. She didn't care what Mel or the waitress thought. That pancake was warm and goddamn good. They could both go to hell. Mel sat still, watching her. Tessa was four bites in when Mel finally moved. She grabbed a napkin from the dispenser on the table.

"Boy, you sure knocked her dick in the dirt pretty good," Mel said.

The expression caught Tessa off guard, and she had to cover her mouth to keep half-chewed pancakes from shooting out. She began to laugh so hard that she couldn't swallow for fear of choking. She had to take deep breaths in and out of her nose with her cheeks puffed full of pancakes. Tears were streaming from the corners of her eyes.

"Careful, Tessa," Mel said. "Come on, now, girl. Spit that pancake out before you choke to death." Tessa shook her head. She took a big breath in through her nose and concentrated on swallowing. The moment she forced it down her throat, she went back to laughing.

"I mean it. You put the fear of God in that poor little featherhead. Jesus, look at you," Mel said. "You're the only woman I know that would rather choke to death than sacrifice a bite of pancakes."

Tessa dabbed at the corners of her eyes and took in another breath. "You did always have a way with words," Tessa said. "I'll give you that."

The talk was lighter after that. They worked their way through the superficial wheres and whats of their lives over the past eight years. It turned out that Mel had been finished with school for a while. She'd been working in a pharmaceutical lab up north the past four years. Mel's mama was worse off than she'd first let on. Her memory was going pretty fast. She had nearly burned the house down a few months back. The fire department had to come. Doreen ended up in the hospital with smoky lungs and third-degree burns on her forearms and hands. That's what had brought Mel back.

Mel paid at the register after they'd finished their pancakes and had two cups of coffee each. Tessa drove her back to work. Mel came around to Tessa's side of the truck out front of Thrifty's. Tessa rolled her window down. "Well," Mel said. She put a hand on the cab of the truck. "That turned out to be a nice surprise."

"Yeah," Tessa said.

"I better get to work," Mel said.

"I hope your mama gets better. I'd ask you to tell her I said hi, but I don't figure she'd like to hear from me," Tessa said.

"Well, you know how Doreen is, but I appreciate the thought," Mel said. Tessa nodded. "See you later, then," Mel said. Tessa smiled and gave a little wave. Mel stuck her hands in her pockets, then turned and headed for the double doors.

"See you later," Tessa said.

Mel was about four paces away when Tessa felt something thrashing around in her throat. She called after Mel. "I lied to get the truck from Angie," she said. It wasn't what had wanted to come out, but it was enough to give her some relief. Mel turned sharply and paced back over.

"I don't want to get mixed up in any trouble," Mel said in a lowered voice.

"I know that." Tessa looked out the windshield in front of her.

"Okay, well then, know it. That's it. You get me, Tess?"

Tessa nodded. She bit her tongue and focused on the sharp pain to keep tears from coming. She put a hand on the steering wheel and reached for the ignition with the other.

"It was good running into you again," Tessa said.

"It was," Mel said.

Mel

Mel walked into Doreen's house and threw her keys and red vest on the entryway table. The smell of pozole was a welcoming comfort after the long, boring day filled with hand sanitizer and pill counting under buzzing fluorescent lights. "Mom," Mel called.

The doctors had recommended that Doreen only use the kitchen under supervision after she had left a pot full of cardboard scraps cooking on the stove, but Doreen didn't like people telling her what to do and she had seemed almost normal since Mel brought her home from the hospital other than a few moments of forgetfulness.

"In here," her mother called from the living room. Doreen was sitting in her recliner across from Ethan Anders, who was now the grade-school PE teacher for the private Catholic school he and Mel had attended as kids. He was sitting straight-backed on the couch. "I ran into Ethan at the grocery store, and I told him you were back in town. I told him to come over for dinner so the two of you could catch up." Ethan was the latest of Doreen's attempts to set Mel up and marry her off to a good Catholic man. Doreen had been inviting men from St. James Parish over for dinner at least twice a week since she'd come back. Many of them were repeat visits, as there weren't a lot of eligible men to choose from, but this was Ethan's first time over for dinner. He stood up and gave a bashful wave that made Mel feel sorry for him.

"Hiya, Mel," he said.

"Hey there, Ethan." Mel reached out to shake his hand. "How you been?"

Mel no longer got worked up over her mother's attempts to fix her up the way she had when she was younger. These days, the suitors never stayed late, and the quest to find Mel a man gave Doreen something to keep her busy. Nearly three weeks had gone by without any sign of her dementia. That was the biggest chunk of incident-free time since Mel had moved back. If the task of finding her a husband kept Doreen awake and engaged with reality, Mel was fine with it. The conversation wasn't always riveting, but the dinners Doreen made these nights were extra good, and they always came with dessert.

Mel saw a pie cooling in the window from where she stood and felt A-OK about good old Ethan being there. She even offered him one of her beers. This, Mel could tell, was not appreciated by her mother, who thought Mel shouldn't drink beer out of the can like she did. That was how men behaved. Mel clinked aluminum with Ethan and eased into the ottoman across from him.

"Wouldn't you be more comfortable on the couch with Ethan?" Doreen said.

"I'm good here," Mel said. She and Ethan sipped their beers in the awkward silences that fell between Doreen's attempts to force conversation.

"Well, would you like to freshen up a bit before we eat? Dinner is almost ready," Doreen finally said after the longest of these pauses.

"Sure," Mel said. She tossed her empty can into the recycling bin and headed down the hallway past her brother Robby's old room to her current and childhood bedroom. Mel flopped down on her twin-size mattress and stared up at the ceiling. She could hear her mother chatting Ethan up with the pleasant, perky voice she would use with these visitors. She worked hard at this, Mel could tell. As if she believed her pleasantness would somehow obscure

Mel's less-than-enthusiastic presence. Doreen was casually bragging about Mel's job at the pharmacy that just happened to "pay pretty darn good." Of course, everyone already knew about her education and job. It was a big part of why Doreen was able to line these dinners up so easily. A decent-paying full-time job with benefits wasn't easy to come by. It meant you could afford to live a little easier, knowing you wouldn't have to scramble at the end of each month.

Mel's income and the fact that she was "pretty" kept these awkward dinner dates regular. The designation had been assigned to her as far as her memory went back. Her mother used to make her compete in junior beauty pageants all over because of it. Mel even placed in a couple. Once, she and Doreen left with a twenty-pound frozen turkey for taking third place in the Temecula Valley Regional. Placing was an impressive feat considering she was often the only brown girl competing, which put her at an automatic disadvantage, just like it would anywhere else.

Of course, Mel was half white and didn't have an accent. Sadly, both of these facts had bettered her chances in those competitions. Mel had never met her father. She once found a picture of him in Doreen's sock drawer. He was hugging Doreen, and they were standing out in front of some hotel with palm trees. He was tall and thin, with some muscle, and had stringy, shoulder-length brown hair and a mustache. The picture had been taken from pretty far away, and her father was wearing big, '70s-style sunglasses, so Mel didn't really have the best idea of what he looked like. She could see that she had his smile, though, and he had the same build and height that her brother once had. She knew his name was Peter because she grew up hearing Doreen and her tías sitting at the kitchen table late at night whispering over shots of tequila about him and other hijos de putas that had double-crossed them. "If only Tío Lalo was still around," Tía Josie would always say, "he would put these m-f'ers in their place." Peter had split right after Mel was born. Robby was just five then.

Mel figured she had time for a quick shower. After she got out and toweled off, she humored her mother and put on a blouse and a pair of blue jeans that she knew Doreen liked seeing her wear. She combed her long, thick hair and hooked the pieces that hung loose around her face behind her ears. She reached into her drawer. The floral-patterned paper that lined it shifted, and she caught a glimpse of something beneath it. Mel pulled the paper back and lifted a picture out.

Tessa and Mel were sitting up on one of the big boulders way out in the middle of nowheres, smiling big and happy as ever. They used to go scrambling up those boulders a lot. Mel had seen the biggest rattlesnake of her life and had once found a duffel bag full of blood-ied clothes out there. It wasn't safe for just the two of them to go out that far, but she and Tessa had done a lot of dumb shit back then.

Mel thumbed the edge of the photo. How strange it was to be back in Doreen's house and to have run into Tessa like she had. She studied their faces. What a couple of dweebs they were. She was glad to be holding that picture. She hadn't thought she'd ever see anything from back then again. Doreen had turned her room over and trashed everything related to Tessa after she sent Mel away. Mel shook her head. Then she slipped the picture back under the floral paper and closed the drawer.

Ethan is such a nice man. I like him. Isn't he so nice, Mel?" Doreen whispered. Mel had followed her mother into the kitchen to help her bring dinner to the table.

"Sure," Mel said. "He seems nice."

Mel already knew he was nice. She already knew everything about everyone Doreen had over. The parish was a small community. She knew Ethan from way back. He was a shy, skinny white boy then too. He used to slouch down in his chair and hide behind his desk so that he could chew crayons. He always had a colorful smile back then and would get in trouble for it all the time. She never understood why he kept at it like he did. He eventually stopped the strange habit sometime during middle school.

She had very little memory of Ethan being at their high school before she was forced to leave it. She thought she remembered him being on the basketball team, but she had smoked a lot of pot and taken a lot of pills her freshman year and couldn't be sure of that fact. Robby had been one of 240 killed in a barracks bombing in Beirut the summer before her freshman year started, and Mel would just as soon not have been clearheaded enough back then to miss him.

Mel had stopped with the pills and eased off the weed some by the time sophomore year rolled around. She was trying to stay out of trouble and do better for Doreen, but ditching the pills and cutting back on the weed wasn't enough. Mel's second year at St. James High School had hardly started before Doreen yanked her out.

The rumors about Mel and Alexus began to spread not long after they started seeing each other. Mel kept her mouth shut when Doreen confronted her about it, but Alexus squealed like a pig. She told her parents it was all Mel's idea, that Mel had put her up to it and made her do the things they did together. The next day, Doreen was signing transfer papers. To help save face and restore her daughter's reputation, Doreen took Mel to Mass five days a week instead of the standard three they'd been going and told anyone who'd listen that Mel was leaving St. James so she could go to Perris High and be part of an honors science program there.

Looking back now, Mel was grateful for the transfer. She had actually ended up joining the honors science program, and that had given her some direction. With the way things had been going before the transfer, Mel probably would have enlisted straight out of high school, just like Robby had. Besides, things would have been hard for her if she'd stayed at good old SJHS. Alexus was her first real girlfriend, and Mel had taken the betrayal pretty hard. She heard Alexus got right back on the straight and narrow after being found out. She started dating a senior on the basketball team and got knocked up two months later to prove her commitment to hetero life.

As far as Mel could tell, not much progress had been made in the direction of the parish accepting lesbos like herself. Everyone with her particular lean seemed to either move away as soon as they could, like she had, or dive back into the closet, have a public come-to-Jesus moment, and let the Holy Spirit heal their wicked ways. Her favorite tía had tried the latter. The prayers and holy waters didn't stick, though. Tía Dede ended up dying of pills and shame when Mel was just a kid. Mel guessed that was a big part of why Doreen had been so fierce in her attempts to keep Mel from being who she was.

Doreen had been skeptical and uneasy when Mel first started hanging out with Tessa back then, but Mel's grades and mood improved after they became friends. That was enough for Doreen to decide to believe that Tessa was a good, straight-girl influence on her daughter, and she began to encourage the friendship. Doreen was always having Mel bring Tessa over for dinner.

"That girl eats like a pig," she would say with big, unbelieving eyes and a shaking head after Tessa left. She was part shocked and part flattered, as she thought Tessa eating so much was a testament to her cooking. "Doesn't her family feed her?!"

In reality, it didn't matter much whether the food was good or not. Tessa ate that way because she never knew when her next meal was coming. It made Mel sick to think of how often Tessa had gone hungry. Mel had always shared what she had with Tessa back then, but she still regretted not having done more to help her.

Ethan had been kind enough to make up an excuse about needing to get back to give his dog medicine shortly after they finished dinner. Doreen was disappointed when he said he had to leave, but she still seemed hopeful of the possible match. She handed him a slice of pie to take home, patted his arm, and gave a friendly smile when she told him to come back soon.

"He seems nice," Doreen said again when she dropped a soaped-up plate into the side of the sink with clean water. Mel scooped it out and began drying.

"Yeah," Mel said.

"He's got a good head on his shoulders," Doreen said.

"Yep," Mel said. She placed the plate atop the stack in the cabinet and started drying the next.

"And he's handsome," Doreen said. When Mel didn't chime in, she continued: "Nice smile and a strong build." Mel's silence made her angry. "You know, Mel, you could try a little. I worked hard to make a nice dinner for us to have with Ethan. You could have at least pretended to enjoy it."

Mel's hands tightened around the plate she was holding. The word *pretend* stuck her and throbbed like a thorn in her foot, so she felt she could hardly stand there. All she had ever done was pretend for Doreen. It had mixed her up so badly that even when she'd left home and moved to the Bay—a place she'd once heard called the gay capital, for Chrissake—she'd ended up pushing away all the women she tried to date there. All the years of pretending and shame had turned her into some weird, warped creature that couldn't accept the one thing it had always wanted.

"You know what?" Mel said, loud and sharp. She threw the plate into the water, and it pinged against the inside of the sink. Doreen's head snapped up from her soapy hands, and her jaw fell slightly open and to the side, like it was broken. She'd had the same wounded, helpless look on her face when Mel came home to find her in a hospital room in a state of bewilderment after she set her kitchen on fire. It had shaken Mel and messed her up inside to see Doreen that way when all she'd ever known of her was the strong, stern woman who'd raised her by the belt.

She considered her next words. Considered how Doreen had been doing so well. Considered that Doreen was just trying to do what she thought was best for her. That this was what she had always tried to do. Mel knew it couldn't have been easy on Doreen, raising her and Robby on her own like she had. She considered the possibility that Doreen would forget about the whole evening by tomorrow. That her mother was slowly slipping away. Mel swallowed the confusion and grief swelling in her throat.

She softened her voice. "You know, I could go for some of that prizewinning pie of yours," she said. Doreen didn't answer. She kept at the dishes. "I can nearly taste it now, that buttery crust that dissolves on the tongue." She looked to see if Doreen was coming around. She wasn't. "The way the blueberry filling, when just warm enough, reminds you of the best jam you ever had in your

life and the sweetest story anyone ever told you at the same time."
Doreen dropped another dish into the lukewarm water with a
blank face. Mel cleared her throat and continued. "I'll tell you
what, my stomach is getting warm and fuzzy just thinking about
that pie of yours."

"Well, get a plate and have a slice already, dummy," Doreen
said. "And don't ever throw my china around like that. You better
pray you didn't put a chip in it."

Mel wiped her hands on her jeans and moved the pie to the table. She took a knife from the block and a spatula from the drawer.
"I'm sure looking forward to this pie of yours. Boy, is it ever good,
though." Doreen was pursing her lips to fight the smile that was
coming. "Best thing I ever tasted on this earth," Mel said.

"Would you quit it?" Doreen said. "Give me that knife, and
stop talking that way. To think of the money I spent to send you
and Robby to private school. Two jobs, working 'round the clock,
and the both of you ended up sounding like a couple of fools. With
all the good kids you two could have made friends with in the parish, you decided to go out and roll around in the dirt with a bunch
of hoodlums and bumpkins. I swear, you did it just to spite me."
She took the pie from Mel. "We'll have to warm it in the oven," she
said. "There's no use in going through all that work to eat cold pie.
Besides, you always butcher it when I give it to you to cut and
serve. You'd think a wild animal got to it."

Mel put a pot of coffee on to have with the pie. She was reaching up into the cupboard for a couple of mugs when she felt Doreen's hand on her shoulder.

"I won't be around forever, you know. I could have died and
burned up the house and left you with nothing. And with Robby

gone . . ." Doreen paused, and Mel heard her taking little breaths to keep herself from crying. "Tía Josie is getting older. Soon you won't have any family left. I just want to make sure that you have someone to look after you when I'm gone," Doreen said. Mel stayed quiet and still there for a moment with her back to her mother.

"I know," she finally said.

1985

Mel

Mel flattened the empty bag of knock-off brand Sour Patch Kids, Sour Friends, tilted her head back, and dumped the remaining sour crumbs into her mouth before chucking the plastic wrapper in the trash. She was coming up on the basketball courts at the park around the way from her tía Josie's place. Her brother and a bunch of dudes from around would meet there to play most afternoons until it got too dark to see and the ball would go slipping through their hands to pop them in the face.

It was around four, and there was plenty of sun left in the day when Mel came walking past the benches near the court. There was a group of high school girls gathered by the sideline. They'd come to watch Robby, who always played shirtless, regardless of the temperature outside. That day it was warm, and the sun reflected off the sheen of sweat on his skin and amplified the lean muscles of his stomach and chest. It drove the girls crazy. They all wanted Robby bad. It was painful to watch the way they'd throw themselves at him. The guys were that way with Robby too. They weren't trying to get him to be their boyfriend like the girls were—Mel didn't think so, at least—but they were just as desperate for his approval.

Everyone loved Robby. Not just the kids who went to St. James either. He knew everyone from all over Perris. Robby rode dirt bikes with his buddies in the sticks; he played basketball and baseball with the jocks at the park; and he gamed with the nerds who spent all their time and coins trying to set best records on Pac-Man and Donkey Kong and the other arcade machines scattered throughout town. Robby had the reigning highest scores on all three machines at the Chicken King down by the old train station on First and Main.

Mel sat on the edge of one of the benches and shaded her eyes to see who all was out playing that day. Robby saw her from downcourt and gave a wave. She waved back, but he had already turned to sprint away in the other direction, and Gary, a short, loudmouthed boy two grades ahead of her, saw the wave meant for her brother and gave a kissy-face in return.

Mel let her hand fall and looked away. "You're Robby's little sister, right?" one of the girls said. Mel turned to see the group of featherheads staring at her.

"Yep," she said and went back to watching the court. She heard them whisper, and one of the girls let out a high-pitched giggle.

"Stupid," she heard one of them say and saw that girl bump into another, which made them all stumble and laugh. They always acted all flimsy and clumsy like that.

"Hey, little girl." The one who walked over and said this had big brown bangs rounded like a half bubble on her forehead. They were so crispy looking that Mel thought she could reach up and snap them off if she wanted to, which she didn't. She didn't want to get that close. This girl, like all of them, reeked of perfume and hair spray and popped her gum loudly. Mel tried to look past the girl toward the game, but the girl bent down and got close to her face. Mel drew her chin back and away from the cloud of stink and the sour smell of overchewed gum coming off the girl's breath. The girl put her hands on her knees and bent closer still.

"Can you do me a favor, little girl?"

"Sure," Mel said, trying hard not to breathe.

"Can you give this to your brother?"

"Sure," Mel said.

"Now, don't open it, 'kay?" the girl said and patted Mel on the head. "That's for your brother to read."

"Alright," Mel said. The girl walked back over to the others, and they all started up again with their "shut ups" and their laughing and their drunken-looking staggering and their bumping into each other. Mel exhaled and took in a fresh breath of air. She shoved the note into the pocket of her corduroy pants. It was too hot out to be wearing those pants, but Doreen only bought her shorts that came in pastel colors and went too high on her waist and too short on her thighs. The only non-pants Mel had that she didn't mind wearing were her gym shorts, and all three pairs were crumpled at the bottom of her laundry basket, due for a wash.

Mel pulled her T-shirt away from her stomach and flapped it a few times to let some cool air in. "Sup?" Niko said as he came walking over. He was in the sixth grade, like Mel, but he went to public school.

"Hey, Niko," Mel said. Niko kept his eyes on the ground by his feet. He always did that. He liked to walk around that way, collecting junk like beer bottle caps, pieces of broken glass, and hair ties. Sometimes he'd luck out and find a nickel or a small lost toy, like the little army man he was so proud to have discovered in the sand under the monkey bars at the park. He was a weird kid. Mel didn't mind him talking to her and showing her the things he found, though. It seemed to make him happy, showing her that stuff, and once he gave her a pretty cool pocketknife that he'd found in the gutter, just because she'd said that she liked it.

Niko sat down a couple feet away from her and started to unload his pockets, setting the junk that came from them on the bench space between them.

"Anything good today?" Mel asked.

"Not really," Niko said. "Think I'm going to head over and look around some at the Circle K parking lot. Want to come?"

"No, thanks," Mel said. "You coming back this way?"

"Think so," he said.

"Could you pick me up a couple cans of Coke and a bag of Cheetos?"

"Sure," he said. Mel took three dollars from her wallet and set it on the pile.

"Thanks," Mel said.

"You wanna come over to my place tonight?" he said as he pitched the tab from a soda can back into the dirt where he'd found it and started shoving the rest of the crap back into his pockets. Mel looked at him then. He'd never invited her over to his place or anywhere else before. They weren't friends like that. He'd never talked about anything besides the things he'd found on the ground. "My grandma is out of town to go see my dad in jail," he said.

Mel didn't say anything. She hadn't known that he lived with his grandma or that he had a dad in jail. "My brother, Forest—" Niko stopped and looked at her then. "You know my brother, Forest?" Mel knew him. He was the same age as Robby, but he went to the continuation high school in Perris for girls who got pregnant and guys who went to juvie. Doreen would have called him a low-life drug addict, but Robby said he was alright.

"Yeah," Mel said, "I know him." Mel couldn't remember ever actually looking at Niko's face before then. She wasn't sure that he'd ever looked up from the ground or his piles of trash. She saw a jagged pink scar that ran from the thick black hair at the top of his forehead to just below his left eyebrow.

"Forest is having people over and said I could invite people too. I think your brother is going." Niko crinkled up his nose and squinted into the sun coming from over Mel's shoulder, then dropped his head back down and stood up. "I'll be back," he said and went off in the direction of the Circle K with his nose to the ground before Mel had a chance to answer. Mel watched him stop and kick at something down by his feet. He bent to inspect it and then continued on without picking it up.

Mel had never considered the possibility of hanging out with Robby when he left out his window each night. Doreen would kill Mel if she ever caught her sneaking out, and Robby had never invited her. He always treated her like she was a little kid. Most days, she would meet up with Robby after school and tag along wherever he went until they had to be home for dinner with Doreen. After dinner, they'd all watch TV for an hour. Then Doreen would make sure they had their homework done and their lunch money for the next day, she'd say it was time for bed. Doreen worked early every morning and slept heavy on the nights she didn't pick up graveyard shifts. Most nights, Robby was gone out his window just as soon as he pulled his bedroom door shut. Once in a while, though, Robby wouldn't feel like leaving, and he and Mel would eat junk food and watch late-night television together. Those were Mel's favorite nights.

Niko came back from scouring the Circle K parking lot about an hour later, when things on the court were winding down. The guys were just halfheartedly shooting around and talking crap by then. Niko set the Cokes down on the bench next to Mel and then pulled from his pocket a scrap of cardboard that looked like it was once part of a Cheerios box. She flipped the cardboard over in her hands and saw an address written on the back. Mel waited to see if he would look up from the ground again. He didn't. Instead, he pulled her change out of his shirt pocket and set it down on the bench too.

"Keep it," Mel said. Niko shrugged, took the coins back, and turned to leave. "Maybe I'll see you later," Mel called after him.

"Okay," he said and skipped off.

"Thanks," Robby said when Mel handed him his cola. He popped the can open, leaned his head back, and poured the soda down his throat. He finished the gulp and wiped his mouth with the back of his hand. "Ahhh," he said, smiling at her. The sun was nearly all gone by the time they were walking back home.

"Oh, and this," Mel said, pulling out the note that the girl with bangs had given her.

"What's this?" Robby said and unfolded the notebook paper. A grin grew across his face as his eyes moved down the page until he gave a little embarrassed laugh and put his free hand on his chin. He lifted the metal lid of the trash can on the curb they were walking by and pitched the note inside.

"You didn't read that, did you?"

"Why would I?"

"'Kay, good," he said, still grinning. Then he snapped his fingers and clapped his hands. "You get your homework done?"

"Yes," Mel said. "Did you?"

"Hey, I'm the big brother here. It's me who's supposed to check on you."

"So, that's a no on the homework for you, then," Mel said.

"That's not for you to worry about," Robby said and put his palm on top of her head. Mel swatted his hand away.

"Yeah, okay," Mel said. She put her hand in her pocket and flipped the piece of cardboard Niko had given her between her fingers. "So, you going to Forest's place tonight?" Mel said as casual and chill sounding as possible.

"What do you know about Forest's place?" Robby said and craned his neck back to give her a side-glance. Mel looked away and pretended like she had seen something in the front yard they were passing.

"Niko told me. He said I should come by." She heard Robby laughing at her then. She clenched her jaw against the embarrassment and hurt and tears that were wanting to come.

"Nah, that's not a place you should be going," Robby said.

"But you should?"

"When you are older like me, you can decide where you want to spend your time, but for now, it's on me and Mom to make sure you are staying out of trouble and getting your homework done."

"You never stayed home. Not when you were my age. Not ever." Mel started walking faster so that she got a few steps ahead of Robby.

"That's different. You're a girl, and plus, you're lucky you have someone looking out for you. I never had that. You should be grateful."

"Whatever," Mel said.

"Oh, it's like that?" Robby said.

"I don't know, Robby. Is it? You call all the shots, right?" Mel shouted over her shoulder. She felt herself start to cry and picked up her pace to run.

"Come on, Mel. Don't be like that." Mel wiped at her face and kept on going. "See," she heard him say. "See, this is why you can't go places like that, Mel. You still act like a baby."

Mel stayed quiet all through dinner. Doreen kept asking her questions about her day, but Mel wasn't having it. Robby didn't have much to say either.

"Jeez, you'd think you might want to talk to your mother who worked all day to keep a roof over your head and then came home to make you dinner, but hey, that's okay. Don't worry about giving a few words to the woman who works her fingers to the bone while you two live the life. Tell you what, why don't you two get your quiet little asses up and clear the table if you don't feel like having a conversation?"

"Good job, Robby," Mel said down to the table as she stood and pushed her seat away.

"What's that?" Doreen said.

"Nothing," Mel said.

"Yeah, okay. You two clean up the kitchen, and see if I spend my time making you nice dinners like this the rest of the week." Mel went to the kitchen and set her plate down by the sink. "It's going to be frozen dinners for you, like all the other kids whose parents don't give a crap. We'll see how you like that," Mel heard her mother call from the dining room.

Robby set his and Doreen's plates inside the sink and turned the faucet on. "I'll do the dishes," he said. "That way, you can stay focused on being real mad at me, 'kay?"

"Deal," Mel said. She tried to keep up the appearance of being irritated, but she felt the hurt and anger slipping away from her, and the warm feelings she had for her brother were working on her instead.

Mel, Robby, and Doreen sat on the couch watching *Jeopardy!* together after the dishes and kitchen got cleaned up. Doreen shouted out answers to every question in every category with complete confidence. She got just one out of the whole grid right. "What is purgatory?!" she yelled. When the answer came back as correct, she slapped her hands down on the knees of both Mel and Robby, who were sitting on either side of her. "You see?" she said. "I should go on this show! Make us some real money, huh?" She shoved Robby's shoulder. "You see? Your mom knows this stuff."

Doreen's eyelids were fluttering and sticking shut by the time the Final Jeopardy! round was up, and she was out cold by the credits. Robby tapped her shoulder to wake her, and she stood and started for her bedroom. "You guys do your homework?" she asked.

"Yep," they both replied.

"Good," she said. "That's good. I'll leave your lunch money on the table."

"'Night, Mom," Robby and Mel said.

"'Night," Doreen said and closed her bedroom door behind her.

Mel was lying still and quiet in her bed, listening in the dark for Robby to leave. At a quarter past nine, she heard a car with squeaky brakes roll up outside, and Robby's window slid open, then shut. She heard the gate close and some words and a car door. Then the car drove away, and they were gone. Mel pulled back the blankets and turned on her bedroom light. She grabbed the shirt and pants she'd worn that day off the back of her desk chair and put them on. She smoothed her hair back into a ponytail and checked herself out in the mirror. She dug her hands into her pockets and added a little bend in her knees so that she looked more laid-back. *Good enough*, she thought, and went to grab her hoodie and backpack.

Mel flipped her bedroom light off and climbed out her window. She went around to the back of the house, moving as silently as possible. Still, she managed to wake the neighbor's old pit bull, Fat Boy, who started up with his hoarse, cough-like bark. "Quiet," she whispered, then bent down and stuck her fingers through a diamond in the chain-link fence to scratch his nose. Fat Boy wagged his tail and pressed up against the gate so that she could get to him better.

She came back out front a few minutes later with her bike. She pulled her hood up over her head, checked the cardboard scrap one more time, and then swung her leg over the seat and started to pedal down the street with the cool night air on her face and a buzzing in her chest.

Mel figured it would be about a forty-minute bike ride to Forest and Niko's place. She had recognized the street when she first read the address on the bit of cardboard Niko gave her. Ellis Avenue was across town from where she lived and out a ways in the sticks, where the ruts and potholes in the dirt roads got bigger and the trailers became more spaced out.

Mel thought she was more than halfway there when the nighttime cold started to seep through her sweatshirt. Her hands were starting to ache against the icy wind that her pedaling produced, and the excitement she had felt when she'd first gotten onto her bike was long gone. The streetlamps had ended several miles back, and the glow from town looked weak and distant. Mel had to stop and pull a flashlight from her backpack to hold on her handlebar in order to avoid the craters in the road. The crickets were loud, and Mel couldn't see anything outside the flashlight's circle. She kept hearing small scurrying noises in the darkness that framed the road. She was talking herself into turning back when she heard music and voices echoing from somewhere up ahead. The thought of traveling all the way back home in the dark by herself seemed worse at that point than heading toward those voices and the lights she now saw not more than a quarter mile up the road. Mel began to pedal faster. She decided she'd find Robby and eat crow as soon as she got there. He'd be pissed, and he'd say he told her so, and then he'd take her home. She didn't want to prove anything anymore. If Robby wanted to think she was a baby, that was fine with her. Biking to Forest's place had been a stupid idea.

Mel ditched her bike in the bushes a little ways away from the trailer. There were at least seven beat-up-looking cars and trucks parked out front. Mel bent down behind a silver pickup and watched a group of partiers drinking and smoking on the mustard-colored sofa sitting out in the dirt in front of a sun-beaten baby-blue trailer. The girl who had given her the note to pass on to Robby earlier that day was asleep with her head resting on some guy's shoulder. Mel didn't recognize any of the others sitting there. She was wondering how long she would have to wait for Robby to come out front when a car came driving up behind her, and she was caught crouching and spying in its headlights. Mel stood up and walked toward the party before the people in that car had time to park and get out. She pulled her hood down around her face and went for the trailer's screen door.

"Hey, dude," she heard one of the guys from the couch say in her direction, but she kept on walking up the steps and into the trailer without lifting her head. The music was loud, and the place was dimly lit by the multicolored Christmas lights draped in bunches over the surfaces of the trailer's chairs, tables, counter-tops, and cabinets. It was crowded, and Mel kept accidentally bumping into people. She made two full passes of the small space before the thought that Robby might not be at the party hit her. Her stomach dropped, and she started to sweat. She was hot and feeling dizzy and thought she might be hearing things when a voice coming from the ground whispered up at her: "Mel." She leaned into the wall behind her and softened her knees to rest some and pull herself together. "Mel," the voice said again.

This time, she looked to the ground where the voice had come from and saw Niko's head poking out from behind the couch backed up against the wall to her right. He gestured for her to come down there with him. Figuring she didn't have any better options at the moment, she slid down the wall, dropped to her knees, and crawled over. Niko scooched back behind the couch to make room for her to join him. The back of the couch was pulled out about a foot and a half away from the wall. There was just enough room for Mel to sit back on her heels. When Niko crawled far enough in, he did this kind of awkward sideways wiggle in order to find the room to turn and face her. It was shadowy behind the couch. The faint colorful glow of the Christmas lights somewhere nearby cast a strange hue that highlighted the scar on Niko's forehead and made the whites of his eyes look an eerie glossy pink. He rested his hands on his knees and grinned.

"You made it," he said.

"Yeah," Mel said. It was even warmer down there behind the couch.

"This is where I hang out when Forest has people over," Niko said in a way that made it seem like he thought it was a cool thing, like he was proud to be hiding there. Mel looked down from his face to the carpet that met the baseboard at the bottom of the wall. The crack there was grimy and filled with food crumbs and dirt. Niko reached under the couch. He pulled out a can of warm Coke and handed it to her. Before she could say thanks, he reached back in and pulled out a small bowl of chips, which he sat down in front of her, and then he reached under the couch for a third time and pulled out two big square plastic Tupperware containers. He peeled the lid off the first one and started poking around in the Tupperware of collected junk with a chopstick. He dug around some more, and Mel saw in the shifting of objects a dead, dried-out, smooshed-flat blue-belly lizard with a small, corroded button battery shoved into its mouth. Niko lifted his chopstick from the soup of found objects. Looped around the end of the chopstick he extended in her direction was a cheap plastic ring, the kind that came from a quarter machine, except this one looked warped and wavy, like it had been melted in a microwave.

"Thanks," Mel said and took the sad-looking ring off the end of the chopstick and held it in her hands. Then, because he was watching her intensely with those glossy pink eyes and because she felt like she was being squeezed between the wall and the couch, she slid the ring onto her pointer finger.

He pushed the bowl of chips closer to her with the same eager and expectant stare, so she picked one up and put it in her mouth. She wanted to retch and spit out the stale chip, which had a moldy tang that clung to her tongue and somehow reminded her of dirty feet, but she swallowed and popped the soda can open to wash down the taste with warm cola instead.

A few minutes went by with Niko digging around in the first Tupperware container. Mel was listening to the voices and murmurs inside the trailer for Robby, but she didn't hear him. She was coming to terms with the fact that he wasn't there. She was working up the nerve to go find her bike and start the ride home when Niko opened the second Tupperware container and the stench of something dead and rotting stung her eyes and clawed at her throat. She leaned back and tried to turn away, but the couch caught her shoulder, and she saw sitting on top of the container full of collected crap a dead piglet lying on its side. It was so small that it had to have been just born or somehow taken from its mom's belly undercooked. Its jaw was slung open to the side, and its eyes had turned into a milky white goop that was draining back into its sockets. Mel backed out crawling buttfirst from behind the couch. As soon as she could, she shot up to stand and caught a guy's elbow with her head and then again with her backpack.

"Watch it," the guy said.

"Sorry," Mel said and went for the door. Her throat was still tight, and it felt hard to breathe. That stench was chasing her. She bumped into several more people and said sorry several more times. The last of these times, she turned her head to say sorry back over her shoulder. When she turned it forward again, her face ran straight into a red plastic cup. Pink liquid spilled down the front of the white tank top that clung tightly to the tall, skinny girl standing in front of her.

"What the hell?" the tall, skinny girl with a thick yellow braid running down her shoulder said. Before Mel could say sorry again, a guy about the girl's height but at least three times as wide appeared by the girl's side. "This dude just pushed me," the tall, skinny girl said. At first, Mel felt some relief at the word *dude*, like maybe the girl was talking about someone else, but then she remembered her hood and how the boy on the porch had called her the same thing earlier.

"You push my girl?" The guy stepped closer to her. Mel wanted to speak. She wanted to pull her hood back and explain herself and beg him or anyone who would listen for help, but instead she felt her joints lock up, and her words became cement in her collapsing chest. Next thing she knew, the guy had her by the shoulders and was pushing her back, back, back until the wall stopped her. The back of her rib cage hit first and made a hollow thud. Then her head hit something that felt metal and sharp. The guy put a hand on her chest to hold her there.

"Little piece of shit," he said. She thought he was going to hit her, but he jerked her hood away from her face instead. Mel searched the crowd, but their faces all seemed indistinguishable and fuzzy, except for one. Niko was watching from behind the couch. His eyes were wide, and he looked like he was about to cry. Then he blinked and did begin crying. "Sorry," he mouthed, then slowly backed into his space until she couldn't see him anymore.

"It's a little girl, stupid." The girl who had given her the note for Robby earlier that day staggered out from the crowd toward her and sloppily pushed the triple-wide guy away. The girl hugged Mel to her. Mel put her face against the girl's chest and started to cry. The girl put her hand around the back of Mel's head and then pulled it away quickly. "Your head is bleeding." The girl looked up. Mel did too. There was a shelf built into the wall above them. Her head must have caught the L-shaped metal piece that was anchored to the wall. "Somebody go get Robby," the girl said. "This is his little sister."

"Shit, I didn't mean to. I didn't know it . . ." Mel heard the wide guy's voice waver and trail off as he took the tall, skinny girl's hand and started to move away.

"You better get out of here before Robby sees what you did. He's gonna kick your stupid ass," the girl who had given the note said.

Mel started to feel her body again. Her legs were weak and

rubbery. She let her knees bend and slid down the wall to a crouch. She pulled her knees into her chest, and the girl squatted down beside her and petted the side of her head. Then Mel heard Robby.

"Where is she?" Robby said. The crowd pushed him forward.

"Look," the girl said. She tipped Mel's head forward, and Mel heard Robby suck in air.

"Awww, shit, Mel. You okay?" Robby said. "Does it hurt?" Mel looked up at him, and her eyes blurred with tears.

"Not that bad," she said.

"Come here," he said. Robby hugged her to him for a moment, then lifted her up and carried her toward the door. The familiar smell of his cologne and his heart beating in her ear soothed her, and she let herself cry some more. "Chris," he said. "Where's Chris at?"

"Here," a voice said.

"Hey, can you give me a ride? I gotta take my sister home. Some fool split her head open. We're going to deal with that part of it later," Robby said. He made eye contact with several in the crowd, and they nodded back.

Robby gave Chris directions to their tía Josie's place and told him to wait in the car when they got there. Tía Josie was retired, but she had been an ER nurse for most of her life, and she knew how to keep secrets. Robby stood in front of Mel and knocked on the door until they heard the sound of Tía Josie's slippers on the entryway's tile floor. The porch light came on. Tía Josie was swearing and squinting into the light when she opened the door.

"Robby?" she said. Mel stepped out from behind him, and Tía Josie put her hands on her hips. "What happened?"

"Can we come in, Tía? I need you to look at something." Tía Josie waved them inside. Robby told her that Mel'd had an accident at the house and they hadn't wanted to wake Doreen, so he'd had his friend drive them there instead. Tía pushed the curtain back and looked out the kitchen window at Chris's car parked out front, then shook her head.

"Bullshit," she said. "You were at home dressed in these wannabe gangbanger clothes that stink of cigarettes and weed? What do you take me for, pendejito? You should have more respect for me than to come to my house and lie straight to my face like that." Tía stopped talking then. She put a hand in Robby's face to shut him up when he started to try to explain himself. She pointed for Mel to sit down in the chair under the kitchen light. She cut away a chunk of Mel's hair and cleaned the cut with a washcloth and warm, soapy water. Then she poured something that burned over the back of Mel's scalp. She put a bag of ice to the back of Mel's head and told her to hold it there for a while.

"Keep it clean," she said. Then she pushed a plastic bag with soap, Neosporin, and cotton balls into Robby's stomach. "It doesn't need stitches, but she can't go to sleep. You have to stay up with her the rest of the night to make sure."

"Thank you, Tía," Robby said.

"How could you let this happen to your baby sister? What kind of big brother are you?" Robby started to answer her. "I don't want to hear it," she said and waved him away. "You need to go home, where you should have been in the first place. Your poor mother works so hard for you, and this is how you repay her?" Tía Josie shook her head.

"Sorry," Mel said. Tía Josie put a hand on Mel's cheek.

"No sleeping, mija. You two stay up the rest of the night and come by after school tomorrow." Mel nodded. Tía took her hand away and stood up straight. "Alright, get out of here, then. Lock the door behind you. I'm going back to bed." Tía Josie started for her bedroom.

"Are you going to tell Doreen?" Robby said. Tía Josie turned to him and lifted her eyebrows.

"No, mijo," she said. "I'm not. But that's not to save your ass from the trouble you deserve. It's because I'm looking out for *my* little sister, something you wouldn't know about. Doreen's got enough on her plate. She shouldn't have to worry about you pulling this kind of crap." Robby dropped his head then. "You keep your ass awake tonight and hers too."

"Thank you, Tía," he said softly.

"Sure," she said and went down the hallway.

Chris dropped them off in front of their place and said he was going to go back to see if anyone was still at the party.

Robby wanted to sit out front on the curb for a minute before they went inside.

"You think people will notice the missing hair?" Mel said.

"Nah. Just pull it back into a ponytail." He pulled her hair back and held it loosely and looked at her a second before he let it go. "You can't tell like that."

"Good," Mel said.

"You shouldn't have come to that party. You know that, right?"

"I know," Mel said.

"I can't believe you rode your janky-ass bike all that way," Robby said, laughing.

"Well, it's gone now," Mel said.

"No, don't worry. We'll get it back." They were quiet for a while sitting there. "You know I love you, right?" Robby finally said.

"Yeah," Mel said.

"That's why I don't want you going to places like that. It's not that I don't trust you or think you're a baby, like I said. You're too smart and good to be hanging out with the people that go to those types of things, you know? I mean, look at the people that were there. You want to be friends with any of them? Even your boy Niko, that dude is weird. And I know it's not his fault, but he's going to end up just like Forest, or maybe worse. I just want something better for you."

"What about you?" Mel said.

"What do you mean?"

"What about something better for you?" Mel said. Robby sighed.

"You've got a good point there." He leaned back on his elbow and stretched his legs out long. "But I'm gonna be alright. Hanging out with those guys is just for now. As soon as I graduate, I'm enlisting, and then after I put in my time, Uncle Sam is paying for me to go to college. And I'm going to make lots of money when I'm done with all that." He turned and looked at her with a seriousness. "You and me and Doreen will never have to worry about rent or bills or any of that shit the rest of our lives." Robby reached down into his pocket with his free hand and fished out a lighter and a loose cigarette. He lit the cigarette, took a drag, and exhaled a cloud of smoke. "I won't be doing this much longer either, for the record, so you don't have to say anything about it."

"Sure," Mel said. She picked at the rubber coming loose from the side of her sneaker until the piece came off in her hand and then chucked it away. "Couldn't you go to college without enlisting?" she said.

"No. I don't have the grades for a scholarship, and I'm not wasting my time working my ass off at some shitty job for nothing.

I'm not taking a class here and there at some community college like I see these fools try. That shit never works. This is the way it's gotta be, but it won't be long. You'll see. You better keep your grades up, though, and get your ass a scholarship, because I won't be making big money in time to send you to college. You need to handle that, alright?"

"Okay," Mel said.

"Better be okay. I don't wanna have to come back from wherever it is they send me to keep your ass in line." Robby elbowed her and smiled. "I'm just playing. I know you'll be okay. Shit, you'll probably make more money than me someday. You could be a famous scientist and shit. Find a cure for cancer or something."

"Yeah, right," Mel said.

"I'm serious, Mel. Didn't you win a prize at the science fair last year?"

"Just for my grade."

"Just for your grade? Okay, see, Mel? You gotta start to take some pride. You think I ever won some shit like that? You can have anything you want. You have to believe that, and you can't let anyone tell you different." Robby sat up and brushed away the ash that had fallen on his shirt. "I want to tell you something, okay?"

"Okay," Mel said.

"Your life can look however you want it to look, and if someone doesn't like it, then that's their problem. You get what I'm saying?" He was looking at her like he was talking about some deeper understanding between them. Mel nodded but wasn't sure she knew what it was. "I mean, like, things are different now than they were for Tía Dede, you know?" Mel's mouth went dry, and her face got hot. She wanted to bolt. "I'm not saying you are like her, like that, but um, like, if you were, I'm just saying, like, there's nothing wrong with it, and I would support that, or you, I mean." Robby tripped over his words and seemed to be making an effort to look at her as he spoke, but he couldn't keep his eyes from shifting.

"I'm not like Tía Dede," Mel said quickly and wished to God for Robby to move on so that the moment would pass.

"Okay, cool, but like, I'm just saying if you were, that would be cool too."

"Okay," Mel said and felt all of a sudden like she was grateful for his saying that and for his not dropping it right away. She wanted to hug him and maybe cry, but instead she sat there looking out ahead of her like she wasn't feeling anything.

"I'm your big brother, and I'll always be there for you, no matter what." Robby twisted the cigarette into the cement beside him and flung the butt into the gutter. "Don't go looking all sleepy on me now. You better stay awake, or Tía will kick my ass. Come here," he said. Robby pulled her to him for a side hug, then pushed her away. "Come on, I'll make us some nachos, and we can watch TV. What time is it, anyway?" Robby lifted his shirt to look down at the beeper clipped to his jeans. He'd gotten it used from his friend's dad. It was just for looks, since Doreen wouldn't pay for the service. "Yeah, see?" he said. "We can still catch *Arsenio Hall*."

THREE

1999

Tessa

Tessa put a hand on Henry's shoulder to steady herself before she fixed the strap on the back of her sandal. She was balancing a tray full of deviled eggs in the other hand. Ruby and Preston were running up ahead of them, trying to beat each other to the doorbell. Preston got there first and pushed the button repeatedly until Angie opened the door.

"Well, there you are," she said with a huge smile. She was wearing a big apron, and there were many wiry flyaways breaking free from her thick ponytail. She bent to hug and kiss the kids. "Go on in." She swatted Ruby playfully on the butt with the pot holder in her hand as she passed. "And there's Mama and Daddy." Angie hugged and kissed Tessa and Henry too.

"You're filling out that dress nicely there, girlie," Angie said once they were in the kitchen.

Tessa looked down at herself. "I guess so," she said.

"I think your belly is bigger than it was at this point with Ruby or Preston."

"You think?" Tessa said. She pulled a knife from the block and began slicing tomatoes.

"Oh yes, definitely."

"Henry," Angie called. "Henry, come here a minute. Don't you think Tessa's belly is bigger this time around?"

Tessa looked up at Henry, knife in hand. He rubbed the back of his neck. "Oh, I don't know, Mama. It seems just like it was with the other two."

Angie waved him off. "Men don't notice these things. You're gonna have a big baby there, girlie," Angie said.

"Goody," Tessa whispered down at the tomatoes on the cutting board, thinking of her vagina below.

"What's that?" Angie said.

"How many of these you want sliced?" Tessa said.

"Just the one's enough. Only me, Nathan, and you all here this Sunday. The others are all busy. You want an apron, honey? I think I have one that would still fit." The others—Benny and Gordy and his wife and kids—were always busy. Tessa hadn't seen all them since Ruby was born. Angie always talked as if they made the trip out to visit all the time.

"I'm fine, Angie, thanks. What are Gordy and Benny up to these days anyhow?"

"Well, let's see," Angie said.

Before she could continue the thought, Nathan came in from the TV room, tall and lanky as ever. His white sports socks were pulled up to just below his knees. Above that he had on khaki shorts and an orange-and-brown-striped shirt. He saw Tessa and lit up.

"Tessa," he said and went over to give her a hug around the waist. He bent and rested his head on her shoulder.

"Hey, Nate," she said. She kissed him on the cheek when he pulled away. "How you doing, honey?"

"Good." He smiled, and his cheeks blushed pink.

"What have you got there?" Tessa asked. He opened his hand to show a lump of putty. He put the warm, flesh-toned ball in her hand.

"It can copy stuff. I'll show you." Nathan rushed away, nearly knocking Angie over as he passed and bumped her shoulder.

"Slow down," Angie called after him. She shook her head and rubbed her arm. "That boy is just as sweet on you as he was the first day Henry brung you home." Nathan came running back with a newspaper in his hands. It was always something to see the six-foot-tall thirty-six-year-old man running unabashedly, like a kid on a playground.

"Press it on here," he said.

Tessa flattened the putty on the newspaper just below the local headline.

"Smoosh it good," he said.

Nathan carefully lifted the pressed lump, giddy like he was showing her a magic trick. "See?" he said. A swath of newsprint pulled up with the putty.

"Look at that," Tessa marveled. "That sure is something, Nate."

"Thanks," he said. He grabbed two deviled eggs off the tray and shoved them into his mouth.

"No more of those," Angie said. "You'll spoil your dinner." Nathan ran off again. "Chew and swallow." The screen door slapped shut behind him.

"Can I help with anything else?" Tessa asked.

"No, honey. Get you a cool glass of lemonade and go put your feet up."

"Thanks, Ang." Tessa squeezed Angie's arm. She took the pitcher from the fridge and poured herself a glass. She grabbed a small plate and put two deviled eggs on it. Angie saw and gave a half smile. She shook her head.

"Oh, I don't think just two more is gonna make much difference," Tessa said.

Tessa kissed Angie on the cheek and headed for the porch. Out in the backyard, the sun was shining. Henry was chasing the kids around while Nathan hid behind one of the metal T-posts that held up Angie's clothesline. He was grinning big, with his eyes closed. His fingers were laced excitedly in front of his chest. The width of the pole hardly covered the distance between his eyes.

Nathan, Angie's firstborn, had been kicked in the head by an old nag when he was a toddler. It wasn't anyone's fault. It happened fast, the way Buck told it. Nathan ran up to the horse's pen, and it spooked and kicked him through the bars of the metal fence. Angie left the hospital just once in the two months Nathan stayed there. In the middle of Nathan's third night at the hospital, Angie went home, took her father's antique rifle from the gun case, and put a bullet between that horse's sleeping eyes. Buck and Gus, their neighbor from down the road back then, had the grave dug and horse buried before the sun came up. Nathan's body kept growing and was perfectly healthy, aside from a slight limp in his gait, but his brain stopped developing early on, so he had the sense of a six- or seven-year-old.

Nathan opened one eye to peek out at the others from behind the pole. He must have spotted Tessa sitting on the porch because he came skipping over. She leaned forward and pulled the little plate out from under her chair. He scooped the eggs off it and pushed them into his mouth.

"Thanks," he said. He was chewing the mouthful and staring off in the direction of the house when one of Ruby's high-pitched squeals snapped him out of it. "Can I have some of that?" he said, pointing to Tessa's lemonade. She nodded and handed him the glass. He drank three huge gulps and gave it back to her with a few little hard-boiled floaties bobbing next to the ice cubes. "Thanks," he said and wiped his mouth with the back of his hand. Then he flew back down the porch steps. "Guys, I was behind the pole the whole time!" he yelled and ran after them.

Henry was out of breath and had a goofy grin on his face when he walked up the steps and flopped down in the lawn chair beside Tessa. He wiped the sweat from his temples and brow with the corner of his shirt.

"Can I have some of that?" he said, pointing to the glass still in her hand. She opened her mouth to speak but said nothing and passed it to him. He drank down the floaties along with the rest of the lemonade. "Thanks," he said and put a hand on her thigh. "I'll go get you some more in just a minute here, after I catch my breath."

They were all holding hands around the dinner table a half hour later. Angie was in the middle of one of her never-ending grace sessions. Tessa was rolling her neck from side to side and thinking about the school secretary's smug, pudgy face. She had had a meeting with the principal about their encounter the next day. She felt the table lurch and opened an eye to see Ruby sunken down in her chair, trying to kick at Preston's shins. Preston was making monkey faces at her. Tessa pulled Ruby up by their clasped hands and gave a stern look at the both of them.

"In Jesus's name we pray," Angie said.

"Amen," they all said.

Five minutes into dinner and talk of the repairs Angie was needing to have done around the house, the doorbell rang.

"I'll get it," Angie said before anyone could move. She pushed away from the table and threw her cloth napkin down beside her plate. "Now who could that be . . . ?" Her voice trailed off as she walked down the hall. A moment later, she came back. Big Luke, with his hat off and shoulders bent, came walking in behind her. Tessa had never seen him looking that way before. Her fingers went tingly, and she felt short of breath.

"What's the matter, Luke? Why ain't Carly with you?" Tessa said.

"Give him a minute, Tess," Angie said. "Come on and sit down, honey." Angie pulled out the empty seat at the head of the table—Buck's old seat—and Luke sat down.

"Thank you, Ang," he said. "I didn't mean to interrupt dinner." Angie placed a gentle hand on his shoulder. He reached up and squeezed it. Then he let it go and rested his forearms on the table. He cleared his throat. "I'm here to see if you wouldn't mind coming to look in on Carly, Tess."

"What's Carly need looking in on for?" Tessa kept her voice calm this time. Luke shifted in his seat and scratched at the table with his thumbnail before he spoke.

"She's not doing too well. I thought it was just one of her moods, but she's hardly been out of bed in nearly two weeks. And I ain't seen her eat nothing neither."

Angie sucked her teeth and shook her head. "Tess, wasn't you there visiting just this past Thursday? Was Carly that way when you saw her then?" Luke shot a quick look at Tessa. Before he could speak, Tessa answered.

"I didn't make it out to visit this week." She felt Henry's eyes on her and continued, speaking to Luke. "I had meant to. Had the truck from Angie and all, but the day got away from me."

Luke nodded. "I think it might help her to see you."

"Of course," Tessa said. "I'll come back with you tonight." She looked to Henry, who was still watching her. He nodded. "Angie, you mind getting Pres off to school in the morning and watching Ruby for the day?"

"I can do that," Angie said. Tessa heard the suspicion in her voice. Angie was itching to get to the bottom of things, but Tessa knew she wouldn't question her just then, with Luke and the kids right there.

"I need to get a couple things from the trailer," Tessa said. Henry stood up and pushed his chair into the table.

"I'll come help you with that," he said.

Angie

Angie opened the hidden drawer Buck had built into the shelf above the fireplace and lifted out a pack of cigarettes. No one knew she still smoked. The truth was, she rarely did these days, or at least she didn't as much as she used to. She still liked to have a smoke on her porch sometimes, when it got to be late at night and she wanted to sit and think in the quiet for a while. She sat in her wooden rocking chair, the one Buck had carved for her, and looked out over what little was left of her land. The way things were going, she'd have nothing to leave her boys. She had always imagined they'd all live on the ranch after she and Buck were gone, or before if they were lucky enough to get them back home, but when Buck got sick, Angie had to sell nearly all of it to pay the hospital bills.

The cattle were the first to go. Angie wasn't too sad selling them off. There were just a handful of them left by then, and they'd hardly broke even raising them, with all it took to keep them fed. Raising cattle had mostly amounted to hard work that was just getting harder with the way it seemed each year was getting dryer and hotter than the last. With Buck getting older, he wouldn't have been able to keep up the long days, even if he had gotten better. But he loved ranching—he lived for it—and it had broken her heart to stand next to his hospital bed and tell him that his cattle were sold and gone.

Angie had to sell parcels of land one by one after that. There was no one to keep watch over or care for all of it at the time anyway. Only Henry still lived nearby then, and he had a new baby and a wife to feed and worry after. He did his best during those years to help Angie out. He and Tessa took Nathan in for her when they could manage to, but in the end, Angie was left to do the heavy lifting. She was left to hold everything and everyone, just as she always had.

Angie coughed and reached for the tumbler on the ground beside her. Ice cubes clinked against the glass as she lifted it to her lips. She drank a pour of whiskey most nights as a kind of tribute to Buck. That was his drink. Before he passed, she never touched the stuff, but now she had grown accustomed to the slight burn at the back of her throat and the subtle sense of ease it gave her. Buck had been trying to get her to partake for as long as she had known him, but back when it was the two of them on the porch, she'd preferred a cup of chamomile tea and left the hard stuff to him.

"Come on, sugar," he used to say. "Sit down with me and have a sip or two, and let your limbs get a little heavy for a while." She'd say she had things to do. He'd pull her onto his lap, and she'd pretend like it was some bother, like he was keeping her from work, like she didn't love every second of it. He'd let her go and swat her ass on her way back inside. She'd finish the dishes from dinner, and then she'd come back out with her tea and sit in the quiet with him.

By the time Buck passed, there was less of him without cancer than there was with. Angie and her boys had known Buck was on his way out, but somehow his death still felt like an awful surprise. None of them ever fully recovered from losing him, not really. Angie had always carried the family, but Buck had always been the central figure. It was him they all wanted to make proud.

Angie set the empty tumbler down next to her chair again and lit another cigarette. She had more thinking to do. She'd had cause for worry when Tessa come to pick up the truck Thursday wearing that makeup and looking fresh and done up like she did, but Angie had made herself believe that Tessa just wanted to feel good, that it was just part of her girls' day with Carly. She should have known better. Tessa was nearly floating when she saw her that morning. She looked five years younger without all the weight of that melancholy she had taken to wearing the past few years.

Since the beginning, Angie had always been careful not to overstep and try and fill the space in Tessa's heart that she kept for her mama. She knew that wasn't her place. That woman, her mother, didn't deserve any real estate in Tessa's heart, but there was nothing Angie could do. People are built to love their mamas no matter the kind of suffering it brings them. Angie resisted the urge to try and ease a little of the ache there. She toed the line and let that hurt be.

She loved that girl, though, like one of her own. In some ways, it felt like she loved her more. She adopted Tessa into the family, saved her from that place she'd been living and all the ugliness that came with it. She gave Tessa life in a different way than she had with her own. She got to coax the life out of her. She loved Tessa back to wholeness. Tessa was like a vacuum for care those first few years. Timid and untrusting but starved enough for love that she'd take what was offered of it. There's a special bond that comes from that kind of saving.

Angie squeezed her eyes shut with the weight of all her feelings. She prayed that God wouldn't make her choose between the daughter the world had given her and her own flesh-and-blood son. When she was done, she stood and snuffed out the butt of her cigarette on the sole of her house shoe, then went inside to try and sleep.

ngie was up early. She got started in on breakfast, coffee, and
lunch to have ready for Henry to take with him when he
dropped the kids off. With Tessa gone, she knew he'd be in need of
all three and that he would be halfway to work before he'd notice
he was missing them.

She met Henry and the kids at the door at six sharp. Ruby was
asleep on Henry's shoulder, and Preston was standing beside them
with his backpack on and a plastic grocery bag in each hand.

"Thanks, Mama," Henry said. He laid Ruby down on the
couch. "Preston's got their clothes and some toys for Ruby."

"Alright," Angie said. "Come on in the kitchen. I got a burrito
and coffee ready for you to take for the road."

"Thanks, Mama." Henry followed her.

"Can I watch cartoons?" Preston called after them.

"Yes, for a bit," Angie said. "Don't wake your sister."

Henry reached for the sack lunch and the foil-wrapped burrito
on the table. Angie was at the coffeepot filling him a thermos.
"You hear from Tess?"

"She called late last night after she got Carly to sleep."

"Carly gonna be alright?"

"Tess thinks so. She's gonna spend the day with her. I'll pick
her up on my way home." Henry yawned and stretched his arms
up over his head, then went back to leaning into the counter. "You
okay having the kids until then?"

"Sure, honey." Angie gave him the thermos, put a hand on her
hip, and looked him in the face. He shifted on his feet uncomfort-
ably and fumbled to smooth down the collar of his shirt with the
hand that was holding his sack lunch, just as he might have done

when he was a boy. This thought only made the tender and worried feelings she had for him in her heart grow.

"Tessa says Carly's just got a bad case of the blues. It's hard on her living so far out there without neighbors and all," Henry said.

"'Course it is," Angie said without moving her gaze. Henry sighed.

"I'd better get going." He bent down and kissed her cheek. "Thanks again."

"Honey?" is all Angie had to say.

"Mama, she said the day got away from her. You heard it same as I did. She told me as much again when we went to get her things last night."

"Henry," she said.

"Mama, leave it." His voice was sharp. It stung her, but Angie didn't show it. She nodded.

"Alright, then. I'll leave it."

"Everyone has a right to let a day or two get away from them from time to time, especially Tessa. She's earned it. You know how hard it was for her after Ruby come along. The thought of that must be weighing on her with another one on the way. And you know how tired she must be growing that baby in her belly while minding Ruby and Preston. It ain't easy on her, Mama, and she don't have to answer to me or tell me every living thing she does each day." Henry tightened the lid of the thermos. "That's it. That's all I've got to say about it. I love you, and I thank you for your concern," he said. He gave her half a hug before heading out the door.

Henry

Henry turned onto Highway 74. He was taking deep breaths in through his nose and letting them go slowly out his mouth, something he'd learned to do as a kid when he got overwhelmed. Growing up, he'd get panic attacks that would make him lose his breath and black out. None of his brothers had that problem. In fact, no one in or around the Valley had ever heard of such a thing. They didn't talk about it if they had, at least. Buck thought it was all in Henry's head, and he was hard on him for it. He was afraid of what others might think of his boy flustering and passing out like that. He thought others might see it as a show of weakness that reflected poorly on the family.

It *had* made Henry feel weak—pathetic too. Henry was in the fifth grade the third time it happened. He passed out on the blacktop at school and split his chin open. He'd gotten into a fistfight at recess and was whupping the other boy pretty good. When he'd managed to get the other boy backed up against a wall, he hit the kid square in the nose. The boy's head bounced off the wall, and blood puffed from his nostrils and clouded his face before he dropped to the pavement. Something about the sequence of images made Henry's knees go limp. He had tried to brace himself against the wall, but it wasn't more than a moment or two before his own lights went out.

Angie took him to the doctor, who was about as much help as Buck was. He told Angie that Henry would grow out of it and not to give him too much attention when it happened, as that was likely the desired effect. Henry was sitting right there with his arms across his chest on the crinkly white paper of the exam table when the doctor had said that. Henry had felt so ashamed that he had to pinch his underarm as hard as he could to keep himself from crying like a baby.

Later, in the car, Angie told him not to pay the man any mind. He was an old, washed-up quack, she'd said. Angie dropped Henry off at home and spent the rest of that day in town at the library researching treatments. When she got home, she and Henry went up to his bedroom, shut the door, and practiced breathing until he got the hang of it. She told him it was a secret cure. That he'd never have the problem again. She'd been right, for the most part. There was just a time or two since that Henry had felt even near to passing out.

Once he felt his chest start to loosen, Henry reached into the center console, lifted the fake bottom lining he'd put in, and pulled out a cigarette. That was the other thing that had helped him keep his cool over the years. Tessa knew he smoked sometimes, but the others thought he'd quit for sure. When Buck passed, they'd all promised to kick the habit, but old habits died hard—they did for the people he knew, at least.

Henry chewed on the thumbnail of the hand that held his cigarette and watched the glow of the rising sun begin to cast shadows across the Valley. He had his windows down enough to let the cold, fresh, desert-morning air wake his body and fill his lungs. He liked the feeling, and besides, he had to keep the smell of the smoke out of the truck as best he could for the kids. The drive to work was one of his favorite times of the day. It was the closest he ever got to feeling spiritual. The hour-long drive to Indio gave him time to air out his thoughts and get clear on things. He often wished Tessa could have something like it for herself. She might feel better if she did. Sometimes he thought that was why she kept things to herself, kept secrets. It was her way of making room, of having a little space just for her. The peace that he found driving to work made him understand her wanting that.

Henry could square with wanting space, but the lying was what gave him a sick feeling in the pit of his belly. It made him feel like the life he had built could crumble into nothing, and there wasn't a thing he could do about it. Their talk before Tessa had left for Carly's didn't help put him at ease none.

They had been quiet for the short drive to the trailer. It was only when Henry followed her into their room and sat on the bed that he spoke up.

"Tessa, where'd you go Thursday?" he asked.

She stopped folding clothes and stood still, then took in a breath. "I went to late breakfast with an old friend I ran into a few days earlier."

"What friend?"

"Her name's Mel. We were pals in school. She moved away before you and I got together. Anyway, she's back, and I ran into her in town, and we decided to get together to catch up, is all."

"Why couldn't you've told me that?" he said. Before she could answer, he stood and rested his hands on his head and sighed. "You said that you and Carly had a good visit when I asked you about it. You lied to me, Tess. What was the point in doing that? It just don't add up."

"I'm sorry. I just answered without thinking, you know? Like how you do sometimes when you just get so used to saying things. It come out of my mouth before I realized it wasn't true."

"You expect me to buy that bullshit? Give me a little credit."

Henry shoved his hands into his pockets and kicked the laundry basket so that it flew some before it tipped and skidded into the wall.

Tessa went still. He saw the muscles of her jaw set. His heart beat hard with the fear that he might have gone too far with the outburst, but he wasn't willing to show no remorse or give up any stance on the matter. She threw the shirt in her hand down on the bed and crossed her arms on top of her belly. "I told you where I gone, who I seen, and what we done. You have any other questions for me, ask 'em now. Otherwise, I need to get my bag packed."

"'Least I know you'll be going to see Carly this time with Luke driving you there," he said. He'd let the screen door slam shut behind him on his way out, and that was how they'd left things.

If he hadn't lost his temper, he might have been able to ask her about the makeup and her hair being all done up like it was. What in the hell had she needed to do all that for? The short truck ride back up to the house was as quiet as it was on the way to the trailer. Henry and Tessa had kissed goodbye for show, to put his mother at ease. Then Henry shook Luke's hand, and off him and Tessa went.

By the time Henry pulled into the dusty parking lot near the construction site, he was feeling a little better. He assured himself that he and Tessa would talk things out on the drive home from Carly's that night. Maybe he'd suggest that they get away over the weekend, just the two of them. Maybe they'd go camping at Barton Flats. They both liked it there. Henry felt the worry that had been climbing up the muscles of his neck and gripping at his jawbone loosen up some with the idea. They'd both been so busy. A trip like that was just what they needed. With a little time and space to connect and unwind, they'd sort things out. They'd be alright.

Tessa

A few miles down the road, Luke leveled with Tessa. "I expect you know it's more than a case of the blues with Carly," he said. Tessa nodded.

"How long she been drinking again?" she asked.

"Hard to say. It's usually been going on a while before it gets bad enough for me to catch wind of it."

"How bad is it this time?"

"Worst yet." Luke exhaled. "That's the reason I come to get your help." Luke shifted in his seat so he could pull his wallet out of his back pocket and put it on the dashboard. "I appreciate you coming with me, Tess. I know you got your own family to look after."

Carly's problem with drink had surfaced a few times in the years Tessa had known her. Tessa had helped out before and kept quiet about it. Carly was a good woman. She tried hard and slipped up from time to time. That's just how it was.

She could hardly fault Carly for it this time. Seeing Tessa pregnant again after wanting so badly for so long to be a mama herself probably didn't help matters. Carly had been doing her best to hang on, but she'd been white-knuckling it since Luke had moved them to that trailer out in the middle of nowheres a few months back. Carly just wasn't built to be alone like that. She was made to entertain and socialize and care for others. She had this generous, sparkly way about her around people. She'd light up and capture attention while making everyone else feel special.

It broke Tessa's heart to see Carly running on near empty every time she made the trip out to visit her. Luke liked it that way, though, Tessa was pretty sure. Tessa had always thought he had a nasty, just-barely-hidden jealousy about him that made him want to keep her away from people.

Tessa had met Carly a few years back on account of Luke and Henry being fishing buds. Carly and Tessa had gone to the same high school, but Carly was four years ahead and had already graduated by the time Tessa got there. It wasn't likely they'd have been friends anyhow, even if they had met back then. Carly was one of those pretty cheerleader types. She even had a pretty-girl name. It made Tessa think of butterflies in the spring. Carly wrote notes in that pretty-girl way, with big, looping, ribbonlike cursive. Tessa had always thought her own name sounded like a stifled sneeze, and she wrote her notes in chicken scratch.

"It's like Angie said—you done the right thing getting me," Tessa said. She watched the lights from houses growing fewer and farther between as they drove away from town. She rested her forehead against the cool glass of her window and dozed off a bit.

The air in the trailer was thick and smelled like stale corn chips. The dishes had been piling up for a couple weeks by the looks of it. Luke led Tessa back to the bedroom, where Carly was sleeping. Tessa went to the bed, rolled Carly over, and gently brushed away the thin wisps of soft blond hair that clung to her damp face. She was out cold. A sick-sweet-smelling sheen of alcohol sweat glazed her skin.

"Oh, honey," Tessa whispered. "Luke, see about moving her up against the wall. Prop her up with some pillows there so she's resting on her side. That way, if she gets sick, she don't choke. You and me have to keep an eye on her while we sort stuff out around here. It's just the drink as far as you know, right? She don't have any pills?'"

"I don't think so," he said.

"Suppose we'll find out. Help me turn this place over and pitch all the alcohol. Let me know if you find anything else."

Tessa started in the bedroom and searched her way through the whole trailer. Luke kept shaking his head every time she found another bottle tucked away. "I swear, I never knew she kept that there. Jesus, I can't believe it."

It annoyed Tessa that he wasn't any help in finding the stashes. It was his own trailer, and she kept having to come up with places for him to look. He kept following her around like a dumb puppy. When Tessa opened the fridge and reached for the six-pack of beer on the top shelf, Luke was quick to speak up.

"Those are mine," he said. Tessa went rigid. She kept her hand on the beer and turned her head to give him a hard stare.

"Should probably empty those too, though," he said.

"Yeah," she said. "Probably should."

She was tired by the time she got done cleaning up and looking all over. Tessa finished the last dish and set it on the drying rack. She put her hands on her lower back and closed her eyes to stand still and rest a minute there in front of the sink. Luke came in from searching around outside.

"You were right. I looked up under the wheel well, and sure enough, there it—" He stopped midsentence. Tessa opened her eyes. He let the box of white wine he'd turned up fall to his side. "I never," he stammered. "You alright?"

Tessa followed his gaze down to her belly. The baby was kicking around. It had been kicking around like that for the last hour or so. She'd become used to it and forgot it was happening. Only when it kicked up into her rib cage did the feeling become uncomfortable enough to get her attention, and it hadn't done that in a while.

She had taken her sweater off when the warm, soapy dishwater started to make her bangs and the hairs at the nape of her neck curl up and go damp. Her long-sleeved shirt stretched thin across her belly. You could see the baby's body shifting around; it bowed out and rippled in fits against the surface of her belly. The big-eyed fear on Luke's face was juvenile. It made her laugh.

"He's just having a stretch in there, is all. I think he gets restless the way his father does sometimes and has to fidget around some."

"You know it's a boy, then?"

The question caught her off guard. They hadn't actually found out the baby's sex yet. She surprised herself by talking as if she knew it was a boy. She wondered why that was and when she'd started thinking of this baby that way.

"No," she said. "Just a hunch."

Luke relaxed and laughed a little. "I didn't know that was normal, being able to see it pressing out like that. Seems like there should be more lining to protect it or something," he said. She'd never thought of her body that way—as a liner. "It looked like something out of that movie *Aliens*. Lord, that was something," Luke said. He was laughing more now, with the relief that Tessa guessed had come with the knowledge that an alien wasn't going to explode out of her stomach.

"Well, it's normal," she said in a flat voice. "Anyway, I think I'll go and see if I can't wake Carly now and get her washed up and fresh for bed. She'll feel better for it in the morning. I'll call you in if I need help lifting or moving her. I expect she'll be okay to stand, though. I'll keep an eye on her tonight. You take the couch and get some sleep before you have to wake for work."

Tessa filled a glass with water from the tap in the kitchen on her way to the bedroom. She put it down on the nightstand next to a bottle of aspirin. Then she went to Carly's dresser and laid out fresh clothes for after her shower. She sat down beside Carly and whispered for her to wake up. Carly rolled her eyes open and closed a few times.

"Ain't you a sight," Carly said.

"Hey, sugar," Tessa said and took Carly's hand.

"Luke bring you here?"

Tessa nodded.

"I figured he'd do that," Carly said. "Wished that he wouldn't bother you but figured he would." Carly was drunk, but Tessa thought she could still manage to help her wash.

"How 'bout we get you cleaned up and ready for bed?"

"As you like," Carly said. She pressed up on her forearms, and Tessa helped her sit up. Carly hooked her elbow around the back of Tessa's neck while Tessa held her around the hip for balance. Tessa turned the shower on and helped Carly undress. Her clothes smelled, and her hair was starting to tangle and grease at the roots. It was hard to believe they'd been sharing tea and trading news just a couple weeks before. That's how it was with Carly, though. She always came crashing down when she fell off the wagon. Tessa sat Carly down in the shower, figuring it was safer than having her stand.

She rolled up her sleeves and pulled her own hair into a tight bun before she soaped up the washcloth. Carly hugged her knees to her chest, lifted her chin, and squinted up through the water at Tessa.

"I'm sorry," she said.

"Turn around, honey. I'll get your back," Tessa said. Carly walked her feet around so her back was facing Tessa. Tessa squatted and ran the washcloth over the jutting bones of her rounded spine. Carly was a naturally thin woman, but when she'd start up with the drinking, it seemed like the alcohol leached away what little reserves her body managed to hold on to. Tessa felt the tremors of Carly's silent sobs rattle up her arms as she smoothed the cloth over her.

Tessa worked shampoo into Carly's scalp and held her neck when she tipped her head back to rinse in the spray. She handed Carly the washcloth. "I'm gonna go grab a towel. You stay sitting and finish up. Be right back."

Tessa combed Carly's hair out and helped her get dressed. After she had gotten Carly into bed and settled herself in for the night, she pulled the comforter up over them both, rested the back of her head on the single flat pillow Luke had left for her, and stared up at the ceiling.

"Get you some sleep," Tessa said and turned out the lamp by the bed. The light from the moon was bright coming in the window above them. Tessa sat up and reached to close the blinds.

"Don't," Carly said. "I like the way it makes things look in here. Like the room is all made of white silver."

"'Kay." Tessa dropped her arm and settled back under the blanket. Carly pulled the sheets down a bit and reached for Tessa's stomach and gently traced her fingers over the mound growing there. Tessa had an impulse to move her hand away as soon as she had felt it, but resisted the urge and allowed Carly to continue.

"How'd you get to be so good at this?" Carly said after a few moments with her hand there.

"At what?"

"Living here. Making babies. Saving wayward friends. All of it. Seems to come real natural to you."

"I ain't saving you, Carly. I wish I could, but it don't work that way."

"Lighten up, darling. It ain't as bad as it looks. I come back every time in the past, ain't I?"

"It's awful hard on your body, Carly. I don't like to see you hurting yourself."

Carly took her hand back and propped herself up on her elbow. "We're all hurting, honey. Only difference between you and me is I ain't got as much as you do to keep me from thinking about it."

"Don't talk like that."

"Like what, honey? Like I know how things is? Keep quiet. Wake up, make Luke breakfast and lunch, and sit around here until it's time to make dinner. Be grateful for what I have. What the Lord has blessed me with. Sure, sugar. I won't mention none of it." Carly leaned closer to her. Tessa stayed on her back with laced fingers under her head. She felt Carly's warm, acidic breath on her cheek and temple.

"I won't mention," Carly whispered in a wicked voice that turned Tessa's blood cold, "that Sandy said she saw you with that Mexican girl you used to be buddy-buddy with at Denny's just this week. I won't mention what the girls from the cheer team back then said about just how close you two was in high school before I knowed you. I won't mention what they said about the nature of you and hers friendship back then." Carly put her first and middle fingers to her mouth and stuck her wagging tongue out between them. Tessa sat up and smacked her hard across the face.

Carly's eyes got big. She put a hand to her cheek. Her mouth hung open, and her eyebrows rose way up on her forehead. The look on her face was closer to delight than surprise.

"Hush up now, you ingrate." Tessa got up and feverishly groped around in the half-light for her coat. She touched the coat's felt, swept it off the floor, and swung her arms into it. "Go to sleep before you say something I won't be able to forgive you for."

"You're not as good as you pretend to be," Tessa heard Carly whisper as she left the room.

Tessa slid her feet into her boots and eased the trailer door open so as not to wake Luke on the couch. Once outside, she leaned up against Luke's truck to steady herself. Carly had never gotten that way with her before. She'd heard her say some hateful things about herself and others when she was wrecked, but she'd never thought Carly had it in her to turn on her like that. "Jesus Christ," Tessa breathed. She smoothed her hair back behind her ears and held her hands on her head so she could fill her lungs. Her stomach was sour, and her limbs felt limp and shaky. She pulled down the truck's tailgate and took a seat.

Maybe Carly was right. Maybe Tessa being so busy with the kids all the time kept her from having to think about things, or kept her from thinking things through, anyway. Going to see Mel had been a bad idea. She had only made things worse by lying about it. When she come to think of it, she wondered if she had even needed to lie in the first place. What she had done back then was back then. Things were different now. She could have told Henry she was going to see her old friend, and he wouldn't have cared. Even if there were people in town who liked to talk and spread rumors, Henry wouldn't have paid any of that mind. She couldn't blame him for getting upset like he did about her lying.

She'd let some foolishness get into her head when she ran into Mel. She blamed it on the lost and lonely feelings she'd been having lately and on her uneasiness about the pregnancy this time around. She'd been feeling mixed up, like maybe no one really understood her at all. Like they were all okay with her pretending to be what they wanted her to be for them. She'd been thinking of her mother recently too, and that kind of thinking had never done her no good in the past.

It happened that she started thinking more about Amber Jean when she was pregnant with Pres and Ruby too. Pregnancy makes a person think about motherhood. No way of getting around that. For a while there, she'd let her mind get the best of her after Ruby come along. She couldn't let that happen again. It was hard on Henry and the kids. She hated having the fear of it, and she hated how it made her wary of this baby. It wasn't fair that she'd tried to wish it away like she had. She knew what it was like to have your own mama treat you like you were a burden. That kind of hurt stays with you. All Tessa could do was hope that the baby would forgive her, that her love for it when it finally came along would wash away any seeds of doubt or feelings of imperfection she might have already sown. Tessa felt a tickle at her chin. She wiped at it, thinking it was a mosquito, but felt the wetness of tears there instead. She hadn't noticed she'd started to cry. She shook her head. *No more of that,* she thought. She wiped her face with her sleeves and let out a sigh.

Tessa put her hands to her belly. "We had us a scare back there, didn't we?" she said. "Don't you worry, baby. She ain't gonna cause us no harm." Tessa reached into her coat pocket and pulled out her phone. "I think we better call your daddy and let him know we're doing okay."

Tessa was looking out the kitchen window when Carly came in from the bedroom that morning. She handed Carly a cup of coffee and pulled out a chair at the kitchen table. "Have a seat," Tessa said.

As soon as she landed in the chair, Carly's bottom lip started to tremble. "I'm sorry I said those things. I wasn't in my right mind. Tessa, I—"

"This is the last time I'm coming out here to help you out like this, Carly. You understand? I don't like how the drink turns you ugly the way it does. It's one thing feeling sorry for yourself. It's another saying those nasty things about me. You want to ruin your life? You go right ahead, but don't you try and drag me and my family down with you. I come out here because you're the closest thing I've got to a sister, and I love you, but if you ever say anything like you did last night again, I'll drop your ass faster than you can blink your eye—just as easy as that too. Henry and the kids is the only real thing I got. You threaten that, you and me are gonna have problems. You can ask your dumbshit cheerleader friends how it went for the girls who tested me back then. I've come a long way, but you can bet your ass I still have that ruthlessness in me. You put me in a corner and you'll see it. I know how to survive, Carly, better than anyone I ever met."

Tessa set her coffee cup on the table. She reached her hand down and lifted Carly's chin so she could look her in the eye. "I need to know—we square?"

Carly nodded.

"Say it," Tessa said.

"We're square," Carly whispered.

"Good," Tessa said. "Drink turns you into a loathful person, Carly. Turns you into someone who's either out chasing hurt for yourself or inflicting it on those who love you best. That should be enough for you to keep away from it. I ain't gonna rub your nose in it anymore, but if we wasn't as good of friends as we are, and if I didn't know you was a good woman, I'd've left last night and never come back."

"It won't happen again," Carly said. "None of it."

They didn't hardly talk the rest of the afternoon. They worked quietly together on a thousand-piece puzzle Tessa found in the coat closet that pictured the nation's Capitol. Tessa focused on putting together the blue sky because the white building pieces all looked the same to her. When she heard the tires of Henry's truck on the gravel out front, she stood and made her way to the door. She put a hand on the doorknob, then turned back to Carly.

"I know it ain't easy on you living out here, and I know you've been holding sorrow in your heart about not being able to start a family like you'd wanted to. I'm sorry for that. You stay sober and get your head straight these next couple weeks, and I'll come out and pick you up to stay at our place for a few days. We'll give Luke a chance to grow him some appreciation and perspective in making his own coffee and meals for a change. How's that sound?"

"Sounds nice," she said.

"See you then, sugar," Tessa said and went out the door for the truck.

FOUR

1999

Angie

Angie believed in signs. "Read the signs," she always said when a friend came to ask her for advice. The signs, in those cases, were usually the facts that the friend wasn't wanting to look at, like evidence of a cheating husband, but she also believed in less obvious connections that spoke to more of a divine warning or spiritual type of premonition. She believed if you paid close enough attention, you could see a bad thing coming from a ways off. It would kick up dust and cause a change in the air, the same way a building storm would. Darkness had a gravitational pull, just the same as light. A mountain lion had killed her favorite mare the week before Buck found out his cancer had spread. Buttercup was Angie's blue-ribbon cutting horse. She had raised and trained her since she was a year-old filly. The week before that, the Williams' house, just nine acres over, had burned all the way down to dirt. Angie believed if you could pay close attention and read the signs given, you had a chance to get far enough away to escape the worst of it. You had a chance to make things right.

She hadn't read the signs with Tessa before. She blamed herself for that. It was too late to avoid the worst of it by the time she wised up to things. After Ruby come along, Tessa was nearly all the way gone. It was more than the baby blues that women sometimes get. Angie was pretty sure that was part of it, though. The thing afflicting Tessa was slippery and impossible to get a read on and grab ahold of. There was too much going on below the surface to really see its shape and size. Tessa had always done her best to keep what had come before Henry to herself. Angie was the only one who knew the extent of the nastiness she'd gone through living with Wayne. Tessa had made her promise never to tell another living soul. She'd seen glimpses of the hurt fixed in her by her mama leaving like she had, but Angie also saw how strong Tessa was. For this reason, she had always made efforts to respect her wishes and privacy to the extent that she could. Angie never should have let her go to collect her mother's body when the authorities called and said they had found her in Phoenix at that scuzzy motel. Angie knew that now. Tessa was six months pregnant with Ruby at the time. She had insisted that she wanted to go by herself. She had told Angie it was important to her. So Angie talked Henry, who was all up in arms, down and let Tessa take the truck.

Tessa receded deeper and deeper into herself after that trip. She withdrew from everyone. When Ruby come along, she took good care of her, but for the blank expression she'd wear when she held her baby in her arms, you'd think she was holding a watermelon on her lap. There wasn't hardly any of her left to bring back out after all that. This time around, Angie was paying attention. This time, she'd intervene.

Tessa and Henry came in the front door just as Angie was pulling dinner off the stove. She'd made Henry's favorite: chicken-fried steak, mashed potatoes, and peas. Ruby and Pres jumped up from where they were sitting in front of the TV set and ran to meet them.

"You didn't have to go through all this trouble," Tessa said.

"Nonsense. It's nothing."

"Well, thank you. I'm sure glad to not have to cook tonight."

Angie waited until they were all settled at the table and happily eating the dinner she'd prepared to mention her plan. "Listen, how 'bout we all take a day trip Saturday so we can get off this property and have us some fun?" she said.

Henry looked to Tessa, who busied herself with smoothing her napkin on her lap. "Mama, Tess and I thought maybe we'd go somewhere just us this weekend. We were gonna ask if you wouldn't mind watching the kids," Henry said.

"You and Tessa can go somewhere next weekend. I'll watch the kids for you then. We haven't spent a day away together as a family in a long while. It's overdue."

Henry looked to Tessa again. She quit with the napkin and nodded. "That sounds nice, Angie," she said. "Where you thinking of us all going?"

"Lake Arrowhead sound alright? We always have a good time when we make the trip. You can put your tired little feet in the cool water," Angie said. Nathan's head had snapped up from his plate at the word *lake*, but his mouth was too full of the food he'd piled into it to speak. His eyes widened with alarm at the word *water*. Angie saw him chewing feverishly so he could swallow and object.

"That'll be nice," Tessa said. Nathan reached for his glass of milk and doused down the food he was struggling to swallow. Milk and potatoes came sputtering out of his mouth when he was finally able to speak.

"I don't wanna go," he said.

"'Course you do, Nathan. 'Member how much you liked watching the birds there last time we went?" Angie said.

"Uh-uh. No. I ain't going." Nathan shook his head violently.

"We'll bring the binoculars this time. I'll even get you some film for the Polaroid so you can take pictures," Angie said. Nathan pushed away from the table and ran for his room.

"I ain't going!" he yelled, and the door to his room slammed shut.

"He'll be fine," Angie said. "I'll work on him. In a couple of days, I'll have him excited to be going." Angie sighed. "Damn Benny for telling him that giant wave bullshit." She shook her head.

"Anyway," Angie said, scooting away from the table, "who's ready for pie?"

"Me!" Ruby bounced in her seat.

"Well, come on into the kitchen and help Grandma slice it up." Ruby popped out of her chair and followed Angie to the kitchen.

"Can I have a Polaroid camera for the birds too?" Ruby said. She went skipping ahead of Angie on the linoleum floor and pulled a spatula out of the drawer.

"Let's let that be Nathan's special treat for the day, okay?"

"Alright," Ruby said with all the enthusiasm of a deflated balloon. Angie pulled her marshmallowed sweet potato pie out the oven and set it on the stove. Tessa came in with a stack of dirty plates from the table and set them in the sink. She clicked her tongue.

"I don't know how you manage to make a nice dinner like that and a pie while watching the kids and Nathan and all else you got going on here," Tessa said. "Most nights, I'm hard-pressed to get a frozen dinner heated and on the table before Henry gets home."

"Well, honey, I've had a lot of practice. It wasn't always dinners and pies like this when I had young ones. You just ask Henry about that. There were times I'd have the family eating the same tuna casserole all week. Hell, I remember feeding them popcorn and cut-up hot dogs when time and money was lean. Besides, it's a lot easier to manage when I only have them some of the time, like I do. I got more energy to give that way."

"You said two bad words, Grandma," Ruby said as she crawled out from under the kitchen table, where she'd been scraping at its wooden legs with the spatula for no good reason. Angie turned to her from the oven.

"I did?" she said and put her hands on her hips.

"*Bullshit* and *damn*," Ruby said.

"Ruby!" Tessa hissed.

"I was just repeating," Ruby said.

"I don't want those words coming out of your mouth under any circumstances, understand?" Tessa said. Ruby opened her mouth to defend herself, and Tessa held up her hand. "Grandma is a grown woman and has earned the right to say whatever she *damn* well pleases," Tessa said. She waited to see if Ruby had anything to say about her own use of the word. Ruby knew better, though. Tessa swept a dish towel over her shoulder and took the plate with the piece of pie Angie had just cut and handed it to Ruby. "Go bring Daddy his slice of pie." Ruby carried the plate and a clean fork out the kitchen.

"She sure is a little pill sometimes. Smart as a whip, though, huh?" Angie laughed.

"Born to give her mother grief," Tessa said. The words hung stale in the air. Angie could tell Tessa felt the weight of them land the same way she did. Angie cleared her throat.

"She takes after her mama, being so strong-willed and sharp like that," Angie said. "You bear the brunt of her exercising those gifts now, but those same qualities will make an intelligent and independent woman of her by the time she's grown," she said. Tessa nodded and went back to the sink. "And if she gets half the resilience her mama has, we won't have to worry none about her. That willful little creature in there will have anything she puts her mind to." Angie walked up to stand beside Tessa with a stack of plates in one hand and her pie in the other. She bumped her hip into Tessa's. "Leave those for me to do later," she said. "Come have some pie."

"I'll be out in a minute. I'm just gonna get them soaking, is all," Tessa said.

"Alright, honey. I'll have a big slice waiting." She backed into the kitchen's swinging door and saw Tessa with her head dropped and hands wide, holding herself up on the sink. "Warm pie," Angie said as she came into the dining room and let the door wag shut behind her. Preston and Ruby stopped arguing over the saltshaker and beamed up at her. Nathan slowly crept back to his seat at the table, unwilling to forgo pie to make his point. Henry, the gentleman that he was, sat with his hands folded and his slice untouched in front of him. Angie's heart quickened with the intense love she felt for them just then.

"Thank you, Mama," Henry said. She smiled and blinked back the foolishness that was trying to mist up her eyes. They'd all be okay, she thought. She'd make sure of it.

Tessa

Tessa sat beside Nathan on the sandy shore of Lake Arrowhead. Nathan didn't want to be there, but with everyone at the mandatory family outing, there was no one to keep an eye on him back at home. He was more fidgety than normal, being that close to the water. He had picked up the fear when he was a young boy. Benny, his oldest brother, came home from school one day back then and told him what tsunamis were and how they worked. The science behind tsunamis didn't stick, but the fear of them sure did. It wasn't just the ocean that scared him; Nathan got it into his head that rivers and lakes could make giant waves too. For that reason, he refused to learn to swim and lived with an unshakable dread that, sooner or later, a wave was coming to squash and suffocate him and the whole of California.

Tessa didn't mind the outing, really. If Angie hadn't insisted on it, she'd've had to go away with Henry like he'd asked her to, and the timing just didn't feel right for that. It would've felt strained, and she wasn't in the mood to try and force romance.

Tessa did her best to keep Nathan from worrying by having him read and explain the cards from his Magic: The Gathering deck. Each card showed a creature and gave that creature's particular stats. They all had different abilities and vulnerabilities, ranging from fireball capability to susceptibility to dark charms.

Tessa supposed that, like for Nathan, large bodies of water would go under the category of vulnerabilities for her too. She wasn't afraid like Nathan was, but she couldn't swim neither.

Tessa's mama, Amber Jean, never let her near more than a puddle when she was young. Amber Jean swore that the women of their family had a water curse on them. She used to tell Tessa stories about the curse. These stories mostly featured Tessa's grandma Opal and Opal's twin sister, Oma.

The curse was supposed to have started back in Oklahoma with Opal and Oma's mama, Tessa's great-grandmother. It happened after she'd crossed a jealous woman named Willa, who lived outside of town and sold spells and bundles of herbs to burn for charms or to keep bad luck away. Supposedly, Tessa's great-grandmother had the nerve to suggest that Willa's husband had a wandering eye and that he was causing the trouble, not all the women that Willa went around talking poorly about. A week after the suggestion had been made, Tessa's great-grandmother drowned. She was washing clothes in the river. Opal's nightshirt slipped out of her hands and got away from her. She waded in after it, lost her footing on the slick stones beneath her, and got sucked right under by the current. The river took her with Opal and Oma watching from onshore. Her waterlogged body was found the next day, spat out on the shore seven miles downriver with one of Willa's bundles lying soggy and half-burned beside it.

That story never changed, but the way Opal and Oma kicked the bucket was different and more creative each time Tessa's mama told it. In some fantastic way or another, drowning was always how they went.

It wasn't always death and drowning stories, though. Amber Jean liked telling adventure stories about Opal and Oma too. This, Tessa supposed, was because her mama had always wanted a sister. Tessa figured that was why Amber Jean had treated her more like a sibling than her child when she was around.

Amber Jean didn't talk much about her growing-up years or her life before coming to Perris. Tessa had once heard her mama quietly say that she'd had a very lonely childhood. She was lying in bed and staring out the window. She had been in bed for days at that point and seemed to whisper this to herself as an explanation of things, or maybe it had been a broken fragment of her private inner thoughts that just slipped out of her mouth.

Other details came few and far between in the seven years Tessa had with her mama. Tessa knew Amber Jean's own mama had died when Amber Jean was just a kid and that she was raised by her great-aunt, whose name Tessa never learned. The few times she had spoken of her, Amber Jean had referred to her as "that old, mean, sour-faced Bible-thumper."

Amber Jean had said that her great-aunt only got meaner after Tessa come along. Tessa heard nothing of who her father might have been. Amber Jean hid her being pregnant with Tessa near next to the day she was born. Amber Jean had always said it wasn't hard to hide what people didn't want to see, but when her water broke in the supermarket, the jig was up.

She left Oklahoma three months later. Amber Jean gathered what little possessions she had and skipped town with Tessa in one arm and an old suitcase with a missing handle tucked under the other. She successfully hitchhiked her way across three states with Tessa sitting in her lap.

She was on her way to Hollywood to become a movie star but had to make a pit stop in Perris when the bit of money she had ran out. She got a temporary waitressing job at Jenny's Diner, where she meant to save up enough money to get herself some new clothes to wear to casting calls out in LA. Jenny let her stay with Tessa in a small storage room in the back. Amber Jean used to say that

Jenny and everyone else thought she'd make it as a movie star back then. Tessa had believed her when she said that. Her mama was the kind of pretty that would take your breath away.

One morning, Wayne came into Jenny's for steak and eggs. He told Amber Jean about the house he owned and the people he knew that he could talk to about getting her on the big screen. It worked like a charm. Amber Jean was the most gullible woman to have ever walked this earth. He sweet-talked her into letting him take her out for dinner that night, and that was that. She and Tessa moved out of Jenny's back room and into his place the following week.

The many stories Tessa's mama told about the twins, Opal and Oma, generated images of cartoon characters in Tessa's mind instead of real people. Maybe that was all they ever were anyhow. Tessa could never really know the truth of anything Amber Jean ever said. Everyone on her mama's side was either dead or living somewhere back in Oklahoma, and her mama was the best storyteller Tessa ever met.

Whether it came from fact or fiction, the terror Amber Jean felt about drowning was as real as it got. She wouldn't set foot in a bathtub. She gave Tessa bird baths in the kitchen sink until Tessa was four and old enough to stand in the shower. Even then, her mama was racked with nerves every time Tessa had to wash. She'd sit on the bathroom floor and read her magazines until Tessa was finished, stopping every other minute to pull the curtain back so she could see that Tessa was alright. Tessa didn't mind her mama doing that. She liked it, sort of. It was one of the ways Tessa could tell that her mama loved her.

Tessa hadn't thought about any of that in years. She figured it was a testament to her own sanity that she'd never shared these stories with her family now and that she was looking out on her own children laughing and playing in the water without a bit of concern. She was glad that the foolishness about the water curse would end with her. Still, she couldn't swim and didn't figure she would ever try and learn how to. The stories had at least had that much of an impact on her.

Henry was waist-deep in the water roughhousing with Preston. Angie and Ruby were sitting near the shoreline in shallow water. Ruby was pulling up handfuls of wet sand and then opening her fists to let it plunk back into the lake while they talked.

Preston let out a loud shriek when Henry launched him up into the air. He splashed in, surfaced, and pounded back over to Henry. He reached his arms around his daddy's neck and clung to his back. Henry wiped his face and checked the beach for Tessa. He gave a big smile and wave when he saw she was watching.

"Hi, Mama!" Preston yelled.

Tessa waved back.

Henry had been in high spirits ever since he and Tessa had their talk on the ride home from Carly's a few days back. Looking out the truck window that night, Tessa was trying to decide if she was gonna tell Henry about the doctor's visit the next day. She had gotten the call reminding her of the appointment earlier that afternoon while she was with Carly. She knew telling Henry was the right thing to do. He'd want to be there. He'd be excited to find out the sex and would make a big deal of the sonogram by having it framed, like he'd done with Ruby's and Preston's. With everything going on, Tessa didn't much feel like going to the appointment. She was tired just thinking about the range of emotions she'd have to fake to make everyone feel okay. But the night before, she'd sworn off secrets and wanted with all her heart for things to be alright for her family, so she pressed away from the truck window to look at Henry and willed herself to speak.

"Hen?"

"Hmm?"

"I got a call from the doctor's office reminding me about a checkup tomorrow."

"This the one where we find out if it's a boy or girl?"

"Think so," Tessa said. "I know it's short notice for your work. It's okay if you can't make it."

"What time?"

"Nine thirty."

"I can make it. Jim won't mind if I come in late. Just have to stay a bit longer, is all." Henry smiled and rested his free hand on her belly. "I wouldn't miss it." He stayed quiet like that with his hand there for a few miles before he spoke again.

"I'm sorry I got upset like I did," Henry said.

"You don't have to be," she started.

"No, I do. I shouldn't have acted that way when there was already enough to worry about. I didn't need to add to things with my foolishness." He slipped his hand down from her belly and took ahold of hers. "I trust you. It's like you said—you don't have to tell me every living thing."

Tessa had felt her eyes wanting to water up. She blinked fast a few times and steadied herself. "I think we're both doing our best, Hen. Nobody's perfect." Least of all her, she'd wanted to add, but she didn't. She knew that saying that last part would have been to make herself feel better, or worse maybe. Either way, it wouldn't have been for Henry.

"I sure love you and the kids" is what she'd said instead. She could tell her saying that had put Henry at ease. His shoulders relaxed, and he chewed on the inside of his cheek the way he did when he was trying not to beam too much. He told her he loved her and the kids too, of course. Then he asked her if she would go away with him that weekend, just the two of them, so they could have some time together.

"It'll be good to have some time, just us. We won't have the chance for a while after that little bun comes out the oven. It was almost two years before Ruby would let you out of her sight, wasn't it?" Henry said.

Tessa felt her chest tighten. She put her hands on her thighs and let out a long, quiet breath. "Yeah," she said. "I guess it was."

Tessa had been shocked that next day at the doctor's office when Dr. Albertine told her and Henry that it was a girl she was growing in her belly. She'd made him check twice more after he first said it. Even after that, she had him point out the empty space between the baby's legs from three different angles.

"No sign of a penis," Dr. Albertine had said. "I'm certain. You're having a girl."

Henry got weepy when he found out the sex, just like he had with the first two. Tessa couldn't feel much, save for a profound sense of having been bamboozled. She had been so certain she was carrying a boy. She couldn't shake the stupid idea that the baby had somehow tricked her. That maybe the baby wasn't so helpless after all. Maybe it had more of a handle on things than Tessa had given it—her—credit for. Maybe making Tessa think she was a boy was her way of letting Tessa know she knew what was what.

Tessa continued to stare at the blank monitor after the doctor had shut off the ultrasound machine and left the room.

"A girl. Can you believe it?! I bet she comes out with her fists up and ready for a fight, like Ruby did." Henry laughed, pulled his baseball cap from the back pocket of his jeans, and slapped it into the palm of his other hand. "Hon?" he said. "You believe we're having another baby girl?!" Tessa studied her own dazed expression in the reflection of the dark screen.

"Well, I'll be" is all she could manage to say.

A re you listening?" Nathan asked.

"Yes, go on, I'm listening," Tessa said.

"Okay." Nathan pulled out another card and set it on the blanket in front of him. "This one is Ajani Goldmane," Nathan said. "He's an albino leonin warrior. His card is called"—Nathan wiped his nose with the palm of his hand and bent over the card to read it more closely—"Heroic Intervention. It means you get to be hexproof and indestructible until the end of your turn."

Tessa hunched over to get a better look at the guy. "How long does a turn last?" she said.

Angie came walking up from the water with Ruby a few minutes later. She bent her knees some and then let gravity land her backside heavy on the blanket next to Tessa. She was laughing at something Ruby must've said or done when she patted Tessa on the knee. "How's my honey?" she asked. Ruby was hopping from foot to foot in front of Angie.

"I'm hungry," Ruby said.

"Towel off. Then you can get you a juice box and sandwich from the cooler," Angie said, then turned back to Tessa.

"I'm good," Tessa said in the most upbeat tone she could muster.

"You sure, honey? You're not having any feelings like you did a few years back with Ruby?" Tessa's face flushed. She bent her head and pretended to straighten out the edge of the blanket at her feet.

"Angie," she whispered sharply.

"Ain't no one but you can hear me. Nathan is in his magic zone. Ain't that right, Nathan?" she said. Nathan didn't respond; he had a card about three inches from his face and was squeezing one eye shut like he was looking through the scope of a hunting rifle. He was making that little humming noise in the back of his throat, like he would when he was concentrating on matters of another world.

"I can't find the one that says my name on it!" Ruby yelled from the other side of their setup, where she was digging in the cooler for her sandwich.

"It's in there. Keep looking," Angie hollered back, closer to Tessa's ear than she would have liked.

"I'm fine," Tessa said.

"Okay," Angie said. She let out a sigh. "Okay."

"I can't find it!" Ruby yelled and let the red cooler's lid slam shut.

"Hang on a second," Angie said. She rolled her eyes and made to push herself up. Tessa put a hand on her arm.

"You stay. I'll find it," Tessa said.

"Thanks, honey," Angie said.

Tessa found the sandwich, lifted Ruby up on her hip, and walked back over to sit with Angie. Ruby settled on Tessa's lap with her peanut butter and honey, no crust. She walked the fingers of her free hand along Tessa's thigh, stopping every few paces to squeeze at the flesh there. She'd done that since she was a baby. It must have felt comforting in some way. Back when she was still breastfeeding, Ruby would leave small marks under Tessa's arm wherever her little wandering fingers felt like pinching.

"You have a good time catching up with your old school buddy the other day?" Angie said. Tessa felt her guts bunch up in her stomach under the baby. She snapped her head up from looking down at Ruby in her lap and searched Angie's face.

"The girl who lost her brother. What's her name again?" Angie said.

"Mel," Tessa said.

"Yeah. Her," Angie said.

"How'd you know we met up?"

"Betty's granddaughter told her you two was at her work. She was your-all's waitress." Angie opened her soda can and took a sip. "Betty's granddaughter said you gave her holy hell over a side of butter." Angie was laughing as she said this. "I kept a straight face when Betty told me, but as soon as I got in the truck, I had a good chuckle over that. God bless her little heart. That granddaughter of Betty's is as dumb as a rock. It's a good thing she has her looks going for her." Angie was still laughing a little. Tessa went rigid. Her hands pressed tight around the bottle of sunblock that she'd begun to fiddle with a few moments before. Angie and her nosy-ass ways were getting on her last nerve. She knew it was one of those moments where she was making more out of a thing than it deserved, but the reaction had already started, and she didn't much feel like quelling it.

"I guess you somehow manage to know all about every little thing I do," Tessa said. Angie stopped smiling. "In fact, I should ask *you* how the visit went. You probably have a better recollection of it, with all the eyes you got on me."

Angie clicked her tongue. "Now, come on. I wasn't snooping

around. Betty told me when I run into her the other day. I didn't mean no harm in asking. I was just making conversation," Angie said.

"Uh-huh," Tessa said.

"Don't be like that," Angie said.

"Ang, I just as soon prefer you get out of the habit of telling me how to be," Tessa said. Ruby reached up and felt Tessa's face with her sticky honey fingers.

"Mama?" she said.

"What, sugar?"

"Can we go put our feet in the water?"

"Let's do it," Tessa said. She stood, dropped the sunblock, lifted Ruby up on her hip, and marched down to the lake.

1990

Tessa

Tessa took a drink, then passed the gallon of water to Mel. It was extra hot out for it being so late in October, and the hike up to Perris Lake hadn't offered much shade along the way. Tessa knew she'd be sporting a red neck and farmer's tan for a while. The hat she'd nabbed from her stepbrother's bunk had kept the sun off her face, at least. "FBI," the black baseball cap read in large white letters. Underneath that, in smaller writing, it read "Federal Boob Inspector."

"That's some hat," Mel had said when Tessa arrived at their rendezvous point.

"It's all I could find."

"I'd've let you borrow one, although I don't know that any of mine are quite as clever."

"Well, I didn't think of needing one until the last minute. Anyway, it works, and ain't no one besides you gonna see it."

"That belong to Wayne or his fucked-up offspring?"

"It's Reggie's."

"Couple of princes, those two are."

"Yeah, well."

Tessa had a long drink of water. She wiped her mouth and drew fresh air into her lungs. It was a beautiful spot. The view from up there was worth a sunburn for sure. The sky was clear blue and didn't have a mark on it. The vastness of it seemed both immediate and endless, like the whole thing was always starting and ending in continuous invisible loops. It went on taking up space like that forever. Looking skyward and thinking that way made Tessa feel lightheaded. The dust and dirt and sagebrush around her were more familiar and grounding. Tessa liked the dry heat on her skin. She liked how it radiated down into her bones. Sometimes she felt like if she could just walk long enough in it, that heat could burn up all the thoughts that troubled her and the ache that was always gnawing deep inside her gut. Without all that sitting heavy in her, she thought she might turn into something lighter, more expansive, something like that sky. Mel peeled off her socks and started to undo her jeans.

"What're you doing?" Tessa said.

"Going swimming. What do you think I'm doing? It's gotta be at least a hundred degrees."

"I don't feel like swimming," Tessa said. Mel paused a moment at the button she was undoing on her shirt. Then she shrugged.

"Suit yourself." She pulled her thin white tank top over her head and slipped her boots back on. Off she went, trotting bare-assed down to the water in her boots, the laces undone so they flopped around with each step.

It wasn't very long before Mel came back up to sit under the sparse shade of a scrub oak with Tessa. She had run into the water, kicked around, and swam out a ways before heading back to shore.

"Shit," Mel said. "Water is cold." She had gooseflesh all over. Mel wiped her face and arms off with her tank top, laid it out on a rock in the sun to dry, and sat next to Tessa on her thin flannel button-down.

"Noticed you used my shirt to sit on up here," Mel said.

"Yeah, well, you wasn't using it." Tessa smiled, leaned over, and bumped her shoulder into Mel's.

Mel gave a little chuckle and shook her head. "You know where I got this?" She lifted a sleeve of the shirt and let it fall back down.

"No," Tessa said.

"It belonged to my ex-girlfriend's big brother," Mel said. Tessa's stomach went sour at the word *girlfriend*. She must have gone sheet white, but Mel didn't seem to notice. She kept on grinning like a fool. "I went camping with Wendy—that was her name—and her family. They thought me and her were just good friends, of course." She shook her head. "Anyway, I went out the tent to pee in the middle of the night and spooked a skunk. It wasn't more than a couple feet away, and it managed to spray me pretty good before I could get my pants up to run. The trouble was, I was wearing nearly all the clothes I'd brought with me to keep warm. The next day, I tried washing them in the river, but nothing takes that stink off. We ended up burning those clothes on the campfire that night just to be rid of the smell. I wore her brother's extras for the rest of the trip. Never gave 'em back."

"So you stole them?" Tessa said in a flat, harsh voice. Mel lifted her eyebrows and drew her chin back.

"What's the matter with you?" she said.

"Nothing," Tessa said.

"If you say so," Mel said. She picked up a stick and started to dig into the ground with it. "You sure seem touchy to me." She took the stick between both hands and pressed her boot onto it until it snapped in two. Then she chucked the pieces aside. "You know, I wouldn't get all butthurt if you happened to mention someone you dated before me, if that's what this is about."

"It wouldn't be likely that I would. How many you had, any-way?" Tessa said. Mel looked at her like she didn't know what she was talking about. "Girlfriends?" Tessa said. Mel rolled her eyes. "I mean it," Tessa said.

"Two," Mel said. Tessa flung a rock so that it flew over the water and plopped down into the lake. "And I fooled around with a girl once or twice before them. You?" Mel said.

"None," Tessa said.

"You mad at me now?"

"Nope."

"Haven't you ever had feelings for a girl before?"

"No."

"Boyfriends?" Mel said.

"I kissed Manny Benson under the slide in the third grade," Tessa said. Mel kept on looking at her like Tessa should've had more to say. She didn't, and that look Mel was giving was aggravating her. "That's it," Tessa said.

"You're kidding me!" Mel began to laugh.

Tessa's brain went foggy. She was intensely aware of the heat growing on her skin. She was embarrassed and blindsided by her own stupidity. She was trying to find some mental footing. Up until that moment, she'd felt security in the singularity of their relationship. The tastes of stomach juice, milk, and cornflakes came bubbling up her throat.

Mel stopped laughing and tried to put her arm around Tessa. "Come on, don't be mad," she said. "I think it's sweet you never dated anyone before me." Tessa slung Mel's arm off her.

"I'm sorry I ain't no expert lesbo slut like you," Tessa said. She got up and stomped down to the shore. She had barely enough mind to remember to take off her boots before she walked fully clothed into the lake. Mel wouldn't come after her. She'd think

Tessa going into the water like that was some childish stunt. And maybe she'd be right in thinking that. Maybe she was that immature. She'd been dumb enough to believe that Mel had never kissed no other girl but her.

She felt ice at her waistline, where her shirt soaked up water, and kept walking in until her chin was just above the surface. She took a breath, bent her knees, and went under. She had to let the air out of her lungs in order to sink down and find the lake's sandy bottom. It surprised her that she wasn't panicking. Instead, there was a peaceful sensation spreading in her chest. When she felt her body wanting to float back up to the surface, she grabbed ahold of a large stone and wrestled it into her lap. She looked up and saw the sun shining through the still water above her. It lit up the tiny particles of dust drifting all around her so that she was surrounded by a cloud of shimmering specks of gold. Tessa released the last of the air from her lungs and let the weight of water and stone hold her there. The light from the sun above began to fade, and she felt a deep calm taking her. She blinked her eyes shut for a moment, maybe longer. When she opened them next, she saw a figure moving toward her. As it came closer, she recognized it was her mother, who was swimming down to Tessa in her favorite summer dress. The sun framed the shape of her, and the blue cotton clung to the front of her body where the water pressed against it, and it billowed out at her sides and behind her in gentle waves.

When she was just an arm's length away, Tessa reached out to touch Amber Jean's face, and a deep cry escaped her throat. Just before Tessa's fingertips could meet her mama's cheek, she was yanked away by her collar. Next thing she knew, she was sputtering for air and being pulled along the water's surface. Mel dragged her onto the shore, then let her go. She dropped heavy onto the muddy yellow grass that ran around the lake.

"Goddammit," Mel said. She was bent over and breathing hard, her forearms resting on her thighs. She stood up as if she had more to say. Then she waved Tessa away with her hand and walked back to their packs. "Goddammit," she said again.

Tessa still felt the ache of that cry in her throat and the unbearable longing and hurt that came with it. She pressed up and sat back on her heels. "Breathe," she whispered to calm herself. "Breathe, breathe." That cry came climbing back up her throat and started ringing in her ears. She made fists with her hands and pressed them to her temples, but the ringing wouldn't stop, and she couldn't hold that cry in any longer. It tore its way violently up and out of her throat. After it got loose, her body went weak, and it hurt to swallow. She fell forward and shook with the deep sobs of her pumping chest.

She stayed that way awhile, until all the crying come out of her. Then she was still and quiet. She heard Mel's footsteps coming toward her. Mel gently draped the thin flannel over Tessa's back and shoulders and cleared her throat. "You're getting a little red from the sun," Mel said. "Thought you could use some cover." Tessa sat up.

"Thanks," Tessa said. She hugged her arms in front of her and stared out over the lake. "It ain't about you."

"I know." Mel didn't have to say what she was thinking. Tessa could read it in the worry on her face.

"There is," Tessa said calm and resolute. "There is something wrong with me." She wiped her eyes and cheeks with the cold wet front of her shirt and brushed her hair back out of her face. She sighed. "I guess you're gonna have to decide for yourself if you're okay with that." Tessa stood, let the flannel drop from her shoulders, and went to her boots. She slipped them on and pulled the laces tight. She walked back to Mel, picked the flannel up, and shook it out. She placed it in Mel's lap and put a hand on her shoulder. "I'm going home," she said. "You make your decision." Tessa started for the trailhead, then stopped a few paces away. She turned back to Mel. "Either way, I'd rather not talk about all this again." Mel nodded, and Tessa continued on.

W hat the fuck you got my hat on for, dipshit?" Reggie said when Tessa walked in the front door. He was sitting on the couch with a stupid look on his face and a video game controller in hand. Wayne was in the recliner beside him working a crossword puzzle. "Hey, dipshit, I'm talking to you," Reggie said.

Tessa didn't have the strength for his dumb ass. She felt worked over by the sun and the hike and the nonsense with Mel. *To hell with it,* she thought. She took the hat off her head and whipped it as hard as she could at Reggie. The bill made a snapping sound when it collided with Reggie's forehead. He jumped to his feet and made to go after her, but Wayne was on him fast. He pushed him back down onto the couch.

"Sit your ass down," he said.

"You've gotta be shitting me!" Reggie said. "That bag-of-bones bitch went riffling through my stuff." Reggie sat there with his mouth hanging open. He let out a whiny scoff. "I don't believe this."

"You got your hat back, didn't you?" Wayne said.

"Yeah, but now it's got her whoring-ass germs all over it," Reggie said. "I don't want it no more."

Wayne shrugged. "Well, it sounds settled to me."

Reggie shook his head. "This is bullshit," he said. He was about to spout off some more when Wayne's arm shot out. He grabbed ahold of a chunk of the chin-length hair that ran down the center of Reggie's otherwise shaved head. All the boys Reggie rode dirt bikes with wore the same stupid haircut. Wayne yanked Reggie's ear down close to his mouth.

"I said it sounds settled to me." He gave Reggie's hair another hard tug for emphasis before he let go and went back to the crossword in his lap. Reggie murmured something under his breath and put his headphones back on. Wayne looked up from the paper in his lap. His drugstore reading glasses slid down his nose. He lifted his eyebrows so he could see out over the thin wire frames and gave Tessa a look like he just done something real special for her. It made her stomach shrivel.

Tessa stood in the kitchen and swigged three full glasses of water before she went to her room. She lay down on her twin-size mattress and traced her fingers along the floral pattern in the sheet her mother had stapled up against the wall.

"Better than wallpaper," her mama had said all those years ago. Tessa remembered her mama up on the ladder in her light-washed denim overalls with a staple gun in hand. It had been one of her mama's better days. That day, she was managing to make sugar out of shit pies, is how her mama would've put it.

"Softer," her mama had said as she smoothed her hand against the sheeted wall. Amber Jean stepped back to admire her work. She stood next to Tessa, who was grinning from ear to ear while looking at the peach-colored sheet patterned with little clumps of lilac. Her mama had let her pick the sheet out of a bargain bin at the Goodwill earlier that day. "Helluva lot easier too."

"They call that an accent wall," her mama had said. "I seen it in a house-and-home magazine." She seemed real proud of herself for knowing what *they* called it. Even back then, Tessa knew that the walls in the magazines were likely painted or papered and that the sheet-and-staple-gun approach had been an idea of her mother's alone.

The sheet had faded from the sun wearing away at it through the window over the years. It had balded down to just a few threads in some places. It bothered Tessa to think that it might disintegrate to nothing someday. She rolled away from the wall to face the door. She sighed and sat up to take off her boots and socks. From the sock lines up, her legs were brown with dirt from the trail. She needed a shower, and she needed to be gone somewhere else not too long from then, but her body was heavy from the wear of the day, and her mind was just about as spent. She needed to lie down for just a few minutes. After those few minutes of resting, she'd make some coffee and get out to the barn to do her homework. She'd be safe awhile longer with Reggie sitting out there in the living room with Wayne.

It didn't feel like more than a moment later when Tessa heard the creak of her door as it was pressed open. It was, though. She'd stupidly allowed herself to fall asleep, and hours had gone by. She could tell that now from the long shadow Wayne's body cast in the hallway light.

Her heart sank. She'd let herself down, let herself get caught, and now she'd pay for it. She'd been able to avoid Wayne slinking up on her for going on a year. Now it would happen again, and there was nothing she could do about it. She betrayed herself further when she started to cry and a whimper squeezed past her clenched teeth.

"Sh, sh, sh," Wayne said as he sidled up to the bed with that sickeningly particular bowed-out, left-legged limp he had from his days as a rodeo clown. She tried to turn away to face the sheet-covered wall, but he caught her hard by the shoulder and lay down heavy on top of her. He started at her throat with saliva-wet kisses that traveled down her neck and chest. She felt him stiffen against her and tried to squirm out from under him.

"Keep still," he said. He put a hand over her mouth and twisted a knuckle into her rib cage. He was working that knuckle deep into her side. The ache of it took the wind from her so that she felt like she could hardly get enough breath through her nostrils. The relentlessness of that knuckle grinding into her and the heavy elbow pinning her down at her collarbone were enough for her to stop trying to get free. She knew how it went from there. She'd tried to fight him plenty of times before. If she stopped struggling and focused on making her mind go blank, whatever it was he was going to do would be over quicker, and she'd end up hurting a lot less.

Wayne pressed in close while he jerked himself off, so the bulk of his weight was digging into her at the sharp of his elbow, and his fist was rubbing against her stomach. When he got close to finishing, Wayne put a hand around the base of her throat and squeezed. Then he slid his palm up under the side of her chin and pushed it away so hard that she thought her jaw might come loose or that her throat might tear open, separate, and send her head back like a Pez dispenser.

His palm would leave a mark. First, it would go purple, then green. Then it would blend into the yellowing-brown one that started high up on her cheekbone that wasn't yet done healing. Wayne had put that one there the week before when he came up on her from out of nowhere and slammed a coffee mug against the side of her face for "being mouthy." She hadn't said a word. Wayne collapsed heavy on top of her, panting. *Bruise on top of bruise,* she thought.

After a few minutes, he rolled off her and fell asleep with one of his arms still draped across her chest. She waited until she was sure he was deep enough asleep that she wouldn't wake him. She carefully lifted his arm and slid out from underneath it. With the same care, she lifted the bottom corner of the mattress and grabbed the worn brown leather purse that she kept hidden there. She wiped her neck, chest, and stomach with the edge of the sheet that had been kicked down to the foot of the bed. Then she picked up her boots, pulled on a pair of jeans, and snuck out the slider door to make for the abandoned barn that sat rickety on foreclosed property a quarter of a mile up the dirt road.

She heard the scurrying of small animals when she rolled the barn door back far enough to squeeze inside. There was plenty of the moon coming in through the barn's windows for her to see her way up a half-busted ladder to the hayloft. She felt around in the sparse piles of straw strewn across the floorboards underfoot for the screwdriver she kept up there. Her hands grasped its cool plastic handle, and she picked it up to wedge in between two slats of wood against the wall. The bottom board came loose. She reached in and pulled out a flashlight, a sleeping bag, and a beat-up copy of the novel *Watership Down*. Tessa leaned up against the wall and sat still for a minute. She could see her breath and wondered if the sleeping bag would be enough to keep her warm until the sun came up. She wished she had grabbed an extra blanket before she left the house. Tessa climbed into the bag and propped herself up. She felt for the purse at her side and pulled a small lump of clothing from it. She cradled the heap for a moment before she pressed her face into it. Then she drew her knees in and hugged her whole body around the bundle. Any trace of her mama's scent that had once been there in the few clothes she'd left behind was gone by then for sure, but when she pressed her face hard against that ball of clothes, it helped her remember her mama's smell. Sometimes, if Tessa concentrated hard enough, she could imagine it was the soft of her mama's belly she was pressing her face into, and she could almost feel her mama's arms around her, hugging her back.

Tessa could've run away. A long time ago, she could've done that. She could've left after the first time Wayne snuck into her room, not even a full month after her mama had split. She would've needed help getting away, being so young then, but being sixteen now, she knew she could make it on her own. She could find a job in some other small town at a restaurant or grocery store, no problem, but every time she got herself packed up, she couldn't manage to leave for the thought that her mama was coming back for her and the fear that she'd miss her when she did. If Tessa went, she'd have to leave no trail for Wayne to follow, like her mother had. There'd be no way for her mama to find her. That would be it.

Working these thoughts over in her head kicked up an electric anger inside of her that made her shiver and clench her jaw. She couldn't shake the image of her mama off laughing happily somewhere, warm and worry-free. Tessa gripped her mama's teal cotton shirt in her fists and squeezed until her fingers turned white. She got her hands inside the collar of the shirt and pulled until it ripped clear down the back. She kicked herself free of the bag, then stepped on an edge of the shirt for leverage and tore it down the front. She took to ripping into all the clothes that way. She tore at them and threw them around and spat on the pile when she was done working it over. Tessa wiped at the spit that had caught on her chin with the back of her hand. She stood panting and dazed for a moment before she climbed back into her sleeping bag, opened her book, and began to read.

The next morning, Tessa woke with the ripped-up shirt tucked under her head as a pillow. She crawled out of the sleeping bag feeling stiff. The cold night had settled into her joints, and there was a steady throb at her jawline. She picked the scattered clothes up off the floor, folded them as best she could, and shoved them back into the purse before making her way down the ladder.

1999

Tessa

Tessa was restless that night after the family trip to Lake Arrowhead. She and Angie never did end up smoothing things over. They had both kept quiet after the exchange on the blanket, so later, when Tessa and Henry were back home in their trailer, he asked, "Did I miss something?"

"Yeah, bud," she had wanted to say, "ya did." But instead she said that the sun had just made her tired. "In a good way," she said, to reassure him after she saw his face drop. "It was a good day," she'd said. Then she'd grasped his chin like she used to and kissed him. The gesture had surprised her as much as him. Memories and feelings from their early years together swept through her. And she felt, for a moment, a hint of the desire for him that used to be so overpowering.

The moment was brief, and the feelings it brought passed quickly, but the gesture had sent a signal, she figured, because later that night in bed, Henry reached his hand around to grab hold of her breast as he hugged in close behind her. She felt his breath on the nape of her neck and turned her cheek to speak over her shoulder. "I'm awful tired, Hen," she whispered.

"'Course," he said. He moved his hand from her breast and patted her once on the hip. He kissed her flatly on her shoulder blade. Then he got up and went to the bathroom. She fell asleep almost as soon as he shut the door.

Some hours later, Tessa woke from a dream with cotton mouth and a heat pulsing between her legs. It was still dark out. She couldn't remember anything about the dream except the moment she'd just woken from. Mel had been behind her. Mel's hand had been between Tessa's legs. They were lying on a cold, severely polished wooden floor in an empty and unfamiliar room. The lighting was fractured and came in pieces, as though it were being filtered through stained-glass windows. It cast geometric patterns in primary colors on her bare skin. Right before Tessa woke, Mel had moved one of her hands to Tessa's throat. She squeezed there while her other hand worked to make Tessa come. Tessa was just getting there when Mel moved her lips close to Tessa's ear. "Cunt," she whispered in a harsh, sharp clip. The word landed and sliced into Tessa like the edge of a belt.

Tessa sat up in bed and wiped her hair away from her face. The warmth between her legs was still radiating. The intensity of the want she woke up feeling gave her a stomachache. She closed her eyes tight and tried to shake the feeling by thinking of all she had to do the next day, but the sensation coursing through her was only getting stronger as little snippets of the dream cut into her thoughts.

"Cunt," she heard herself whisper. "C-uhhn-t," she said trying the word out again.

Tessa shook her head and pulled the covers away. She went to the kitchen for water. She made her way back to the bedroom and put the glass down on the nightstand without having taken a drink. Tessa rolled Henry over onto his back and climbed on top of him. His body responded to hers before his mind fully woke. When he opened his eyes, she saw the confusion in them and leaned down to slip her tongue between his lips.

"I changed my mind. You think you could wake up for a bit?" Tessa said.

"For you," he smiled and said, "anything."

Tessa leaned away again and braced herself with her palms on his thighs. She felt his hand land on her chest to rest over her heart. She arched her back and chased after the sounds of the word that Mel had whispered into her ear until she could think of nothing else.

FIVE

1999

Tessa

Preston woke up the next morning with what looked like the start of impetigo on his chin. Tessa put a big Band-Aid over it and told him not to itch. Then she handed him a sandwich bag filled with ice cubes. "Hold that to it. It'll take the itch away. If it's bothering you bad at school, ask the nurse for another bag of ice. You tell her it's for the scrape on your chin. And tell her your mama said she doesn't want nobody messing with that Band-Aid."

If the school nurse saw it, she'd send Preston home until it was gone, and he'd missed enough school already that year. Tessa would make a doctor's appointment for him. She'd take him after school. *Lord,* she thought, *it's one thing after another.* Right then, Ruby came running by and whacked the back of Tessa's head with the cardboard tube from a used-up paper towel roll. Tessa made to say something but decided to save her energy. She had a nine o'clock appointment with the principal at Preston's school that she was starting to worry over. She'd called and successfully rescheduled three times already and didn't figure she could do that again.

Angie had volunteered to go in her stead two weeks ago when she'd overheard one of Tessa's phone calls. At the time, Tessa declined and saw the offer as another one of Angie's annoying intrusions, but now that the day had come, she wished she and Angie were on better terms so she could take her up on the offer. Angie was good at handling these kinds of things. Still, the principal had requested to see her, Tessa, the woman who'd threatened his secretary with violence, not her mother-in-law. It was time to stomach a slice of humble pie, as Angie would've said it.

Tessa sent Preston to Angie's door with Ruby so he could get the keys to her truck. Tessa had Henry call the night before to remind Angie that she would be back with the truck a little later than usual on account of her needing to meet with the principal. Tessa stood at the end of the gravel pathway and gave a small wave when Angie looked over Preston's shoulder toward her. Angie's lips pressed together tight in a straight line before she faked a bright smile and gave a flutter of fingers in response. Ruby pasted herself against Angie's front, doing her best to stretch her arms around Angie's soft waist. The intensity of that hug made Angie laugh and glow. Ruby didn't let go, not even when Angie bent to give Preston a kiss on the cheek. She handed him the keys, and he bounced back down the pathway to Tessa.

"Little girl, you're about to squeeze the life out of me," Angie said, laughing and tickling Ruby's ribs until she let go. Then Angie shooed Ruby inside.

"Bye, Mama," Ruby hollered just before the door shut.

Tessa looked up from buckling herself in to see Preston shining up at her with just about the sweetest smile she ever saw.

"What?" she said with a little laugh.

"I love you, Mama."

"I love you too, mister."

Tessa tucked the seat belt below her belly and reached for the gearshift. Next to the little lit-up *R* for "reverse," Tessa saw that the odometer had been zeroed out. She shook her head and backed out down the driveway.

Tessa walked Preston to his class and spent the hour she had to wait before the meeting pacing the perimeter of the school's empty playground, preparing herself for the crow she'd have to eat. She didn't like the school principal as it was. Theodore Threadgoode, or Principal Teddy as he was known at school, was tall and wormy and always looking down and picking at his fingernails when he spoke to people, like he had something better he'd rather be doing. A few weeks back, he had told Preston he couldn't bring his new remote-controlled car to school for show-and-tell because it had batteries in it. He was the kind of guy who liked that sort of thing—telling people what they could and couldn't do. He liked making up rules on the spot like that, just to remind others that he could. Preston had been so disappointed that he ended up bringing nothing at all to show.

Five minutes to nine, Tessa walked into the front office and was pleased to discover that the seat where the school secretary usually sat was empty. She signed in on a clipboard and settled into a folding chair across the way from the door that led back into the principal's office. At ten minutes past nine, the school secretary came out of that door and stopped mid-laugh to look Tessa over before she pulled the door shut behind her.

"Did you sign in?" she asked.

"Yup," Tessa said. Then the woman walked over to the clipboard, picked it up, and inspected the page fixed to it.

"You didn't write down the time you arrived."

"It was a little before nine."

"There's a space next to the place for your name where you're supposed to write the time you arrived."

"Okay," Tessa said. Tessa watched the woman lean out over the desk to look at the clock that was hanging above it.

"I'll just put the time now," she said.

"Sure," Tessa said. Tessa took a deep breath and remembered her affirmations. *I am peaceful,* she thought, *I am calm.*

"Tessa Jason?" the woman said, still looking at the paper.

"Jenson," Tessa said. Of course, the woman knew Tessa's name, and Tessa knew hers. They'd grown up in the Valley together, just like every other person who lived there.

"Hard to read your writing," the woman said. Tessa ditched the affirmations and went to an old-fashioned desperate prayer. *Lord,* she thought, *give me the strength not to kill this woman.*

Thirty more minutes went by with the woman chomping on a piece of gum like a cow working cud in its maw. She was fiddling around on the computer while Tessa sat there waiting. "Teddy know I'm here?" Tessa finally asked.

"What?" The woman looked up from the computer, pretending to be startled, as if she had forgotten Tessa was there, as if she weren't relishing in Tessa's having to sit there all that time like a damn fool.

"Does Principal Teddy know I'm here for our appointment?" Tessa said, calm and steady. "Does he know I've been waiting to see him?"

"Well, of course. You signed in. I always let him know when a person signs the clipboard. He's a very busy man, you know." The way she seemed to exude pride when she said this made Tessa wonder if Ruth and Teddy were involved. The thought of those two making it was something she could do without.

"Alrighty." Tessa got up, wrapped her scarf around her neck, and bent to pick up her purse. "That's enough of that." She was hungry, and she was done waiting. Tessa went to the desk. "It's been a pleasure, as always, Ruth Ann." She knocked her knuckles on the surface of the desk and headed out the door.

Tessa checked the odometer as she pulled out onto Highway 74. Nineteen miles so far. She took the next exit toward Beth's Donuts. A couple extra miles out of the way and she could have the best old-fashioned glazed doughnut and a cup of the strongest coffee around.

Tessa pointed to the biggest, most heavily glazed doughnut on the tray. "And a small cup of coffee," she said.

"Decaf?" the man behind the counter asked. Tessa hesitated. "My wife," he said, "she always forgets to say decaf when she's carrying. We have four little ones. We're always having to double back to switch out." He gave a little shake of his head and chuckled. "You must be near nine months?"

Tessa paused a moment to take in the cluster of signs with little sayings hanging on the wall behind the register. Signs that said things like "Happy Wife, Happy Life" and "It Takes a Lot of Balls to Golf like Me." Thumbtacked to the wall just to the side of these signs hung an extra-large white T-shirt painted with a woman's body in a neon-pink string bikini. It read "Beach Body Ready."

"Ain't Beth around anymore?" Tessa said.

"Beth? No. She sold when her health started to go a few years back. Last I heard, she moved up north to be closer to her kids. Eddy Travert, of Travert Feed and Seed, owns it now. Kept the name on account of it being a town fixture and all."

"Uh-huh. I'm noticing some of the differences," Tessa said. "Make it a regular coffee." She pulled three one-dollar bills from her wallet and slapped them onto the counter. "And make it strong like Beth used to brew it," she said.

Tessa sat in the corner booth by the window, where she could watch the road and guess at the price of each car as it drove past. Halfway through her doughnut, a beat-up Toyota bounced off the curb and parked out front. The car was red and rusting where the paint had been worked over by the sun. Its windshield was cracked clear down the middle. It couldn't have been worth more than $500 at best. A big man, Tessa guessed somewhere in his upper sixties, braced himself on the open doorframe, and with what seemed like great effort, he lifted his back end from his seat to stand. Then he popped the seat forward and lugged a box out from the back of the car. He waved to the man behind the counter and set the box beside a folding chair out in front of the store. The man sat down heavy in the chair with a throaty exhale Tessa could hear through the glass of the window. He bent to open the box.

"He's got puppies to give away," the man behind the counter said in answer to the question she was thinking. Tessa nodded and watched the big man lift two small heaps of fur out of the box and hug them to his chest. The big man tucked his chin and grinned down at the puppies. His lip gathered and pulled funny on the side of his mouth that Tessa could see. She popped the last bite of her doughnut into her mouth, wiped the glaze from her fingers, and took up her coffee. She gave a two-finger wave to the man behind the counter and walked out front.

"Those are some fine pups you've got there," Tessa said.

"Thank you," the big man said, seeming both a little shy and proud. He met her eyes momentarily, then looked down into the box. Tessa thought that was all he was going to say. She took a step toward the truck but turned back when he started to speak in quick clipped sentences. "My Sheba, she's such a sweet girl. She gave me these. It's her fourth litter. She's a husky mix. Don't know what these are. Don't know who the daddy is. Never do." He let out a short laugh and kept his head down, but Tessa could see from his lifted bottlebrush brows that he was straining to watch her response.

"Oh?" Tessa said. She looked into the box again. "Are they old enough to be without their mama?" They seemed to have just barely opened their eyes. The four of them were still squinting and blinking and bumbling around in that groggy newborn daze when the world must look like it's made up of a blur of bright, smudged lights. It was that pure, innocent, what-the-fuck-just-happened-to-me state of newborns that made it so a person couldn't help but want to care for them. That was evolution's doing for sure.

"I gave 'em away younger before. They'll be fine. Just have to give 'em wet food in the beginning, is all." The man put one of the pups he was holding down, then the other. "Or sometimes they like chicken broth."

"May I?" Tessa gestured toward the box, and the man nodded. She reached down and picked up the puff of black fur that was nosing at an empty corner of the box. "Kind of funny-looking in the face, aren't they?" Tessa said. She held the puppy under its arms at eye level. "Almost like a shar-pei or something."

"They're probably part pit. There's lots of pit mixes out where we live. They sometimes got smooshed-up faces like that too." The man seemed to be easing to her presence. He sat back and shielded his eyes from the sun as he spoke.

"There were five puppies," he said. "One came out dead already."

"I'm sorry," Tessa said.

"I tried to breathe into its mouth and put it in the oven to warm in a casserole dish, like my cousin told me to. I brung back two from other litters that way before, but this one stayed dead."

Tessa could feel the puppy's heartbeat in her right thumb as its little legs cycled in midair and its snout searched for something to press against. It was more than she could resist. She pulled the pup close to her chest.

"They do okay in the car on the way here?"

"Oh, sure. They don't mind. I been here three days this week, and it's a forty-minute trip one way. Nearest place to mine is twelve miles out. I got my Sheba to keep me company out there, so it ain't so lonely." Tessa thought on what he had said for a moment.

"Can I have this one?" she asked.

"You know how to take care of a puppy?"

"Yes."

"You'll give him a nice home?"

"He'll have a good home."

"I promised Sheba I would only give her pups to good people." He searched her face. She could see now that the skin on one side of his face drooped heavily, like it was melting off the bone. The eye on that side was nearly shut. "Yeah, okay," he said. "You can have him."

Tessa grabbed a blanket from the back of the truck and set it down on the floor of the passenger side, then put the puppy on top of it. She could tell he wasn't going to stay put as soon as she sat him down, so she moved the blanket and pup to her lap.

"There we go," she said. Tessa pulled out onto the highway heading in the opposite direction of home and watched the numbers on the odometer roll up. Fifteen miles down the way, she pulled off the road to use a gas station's restroom. She bought a pack of bubble gum, a bottle of water, a stick of beef jerky, and a couple cans of wet dog food from the mini-mart. Since her cell phone had run out of battery at the doughnut shop, she used the pay phone out front to call Henry's work and was relieved when the man who answered said Henry couldn't come to the phone just then. She left a message. "Tell him to let his mama know I'll be back with the truck after I get Preston from school."

Back at the truck, she poured water into her cupped hand for the pup. She pressed its smooshed little mouth into the water. It took a single lap, then turned its tiny head away. "Okay, pal," she said. "More later, then." The pup had settled into the passenger seat. It sat on its haunches and looked out ahead, calm, cool, and collected. The way it had settled in like that made Tessa laugh, and the pup turned its head and looked over at her like, *We hitting the road or what?*

It was twelve miles farther to the narrow, bumpy dirt road that led to the small cemetery where her mama was buried. There wasn't no fancy headstones there. Everyone who came to their final rest in that cemetery arrived same as the next—broke. It was the cheapest plot Tessa could find at the time, and even then she and Henry couldn't cover the whole cost. It would have been cheaper to have had her cremated and been done with it, but Amber Jean had been very clear with Tessa from a young age that she didn't want no fire burning her up when she went. "Let the worms eat me," she'd said. "That's how it's supposed to be." It'd always made Tessa sick to her stomach when her mama talked like that.

Even now, it was hard not to think of worms squirming in her mama's rotting organs and dead flesh, not that any of that was still around down there. She was probably just bones by now. Hell, Tessa thought, she was nearly just bones when she was this side of the dirt. When she wasn't in bed with the blues, Amber Jean lived in a constant state of unfocused jitter. Either way, Tessa was always trying to get her to eat something.

Angie had to pitch in to have Amber Jean buried like she'd wanted, and Tessa had to be grateful. Tessa found the plot, and they spent the money to have her body flown back from the shithole motel in Phoenix where she'd been found. God only knows what she was doing out there. The circumstances surrounding her death were unclear, but the cause of death was deemed natural on the death certificate.

"Heart failure, most likely," the woman at the morgue had said.

"Ain't there some way to find out?" Tessa had asked.

"We could do a more extensive autopsy, but—"

"But that'd cost me." The woman nodded. "I figured as much." Tessa could read the pity and judgment on the woman's face. She knew that look well. This woman—who had gone to college, who talked in clean, confident, proper sentences—she knew without a doubt that she was better than Tessa, and the saddest part, the woman was thinking, was that Tessa didn't even have the wherewithal to know it.

"She's not important enough for you, I guess," Tessa said. "Suppose it was your mama lying here and that autopsy was the last little bit of information you'd ever have from her, the last thing she'd ever tell you before she was gone for good. How'd you feel if someone kept you from hearing that?"

The woman crossed her arms and looked down at the ground.

"It's just policy," she said. Tessa didn't ask Angie for the extra money the autopsy would have cost. She knew Angie didn't have much to spare, and it would have been one more debt hanging over Tessa's head anyhow. Instead, she gave her mama's hand one last squeeze and let the woman pull the sheet over her head. Case closed. Heart failure had seemed about right to Tessa anyhow.

The wrought-iron fence that circled the cemetery was leaning in at some parts and all the way fallen in at others. The entry gate was stuck shut and wouldn't budge when Tessa tried it. She walked a few paces to the right, where a chunk of the fence was lying on its side, and stepped through. She counted fourteen rows in and walked across six spaces, each with an identical little concrete plaque overgrown by tufts of crabgrass, until she came to her mama's spot. "Amber Jean Crawford-Heins," it said, "1955–1995." Her mama had insisted on keeping the Heins part of her name when she married Wayne. "You and me will still have that little part to share, baby," she'd told Tessa.

Tessa had left the inscription on her mother's grave to just the name and date. There wasn't much that could be said beyond that. Amber Jean wasn't the kind of woman who could be summed up in a line or two or by a title like "mother" or "wife," and there wasn't any scripture that would suit her neither. The phrase "a feather in the wind" came to Tessa then, because of the way her mama had drifted around in life, but she shook her head. That wouldn't have been right. That would have made it seem like Amber Jean was light and free, and you just had to take one look at her when she was living to know that she'd never felt neither of those things.

Tessa pulled a stick of bubble gum out of her pocket and sighed as she popped it into her mouth. She twisted and folded the little foil wrapper until it made the shape of a long-stemmed flower.

Then she bent and placed it on the plaque next to her mama's name. "You were something, Amber Jean," she said. Tessa heard the early-afternoon crickets and figured she'd better get going if she was going to make it back in time to pick Preston up from school.

1980

Tessa

Tessa was lying with her ear on her mama's chest. She liked to listen to her mama's heartbeat. She liked to hear the ocean sound it made when her mama put her cigarette to her mouth and took in breath. It was just like when she'd hold the big conch shell her mama had bought at a garage sale up to her ear. Her mama was reading her magazines and smoking in bed the way she liked to. Tessa was walking her fingers along her mama's collarbone and watching the little rainbow shapes the crystal hanging in the window made bounce around on the white sheet beside her.

"I'm six today, Mama?" she said.

"Yes, baby. Today you're six." Amber Jean put her cigarette in her mouth so she could turn the page.

"Today I'm six," Tessa whispered to herself. "One, two, three, four." She counted her mama's heartbeats as she tapped out the numbers on her own belly.

"Five, six," Amber Jean said, faster than the beat. "Now why don't you go play outside, hmm?" Tessa rolled off her mama's chest, sat up, and brushed her hair out of her face.

"Okay," she said.

"Wayne said he'd bring home cupcakes. We can put a candle in yours so you can make you a six-year-old-birthday wish. How's that sound?" Tessa beamed, then hugged Amber Jean's neck and squished her cheek into her mama's cheek hard. She liked the feeling of being that close to her mama. Amber Jean laughed a little. "Ouch, okay. That's enough, you little screwball. Cupcake later. You go out and play."

Tessa skipped to the gate in the front yard and made sure to close it behind her good so it stayed shut. Wayne had gotten mad and yelled at her mama once when she'd forgotten to double-check that stupid gate. Tessa took ahold of a couple of the wooden slats. She rattled them to make triple sure it wasn't gonna pop open. She smiled. It seemed like her mama was having a good day, and Tessa was glad in her heart for it.

It was hot out, but Tessa didn't mind. Next to being with her mama, she loved being outside best. She figured she'd go play under the peppertrees and wait for the hottest part of the day to pass. Tessa had a book buried at the trunk of one of those peppertrees. She'd dug the hole with a stick and put the book in a plastic grocery bag. She'd laid a thin plank of wood over the book in the hole and then piled dirt on top of that. It was one of her best hiding places. There were other things in that hole too: some spent shotgun shells she'd found, a little glass baby-food jar, and the stick she'd used to dig the hole in the first place. Tessa pushed aside the hanging branches of the tree and tugged down on the end of one of those branches so the leaves slipped off their stems into her hand. They made her palm sticky. She cupped her hands around her nose and breathed in the spice.

Tessa brushed away the top dirt and pried up the small plank. She reached in and took out her book. She'd gotten the book from the Perris Library. Her and her mama had made the trip there a long time ago it seemed like. They hadn't been back since. It was a book of scary stories. There was a skeleton squeezing a bloody heart on the cover. Tessa had found it in the grown-up section.

Tessa and her mama had signed up for and gotten library cards the day they went so her mama could rent some workout videos. She had said Tessa could get her one book. Her mama had handed the videos to the woman in charge of checking people out. Those videos had pretty, feathery-haired ladies in leotards on the covers. Tessa never saw her mama watch any of those workout videos. She was pretty sure they were still shoved under the seat of Wayne's truck. The woman who had checked them out gave a concerned look when Tessa put her choice up on the counter.

"Maybe you'd like to look in the children's section for a book? There's lots of nice books for little girls there." Tessa shook her head.

"This one," she said and bounced up and down on her toes.

"Can you read yet, honey?" The woman opened the book and showed it to her. "See? Its pages are full of words."

"It's got some pictures," Tessa said. It did, and they were *very* grown up and scary. The woman looked to her mama then. Amber Jean seemed bored with the conversation. She had just put a cigarette between her lips and was fishing around in her pockets for her lighter.

"There's no smoking in here," the woman said. Amber Jean raised her eyebrows.

"Oh," she said. "Okay." She took the unlit cigarette out of her mouth and held it between her fingers. She slid her sunglasses from the top of her head down over her eyes. "We square, then? Good to go?"

"This book," the woman started, "it's a little . . ." She made a kind of I'm-not-so-sure face.

Amber Jean shrugged and said, "She likes the pictures."

Tessa flipped the book open to the worst, most scary of all the pictures. It was of a man hanging from a rope with his stomach torn open and his guts coming out. She held the page and studied it while she counted to ten. She had been training that way since she got the book. At first, she could only glance at the page for a second before she had to quit. Now that she was six, she was getting to be very brave. Tessa put the book back in its secret hiding place and decided she'd spend a little time climbing that pepper-tree. She had tied a jump rope around a branch way up high a while back and hadn't been able to get that far up to untie it and bring it down since. She gave up on the jump rope after trying for it several times and scraping her shin. She was thirsty. The coast was clear. Wayne's truck wasn't parked in front of the house. She'd get a drink from the hose before she decided on what to do next.

She liked the way water from the hose tasted, kinda like plastic. She also liked how at first it would come out warm or even hot before it turned cold. She always let the warm or hot water run over her hands and feet, if she didn't have shoes on. She took three big gulps when the cool water come. Then she dropped the hose and turned the spigot off. She wiped at her mouth with her shirt and stood for a minute before she had the thought that she might like to try and catch some lizards next.

They liked to sunbathe on the scrap pile out front of the abandoned trailer that sat on land no one owned. The trailer was supposed to have poison on it, and you weren't meant to go inside it or touch none of it. That was fine with Tessa. She didn't want to go in there or mess around with it anyway. She thought it looked spooky, the way it was half burned up and left to rot and fall apart.

She went and plucked a tall green foxtail. She cleaned off all the leaves and brush from its long stem and tied a loop at the end of it. She would creep up on a lizard and put that loop around its neck to catch it. Most of the time, if she was sneaky and her hand didn't shake none, she could get one pretty easy. The lizard would think it was a piece of harmless grass moving in the wind or something. She'd drop the snare over the lizard's head, and then she'd move a little so the lizard would try and run. The loop would tighten around its neck so it couldn't get away while she bent to scoop it up.

Tessa would never hurt those lizards. She just liked to catch them and hold them in her hands for a bit. Sometimes she would pet their bellies. Some of them seemed to like that. They'd close their eyes and smile the same way a cat being pet would. Tessa bet those ones would purr if they could. Others didn't like her petting them none. They'd squirm around, and she could feel their hearts beating up into her fingers. Those ones she'd let free sooner. She caught three that day. Two baby ones, they were the easiest to catch. They were quicker, but had less sense. And one big one, a mama maybe. She let the last one she'd caught go, wiped the sweat from her forehead, and looked for somewhere she could rest in the shade.

She made for one of her favorite hideouts under the short, fat palm tree near the house. It wasn't like the tall, skinny ones she saw in cartoons and posters. It squat close to the ground. Its leaves reminded her of elephant ears. They were so big they scraped the dirt when she pushed them aside. Tessa liked to slip inside the cover and look out from behind the leaves while she relaxed in the shade unseen. She laid down on her belly under that nice, fat tree. She rested her chin on her palms, flat and stacked one on top of the other, and watched the weeds sway in the gentle breeze that had started up.

She fell asleep like that. She didn't know how long she'd been out when she come to. She blinked her eyes open and thought for a moment that the clods of dirt by her hands looked good enough to eat. That happened sometimes. She'd get so hungry that sometimes different types of dirt made her want to eat them. Sometimes she did eat them, but she didn't tell nobody that. Wayne never shared food with her. She wasn't supposed to touch nothing of his in the fridge. He only was nice to and shared with Reggie. Her mama never hardly thought to eat, so she wasn't no help in getting Tessa fed. Tessa had to sneak little bits to eat from the kitchen at home and bum off the other kids at school when she went there. She didn't make it to school all that often. The bus didn't come out as far as they lived, and she wasn't big enough yet to make the long walk to meet it. They told Tessa's mama that she was going to have to repeat kindergarten with all the days she'd already missed. Sometimes the school gave her lunch when they had extra. Tessa liked going the days she did for the chance of that, at least.

Thinking about school somehow made her remember that she'd turned six that day and that her mama had said there'd be a cupcake for her to have that night. She stepped out from under the leaves of the palm tree and stretched. It was near dark. The kitchen light was already on, and Wayne's truck was parked out front. Tessa wiped the dirt off her front and ran for the house. She had just come in the side door when she realized coming back right then was a mistake. Her mama was leaning into the kitchen cupboards behind her with the empty look on her face that she'd get when Wayne was ripping into her about something. He was all worked up and spitting angry.

Tessa saw the fishing pole he was waving around, and her stomach turned. The tip was hanging off by the little bit of clear tape Tessa had used to try and fix it back together. She'd stepped on it like a fool a couple weeks back when she was in the garage looking for a neighbor's lost cat. She was worried sick for a long while after she'd done that, but somehow, she'd stupidly forgotten all about breaking it. Maybe she had made herself believe that the tape would hold the pole together. Maybe she'd thought it was really fixed. She hated herself for it now. Now Wayne was yelling and screaming about the fishing trip he was supposed to go on the next day. Tessa tried to shrink behind the refrigerator unseen, but her mama had already given her away by looking in her direction. Wayne spun around and let the fishing pole drop from his hand. He grabbed Tessa up under her armpit and jerked her to stand in front of her mama.

"Take a look at the little brat you're raising." Tessa had just enough time to give her mama a sorrowful look before Wayne turned her to face him. He had her by the shoulders then. He got down in her face and spoke through grinding teeth. "Did you break my pole?" Tessa could've sworn that one of the bulging veins in his neck was gonna burst.

"I didn't mean to." Tessa's lip was shaking bad, and tears were coming down her face. He squeezed her shoulders tight. His thumbs dug into her like hot fire irons. It hurt like sin.

"Come on, now, Wayne," her mama said. "She said she didn't mean to." Wayne let go of Tessa and gave her a shove so she landed on her backside hard. He spun around and turned on her mama again.

"You shut up. You're the reason this happened. You aren't raising her right. You're spoiling her." He put his hand around her mama's face, and his dirty fingers squeezed her cheeks in. "You hearin' me?" Her mama looked away from him to the ceiling above. "Look at me," he snarled and got closer to her face. Tessa wished her mama would look at him like he was asking her to and maybe things could be over sooner that way, but she wouldn't. Her mama could be as stubborn as an ass. Wayne got rabid-dog mad. He pressed her mama's head back into the cupboard behind her. It made a loud bang.

Tessa hooked her fingers over her bottom teeth and bit down so she wouldn't make the crying sound that was wanting to come out. Wayne stood up tall over her mama so she'd have to meet his eyes, but it didn't work. She looked down at the counter beside her then. Wayne looked that way too. He grabbed up one of the four cupcakes sitting on a plate there. "This what you looking at?" he said. He kept ahold of her face with the one hand still pressing her head back, and with the other he smashed the cupcake into her temple and ground the chocolate frosting and cake into and down the side of her face. Then he picked up another one and crammed it into her closed-tight lips. "Open your mouth." Her mama shook her head as much as she could with his hand holding her face the way it was. "Open," he barked. Her mama's expression didn't change none, but the way he was squeezing her cheeks so hard must've hurt, because tears Tessa knew her mama didn't want to show were filling up her eyes. "There's your fucking cupcakes," he said and slammed her head back into the cupboard again. "You're welcome." He let go of her face. Tessa could see blood at the corners of her mama's mouth from where her teeth must have cut into the insides of her cheeks.

"I'm sorry, Mama," Tessa cried. Wayne flicked the rest of the cupcake left on his hand to the floor and went and yanked Tessa up by the hair on her head. She was so shocked at first she didn't fully realize it was happening. Wayne usually never put a hand on her. He did that to her mama plenty, but normally he wouldn't have nothing to do with Tessa. He made it a point to act as if Tessa didn't exist. He never looked at her. Never said her name. He'd only yell at her mama about how stupid *her child* was sometimes. Now he had Tessa by the hair and was dragging her down the hallway so quickly she couldn't get her feet under her. He was swinging her body around so it went banging into the walls. She thought her neck might break.

He stopped when he got to the door to the junk closet. He opened it, threw her inside, and slammed the door shut. It was dark in there, and she had landed on something that jabbed into her back. Wayne pounded on the door once.

"You better not come out until I say you can, or you'll get much worse. You hear me?" He pounded the door again, and Tessa heard him walk away. She tried hard to listen to what might be happening in the kitchen, but she couldn't hear nothing. Mostly, she was thinking about the burning pain in her back and blinking into the dark in hopes that her eyes would adjust and find some bit of light. She hated the dark. It scared her more than anything. Wayne knew that. It wasn't the first time he'd made her sit in there. He'd made her mama put her in there as punishment a few times before. Those times wasn't so bad. Tessa knew it was coming those times and had been quick to slip a flashlight into that closet while Wayne was yelling at her mama. This time she wasn't so lucky. That flashlight was under the pillow on her bed right then.

Tessa hugged her knees into her chest and squeezed her eyes shut to try and fool herself into thinking that the light was on in that closet, that it was keeping watch. She only had her eyes shut, is all, she tried to tell herself. Tessa hummed a melody she was making up on the spot, quietly so Wayne wouldn't hear. At some point, that melody turned into the "Happy Birthday" song. She thought then of the cupcake she didn't get to eat. She worried about her mama. She hoped Wayne was drinking in the garage and leaving her mama be. Tessa felt the ache of her empty stomach. She opened her eyes and took in the pitch black all around her. The images from the scary book started to run through her head. She tried to be brave. She tried to count to ten, but it was no good. She saw that man with his guts out, and she saw the skeleton with the bloody heart in its hands, and knew they were in the dark of that closet with her. She hugged her knees in tighter. She heard the squish of guts moving toward her and felt the skeleton's bony fingers tracing lines across her back. Tessa cried into her knees. She gave up on counting and whispered over and over *Please go away* instead.

She woke curled up in a tight ball on her side. She blinked her eyes open and winced at the sting she felt when she pulled a chunk of her snot-crusted hair from her cheek. Tessa saw a faint line of light at the bottom of the door. She sat up and went still as she could to listen for any noise. She didn't hear nothing. If it was morning, there was a chance that Wayne's buddy had picked him up to go fishing already. Tessa hoped she hadn't ruined her chances of a Wayne-free day by breaking that stupid pole.

She waited for what could have been an hour before she got the nerve to reach up and feel for the door handle. She turned it and flinched at the clicking noise the door made when it popped open. Tessa crawled out on her hands and knees and closed the door carefully behind her. She made her way down the hallway as stealthily as she could. The living room was quiet, aside from Reggie snoring on the couch. She stood up and walked to the kitchen and felt her chest loosen when she touched the coffeepot. It was still warm and more than half gone. Next, she snuck out to the garage to make sure Wayne's flannel, tackle box, and other two poles weren't there.

She relaxed some after she knew for sure Wayne was gone. She thought maybe she'd like to go watch cartoons. If she kept the sound off, Reggie wouldn't wake up and take over the TV for a good while longer. When she came back to the living room and walked by Reggie on the couch again, the chocolate frosting circling his slung-open mouth caught her eye. A deep, deep hatred gripped her. She wanted to spit in his mouth and pull out his hair. That feeling was shoved aside by the intense hunger and desperate hope she felt next. She looked down at his dumb face and thought, *You've got a world of hurt coming for you, you rotten, no-good punk.* She made a tight, silent fist over his face and gave it one good shake in the air. She was impressed with the words she'd thought and with the tough fist. That was some outlaw stuff, like she'd seen in movies.

She turned for the kitchen, where she'd search for any sign of a surviving cupcake. The plate the cupcakes had been on was sitting at the bottom of the sink, sunk down in soapy water. There was no sign of the pieces that had fallen to the floor when Wayne smashed the cupcake into her mama's cheek. She looked under the sink only to discover someone had already taken the trash out. Tessa's chest started to pump with little sobs as she opened and closed cupboards that she knew would be empty. Her eyes stopped when they hit the plastic four-pack container that had held the cupcakes. Wedged in the space between the counter and the refrigerator, it must have fallen down there and gone unnoticed. Tessa stuck her arm into the crack and was barely able to reach far enough to pull the thing out. There was some frosting left in the little dips and corners of the container and a big smear of chocolate inside at the top. She opened the lid, wiped the top with her finger, and put that sweet goodness to her lips. After she licked the top clean, she started in on the corners and edges. She had gotten every last bit of frosting out of that container when she heard footsteps behind her. She turned to see her mama standing there with her hands on her hips.

"What are you doing, little girl?" One of her mama's cheeks was red and puffed out some. Tessa set the plastic down and swallowed the last little bit of sweetness in her mouth.

"Nothing," she said.

"Uh-huh." Amber Jean looked at the plastic cupcake container in her hands and went to pour herself a cup of coffee. "You don't like coffee yet, do you?" Tessa shook her head. She hated the mean taste of it, and it'd made her stomach feel emptier every time she'd ever tried it. "Okay, well, let's see here." Amber Jean opened the refrigerator and bent down to have a look inside. "Not much in there, huh? Here"—she pulled out some of Wayne's milk—"we'll only use a little." She put a splash of milk in a mug, then filled it the rest of the way up at the sink. Then she went to the cupboard, pulled out a bottle of old corn syrup from the back, and squeezed some into the mug. She put it in the microwave and pressed the button to make it start.

All the while, Tessa watched her mama with a curious fascination. She wondered what had gotten into her. Why was she so happy-seeming and light on her feet? Why was she out of bed, drinking coffee and heating up something for Tessa to have? Her mama took the mug out of the microwave and stirred it with a spoon. "Voilà," she said and handed it to Tessa. "Blow on it. It's hot."

Tessa took the mug from her mama in disbelief. She didn't take her eyes off of her mama. She tried a sip of the hot milk-water without thinking, and it burned down her throat and into her chest. It tasted good, at least. She blew on it awhile and watched her mama some more. Her mama had a sip of coffee and pulled one of the wooden chairs from the kitchen table over to the fridge. She climbed up on that chair to stand and started to collect the change that was up there. Wayne had a habit of emptying his pockets on top of the fridge when he got home. Tessa even saw her mama pick up a couple bills from up there. Wayne sure wouldn't like her doing that.

After the fridge, her mama went all around the house scrounging up change. When she'd turned over the rest of the place, she went to the living room, where Reggie was sleeping. She shook him. "Get up," she said. He pushed her hand away. "Up, up." She pulled on his arm so he come to a seat.

"What the hell?" he said.

"Go lay down in your bed," she said. He flung her arm away, then stood and staggered down the hallway mumbling under his breath. Amber Jean lifted the couch cushions and turned up a few more coins. She took all that she had found and put it in the pocket of her purse. Tessa followed her down the hallway to her mama's bedroom, where Amber Jean put on her good jeans and a pretty green blouse Tessa had never seen her wear before. Next, her mama put on red, red lipstick and used powder to hide the mark on her cheekbone. Then she put her hair up fancy with bobby pins. She turned to Tessa when she was done. "How does Mama look?" Tessa couldn't hardly speak. Besides being shocked by the way her mama was up and sweeping around all happy-like, the way her mama looked made her mind go blank.

"Beautiful," Tessa finally croaked out through a rusty-feeling throat. Amber Jean laughed.

"Well, thank you, honey," she said. She took a duffel bag from the closet and shoved lots of clothes into it. Tessa had to help her hold the bag shut in order to get it zipped. "Now you," she said.

She picked out a shirt and shorts for Tessa to wear. "Arms up," her mama said. Tessa did as she was told, and her mama lifted the dirty shirt she'd been wearing for days on end over her head and whipped it to the corner of the room. She couldn't remember the last time her mama had dressed her like that. She was caught in her thoughts and the strange feelings she was having just then when a flash of pain snapped her attention back. Her mama had touched the spot where the thing in the closet had gone jabbing into her back the night before. Tessa jumped, and her mama made a sour, crinkled-up face.

"Ouch," her mama said. "How the hell did you get a bruise like that?" Tessa studied her mama's face and then just shrugged. Amber Jean told Tessa to put a change or two of clothes in the plastic grocery bag she grabbed from under the sink. Then she took Wayne's truck keys off the hook hanging by the door. Wayne sure wouldn't like that neither.

Tessa waited until they'd been on the road awhile to ask her mama where they were going, for fear that the question would make her mama turn back.

"We're busting out. We're getting out of Perris and going on an adventure to find somewhere new and better for us to live. How does that sound?" Tessa wasn't sure she was hearing her mama right. She'd begged her mama to leave so many times before. "Well," Amber Jean said, "say something. I'm hanging in the wind here."

"To live somewhere else?"

"Yup."

"Somewhere Wayne can't find us?"

"Better make sure it is. He'll be angrier than a hornet when he finds out we took the truck."

"Can we get a dog where we're moving?"

"Don't see why not. Hell, I'd like to get us a cat and some chickens too." Tessa couldn't believe it. They were leaving and getting the pets Wayne would never let them have to boot. Amber Jean stopped at the gas station for cigarettes and told Tessa to wait in the truck.

She came out the door, drew a cigarette from the box, and put it between her lips to light. She tucked the lighter in her pocket and winked at Tessa as she made her way back to the truck. Once she was sitting inside with Tessa, she reached down into her pants and pulled out a smooshed Ding Dong and gave it to Tessa. "Don't say your mama never did nothing for you. Sorry you didn't get no cupcake last night." Tessa peeled the tinfoil off. She bit into the Ding Dong and felt pure bliss.

"That's okay, Mama," she said, sugar running through her blood and buzzing in her head. "I love this Ding Dong better."

"You do, huh?" her mama said. Tessa nodded. Tears were forming in her eyes for the happiness she was feeling.

"You're a strange little creature, you know that?" Amber Jean popped open the glove compartment and rummaged around until she found a couple maps. Tessa ate her Ding Dong while her mama looked the maps over. It startled them both when someone came knocking on the driver's-side window. Amber Jean set the map down on her lap and cranked the handle by her knee in quick circles to get the window down. She took the cigarette out from between her lips.

"Yes?" she said. A woman that looked like a grandma was

standing there with a purse hanging off her forearm and a silk scarf tied around her neck.

"You shouldn't be smoking like that with the windows up and that little girl sitting there breathing it all in." Her mama stared blankly at the woman. "Secondhand smoke. It's worse than if she were smoking the cigarette herself." Amber Jean didn't say nothing or make no move. Tessa wished the woman would take a hint and leave. She didn't want her spoiling things. "I'm not trying to tell you what to do. I only thought I might say something, you know?" The woman nodded her chin in Tessa's direction, and Tessa looked down at her feet. "For the kid." Tessa could feel her mama's temper boiling up from where she sat. She could tell, too, that her mama was feeling embarrassed or nervous, maybe because she was starting to flush and sweat. Tessa knew why her mama was getting angry, but she couldn't understand why her mama would be having those other feelings right then.

"Of course," Amber Jean said, still watching the woman.

"Well, I better get going," the woman said. Amber Jean put the cigarette to her mouth for a breath, then, with the cigarette resting between her fingers, gave a fake half smile and wave to the woman.

"Bye now," Amber Jean said. She cranked the window up as the woman walked away toward the gas station's store. "The nerve. When did people get so comfortable sticking their noses into other people's business, huh?" Tessa didn't have no answer for that. She'd finished the Ding Dong and was rolling the foil into a tight ball. "Hmm," Amber Jean said. She folded up the map all mad-like and threw it between them. "We better leave before she comes back out and has more to say." Amber Jean pulled onto the road. Tessa could sense her mama's mood dropping and her lights dimming. She tried to save things. She tried to get her mama laughing like she sometimes could by retelling the jokes they'd heard on the late-night television they watched when Wayne wasn't around. Her mama wasn't in the laughing mood.

She turned into the Family Basket drive-through and ordered an Orange Bang and paid with the change she pulled from her pocket. "Here," she said and handed the Orange Bang to Tessa. "It's got orange juice and egg whites in it. It's good growing food. Good breakfast for a kid." She seemed to be making some case, like she was telling that to someone who wasn't there. Tessa took the Orange Bang and sipped. The sweet, thick drink felt cool on her tongue. She'd never had a drink that tasted so good. It was kinda like the orange Tang that she got at school sometimes but creamier and less sour. Amber Jean sat at the wheel with her arms crossed. Tessa set the cup to hold between her legs so that it felt cold on the inside of her thighs.

"How many chickens you think you might want, Mama?" she said. Amber Jean didn't say nothing. "You want the brown ones? Or maybe some of the ones that are black and white? You want that kind, Mama?"

Amber Jean started the car back up. "Roll your window down," she said as she lit another cigarette. "I don't need you getting me in trouble again." Tessa rolled down her window. Amber Jean turned back onto the road going the direction they'd come from.

"Where we going, Mama?" Amber Jean didn't answer. "Mama?"

"Where you think we're going?" Tessa started to cry. "Don't start with that."

"Please don't take us back there, Mama." Tessa's chest was heaving like it would when she was trying to breathe and not cry. "Please, Mama. We got our clothes packed."

"Stop that. I mean it. It was just pretend. We were never really leaving. It was a stupid game. Aren't you always asking me to play with you? Huh? Is this what I get for playing and buying you treats? Well, now you know why I don't play with you so much, don't you? Crying like that after all I done for you today. And with all the shit I'll catch for it." Tessa covered her face and started to sob.

"Please, Mama? We can find somewhere else. I'll be good and help you. I promise."

"Stop it, now. I mean it." Tessa couldn't stop. She sobbed as hard as she ever had. "Didn't I get you that Orange Bang? I could've spent the money on gas or magazines. Tessa, quit it. Quit crying. It was just a game. We don't have the money to get to anywhere. You're making your mama upset now." Amber Jean flipped the radio on and turned the music up loud. "There," she shouted. "Now I don't have to hear it, at least."

Tessa stopped crying a few miles down the road. She leaned against the door, rested her forehead on the glass, and counted the telephone poles as they went by. She was trying to get to ten. She wondered if Wayne would remember the night before and expect her to still be in that closet. She wondered if she should climb back in when they got home so he wouldn't get mad about her coming out before he said she could. She felt the sweet orange liquid slopping around in her stomach and swallowed. She closed her eyes tight and concentrated hard on not getting sick.

1999

Tessa

Tessa had to dig the puppy out from under the seat where it had gotten itself stuck when she arrived back at the truck from her mama's grave. She spat her gum out into her empty coffee cup, slipped open the beef jerky, and took a bite. "Okay, fella. Let's take you home."

The puppy was small enough to fit snug in her coat pocket, where she tucked it away before she walked up and knocked on Carly's trailer door. It was looking up at her from the shadows of her pocket with curious, wet eyes. "You'll like it here," she said. "I promise."

Tessa began to worry when it took two full minutes of knocking for Carly to open up, but when the door swung back, she could see right away that Carly was awake and sober.

"Honey!" Carly said. Her bright, big-toothed smile made her eyes squeeze all the way shut. Tessa hadn't seen her face light up like that in a long time. "What're you doing here?"

"I got the truck for the day. Figured I'd swing by," Tessa said. They stood there looking at one another for a moment like that, and then Carly opened the door wider.

"Well, come on in. I was just fixing up the floorboards in the bedroom." Carly had splotches of dried white spackle on the tips of her fingers and the backs of her hands. "You weren't waiting long, were you? I barely heard you over the radio." Carly's face was just starting to show gentle signs of age. The creases at the corners of her eyes only made her smile more charming. Tessa could tell the years would be kind to her. That she was among the small population of women in their valley that would age handsomely, the way square-jawed men always seemed to. The way her Henry would.

"No, not long," Tessa said. She stepped in and wiped her shoes on the welcome mat. The place was spotless, the way Carly always kept it when she was well. "You look good," Tessa said. Carly reached out and squeezed Tessa's hand.

"Thank you, honey," she said and let go. "Tea?"

"No, I can't stay long this time," Tessa said. Carly's smile dropped. "I just have to be back to pick Preston up, is all. I brought you something." Tessa reached down and pulled the sleepy puppy out of her pocket.

"Oh my God" was all Carly could say, and then she went straight to crying.

"Lord, you are a softy," Tessa said, laughing.

"Hush, you," Carly said and dabbed at her cheeks. "Give him over to me." Tessa handed her the puppy. "Is it a him?"

"It is," Tessa said. "What are you gonna name him?"

"Oh, I don't know. Let me get a good look at him." Carly held the puppy out in front of her the same way Tessa had when she gave him a first look over. His little belly was puffed out, still swollen from his morning feed, Tessa guessed. "Willie, maybe?" Carly said.

"Really?" Tessa started laughing again.

"Yes, really. I was just listening to Willie Nelson when you pulled up, and looking at him now, I think the name suits him." Carly went and sat down on the sofa so she could pet the puppy on her lap. She was grinning even bigger than when she'd first opened the door, and Tessa knew she'd done the right thing giving her that pup.

"I love him already," Carly said.

"Knew you would," Tessa said. She brushed Willie's shoulder with the back of her finger.

"You doing alright, sugar?" Carly reached up and gave a little tug on the drawstring of Tessa's jacket.

"Think so. Could be otherwise, I guess," Tessa said. Before Carly could respond, Tessa leaned down and kissed her on the top of her head. "I've gotta be going to get Pres now."

Carly nodded. "Thanks for stopping by, babe."

Tessa made it back to pick Preston up with time to spare. She was parked and waiting out front under the sycamore tree where they met each day when he came bouncing up to the truck. He opened the door and swung himself into the passenger seat.

"Hi, Mama," he said.

"Hi, ba—"

"It's wet!" Preston shot up out of the seat. He swept the blanket that the puppy had been resting on away to reveal a damp spot on the seat beneath. Tessa brushed it with her hand and took a whiff.

"Darn," she said. "I'm sorry, honey."

"It's pee!" he said before she could explain.

"Yes, I'm sorry, honey. I didn't know. I brought Auntie Carly a puppy today, and—"

"You got her a puppy?!"

"Yes, I brought Auntie Carly a puppy today, and it must have peed on the seat when I wasn't watching." Preston began to cry. "Oh, baby, I'm so sorry. We'll get you cleaned up. Don't cry. Come here." Tessa reached for him, and Preston tugged away so hard that he slipped back and fell out the truck door. He landed on his butt in the hard dirt beneath the tree. Tessa jumped out the truck and ran over to him. She tried to reach for him again.

"Don't!" he screeched and took little puffs of air between sobs. He stood up and wiped at his face.

"Pres, what's wrong? It's just a bit of puppy pee, is all. We'll clean you up."

"You got Carly a puppy," he said.

"Yes, baby. I got Auntie Carly a puppy."

"I wanted a puppy!" Preston pounded his chest with his fist when he said it. His cheeks went fire red. "I've wanted a puppy for forever and ever. I told you so many times." He started to sob again.

"Honey, I know you do. I know you want a puppy. We just ain't got the space for it now, is all. We'll get you one when we have our own place with a fenced-in area for it."

"You been saying that for years, Mama. I want a puppy. You got Carly a puppy, and I wanted one. Me, your son." Preston sat back down and hugged his knees to his chest. Tessa let him be for a moment. She waited until his back stopped shuddering and his breath became quiet. Tessa used the trunk of the tree to help her get down to her knees next to him.

"You're right, Preston. I been telling you that a long time, and it ain't fair. I should've thought how you might get upset knowing that I brought Carly that puppy," Tessa said. Preston stayed hugged in a tight ball with his head tucked between his knees.

"How 'bout you and me go get you a puppy tomorrow morning? What do you think about that?" Preston lifted his head.

"Really?"

"Really."

"I want it to be the kind that will be a big dog when it grows up." Preston wiped his nose on his shirt.

"I think we can manage that."

Betty Kinch's bright yellow Beetle was parked out front of Angie's place when Tessa and Preston pulled up. Betty was Angie's best friend and made it her business to know everyone's business even more than Angie did. They were two peas in a nosy-ass pod. No doubt Betty had brought her youngest granddaughter, Shelby, along with her. Tessa didn't like Ruby spending time with Shelby. She was a bad influence. Shelby was only two years older than Ruby and already pursing her lips and swishing her hips when she walked and her mama had her carrying a little plastic purse on her arm. The last time Ruby came home from a playdate with Shelby, she wouldn't make mud pies with Preston in the back-yard because she was afraid of getting dirt stuck under her nails. Ruby had sat glum at the kitchen table, watching out the window as Preston stomped around in the big puddles made from a week's worth of rain. She gave up her foolishness and followed when Tessa went outside in Henry's waders to join him.

Tessa turned to Preston before they left the truck. "Don't say nothing about the pup yet, okey dokey?"

"Okey doke," he said, grinning from ear to ear. It was the sec-ond time that day she'd managed to make someone she loved dearly happy in a way she'd not been able to for a long while. It felt real good. Tessa reached to press the button that would clear the odometer, then decided she'd leave the numbers for Angie to wonder after instead.

"There you are!" Angie called before they were all the way inside the front door.

"Hi, Angie," Tessa said.

"Hi, Grandma," Preston said.

"What happened to your chin?" Angie asked.

"He's got impetigo," Tessa said. "We just come from the doctor."

"I got something for that in the medicine cabinet."

"We already got cream for it. We just come from the doctor."

"This stuff I got is better. It'll have his chin cleared up in half the time of that antibiotic crap." Angie turned to walk down the hallway.

"We're using the cream they gave us, Angie," Tessa said with more of an edge than she meant to.

"Well, okay. No need to get sharp with me."

"No one's being sharp. I just want to use the cream the doctor gave, is all."

"Where you been all this time?" Angie said.

"Did you need the truck?"

"Well, no, but I was worried, is all." Tessa could tell Angie was embarrassed to have Tessa talking to her like that in front of Betty.

"I told Henry to get you a message saying when you could expect me back." Angie stood there watching her, waiting on Tessa to explain herself. "I went to see Carly," Tessa said. Angie let out a puff of air and gave a side-look to Betty, who was beside herself with glee. Tessa could imagine the same look on Betty's face as she sat her fat ass on her plastic-covered floral couch watching her soap operas at home.

"You can call her and ask if you don't believe me," Tessa said.

"What has gotten into you?" Angie said.

"Nothing, Angie. Please, I don't want all this. I'm tired. Is Ruby ready to come back with me?"

"Maybe you ought to leave the kids here if you're so tired. You can go home and rest. I'll tell Henry to come by and pick them up on his way home."

"No, Angie, you don't need to be calling my husband because I'm taking the kids with me now. We got plans." Just then, Tessa heard the clicks, scrapes, and drags of heels on feet too small to be wearing them. She knew what was coming down the hallway before she turned to see the pair of them. Ruby and Shelby came clomping shaky-ankled down the hallway, all dolled up.

"Look, Mama, I'm sexy." Ruby flipped her teased-out baby hair over her shoulder with the back of her hand when she said this, and Tessa felt her stomach spoil. She marched down the hallway, lifted Ruby out of the heels, and started to wipe the makeup off her face.

"Stop it," Ruby said and tried to bat her hand away.

"Take these off," Tessa said, and she worked at undoing the knot of material at Ruby's back that pulled the blue silk shirt tight to her chest and belly.

"They're just playing," Angie said.

"You okay with Ruby playing sexy, Angie? 'Cause I'm not."

"Tessa, she doesn't even know what that word means."

"Yeah, and I'd like to keep it that way. And where do you

imagine she heard that word anyway?" Tessa looked from Shelby to Betty, then back to Angie. "'Cause it sure as hell wasn't on my watch."

"You're ruining it," Ruby wailed. "We were having fun. You always ruin it."

"Where are your clothes?" Tessa asked. Ruby had collapsed into a puddle on the floor. She was in the throes of a full-blown meltdown where she could no longer be reached. Tessa turned from her to Angie. "Where are her clothes?" Angie went down the hallway to the bedroom and came back out a moment later with Ruby's little purple backpack. Tessa took it from her and lifted Ruby up from the floor.

"This is your fault," Tessa said, looking sideways at Angie over the top of Ruby's head, which was lifting and banging into her collarbone in fits. Ruby started to kick, and Tessa swatted her butt with her free hand. "Stop that," she said. "You'll kick Mama's stomach." She turned her attention back to Angie. "You know I don't want her dressing up like that, Angie. You know it." Tessa felt acid rising up her throat. She needed to leave quick, before she got sick or said something she couldn't take back. "Preston," Tessa called. Before she had to call for him a second time, Preston was at her side with a mouth stuffed full of cookies from the plate on the kitchen counter. "We're leaving," she said.

"Bye," Preston said, giving a wave to his grandma. White powder from the cookies puffed out of his mouth.

Tessa walked back to their place with Ruby limp and sobbing on her shoulder and Preston skipping out ahead of her. She let Ruby down off her hip when she got the trailer door open. Ruby ran down the hallway and pulled the divider curtain shut. Tessa heard her plop down in her bunk bed, where she began to kick at the wall. Tessa tossed her keys onto the counter and took a seat.

"What plans we got?" Preston said.

"Huh?" Tessa said.

"You told Grandma we got plans. What are they?"

"We're gonna make dinner."

"That's the plans?" Preston said.

"I got other plans to think about too. About tomorrow morning." Tessa gave him a look, and he gave her a wink in reply.

"Can I help?"

"Why don't you see if you can cheer your sister up? But, remember, don't tell her about the puppy yet. I have to tell Daddy first, and you know she won't be able to keep it a secret once she finds out." Preston gave her a thumbs-up and bounded down the hallway to where Ruby was sulking in her bunk. Tessa heard him start to work on her using a series of improvised knock-knock jokes with punch lines involving fart noises and cameos from her favorite cartoon characters, and she knew it wouldn't be long before Ruby came around. He had his daddy's charm and good heart. That was for sure.

1992

Tessa

Tessa had worked up the guts to stop by Mel's place after a month of no sign of her. Mel hadn't told her nothing. She hadn't come back to school when it started up again a week after her mama had caught them together, and that was it. She was gone.

Mel's mama had spoken to Tessa behind the shadows of the screen door. "She's away at school," she said. "And you're not welcome here." She punctuated this last statement by opening the screen door to spit down at Tessa's feet. "Now get off my porch." She let the screen slap shut and slammed the door behind that. Tessa walked away heartbroke with spittle clinging to the toe of her shoe.

Things were worse off at school, as she'd expected they'd be. Without Mel around, the mean girls jumped back on her like a pack of coyotes on a stray dog. They were relentless. Tessa was too sad to pay them much mind. They made her life harder for sure, but nothing they did hurt the way Mel's being gone did.

Two months into life without Mel, Tessa began to feel something different. She began to feel mad. So mad, all the time. The girls picking on her gave her reason to get into fights at school every day. She was on the losing end of those fights for the first bit. The losing didn't last long, though. Tessa became a scrappy fighter with unmatched endurance. She could take the first few minutes of raw, unfocused walloping and hairpulling the girls had to give, even when there were two or three of them at a time. She'd keep her guard up as best she could and even land a blow or two if the opportunity presented itself. Then, when they'd tire out, she'd turn on them and give back double what they'd given with a ruthless precision. They'd be so tired by the time she'd round on them they didn't have the strength to lift an arm, not even to protect their faces.

It wasn't long before she was made up of lean, ropy muscles and sharp bones. It wasn't just the fighting that was making her that way—she'd started running too. She was running eight to fifteen miles a day. It wasn't planned on or nothing. What started it was the Prescotts' big German shepherd mix, Nanna. Nanna had a new litter of pups and must've felt Tessa was walking too close to the yard. The bitch jumped a six-foot fence and tore after Tessa, who was just heading home from the mini-mart up the way from school. Tessa dropped the bag of chips she'd just sprung for and hauled ass down the dirt road. A quarter of a mile into the chase, her legs and lungs were burning something fierce, and there was no sign of that dog stopping. Something kicked over in her when her legs wanted to give out. It was the same feeling she'd get when she was beating off a gang of girls. Exhaustion and adrenaline mixed in her blood. She pushed harder. She burned up everything in her body and started to run on something different. Something clean—a pure energy that felt like it was gutting her out and filling her up at the same time.

Her lungs were working so hard running from that dog that she tasted metallic blood. The bitch stopped chasing half a mile in, and Tessa kept going, running after that burned-out, nothing feeling. It was good the running come to her when it did because the girls at school had caught enough ass-whuppings to last them a lifetime. They gave her a wide berth in the hallways. She had a whole table to herself every lunch.

Springtime came around that year and Tessa was as strong and solid as she'd ever been. She ran all over the Valley so that people started calling her Jacky Rabbit, which was fine by her; it was better than any nickname she'd earned before, anyway. It even got to be that people would ask her to deliver messages for them across town or out in the sticks when they'd see her running by. Sometimes they'd ask her to drop a letter off at the post office or grab an item from the grocery store. She didn't mind them asking her to do that stuff. She was bound to be going in the direction of the errand at some point anyhow, and they'd give her a little something for her trouble, which helped out greatly now that she was always hungry and having to eat like a horse when she could afford to. Before the running, Tessa got by on handouts at school, ketchup and mayonnaise packets, and watered-down coffee. Now she found that if she couldn't get at least one halfway decent meal in her each day, she couldn't run but four miles before her legs and arms got lead heavy, and there wasn't no pushing past that for more than a day or two.

It was around three o'clock on a clear, blue-skied day, and Tessa was out in the sticks cutting across the Jensons' property like she'd taken to doing to avoid the awful pig-shit smell downwind of the Milfords' farm. She was six miles in and felt like she was just catching her stride when the ball of her right foot landed in a gopher hole, sunk down, and caused her ankle to bow out funny. She crumpled right down to the ground with the next stride she tried to take on that foot.

"Fuck," she said. Her body curled up into a ball by its own

doing. She rested her forehead in the dirt and held her stomach for the sudden wave of nausea thrashing around in there. She tasted the mayonnaise and hard-boiled egg she'd eaten at lunch on the back of her tongue. "Oh Christ," she breathed and rocked over to her side. After a solid minute of curses, Tessa pushed herself up to a seat. She made to move her ankle, but it may as well have been a noodle for the limpness she felt and saw there. She bit her tongue for the pain and tied the shoe on that foot tighter to try and curb the swelling that had already doubled the size of her ankle. With the wild grass growing all around her and her ankle busted up like that, Tessa couldn't help but think of Mel and their sledding adventure just then. It made her awful mad to have the thought creep up on her in a moment like that. She'd managed to put Mel out of her mind for some time now, and to have her come back to her just after she'd eaten shit in a cow field was a real point of agitation.

She was in the middle of thinking on what she was going to do when the shadow of someone coming up behind her bumped her from her thoughts. She spun around and shaded her eyes so she could make out who it was. A tall, thin-framed boy with mousy-brown hair and a dumb-looking grin on his face was standing there in a jumpsuit with grease spots all over it.

"You must be the girl my mama's been seeing running through here every day," he said.

"Could be. What difference it make to you?" Her ankle was hurting bad, and she didn't have the energy to suffer a fool just then.

"I heard you were a feisty one," the boy said. "Why're you sitting there on your cottontail? Why ain't you running, Jacky Rabbit?"

"'Cause I fell and rolled my ankle in a goddamn gopher hole running across the piss-poor kept field you got here," Tessa said.

"This field ain't meant for running. It's meant for grazing, which I'm sure you know on account of how you been spooking our cattle every day when you tear through here like a wild banshee."

"Well, it don't look like I'm gonna be tearing through nothing for a while," Tessa said, pointing to her blown-up ankle. As soon as she said the words, she felt a panic seizing up her chest.

"Ouch. Lemme take a look at that." The boy took a knee and got closer to her. She made to protest but couldn't get air into her lungs. Her head was pounding with the fear of not being able to run. It was the only thing she liked about her sorry-ass existence. The only reason she was getting by. She was starting to see spots, and a black curtain was coming in on her from all sides.

"Whoa there, girl." The boy popped his head down in front of her in the small circle of vision she still had. "You're looking green," he said. *Stupid thing to say,* she thought, but she was going out like a light and couldn't speak to that point now.

When she come to, the back of her head was resting on his shoulder. He was sitting up behind her and waving his sweat-stained baseball hat in her face.

"Get that out of here," she said and swatted the hat away. "How's that supposed to be helping matters anyhow?" Tessa sat up and away from him.

"Easy," he said. Tessa blinked a few times to get her bearings. It all come back to her when she rolled onto her knees and made to get to her feet. She felt a shock of pain shoot up her leg like reverse lightning.

"Well, that ain't no better," she mumbled to herself.

"What?" The boy leaned down to crowd her space some more.

"Don't you have some cow to be milking?" She looked him over. "Or some grease to be rolling around in?" He didn't say nothing to that. Just laughed. "What are you laughing for?" she said. "Can't you see I'm injured and just passed out?"

"I ain't laughing at your ankle. That ain't funny. It looks like you twisted it awful bad. Must hurt like hell. I'm laughing because you're more interested in insulting me than you are in letting me help you get some medical attention. Makes me wonder, is all."

"Makes you wonder what?"

"Makes me wonder how much pain you'd have to be in to shut up and let me carry you back to the house where my mama can help you."

"Well, I ain't there yet," she said.

"Alright. What's the game plan, then? It don't look like you're getting too far on foot. And it would be an awful long crawl for help in any direction." It pissed her off to concede, but he had a point.

"You can carry me piggyback. That way I can hold on around your neck. I'm not having you carrying me in your arms like some hillbilly romance novel."

"Thank you for the honor, Miss Jacky."

"It's Tessa, and you're not welcome. Let's get this over with." He bent down in front of her. She climbed up on his back and held on to him around the neck. He looped his arms under her legs.

"Watch it," she said and gave a little kick with her good leg.

"I have to hold you up somehow. Otherwise, you'll choke me to death grabbing on to my neck like that."

"Fine," she said. "But don't get no ideas."

"Jacky, I'd sooner climb into a sleeping bag full of rattlesnakes than get any ideas with you."

"We're on the same page in that book, pal." The boy started toward the ranch house with a little spring in his step, like he felt proud of himself for doing a good deed. Halfway there, he spoke up again. Tessa knew he couldn't keep quiet.

"Would two broken legs and sudden blindness have done it? Would you've let me carry you in my arms hillbilly-romance-novel-style, then?"

"I wouldn't count on it, bud."

"My name's Henry. My oldest brother, Benny, goes by Bud."

"If you say so," she said.

"And you're Tessa Heins," he said. She didn't answer him. It was quiet traveling the rest of the way until they got to the house, where he hiked her up on his back so he could slide an arm out from under one of her legs and bang on the front door.

A sturdy-built woman with an oven mitt in hand opened the door. Henry's mama, Tessa guessed.

"What in the hell we have here?" the woman said.

"She hurt her ankle," Henry said and nodded toward one of Tessa's dangling legs. The woman bent down to look closer.

"Sure did." The woman stood upright again. "Bring her in the kitchen," she said. The woman moved out of the way to let Henry pass. "Set her up on the counter." The woman followed them into the kitchen, where Henry backed up to the counter and let Tessa down to sit. "Henry's always bringing home wounded animals for me to fix." The woman laughed. "Today he brought me a trespassing jackrabbit with a turned ankle." Tessa kept quiet and wondered what it was about this family that made them talk all cheerful and knowing, like they had some joyful and funny secret between them that they were keeping from her. The woman came over with a glass of water and a couple pills. "Take these," she said and handed them to Tessa. "For the pain and swelling." She bent and reached to lift Tessa's ankle. Tessa jumped at her touch. "Good Lord, you sure tweaked the hell out of it. I bet it hurts like a son of a bitch. I'm gonna touch around a bit and see if I can tell if something is broken. This won't feel so good." Tessa nodded, and the woman pressed on her ankle and moved it around. It hurt worse than when she'd twisted it in the gopher hole, but Tessa didn't make a peep or let her face show it. The woman let go, and Tessa felt like she could breathe again. "I don't think it's broke. I think it's a bad sprain. Best if we took you to the emergency for an X-ray to make sure, though."

"I can't afford no doctors."

"You'll want to know if it's broke, girl. If it is, you'll need a cast. Otherwise, it won't heal right."

"With respect, ma'am, it's like I said—I can't afford it, and I ain't going."

"Suit yourself." The woman went away for a minute, then came back over with a bucketful of ice water. Put your foot in here. All the way up to your shin. This won't feel good neither." Tessa didn't let herself flinch when her foot hit the water.

"Thank you," Tessa said.

"You're welcome." The woman stepped back and crossed her arms. "You're a tough little pissant, aren't you?"

"Mama," Henry interjected.

"I meant it as a compliment." Tessa didn't say nothing to that. "Tessa Heins," the woman continued. "You're Amber Jean's girl."

"Yes, ma'am."

"I thought so. I'm Angie Jenson. You already know my son Henry, I imagine."

"Yes, ma'am."

"You're awful polite for a trespasser."

"I only cut through the property for running. I ain't causing no harm."

"You seen the signs posted, though?"

"Yes, ma'am."

"You ought to be more careful cutting through people's property. You're liable to get your ass shot off with some of the gun nuts around here. People out here like their privacy, but I suspect you know all that and choose to hop fences anyway." Tessa nodded. "Alright, well, I'm not gonna rub your nose in what you've already stepped in. I'm sorry your ankle's hurt."

Tessa's foot and ankle were going numb, and whatever the woman had given her felt like it was kicking in and putting her at ease. "Thank you," Tessa said. The woman leaned up against the sink and looked Tessa over.

"Here, darling," the woman said. She wet a dish towel and moved it toward Tessa's face. Tessa leaned back quick so that the back of her head banged into the cupboard behind her. Her arm shot up to bat the woman's hand away. "Will you let me help you or not? There's some dirt on your face—I'm hoping it's dirt, at least. Out in that field you keep cutting through, it's twice as likely to be something else." Tessa put her hand down and let the woman wipe at her forehead, which, as she remembered just then, had been resting on the ground not too long ago. The woman wrinkled her nose and made a sour face. She went and rinsed the dish towel and came back to work on Tessa's forehead some more.

There must have been a lot caked on there, because Tessa felt big flecks of it sprinkle down her face as the woman wiped. It was cow shit for sure. Tessa didn't know how she'd missed the smell before. She looked hard at Henry, who up until that moment had been sitting quietly on the counter across from her. Now, though, he was having himself a good laugh.

"I'd've told you about the shit on your forehead, but then I wouldn't've had anything to focus on while you were busy putting me in my place," Henry said. Angie smiled at this and threw the balled-up dish towel at Henry.

"I've got some old crutches a couple of my boys have used after they done something stupid. I'll adjust them to fit. You'll stay off that ankle and let it heal if you don't want to have a limp for the rest of your life. And I want you to come back here in four days so I can check on how it's healing."

"I'll be alright."

"I know you will, because I'm going to see to it. I'm not asking. I'm telling. The only way I'm letting you leave here and not see the doctor is if you promise you'll come back so I can take a look at that ankle. Understand?"

"Yes, ma'am."

"Alright, then. Henry will give you a lift home. Don't make me have to go chasing you down. I done you a favor today."

"Yes, ma'am."

"I'm gonna fix you a couple sandwiches to take with you. We gotta see about getting some meat on these bones." Angie patted Tessa's thigh and gave Henry a look that Tessa couldn't quite read.

You can let me out here," Tessa said when Henry turned down the unmarked gravel road that led up to the house. They were coming up on the big peppertree that marked the start of Wayne's property.

"Come on." Henry rolled his eyes. "I can't let you walk all that way on crutches." He kept driving, so Tessa put a hand on the wheel and jerked it to the side. Henry hit the brakes.

"I'm serious. I'll be in trouble if you take me any closer." Her voice and the look she gave him then were the most honest she'd given anyone in a long time. It caught her off guard, the same way it must've caught him. Tessa looked down at the worn floor mat beneath her feet. "My stepfather don't like strangers coming around."

"Okay," he said.

"Okay," she said back. She opened the door, and Henry reached behind the seat, then lifted over the crutches his mama had given her. "See ya, then," Tessa said.

"See ya," he said. Tessa put the crutches under her arms and started the quarter-mile walk up to the house. She heard the sound of the gravel under Henry's truck tires begin to move away from her. Tessa didn't look back to see him drive away, as maybe he was waiting on or wanting her to do. Her mind was already figuring how she'd hide her sprained ankle from Wayne and Reggie. She didn't need them thinking she was back to being weak again. Her running had given her a confidence that seemed to keep the both of them from bothering her too much of late. She still spent her nights reading and sleeping in the barn, which had always helped matters, but since she'd started running, daytime interactions at the house had been close to civil. The two of them seemed almost spooked by how she moved around the house like she had a right to be there, instead of sneaking around on eggshells like she'd always done before.

She set the crutches down for a second to see if she could walk in a way that would hide her being hurt, but it was no good. She couldn't put a feather's weight on that ankle. She'd have to lie low until she could at least pretend that there was nothing wrong with her. She changed directions and started off the road, through the sagebrush toward the barn, where she'd have to hide out for a bit. When Wayne wasn't around, she could slip a note under the door telling him she was going on a school camping trip, like she'd done before in the past. He wouldn't care. She could shower in the locker room at school and snag some clothes from the lost and found if she needed to. She had the thought then that school might be trouble for her now too. The girls would be on her again once they saw her on crutches. Nothing she could do there. Tessa had stopped going to school for a while after she learned Mel wasn't coming back. She couldn't miss no more school. Otherwise, the truancy officer would pay another home visit, and Wayne's wallopings were worse than anything she'd catch on campus. Plus, she'd been thinking recently it might help her in the long run if she were able to graduate.

She was sitting right there next to Wayne when the truancy officer had said that Tessa was among the few students he thought could actually make something of themselves. With her grades and smarts, he'd said, if she stuck to it and got a diploma, she could get into the local junior college. Maybe even better. Tessa's ears got warm hearing that. She'd never given more than a week's time out any forethought. It struck her then that school could be her ticket to a future somewhere else, and the heat in her ears got turned up and meshed with a floaty sensation that made her feel like she was half-drunk.

Tessa could see that Wayne wasn't interested in hearing anything the man had to say. He was wanting that man gone off his property. Wayne nodded his head and got the man out the door with his word that Tessa would be at school the very next day. The door had hardly clicked shut before Wayne turned to send her head into the wall.

By the time she made it to the barn, Tessa's underarms were chafed and her wrists were spent. She steadied herself against the side of the barn and wiped the sweat from her face with the front of her shirt before she rolled back the door. Once inside, Tessa let out a long breath and leaned the crutches up against the bottom of the wooden ladder that led up to the hayloft. She hadn't thought about needing to climb that ladder. She felt her throat tighten, and her eyes started to water up, but she clenched her jaw and fought off the cry that was wanting to come. Feeling sorry for herself had never done her no good, and she wasn't no stranger to impossible situations. Tessa started in on climbing the ladder with her good foot, hopping from one half-broke step to the next as lightly as she could.

SIX

1999

Henry

Henry wanted to do something to prepare himself before he climbed the steps to the trailer. If he were a Catholic, he'd've made the sign of the cross. Being that he wasn't raised on any religion and didn't much believe in God, he figured it was careful words and good sense that would get him through, so he tapped the mud off his boots and took a deep breath before he reached for the door, and left the preparing at that.

Tessa was sitting at the table in the kitchen with her folded hands resting on its plastic surface. He could hear the kids playing back by the bunks.

"Kids ate already," she said. "Yours and mine is in the oven to keep warm." She made to get up.

"I'll get it," he said. Henry grabbed a dish towel, then took the two warm plates from the oven and set them on the table. He turned the kitchen faucet on and soaped from his hands up to his elbows. He'd had an earful from his mama on the drive home. Henry longed for the days before cell phones and his mama's daily calls. He'd hoped this thing that had started at the lake between his mama and Tessa would have blown over by now, but it seemed to have blown right up instead. He'd tried to keep himself out of it for the same reason a person tries to keep out of a dogfight. You get in the middle of things and you're the one that's ending up worst bit.

His mama had hardly come up for air during that phone call. She'd told him that Tessa's strings were wound up and pulling dangerously tight. Her voice got shaky when she told him she'd never imagined Tessa could talk to her like that and how it had made her feel embarrassed in front of the kids and Betty. She'd told Henry he'd better be real careful how he handled things, because the way she saw it, Tessa was ready to snap.

The only time he'd had room to speak was when she'd pressed him to tell her what he was going to do about things. Fortunately, he'd made it home by that point. He parked out in front of the trailer and told his mama he was heading in to have supper and that he'd talk to her the next day.

"Alright, then. I'll be thinking and working on the situation here," his mama had said, getting off the phone. Henry didn't know what she had meant by "working on the situation," but he figured he'd have to worry about that later.

It took a lot to get his mama shaken up like she was, and Henry knew, of course, that something had to be done or said to smooth things over. He was glad not to have his mama's worked-up voice pressed right up against his ear anymore, but now he was faced with something different—the unknown waiting in the quiet and composed woman sitting at the kitchen table behind him.

"Milk?" he said, reaching for the carton in the fridge.

"Sure," Tessa said. Henry took two glasses down from the cupboard. He placed them on the table and filled one after the other.

"So," he said, trying to sound lighthearted, "how was your day?" Tessa tilted her head and rested her jaw in the hand propped up by her elbow.

"I suppose you talked to your mama on the drive home," she said.

"I did," he said.

"There's your answer," she said. Henry waited for her to give him more. He needed to know what he was getting into and how she was situated within it; that way, he'd know what angle to approach from. "She tell you how badly behaved I was in front of her friend?" Tessa said.

"She mentioned something to that effect."

"She tell you what Ruby said and how they had her dressed?"

"She told me you had a real strong reaction to both."

"You saying you wouldn't?"

"No, I'm not saying that."

"Okay, well, what are you saying?"

"Mama was just really upset. That's all I'm saying."

"Henry, if you think I'm worried about that right now, we got bigger problems than I thought."

"Tessa, you doing okay?" He didn't mean to blurt the question out like that, but it had been on his mind for weeks, and the worry in his mama's voice had gotten inside his head. "I mean, with this baby coming and all. I just don't want you to feel like you did."

"Oh, here we go with all this again."

"You can't blame me for asking or being concerned. I'm just trying to understand where all this is coming from."

"Jesus Christ! It ain't this baby. I can't believe you're taking her side on this," Tessa said.

Henry looked over his shoulder toward the back of the trailer. "Keep your voice down," he said. He could feel the heat coming off Tess from across the table. "The kids," he tried.

"You're so scared of offending your mama that you can't see straight on nothing anymore. This is our Ruby we're talking about. Don't you care if she gets the chance to be a kid for a while before she has to worry about all that crap? She's four years old. They have her practicing to be a hooker, and I'm the one that's made out to be unwell? That's what's crazy, Henry. Not me. I'm sick of you and your mama holding what happened when Ruby come along over my head. It ain't right. It's bullshit. And I'm tired of it. You're just trying to understand where all this is coming from? What a crock of shit that is."

"Real nice, Tess." Henry shook his head and dropped back in his seat.

"I mean it. You've known where I've been coming from since day one. You just ain't cared to pay it mind because you're happy pretending things is always fine." Tessa slapped her palms down on the table and leaned in toward him. "And you're damn right I had a strong reaction, Henry. I'm at a loss trying to figure out what kind of father wouldn't." Tessa shook her head. She slid her arms from the table and sat back. "And now you're sitting there with your wide eyes and big heart, looking all wounded and scared, and it squeezes in on me and don't give me room to have the way I'm feeling. It never does. And—"

"And what?" Henry said in a harsh, angry voice he didn't hardly recognize as being his own. "It makes you wonder? Jesus

Christ, Tessa. Where do you get off saying something like that to me? I'm a good father and husband. It ain't fair of you to suggest otherwise, and you know it." Her eyes went blank then, like something in her had shut off. He felt his insides twisting up and tangling. The flash of anger giving him legs to stand on left him quick, like a rug pulled out from under his feet. Now he felt himself falling into a panic. Henry had the unshakable feeling that she'd given up on him in that very moment in some devastating and irreversible way. The walls of his lungs were collapsing in on themselves and sticking together like flypaper. He tried to concentrate on taking long, easy breaths in through his nose.

"I just," she said. The words sounded forced. Nothing in her face had changed, but hopelessness came through the wet gathering in her eyes and the defeated tone of her voice. Tessa dropped her head and pressed her eyes closed. Big tears ran down the bridge of her nose and made little spots on the light-blue sweater stretched thin across her belly. She looked up at him. "I just can't."

The hurt on her face then felt like a punch to his already troubled gut. He could hardly stand to see that kind of sad on her. He leaned forward and tried to reach for her. She shook her head and held her hand out for him to stop. "Uh-uh," she said. "No. It's past time for that." Tessa cleared her throat. He saw the muscles at her jaw flex. She wiped at the stray tear running down her neck. "We need our own life, Henry. If we are going to have a chance at making it, we have to move off your mama's property."

"Tess, believe me, I know how my mama can work you down to your last nerve. I just spent the whole of my drive home listening to her and feeling about ready to jump out the moving truck, but she helps us. Without her—"

"Without her, what?"

"We ain't got the money to move, Tess. We don't."

"You better figure something out, Henry, and real quick." Tessa moved out from behind the table and stood with her hands resting on her head. She began to pace the short length of the kitchen. "And I want my own car by the end of this month."

"Tessa, come on." Henry threw the napkin from his lap on the table. "Be reasonable."

"I mean it. I'm done depending on that woman. Done. You either hear me this time when I say it or you don't, but I'm telling you right now, I mean it." Tessa's stare cut straight through him. Henry wanted to look away, but he knew better.

"Alright," he said. "I hear you."

"And Ruby is not allowed to be around Betty's granddaughter no more, and she ain't playing that kind of dress-up ever again."

"That's fine by me, Tess. I don't want her doing that neither."

"Okay, then." Tessa walked toward the counter, stopped, sighed, and dropped her hands to her sides.

"There's more?" Henry said. She turned to him and crossed her arms over her belly.

"I told Preston I'd get him a puppy tomorrow morning." Henry's mouth opened to speak, but nothing came out. "I know we ain't got the space for it and it's the last thing we need right now, but I promised, and we've been stringing him along about getting him one for years."

Henry considered his options in that moment and thought of his mama's warning earlier. He nodded. "I'll pick up some fencing on the way home tomorrow."

"'Kay," Tessa said. She uncrossed her arms, and her shoulders relaxed. She made her way back to the table to sit. She had just set the saltshaker down when Henry stood and picked up his plate to put back in the oven.

"You ain't gonna eat?" Tessa said.

"I need a hot shower first, I think. You go ahead while it's still warm. I'll have mine after a bit."

Tessa

Saying her piece the night before had lifted a weight off Tessa that gave way to a deep, heavy sleep. She didn't wake or even stir when Henry got up for work. He was gone before she was out of bed. She let the kids sleep in on account of Preston not needing to be up for school. The doctor had said he was highly contagious, and Tessa knew it was likely that this news had already traveled from the doctor's office to Preston's school. It was just as well, seeing as she had promised to take him to get a puppy that morning.

Tessa was organizing her thoughts at the kitchen table with a cup of coffee when someone came banging on the trailer door. She couldn't move fast enough. With the way that banging was going, it would wake the kids up for sure, and the few minutes she had to herself for the day would be gone. Tessa was ready to let whoever it was have it. She whipped the door open, fixed to let her tongue fly, but there in front of her was all six foot three of Nathan grinning big as ever. He was standing there in his swimming trunks and flip-flops. The outfit was topped off by a down jacket and a beach towel swung over his shoulder.

"Well, hey there, Nate."

"Mama said to ask if I could spend the day with you." Nathan looked back to his mama's house. Tessa did too. Angie was standing in the doorway, watching to make sure he made it over okay. Angie gave a wave. Tessa waved back.

"Sure, honey. We'd be glad to have you over. Is your mama going somewhere?" To this, Nathan shrugged and pushed past Tessa to get inside.

"Is Preston awake?" Nathan asked. Tessa was still watching Angie's place. Angie came back out of the house with her purse and climbed into the truck. Tessa stepped inside and shut the door before Angie could drive by and see her watching. She turned to see that her two little towheads were out of bed rubbing their eyes and stretching.

"When we leaving to get my puppy?" Preston said.

"Good morning, Preston," Tessa said.

"Morning, Mama. After breakfast?"

"Mama sent these." Nathan lifted a plastic bag with four warm, foil-wrapped breakfast burritos in it and dropped it heavy on the counter. "And this." He then pulled a carton of orange juice out of his duffel bag and thunked it down on the table.

"What puppy?" Ruby said. Tessa grabbed a roll of paper towels and four glasses to set the table.

"Come eat breakfast," Tessa said.

"What puppy?" Ruby said again with an edge in her voice that warned against making her ask a third time. Preston came popping up to the table.

"Mama and me are picking me up a puppy today," Preston said. Both Nathan and Ruby froze blank-faced, like the statement had caused a glitch in their brains. It was Ruby who caught her lost senses first. She turned on Tessa quick.

"Preston's getting a puppy?" Her face was twisting up and flushing red.

"Yup," Preston said. He slid one foot under his seat, flipped open the notebook he'd left on the table the night before, and took a big bite of his burrito. Just then, Tessa caught a glimpse of his chin.

"Shit," she said. She took ahold of the sides of his face in both hands. "Well, that ain't no better." The impetigo had spread. The dime-size patch had doubled to a nasty-looking half-dollar blotch.

"Band-Aid fall off when you were sleeping?" Tessa said. Preston nodded. "Honey, you gotta do Mama a favor and not itch. Okay?"

"Okay," he said. Then he lifted his hand and scratched at the gooey mess on his chin. Tessa grabbed his wrist.

"No. See, honey? That's what I mean. That's gonna spread it more. Go wash your hands at the sink now. You have to wash your hands—we all have to wash our hands all day long until we get this thing whipped." Preston went back to doodling in his notebook. Ruby was screeching something about the puppy, which Tessa was choosing to ignore, and Nathan had checked out and was staring off into the void while peacefully eating his burrito. Tessa got up and went to the medicine cabinet. The cream the doctor had given hadn't done shit. Maybe it had even made things worse. She reached for the big Ace bandage and sports tape at the back of the cupboard.

"Look at Mama," Tessa said. Preston lifted his head from his notebook, and she wrapped the Ace bandage from his chin to the top of his head and back around again a few times. She taped it in place.

"Can you open your mouth to eat alright?" Tessa said. Preston opened his mouth and gave a thumbs-up.

"Mama," Preston started.

"Wash hands and eat," she said. Tessa saw the flash of Ruby's little body dart for her bunk bed. A moment later, the wall-kicking started up. Tessa went and filled a bucket with hot water, dish soap, and bleach. She started in on wiping down door handles and exposed surfaces around the trailer. After giving the trailer a once-over, Tessa dumped the bucket out front and chucked it and the washcloth in the sink. She marched down the hallway, forcing out halfhearted affirmations about patience and courage between gritted teeth. Tessa dropped to her knees next to Ruby's bottom bunk.

"Hey, you wanna talk about this puppy or what?" Tessa said. Ruby's kicking stopped.

"We getting a puppy?" Ruby said.

"Yes."

"Is it going to be Preston's puppy?"

"It's going to be all of our puppy some, but mostly it's going to be Preston's puppy, yes."

"Why." Ruby stomped the wall. "Does." She stomped again. "Preston." Stomp. "Get—" Tessa grabbed Ruby's legs and spun her around to sit up and face her.

"Because he is big enough to take care of a puppy, and because we've been telling him he can have a puppy for a long while, and when we say things in this family, we mean them. And it ain't right for you to be kicking the wall like that. You know better. I don't want you doing that anymore. Not even if you're mad. If you're mad about something, you say you're mad about it. You don't go kicking things your daddy works hard to pay for."

"I'm maaaaadddddd!" she shouted.

"Okay. That's okay. Be mad. Why are you mad?"

"'Cause you always be nice to Preston and get him things and not me."

"Aren't I nice to you when you're behaved? Didn't I get you a couple Ring Pops and a Pixy Stix just last week and Preston just one Abba-Zaba?"

"But you never got me a puppy."

"You aren't big enough yet. When you are, you can have one."

"I'm big enough. I can take care of it."

Tessa lowered her voice. "You know, Preston is going to have to pick up puppy poop, it being his pup and all." Ruby stayed quiet and still, signaling her interest in hearing out this line of thinking. "And when that puppy gets sick to its stomach, he's gonna have to clean up after it then too." Ruby was looking at Tessa now. "He's going to have to wake up earlier every day to feed that puppy and make sure it's set for the day before he leaves for school. You won't have to do any of that, Ruby. You get to just pet and play with and love on it like the rest of the family will." Tessa watched the wheels turning in Ruby's head and steadied herself for the counteroffer Ruby was brewing up.

"Mama?" Ruby said soft and sweet.

"Yes?"

"Can I at least have a bunny? They only make little poops and eat hay."

"Come eat breakfast. I'll think about it," Tessa said.

"Mama, I really want one. I'm big enough for it."

"I hear you, Rube. Let Mama think on it."

Ruby skipped down the hall to the kitchen table. She flopped down next to Nathan and cheerily started in on her burrito. She took a sip of her orange juice and clapped her hands together.

"Pres, you're gonna have to pick up puppy poop," Ruby said. "And I'm getting a bunny!" These two consecutive statements were enough to snap Nathan back from whatever it was he was daydreaming about. His eyes got big. It took him a moment to speak.

"Ruby's getting a bunny?! What about me?" he said. Tessa

took a big bite of her burrito, chewed, and exhaled through her nose. The baby kicked and squirmed up under her rib cage at an uncomfortable angle just then. Tessa figured it was to make sure she wasn't being forgotten about neither.

"No more questions or bothering me until I eat this entire burrito." Tessa held her burrito up and made eye contact with each one of them at the table. Then she took a page out of Nathan's book and stared out the window. She ignored Ruby's bumping and tugging on her arm while she ate her burrito and tried to dream up a scenario in which she had some personal space.

Tessa popped the last bite of her burrito into her mouth and turned from the window to see all three faces watching her.

"What?" Tessa said.

"When we leaving?" Preston asked.

"Honey, Grandma has the truck. We have to wait until she gets back so we can borrow it."

"You said we'd go first thing in the morning," Preston said.

"I didn't know Grandma would be using the truck. There's nowhere walking distance to get a puppy," Tessa said. Preston slouched down in his seat, crossed his arms, and put a sour look on his face. "You better straighten yourself up and change your attitude real quick. You ain't acting like a boy whose mama is getting him a dog."

"Sorry, Mama," Preston said and pressed upright in his seat. It was so much easier with him. As if she were overhearing Tessa's thoughts, Ruby spoke up.

"What are we going to do now, then?" Ruby said.

"Mama said it was going to be warm enough for the sprinklers maybe," Nathan said. Tessa was certain Angie hadn't said that, and that she'd most likely had to fight him tooth and nail into the jacket he was wearing. There was an early-spring cold snap, and it hadn't been warmer than sixty-five degrees all week, but Nathan loved playing in the sprinklers, which explained both this hopeful suggestion and his getup.

"Let's go on an adventure," Tessa said. As soon as it come out of her mouth, Tessa felt the idea lifting her spirits. "You two get dressed in layers and brush your teeth. Me and Nathan will walk over and get him some shoes and pants from his place. Sound good, Nate?" she said. Nathan nodded.

"Maybe after we can go in the sprinklers," Nathan tried.

"Sure, honey, if it gets warm enough, we can do that."

They used the spare key Angie left taped inside the wheel well of a brokedown lawn mower covered in rust and cobwebs. It was a good spot to keep that key safe. Wasn't no one wanting to go sticking their hand in there, least of all Tessa, but after scraping a twig around in the hollowed-out space, she did reach up and feel about until she found the key.

Nathan was in his bedroom, putting on his boots and getting dressed in layers like Tessa had asked. Tessa was looking through Angie's medicine cabinet for the salve she'd offered for Preston's chin the day before. Nothing in that cabinet was labeled, and Angie had a habit of reusing old bottles so that the current contents of one of these used containers had nothing to do with what might have originally come in it or what it was advertising itself to be. Tessa figured this was just another way in which Angie made it so she was involved in everything, another way in which she had to be depended on.

Her doing that with the bottles was how it turned out to be that Gordy had been sprinkling ant repellent in his shoes instead of Gold Bond powder for nearly three months. His athlete's foot had gotten worse in that span of time, but the ants hadn't bothered his shoes none.

Tessa couldn't tell one thing from the next in that medicine cabinet. She heard Nathan coming up behind her, shut the cabinet door quick, and spun around to face him.

"Ready?" she said.

"Uh-huh," Nathan said. He had running shorts on over bulky sweatpants. Tessa suspected he still had his swimming trunks on under that. Up top, he was wearing a hoodie and a vest.

"Alrighty," Tessa said.

She tightened up her boots by the trailer door while she waited on Preston and Ruby to meet her and Nathan out front. "All set?" she asked when they came down the entry steps. She looked the three of them over and smiled. She felt her lungs expanding in the fresh air outside and locked the trailer up behind them.

They walked out into the field of weeds back behind Angie's place, beyond the old chicken coop and horse pen. Tessa pointed out the pasture where they used to keep the cattle. That property belonged to someone else now, but they hadn't done much with the land since they'd bought it. They had only been seen walking it a time or two with a team of men in neon-orange vests. The last time they were out there like that was over a year ago. For that reason, Tessa figured it would be okay to walk the kids through it. She was careful to tell them that they shouldn't never go out that far on their own. They walked through the pasture to the property line. Tessa unhooked the wire circling a rotting fence post. She swung the fence open, and they kept on going. She wasn't sure the land beyond the old pasture belonged to anyone. Since she'd known it, that land had been overgrown with mustard plants in the spring and bone-dry dirt and boulders in the summer and fall.

The cool air on Tessa's face and the hiking boots on her feet felt alright. Tension she didn't know she was holding on to was draining from her shoulders. It was freeing up her neck. Her smile wasn't feeling like work. She didn't want to think too much about why it was she was feeling like that, for fear the reasoning would make it go away.

"We found a nest of baby kangaroo rats once in that woodpile over there," she said and pointed to a sprawling heap of rotting scrap wood. They walked over, and Tessa crouched and looked into a little hollow space close to the ground in a stack of old railroad ties. "Right in there. They were cute and ugly in equal parts. We picked them up and held them squirming and pawing at our hands, but we shouldn't have done that." Tessa was talking quickly, as if the amount of time she had to tell about the baby kangaroo rats was going to run out. She wasn't sure the kids were even listening. Maybe it was that she was talking more to herself than to the kids anyhow. "Our scent scared their mama off. She didn't come back to take care of her babies after she smelled us on them. We didn't know that would happen, of course." Tessa sniffed and wiped at the snot that had started leaking from her nose with her sleeve. "We came back to check on them a week later, and those little mice pups were all starved and frozen dead." Tessa looked up from peering into the small, empty space to see three somber and captivated faces. "That's why you shouldn't never try and pick up no living creature in nature. Just appreciate things with your eyes and leave them be." Now that Tessa was becoming more aware of her audience again, she was trying to make the story into a lesson that would offer a purpose for her telling it.

"Why didn't the mama come back for them?" Ruby said.

"Spooked, I guess. Wild animals do that. It's their survival instincts that kick in and tell them to leave. They can't reason like we can." She hadn't meant to go so dark there. The abandoned, dead baby kangaroo rats story was a bit much, probably—at least for her four-year-old, it was. But when she and Mel had come back and found them dead all those years ago, Tessa couldn't remember feeling sad at all. Maybe a little guilty after realizing what they'd caused, but more than anything, it'd just felt like they were observing a fact of life. They'd even picked them up again to see how they felt different being dead. That's the way it was back then with Mel. Things could be boiled down to simple cause and effect. You didn't have to worry about what end of the equation you was on, as long as you saw things for what they were and didn't try and pick up and carry none of it around on your back.

"My brother used to say that our backs were already strained and bent just from living here and scraping by. He'd say, 'You don't need to go bending down to reach for more to add to it. You'll get too hunched and heavy that way. Then you're never getting out.'"

Mel had said that once, way back in the days when she and Tessa would go out exploring together. It was one of the few times that she had ever mentioned her brother to Tessa. Tessa knew then that Mel didn't understand just how hunched and heavy Tessa already was. That she was already stuck.

"Who was with you?" Preston said.

"Huh?"

"You said *we*. Was it Daddy you found and killed those mice with?"

"No, honey, that was before I knew your daddy. I was with my best friend, and we didn't kill them. The mama didn't come back for them. That's how come they died."

"What best friend?"

"Mel."

"Never heard of her."

"Well, we ain't best friends anymore." Tessa heard the words echo back from an empty space inside of her that she'd forgotten about, or had tried to, anyway. "But maybe you should know her. She was my favorite person back then. Maybe one day you'll meet."

This answer seemed to satisfy Preston enough for him to move on. More than likely, he had stopped listening before she'd finished speaking. His attention had been diverted to something in the grass by his feet. Tessa looked in time to see him stab a dead, bloated squirrel through the eye with a stick. He lifted the stick with the squirrel hanging off by its eye socket. Before Tessa could shout at him not to, Preston whipped the dead carcass at Nathan. Nathan squealed, turned away, and tried to dodge it. The squirrel thumped between his shoulder blades and slid down his jacket to the ground. Both boys found the noise it made against Nathan's back incredibly funny. Nathan chased Preston across the open field. They both took turns saying "Thud!" between fits of laughter. Ruby came walking up beside Tessa and took her hand. "Dumb boys," she said. Tessa looked down and saw the uneven part approximating the middle of Ruby's two ponytails. She made to say something but closed her mouth and nodded instead.

They walked along a coyote trail single file. The grass and mustard plants on either side of them would be scorched away by the heat in just a couple more weeks, but right then, they were alive and green and so tall she could only just spy the top of Ruby's head over them. Preston and Nathan kept pushing each other into the thick, fog-dampened walls of growth at their sides. They'd go falling over and flatten the growth beneath them. That's what gave Preston the idea to crawl into the grass and weeds and mash them down to make a tunnel. Nathan got on his hands and knees and followed suit. Tessa wasn't sure she should be letting them do that. There could be rattlesnakes in that grass, but she figured it was still cold enough, maybe, that they wouldn't be out. If they made enough noise, she figured, they'd be alright. She remembered how much playing and running wild and free in fields like this one had meant to her when she was young, and she didn't want to rob them of something like that. When Ruby tugged on her hand, wanting to join the boys, Tessa nodded and said, "But let Mama go first."

That's how it come to be that they spent the next hour and a half building an elaborate grass tunnel system. It included several small clearings of mashed-down growth that served as rendezvous points and one larger clearing that they called Home Base. The knees of all their pants were wet and green and brown, and their hands were covered in mud and minor scrapes. They'd had to stop several times to try and rinse hands that had accidentally pressed into patches of stinging nettle. They came upon big hunks of rusting vehicles; soggy and disintegrating sofas and mattresses; and worn-out appliances that had been dumped. These things became part of the mapped landscape and tunnel system. If one of them were to get separated from the group, they were to climb up on the washing machine to spot the others in the grass. That was the lookout. If they needed to rinse their hands, they'd make their way over to the big tractor wheel that held pockets of rainwater.

Now Tessa was following on all fours behind the three of them. Her belly was in the way of her crawling, so her legs had to work harder by taking shorter, quicker strides in order to keep up. She had to keep stealing little breaks, where she'd sit back on her heels and catch her breath. Preston was leading the way through uncharted territory. They all did their best to mash the plants down beneath them as they crawled along. The tunneling stopped abruptly when the wall of growth ended, dropped off to just dirt, and opened out onto a row of peppertrees. They all took turns getting up on their feet. They brushed their pants off and blinked into the sun and open space around them, like they'd just woken from a dream. Tessa couldn't tell, exactly, where it was they were. She wondered how much ground they could have covered on their hands and knees.

"We going back in?" Nathan said and pointed to the tunnel from where they'd emerged.

Tessa shaded her eyes from the sun and looked around some. "I think I better figure out where we are first. Maybe it's time to start heading back." Tessa walked between a couple peppertrees. She brushed their long-hanging branches out of the way as she went.

What she saw when she came out on the other side stole the air from her lungs and the blood from her face. Not more than a hundred yards straight out in front of her was what was left of Wilkinson's old barn. Tessa had been careful to stay away from that barn and Wayne's old place since she'd left. The entire two square miles that surrounded those two buildings had dropped off her grid of existence. It didn't matter where she was trying to get to—she didn't cross the boundary lines she'd built up around them in her head. Seeing that barn now felt like looking up just in time to see the bright light of a train before it hit. Tessa's legs buckled and brought her to an unsteady crouch on the ground. When Ruby come up on her, she willed her lungs to open so she could take a breath. It was then that she felt the weight of her grown belly between her thighs and remembered what was resting inside it. Preston and Nathan came walking up then too.

"Who's hungry for lunch?" Tessa forced the words out.

"I want to make more tunnels, Mama," Ruby said.

"No, I think it's time we get back." Tessa closed her eyes for a moment to think of the fastest way home. She concentrated hard and beat back all the other thoughts that were coming to her then. She remembered the dirt bike path that cut through Gus and Millie's property. It wasn't too far from where they were. Once on that path, it was a near straight shot to Angie's place.

Right then she remembered the last time she'd taken that route. She broke into a cold sweat, and violent images started flashing through her head. Those images were starting to fix themselves together so that they were turning into something terribly solid and unsurmountable. She couldn't let them keep coming together that way—she'd be in deep if she did. *Nathan, Preston, Ruby.* She thought the names loud as she could in her head. *Nathan, Preston, Ruby. Nathan, Preston, Ruby. Nathan, Preston, Ruby—Baby.* Tessa opened her eyes, shook her head clean of those images, and turned in the direction of the bike path. "This way," she said. "If you hurry up, I'll make us pancakes for lunch."

"With chocolate chips?" Nathan said.

"With whatever you'd like." The three of them were on her heels with that promise, all dreaming up different candied pancake variations that she'd have to deliver on, no doubt.

After they all washed up, Tessa set about whipping up some pancakes. She let Ruby, Preston, and Nathan raid their grandma's pantry for whatever ingredients they wanted to add to their pancakes. In the end, Preston came up with the best-tasting combo of peanut butter and Abba-Zaba pancakes topped with powdered sugar. Nathan, both overwhelmed and excited to an extent that bordered on euphoria by the freedom of being allowed to make his own decision, doubled down and insisted Tessa add all seven ingredients he'd picked out: strawberry jam, a fistful of rainbows from Lucky Charms, smashed corn chips, sprinkles, eight yellow gummy bears, three spoonfuls of Fruity Pebbles pounded down to brightly colored dust, and chocolate syrup.

His pancakes stuck to the pan and came out looking like tar. They couldn't have been any good, but Nathan boasted that they were the best pancakes he'd ever had. He kept trying to get someone to give his pancakes a taste. They all passed on the offer, several times each. When Nathan put down his fork and frowned at his plate, Tessa caved and took one for the team.

"Gimme a bite of those fine-looking pancakes," Tessa said. She reached over the table and used her fork to saw through the sticky glob on his plate. Nathan watched her put the bite in her mouth, his face bright and expectant.

"Oh boy," Tessa said. Her teeth were sticking together like she'd taken a bite of cement glue. She was having a hard time distinguishing any of the seven flavors. Instead, it was as if Tessa had leaned down and put a hand cupped full of swamp water from Candy Land in her mouth. She reached for her glass of milk to wash it down. It gripped her throat as she swallowed. "That was real good, Nathan. Maybe you should be a chef."

"See!" he said. "See"—he pointed his fork to Ruby, then Preston—"I made them good!"

They all felt sluggish and weighed down by mild stomachaches post-pancakes. After the worst of the sugar crash and general complaints about everything had passed, they settled on having some tea and playing a game of Monopoly. The game ended abruptly forty-five minutes in when Ruby landed in jail. Nathan let out a celebratory hoot, which set Ruby off. She hopped up and kicked the board so the pieces went flying everywhere. Ruby was currently serving time with her nose in the corner.

"Mama, can I come out yet?"

"No," Tessa said.

"But there's a daddy longlegs up in the corner looking at me."

"Should've thought of that before you spoiled the game." In truth, Tessa had been grateful that the game had ended. Playing board games with the three of them was like being a referee in a rugby match. It was real rough, and there weren't no way of winning or pleasing anyone. Plus, Monopoly was the worst, longest, and most boring board game of them all. She had winced and reluctantly resigned herself to the task when she was outvoted three to one on playing it. It was an especially hard defeat to swallow knowing the only reason Nathan had voted for the game was for the pleasure of choosing the wheelbarrow as his totem and that Tessa would have to be the banker while managing her, Nathan's, and Ruby's money.

"He's crawling down to get me now, Mama," Ruby whimpered.

"I see him, and he ain't bothering you none."

It was three o'clock, and there was no sign of Angie. It hadn't occurred to Tessa that she might be gone that long, and she was starting to worry that the man with the puppies at the doughnut shop would be gone by the time they could get there.

"Angie say how long she'd be away?" Tessa asked Nathan, who had his Walkman on and was listening to one of Buck's old books on tape. *Lonesome Dove*, Nathan's favorite, if Tessa had to guess. Nathan didn't answer.

"Can me and Nate go play outside?" Preston asked.

"Okay, but stay within shouting distance."

"Okay, Mama," Preston said. Preston lifted the headphones off Nathan's head. "Let's go outside." Nathan looked to Tessa for permission.

"Go play awhile. I'll holler when it's time to come back." Tessa expected Ruby to whine about wanting to go with them, but she was quiet and content with her crayons and coloring book for the moment. She had snuck out of the corner just a few minutes before and was most likely trying to keep a low profile. For this, Tessa was grateful.

Tessa picked up the cushion and cover board on the bench at the table to get to the compartment below. She lifted out the phone book and flipped it open to the *B*'s so she could ring Beth's Donuts.

"Big Bill left about an hour ago, when he gave away the last pup," the man on the phone said.

"Shit," Tessa said.

"Excuse me?"

"Nothing. Thanks." Tessa hung up the phone. Next, she turned to *P* for "pound." The closest one was a twenty-minute drive. Not bad. They closed at five. Tessa looked at the clock on the microwave. It was nearing three thirty. She chewed on her lip and stared at the tarred-up frying pan that was soaking in soapy dishwater while she thought. She settled on an idea and dialed the Perris Pound.

"You have any puppies in?"

"A few," the woman who answered said.

"Any that look like they'll grow into big dogs?"

"A couple have good-sized paws on them."

"Can you hold on to the big-pawed ones until I can get there?"

"We don't hold. It's first come, first serve."

"Alright. Well, I'll be there soon anyhow."

Tessa hung up and looked down at the number pad on the cordless phone. She remembered the number easy. It come right to her—four, two, two, six, five, four, two. The numbers all lay within the same triangle on the keypad, except for the area code, which didn't count, seeing as she didn't have to dial it. Mel had told her about the triangle shape of her home phone number the day she first gave it to Tessa all those years back, on account of Tessa being in a hurry and not having no paper or pen on her at the time. Mel's number had stuck with Tessa ever since.

Tessa pressed the triangle of numbers and put the phone to her ear. Doreen picked up on the second ring. Tessa recognized it was her right away.

"Hello?" she said. The rasp and distance of Doreen's voice brought Tessa right back to the feelings of shame and desperation she had experienced standing on Doreen's porch asking after Mel years before. Tessa's voice got tangled up with her thoughts in her throat.

"Hello?" Doreen said again.

"Hi," Tessa choked out. "Is Mel there?"

"Who's calling?" Doreen said. Tessa thought to lie, but she had decided on not doing that anymore. Maybe with the dementia, Doreen wouldn't remember who she was anyhow.

"Tessa." Tessa strained to listen for something in the silence that followed. She was hopeful when she heard Mel in the background ask, "Who is it?"

"She's not here." The three stern words were followed by a click and a dial tone. Tessa set the phone down on the table and thought for a minute before she picked it back up and dialed again. One ring.

"Hello," Doreen snapped.

"Hi, Doreen. May I speak to Mel?" There were no words this time. It went straight to the dial tone. Tessa gave her calling Mel another thought. Maybe it was for the best Doreen had hung up on her. Maybe she was just stirring up trouble anyhow. She didn't want more of that. Tessa knocked her knuckles on the table and stood to walk the phone back over to the charger. She nearly jumped through the roof when the phone in her hand began ringing.

"Hello?" Tessa answered.

"Everything okay?" Mel said.

"Mel. I— Yes, everything is fine."

"Well, what are you calling here for? You scared me. I thought maybe something bad had happened," Mel said.

"I'm sorry. I didn't mean to bother. I—" Tessa grasped at her line of thought for calling. The seemingly solid reasoning she was now being asked to present was dissolving into a greasy pretense that was slipping through her hands. "We were out on a kind of adventure today. The kids and I. Anyway, we come across that pile of wood where we—you and me—once come up on that kangaroo rat nest. Remember that?" Tessa paused for a response that didn't come fast enough. "Anyway, I was telling them about it, and my boy, Preston, said he'd never heard of you before. And, well, I thought that ain't right. You know, him not knowing you."

"Tess," Mel started, but Tessa had caught a momentum with her blurted words, and that momentum was needing her to try and finish whatever it was she was saying.

"And, well, I promised Preston that I'd get him a puppy today, but Angie took the truck, and I ain't got no way of getting him that puppy. And I been trying real hard to say things square, you know, to show the kids it's important to keep your word. I was just sitting here thinking about all of that and thought maybe you might come and take us to get that pup. That way, I could keep my word, and that way, my kids could get to know you. Because, Mel, you was awful important to me back then and awful important to who I come to be." Tessa felt her insides swelling up like water balloons. She felt like if she let herself start to cry right then, she might lose what little handle she had on things. Mel was staying quiet, so Tessa kept talking to try and stay out ahead of the swelling and the cry.

"I saw the old barn. The one I told you about back then. I'd sleep there sometimes to keep away from Wayne and Reggie." Tessa knew then that her seeing that barn, that was why she had called Mel all along, and that instead of running from all the feelings trying to catch her right then, she was headed straight for them. Seeing that barn had scared her so bad. It had kicked up old, twisted feelings in her body and scrambled her brain. Those memories and feelings tore back the curtain of her flesh and the life she'd gummed to it and exposed the hollowed-out lonely that had been festering there all along. For the kids' sake, she'd had to pretend she hadn't felt or seen it in the moment, but it was pressing back up into her awareness something fierce and uncontrollable now. She put a hand over her mouth to catch the sound of the sudden sobbing that started. She pulled the receiver away from her mouth and went back into her room, where Ruby couldn't see her.

"Tess? Tess, you sure you're alright?" Mel said. Tessa breathed deep into the pillow she'd pressed to her face. She pulled the pillow away. She closed her eyes and watched the little electric fits of light playing on her eyelids. She sniffed and wiped at the snot smeared across her upper lip and cheek. The stillness that came after the out-burst offered a moment of clarity that helped her come to her senses.

"I'm sorry if my calling caused you trouble with Doreen," Tessa said. "I guess I didn't think things through none."

"Doreen will be fine." Mel let out a little laugh. "She wouldn't tell me who it was that called. I had a feeling it was you, though, by the way she was cursing under her breath after she hung up. I had to get the operator to do a callback to be sure." Tessa didn't know what to say to that. She figured she'd said more than enough, and now it was her turn to stay quiet.

"You still there?" Mel said.

"Yup."

Mel cleared her throat. "I'm not sure me taking you and the kids to the pound is such a good idea."

"No. Of course. I under—"

"Henry know who I am?"

"He knows you're an old friend."

"And how do you figure Henry would feel if he found out we were closer than friends back then and you and me and the kids are all palling around while he's at work?" Tessa couldn't say much to that. She didn't know how Henry would react. With the way talk spread around the Valley, he may have heard about Tessa and Mel from before. If he had, he didn't seem bothered none by it now.

"Mel, you want to be my friend or not? That's what it boils down to. I don't care what people once thought or what they think now. I ain't trying to add burden to your life, and I ain't trying to mess up mine neither. It just seems a shame to have you living back here close by and not get to see you every once in a while. Friends, Mel. That's all I'm asking."

"That simple, huh?" Mel said. "Well, alright, Tess. Sure. Let's do it. Let's be friends." Tessa recognized the not-so-veiled edge in Mel's voice, but she couldn't help but feel a little good hearing the words.

"You mean it?" Tessa said.

"You got a box or something to put this puppy in? I don't want it running around or puking in my car on the drive home."

"I can find something."

"Okay, then. I'll help you keep your promise."

1992

Tessa

Tessa could tell it was Reggie and his dipshit dirt-bike buddy Connor when they rolled the barn door open. The sound of the door woke her. She knew it was them two on account of their loud attempts at whispering, and she knew they were up to no good on account of the fact that they weren't saying things outright at a regular volume. She sunk down in her sleeping bag and strained to listen over the loud pulsing in her ears. Neither Reggie nor Wayne had ever come looking for her there. Nobody had. Maybe it was a coincidence that they'd shown up. Maybe if she kept quiet they'd have their drink or their drugs or jerk each other off or do whatever it was they come to do in secret and then be on their way. She knew that weren't the case when they started shining their flashlights around and calling out her name.

Tessa guessed they were both on crank by the way they were talking too fast to one another and to themselves. They weren't stopping to listen to what the other was saying. They were winding themselves up and speaking in that eerie meth talk that came out in partially discernible fragments and left out chunks of the sentences that were zipping too quickly through their corroded brains to be grabbed by spoken word.

"She's here. Seen her. Window. This way earlier. Know she is," Reggie said. "Tessa," he called out.

She sunk deeper into the bag when she heard footsteps nearing the ladder that led to the hayloft. The pounding in her ears was deafening, and a sickening mix of mobilizing adrenaline and paralyzing terror crashed against and coursed through her body.

"Up there," Connor said. Tessa saw lights through the cloth of her sleeping bag jetting around on the ceiling above her. Maybe she could fight Reggie off if he were by himself and if he weren't cranked up, but as it was, he wasn't alone, and the same chemicals that were eating out his brain just then were also giving him an edge on any fight she might be able to muster.

Tessa heard the ladder creaking, and she prayed to a God she'd never known to be there, that they'd somehow overlook the lump in the sleeping bag laid out square in the middle of the ten-by-ten loft.

She heard boots come to a stop on the ground near her head. "This snake has it a rat in the belly." Reggie laughed and kicked at the part of the sleeping bag where she was balled up. His boot bounced off her spine. Next, he unzipped the bag enough to reach in and grab her under her arms. He hauled her out kicking and thrashing. Before she could get her scrambling feet under her, he let her go, and she landed hard on her tailbone. She spun to face him and ended up turning into the plank of wood that was already swinging toward her head. It clocked her good at her temple and upper cheek and made things go bright behind her eyes for a second. She went back down to the ground again.

Reggie flipped her onto her back, climbed on top of her, and clapped a dirty hand over her mouth when she started to yell. She tasted metal and battery acid. He leaned in close to her face and said, "Hush up." A harrowing clarity and focus crystallized in his horrible blue eyes just then. He looked her dead in the eye and said, "If you can do it for Wayne, you can do it for us."

Her chest tightened, and she drove her knee up hard between his legs. He bucked over and rolled off onto his side. "Bitch," he groaned. Tessa went for the ladder, but a quick-moving figure, Connor, came out of the shadow where he was standing. He caught her tight by a fistful of her hair and yanked her down to the hay-strewn floor. It was his turn to pin her down. Tessa reached up and scratched at the flesh of his face. She grabbed ahold of his bottom lip and twisted and tore into it with her nails. Connor let out a shriek and batted her hands away. Her arms were moving too fast for him to take ahold of, so he grabbed around her neck with both of his hands. Spit came bubbling out of his mouth like he was blowing raspberries. He gurgled and squeezed and throttled her neck. She couldn't take in breath. Her clawing hands weakened as her arms started to go limp. Right before she blacked out, she heard Reggie's voice and felt a steel-toed boot dent her side.

When she come to next, she heard their voices again. Connor and Reggie were arguing this time. Reggie was on top of her. Her head was turned to the side, and his hand was pressing her right cheek into the floor. There was a searing pain in her side that was making her sweat and keeping her from taking a full breath.

"We gone too far," Connor said. Tessa felt the cold on her bare legs. She swallowed the wave of sick that came with the realization that they'd taken off her pants.

"Yeah?" Reggie said. "Leave, then."

"Fuck you, Reggie. I ain't getting strung up for this," Connor said, and then she heard him stomp over to and down the ladder.

"Fuck you," Reggie called after the barn door slammed shut.

Tessa knew she was hurt pretty bad. She blinked her eyes open and closed, or tried to. One of them was sticking shut. She could just make Reggie out in her periphery. He turned his attention back to her unmoving body. He hadn't noticed she'd come to. She meant to keep it that way. He kicked her legs wider. Tessa knew he had it in him to kill her and that if she stayed still and let him do what he was wanting to, there was a chance he'd leave her be after. She couldn't count on that chance, though. Even if she could, she knew she wouldn't be able to live with herself if she didn't try and keep this ugliness from happening.

She closed her eye and thought hard on how she could get out from under Reggie. An idea come to her, and she began to crawl her fingers out along her side, searching the floor as discreetly as possible. She nearly let out a whimper with the grace she felt when she touched the cool handle of her screwdriver.

Reggie was panting and struggling to get his pants down. Spit from his slung-open mouth dripped out over his bottom lip and landed on her collarbone. He got his belt undone with his free hand and folded back his fly. When he leaned in close with his dick in hand, she drove the screwdriver up under his rib cage. He took a sharp, wheezing breath and dropped down heavy on her chest. She pressed him off and crawled away quick. He was fighting for air and not moving none when she started to make her way down the ladder. Halfway down, her foot broke through the step it was pressing on, and the whole ladder gave and split apart. She fell the five or six feet it was to the ground. The impact strummed the pain in her side, and she let out a dry-throated cry. She rolled onto her hip and pushed up. She knew she had to keep moving, else she might just lie where she landed and let the pain take her.

Reggie was dead, probably. After the initial force it took to break the skin, the screwdriver had glided in up past the handle as easy as though she were poking open a bag of feed. Even if he wasn't dead, he was in no shape to be chasing after her—at least she had that going for her. Connor could still be nearby. For that reason, she cut through a swath of thorny milk thistle wouldn't nobody like to take in the dark. All the hurt that the adrenaline had been staving off was now bearing down on her. It felt like someone was thumping on her with a bag of bricks with every limping step she took. Tessa kept tripping over rocks and scraping up her hands when she landed. She was grateful to have had the wherewithal to pull on her jeans before she climbed down the ladder, but she wished she'd taken the extra moment to grab her boots. Her feet were tearing open every which way on the spines of thistle and jagged rock. A mean tumble over a boulder caught her at the shin. Tessa picked herself up and squinted into the dark to get her bearings. She caught the twinkle of a second-story bedroom light that seemed not too far away. She figured it was Gus and Millie's place, which meant if she kept going, cutting across at a diagonal, she'd hit the dirt path she was looking for. Then it wasn't but a mile and a half of smooth walking to Henry's place. She could do that.

Forty minutes later, Tessa was leaning up against the Jenson house. She could give way to the pain and fatigue now. Angie would help her. She reached up and tapped on Angie and Buck's bedroom window and waited a minute. Then she reached up and tapped again. A moment later, light was shining in her eye, and a moment after that, Angie and Buck come running out to her.

Judging by the pained and twisted expressions on both their faces, Tessa must've looked as bad as she was feeling—maybe worse, even. Buck tried to be gentle when he lifted her up to carry her inside, but the movement shifted her splintered ribs so they poked into her at an excruciating angle and made her wish she were dead. She let out a hoarse moan and begged to God that the pain would be enough to black her out again. It wasn't, though, and she was acutely awake to every touch as Angie laid careful searching hands on her body.

Angie gave her a good look over, cleaned her up some, and put her in fresh clothes. The bags of ice and the pills Angie gave her turned the pain down enough for Tessa to answer questions in short sentences. She blamed those pills for loosening her lips when it come to Angie's asking about the way Wayne had been with her in the past and about what Reggie and Connor had tried to do to her that night. She didn't want nobody knowing about that, and she made Angie swear to her that she'd keep that part of things between the two of them.

"Forever," Tessa said and took Angie's face between her hands so Angie had to look her in the eye.

"To my grave," Angie said. Tessa let her hands slip from Angie's face and fall to her own lap. She leaned back into the pillows propping her up. She could relax a little knowing Angie wouldn't never say nothing after giving her word like that. Women who lived out their way knew that their word was just about the only thing they could ever count on truly owning outright, and they didn't make a promise unless they meaned to keep it.

Angie left Tessa so she could talk with Buck. He would go collect her things. Tessa had agreed that her moving in with them would be for the best. She told Angie there wasn't much for Buck to gather. It was just some clothes, a shoebox of pictures, and her mama's purse that she wanted.

When Angie stepped out, Tessa took the opportunity to try and doze off a bit. It didn't seem like she had but a moment before she heard the door open again. Henry stepped inside, and she did her best to push up to a seat and make herself appear less crumpled.

Angie must have prepared him good, because he didn't make no face or show the sick he must have felt seeing her all busted up like she was. He couldn't talk none, though. His seeing her like that had made him go mute. He went to her side, sat lightly on the edge of the bed, and put his hand like a feather on top of hers. She didn't like the silence or the feeling of his hand being so cautious of hers. She was needing him to hold her hand like he meant it just then.

"You should see the other guy," Tessa said. She regretted the words as soon as they come out, and she forced herself to let out a little laugh after saying them. Using the muscles it took to let that laugh out felt like someone was running a fire iron clean through her, but she didn't show that hurt none. The sad, pitying look on Henry's face then made all of it feel about a hundred times worse. She reasoned it wasn't his fault, but she couldn't help feeling betrayed by his looking at her that way. She knew that somehow, his looking at her like that, it changed things between them.

Tessa wished that instead of seeing her lying there as some broken victim, Henry could see that she had survived because she was strong, and that now that it was over and she was moving in, they could put all of it behind them. That weren't the way he was taking things in, though. He was coming to different conclusions.

"It's not as bad as it looks," she tried. Henry gave a little nod and looked away from her to the lamp beside the bed. She could see then that the corners of his eyes were welling up and that he was trying awful hard not to cry. His cheek was pulling in on one side from where he was biting down on it. He opened his mouth several times to try and speak, but the only thing he got out was a half-audible croak. He pressed his shaking lips together then. Tessa waited. It was painful, but she waited. She hoped that he might be able to pull himself together and talk to her, but he didn't. He couldn't.

Until that moment, Henry and her had been something completely separate and untouched by her other realities. That was one of the things she'd loved best about being with him. Now she could see that Wayne, Reggie, and her mama had finally taken that from her too.

"I should probably try and rest some," Tessa said after the long silence. Henry nodded again. He leaned down and kissed her forehead. Tessa gave him a little smile when he pulled his lips away. She waited until the door was closed to let go of all the tension and effort it took to hold herself up. She adjusted herself so that she was on the side that hurt less to be lying on. The cheek that didn't feel broken was resting on the scratchy afghan blanket Angie had tucked around her. She pulled down the sleeve of the Easter egg–pink sweatshirt Angie had put her in to cover the developing bruises that circled her wrist. She held the end of the sweatshirt sleeve in her closed palm to keep it put.

Tessa stared up at the bright light bulb in the lamp beside the bed until it burned a jagged yellow hole in her vision. She closed her eyes and found the dark surrounding the formless bright spot soothing somehow, like she was drifting off into space. One day, she thought, she would kill Wayne and Connor, and if Reggie wasn't dead already, she'd finish that job too. They wouldn't get to live. She made herself that promise. Then the light began to shrink and fade, and Tessa let the exhaustion and numbness that had been tugging at her pull her further into the dark, where she found deep, dreamless sleep.

SEVEN

1999

Mel

Tessa and her bunch were waiting out front when Mel drove up in her little white Toyota. Tessa was resting a milk crate lined with a white sheet on her tilted hip. The breeze was kicking up the bottom edge of the long, soft-blue wraparound dress she had on so that it fluttered down at her ankles, just above her worn-out sneakers. She gave a wave with her free hand, and Mel let the breath out her lungs.

"I must be crazy," she whispered and pulled up along the mailbox at the end of the driveway. The little group came walking down to her. Tessa put a hand on top of the car, bent down, and stuck her head in the passenger-side window. "Well, hey there," she said with a playful smile.

"Hey," Mel said.

"Why don't you put her in park and step outside so you can meet everyone?"

"Sure thing," Mel said. She left the keys in the ignition, so there was a loud beeping when she stepped out and swung the door shut.

"Ruby, you remember Mel from the other day?" Tessa said. Ruby nodded and looked Mel over.

"You helped us get the soap for the bugs on Preston's head," Ruby said. The boy made a face and kicked some dirt in Ruby's direction.

"Good to see you again," Mel said.

"And this is Preston," Tessa said, pulling him forward by the shoulder. He fidgeted with the bandage wrapped around his jaw and gave a little wave.

"Hey there, Preston." Mel took a hand out of her pocket to wave back. "You hit your chin or something?" He stepped back and busied himself with kicking at the dirt again.

"Well, this big guy here must be Nathan," Mel said, leaning to the side to see back behind Tessa, where Nathan was standing and looking off toward the house.

"That's right," Tessa said, stepping out of the way. "Nate, can you say hi to my friend Mel?" Nathan didn't respond; he was watching a red-tailed hawk hang in the wind current just above the house. Tessa turned to him and touched his arm. "Nate, buddy, can you say hi?"

"Hi," Nathan said, not moving his gaze.

"Well, should we get going?" Mel said.

"Yeah, okay. Let's get going," Tessa said. "You three climb in the back." Ruby opened the door.

"I want a window seat," Ruby said.

"Me too," Preston said.

"You two are gonna make your uncle sit in the middle?" Tessa said. They didn't answer. Ruby slid in behind Mel's seat, and

Preston motioned for Nathan to go next. Nathan climbed in and scooched over next to Ruby. Tessa shrugged and opened her door.

Mel couldn't see anything in the rearview mirror, save for Nathan's big head. Every time she glanced back that way, she caught him staring right at her. The other two were both looking out at the fields that ran along the road on the way into town. Tessa was sitting with the milk crate in her lap, folding and smoothing and refolding and resmoothing the sheet inside it. It was quiet enough to hear the pebbles the wheels kicked up from the dirt road as they went pelting off the underside of the car.

"It didn't take you long to get here," Tessa finally said.

"Nope," Mel said.

"Car seems to be running well. Seems brand new almost. What's it, like, a ninety-seven or something?"

"Ninety-six. I haven't put much miles on it since I got it. And the lady that had it before hardly drove it."

"It's nice. Still has that new smell inside," Tessa said. Mel nodded. She put her blinker on to turn and again saw that Nathan's eyes were fixed on her in the rearview.

"Jesus, for being on the way to pick up a new puppy, these guys sure don't seem too excited."

"They're just shy at first around new people, is all."

"The big guy seems to be sizing me up pretty good," Mel said. Tessa turned to Nathan.

"Nate, honey, you excited we're going to look at some puppies?"

"You freezed to death baby mice," Nathan said.

"No. Nathan, remember I said it was an accident? Me and Mel didn't mean for those mice to freeze to death," Tessa said.

"Oh, I see. You think I'm a cold-blooded mouse killer. Is that why you've been staring me down?" Mel said. Nathan didn't say anything. "Tessa's right. We didn't know picking those mice up would make their mom split." Nathan didn't respond or move his gaze. "Were you watching that hawk up by the house earlier?" Nothing. "You like bird-watching?" Mel said. She saw a little crease form in the middle of his forehead, like he was trying to figure her out.

"He loves bird-watching. Don't you, Nate?" Tessa said. Nathan nodded.

"You like hawks the best?" Mel said.

"No," Nathan said. "I like them worst. They eat the littler ones that I like the best. Hawks scare off all the good ones."

"Yep, they'll do that. I knew a guy who had a hawk for a pet. Had it trained and everything. People would call him over so he could let it free in their barns, and it would hunt down all the . . ." Mel's voice trailed off, and she swallowed the last part of that sentence when she saw Nathan's eyes growing big with worry. "So it could fly around and show off all the tricks the man taught it. They'd have little private hawk shows in their barns." Nathan's face softened.

"Was it a boy or girl hawk?" Nathan said.

"Girl," Mel said.

"Did she have a hat?" he said.

"Well, sure she did. It was a little yellow hat. A tiny baseball cap to keep the sun out of her eyes." Nathan scrunched up his nose and giggled.

"They don't wear those kinds of hats," he said.

"They don't?" Mel said.

"They wear little brown hats to keep their eyes from seeing."

"Is that right?"

"Uh-huh, so they don't be scared of things."

"I didn't know that." Mel lifted her eyebrows and gave a little who-knew look Tessa's way. "What else you know about birds?"

"Lots of things," Nathan said.

"Like what?" Mel said.

"Tell her about your favorite, Nathan," Tessa said. Nathan smiled at Tessa and acted all shy. "Go on," she said. Before Nathan could speak, Preston turned from the window.

"How much longer until we're there?" Preston said.

"Not much," Tessa said. "Go on, Nate."

"But, like, how much time, Mama?" Preston said. Tessa turned to Mel.

"What do you think? About seven minutes?"

"Just about," Mel said.

"Seven minutes until I get my puppy!" Preston said.

"Mel, Mama said I could have a bunny," Ruby chirped and beamed at Mel in the rearview, as if they'd been talking buddy-buddy-like the whole ride.

"Is that right?" Mel said.

"Honey, I said I'd think about it. That's not the same as saying yes."

"You thought about it for a long time already, Mama, and we could get a bunny for me at the pound," Ruby said.

"They don't have bunnies at the pound, honey. Only cats and dogs."

"They might have a bunny, Mama." Ruby whimpered and kicked at the back of Mel's seat. Tessa grabbed at her legs.

"Look at me a minute. I just don't want you to be disappointed when we get there, Rube. They don't have bunnies at the pound. Okay?" Tessa said. Ruby crossed her arms and slouched down in her seat. "Nate, tell Mel what your favorite bird is."

"A hummingbird!" Nathan said and flickered his fingers, which Mel guessed were supposed to be little wings.

"No shit! That's my favorite bird too," Mel said. She saw Tessa looking at her like she was lying or just trying to get on his good side. "I'm serious."

"I never knew that," Tessa said.

"There's lots of things you don't know," Mel said. Tessa stayed quiet for a beat, then turned back to Nathan.

"You hear that, Nate? Hummingbirds is her favorite too."

"Yup," Nathan said, grinning.

"Tell her why they're your favorite, Nathan."

"Because they got strong hearts!" Nathan made a fist with his hand and pounded his chest hard once so that it made a deep thumping sound. Tessa turned and looked at Mel with an ain't-that-too-sweet look on her face, and Mel had to admit it was pretty damn sweet.

"You know why they're my favorite?" Mel said.

"Why?" Nathan said.

"I like the shiny greens and blues of their feathers. My uncle used to feed them out of his hands. He taught me how. Trick is, you got to sit still for a long time holding the cap of a soda bottle filled with hummingbird nectar in the palm of your hand just when the sun is about setting. Sometimes, when they're first getting used to you, you have to sit still like that for over an hour. I would get all bit up by mosquitoes waiting, but it was worth it when they'd finally come. You can see the shine of them from up that close. That's your reward for being patient and earning their trust." Mel looked at Tessa then and had such a swell of feelings hit her that she thought for a moment she might cry. She snapped her head back forward and felt angry with herself for almost letting that sappiness get the best of her.

It went back to being quiet in the car again. Nathan's eyes had glazed over and he was staring out at the road ahead of them. Mel guessed he was thinking about her feeding those hummingbirds. She was glad when Tessa cleared her throat to speak.

"Your cousin still trying to work as a PI out of that little trailer in Hemet?" Tessa said.

"He's actually pretty successful now. Has a real office."

"Is that right?"

"Yeah. A couple times, the sheriff's department has even hired him to help out on a case."

"Huh, well, good for him," Tessa said. She got fidgety in her seat all of a sudden, like there was a bug caught up in her dress. It was making Mel itchy watching her move that way. Tessa finally settled and chewed on her thumbnail a minute. "He's good at finding people, then?" she said.

"That's the job," Mel said.

Tessa lowered her voice when she spoke next. "You think he could find two or three people for me if I gave you their names on a paper to pass along to him?" Mel looked at her and was about to ask who it was she was needing to find, but Tessa cut the moment short.

"There it is!" She pointed to a big gray building on the corner of the next street.

They were parked and walking through the Perris Pound's double doors a couple minutes later. Tessa stopped short as soon as they set foot inside, and Mel nearly gave her a flat tire.

"Oh, for crying out loud," Tessa said.

Mel caught herself and jerked her head up to see what was the bother. She was bent over laughing as soon as she saw it. Sitting right there on the counter at reception was a cage with a huge black bunny inside. "Patty the Rabbit Needs a Good Home," the sign said.

"Look, Mama!" Ruby shouted and ran to the cage. Up close, the rabbit looked older than dirt. Its eyes were milky white, and it was so fat that Mel wondered if it could even move. "Mama, they have a bunny!"

The older woman behind the desk stood up eager. "Are you all wanting a pet bunny?" she said. The lady was wanting to unload the thing real bad.

"Yes!" Ruby said. She was up on her tippy-toes sticking her fingers in through the wire holes of the cage. Tessa pulled Ruby's hand back.

"Careful, Ruby," she said. "It might bite."

"Oh, she don't bite. She's as gentle as a lamb. Even if she did give a little nip, it wouldn't hurt a bit. Her teeth is wore down near next to nothing."

"Of course they are," Mel said. She sucked in deep to try to catch her breath. "Excuse me," she said. She supported herself against the desk and let out a snort. She looked to Tessa, who wasn't finding things so funny. "I'm sorry. It just—"

"I want her, Mama," Ruby said. The woman behind the counter threw an irritated glance Mel's way.

"She's a real sweet bunny. And very low-maintenance." The woman leaned over her desk to speak quietly next to Tessa's ear, and Mel leaned in thinking she'd like to hear too. "Her owner passed away. Lived way up in Gavilan Hills on her own. She was a kind of shut-in, hermit type. They found her and the bunny after days gone by with her being dead. The paramedics didn't know what to do with Patty. No next of kin. We don't normally take other animals besides the cats and dogs, but well, what could we do?" Tessa leaned away and nodded. Mel elbowed Tessa.

"After all, Tess, what else could they do?" she said. Tessa ignored her and kept looking straight ahead. Mel saw Tessa grinding her teeth like she would when she was getting ready to tell someone what was what, and if that someone was the lady in front of them, well, that was something Mel would enjoy watching.

"We come to look at puppies. Can you show us some of those?" Tessa said. Preston came up beside Tessa and took ahold of her hand.

"Of course. I'll call someone up here to take you back to the kennels." The woman sat down, picked up the phone, and dialed.

"Mama, please, please, pleeeeeeeease!" Ruby grabbed at Tessa's free hand and pulled her arm in the direction of the caged rabbit. A high-school-aged boy came walking in from the back.

"You here to look for a dog?" he said.

"We're hoping for a puppy," Tessa replied and tugged her hand free from Ruby, who stumbled back, ran to the cage, dropped down to the ground in front of it, and started to sob.

"We have some of those," the boy said. Tessa turned to look at Ruby. Seeing that Tessa was about at her wits' end with the girl, Mel figured she'd step in.

"I'll stay with her," Mel said. "You two go."

"Thank you," Tessa said. "Nate, honey, what about you? You want to come look at puppies with us?" Nathan lifted his nose from the kids' magazine he'd found. Tessa smiled and held out her free hand for him to grab ahold of, and he skipped toward her. The three of them followed the boy into the back.

"Can we take this thing out of its cage?" Mel said to the lady behind the desk. Ruby lifted her forehead from the linoleum floor. She sat up and wiped the hair out of her face.

"Sure," the woman said. "Just be careful with her."

Mel turned the cage around so she could unhinge the little gate. She reached in and got her hands under the rabbit's front legs, then pulled it toward her until it was close enough to lift out of the cage and hold next to her chest. It was heavy and warm in her arms. There were spots along its back and by its haunches, where its fur was matted and clumped. Mel bent down next to Ruby with the rabbit.

"You want to pet her?" Mel said. Ruby sniffed and nodded. Mel sat down on the ground with her legs crossed and let the rabbit rest in her lap. "Go on," Mel said. Ruby stroked the bunny's back and brushed its twitching nose with her fingers. The girl looked so much like Tessa right then. "I think she likes you," Mel said. Ruby nodded and wiped snot from her nose.

"She does," Ruby said.

Twenty minutes later, Tessa came back out with Preston walking by her side and holding a brown fur ball about the size of the bunny in his arms. Nathan was following behind them.

"Courtney will get you all squared away with the paperwork." The young man handed a few slips of paper over to the woman behind the desk.

"Isn't he cute?" the woman said, smiling down at the puppy in Preston's arms. Preston smiled back up at her, proud as a new father. "Okay, let's get you sorted so you can get that pup home." The woman busied herself at the computer for a couple minutes while they all waited. Then she got up and pulled a few pieces of paper from the printing tray.

"Alright," she said, walking back over. "We just need payment for the adoption and vaccination fees. Then you're all set."

"What's that going to run?" Tessa said.

"Let's see here . . ." The woman squinted down at the paper.

"With the tags and all, it's going to be one hundred and seven dollars." Tessa sucked her teeth.

"That much to take a dog off your hands?" Tessa said. Mel moved to the counter next to Tessa.

"Well, the vaccinations and—"

"Yeah, but you're about to have one less mouth to feed around here, and I'm about to have one more. A hundred and seven dollars? That don't make sense. That make sense to you, Mel?" Mel shrugged, hoping to remain a spectator. It seemed she might get to see Tessa tell this lady what was what after all.

"Is there some sort of discount you can give, or is there someone I could talk to? I don't have that kind of money to be spending."

"I'm sorry. That's how much it costs to adopt. It's the best we can do."

"Lord, I didn't think it would be so much."

"Mama, we're still getting him, aren't we?"

"Hold on, honey. Let Mama think and talk to this nice lady." Tessa lowered her voice. "Ain't there anything we can do? I mean, could I pay in installments?"

"I'm sorry. That's what it costs, and we can't take partial payments. I wish we could." Mel sighed. This wasn't what she had been hoping for, and she felt guilty for letting it go on as long as she already had.

"How much you short?" Mel said. Tessa looked up at her.

"Eighty-seven dollars," she said quietly.

"You thought you'd get a puppy for twenty dollars?"

"I thought I'd get a puppy for free. I'm doing them all a favor." Tessa turned and looked hard at the woman. "I thought I'd be able to use some of that twenty dollars to spend on dog food." Mel rolled her eyes and reached into her back pocket for her wallet.

"I'll pay the difference." Mel took out her card.

"You don't have to do that," Tessa said. "I can figure something out."

"Will you quit? I said I'll pay the difference. It's no biggie. Besides, you think I'm going to sit here and watch them take that puppy back from him?" Mel gestured to Preston, who was hugging the puppy close and looking up at them with pleading eyes.

"Let your friend help out, darlin'," the woman butted in. Both Mel and Tessa shot her a look then, and she swallowed like her mouth had gone cotton dry. Mel handed the woman her card, and Tessa pulled several sad, crumpled bills from her change purse.

"Thank you," Tessa said, not meeting Mel's eyes.

"Mama"—Ruby came tiptoeing over, talking low, soft, and sweet—"am I going to get my bunny?" Tessa put her hands on her hips.

"Ruby, baby," she started, then stopped. "The hell with it." She turned to the woman. "Don't you run that card yet."

"I already done it," the woman said.

"Doesn't matter. We could make you void it. We're taking the bunny with us," Tessa said. The woman brightened. Ruby jumped up and down and squealed.

"That's wonderful—"

"For free, with the cage and all. And we'll take whatever food you have back there you been feeding it," Tessa said.

"Oh, well, we can't. I mean, there's an adoption fee," the woman said. Tessa stepped closer and gave a quick wave of her hand for the woman to lean toward her.

"Bullshit," Tessa whispered. She went heavy on the *t* sound and waited for it to land. Mel had to choke down a laugh when she saw the woman go slack-jawed from shock. "You said you all only ever took cats and dogs before. That means you don't have no policies to follow for this rabbit. And I know plenty damn well you want this thing gone as much as I don't want to be taking it. So if you want to make your money by making me buy a dog you got for free off the streets, then you're going to throw the geriatric rabbit and all its things in no charge, because you know damn well I'm doing you a favor."

The woman opened her mouth to speak, then closed it. Then opened and closed it again. She pressed her lips together in a tight line. "Fine," she finally said.

"Wonderful," Tessa said. She turned and gave Mel a satisfied nod.

Back in the car, Preston held the crate with the puppy in his lap, Ruby held the rabbit in the cage in hers, and Nathan was sandwiched in between the two of them looking glum for not having anything of his own to hold. He had the palms of his hands pressed together between his knees and was taking turns looking from Ruby's lap to Preston's. Tessa had tried to get him to talk about several of what she'd said were his favorite topics, including the Teenage Mutant Ninja Turtles, songbirds, and things that stick to the bottom of your shoes, but he wasn't interested.

"Hey, big guy," Mel said. "How about we stop and buy some hummingbird feeders on the way home? You and me can put them up when we get back to your place, if that's alright with Tessa?" Mel said.

"Sure," Tessa said. "That sound good to you, Nate?"

"Uh-huh," Nathan said.

"After a while, when they start coming around and getting used to the place, I can teach you how to feed them from your hands, like my uncle taught me. Would you like that?"

"Uh-huh," Nathan said. "I want that." Nathan sat up in his seat. "Mel?" he said.

"Yeah, big guy?"

"Can you bring that hawk for a hawk show?"

"I'm not sure that hawk is still around, but I'll see what I can do."

"Okay," he said.

"But we can get those hummingbird feeders for sure." Mel turned to Tessa. "We can pick up dog food then too."

"Really?" Tessa said.

"May as well," Mel said.

"I'll pay you back," Tessa said.

"Alright. We'll stop at the feed and seed."

"What a fine day it's turning out be," Tessa said. She was grinning like a happy fool. Mel shook her head and laughed a little.

"Well, it is," Tessa said. "It's a real nice day." She hung her arm out the window and leaned her cheek against the door so that the wind was blowing her bangs away from her face. She squinted up at the sun. Lines formed at the corners of her eyes and nearly met the ones that framed her big smile.

Nathan convinced Mel to buy four feeders, and they got enough puppy food to last for a couple weeks. The feed and seed was next door to Shakey's Pizza. Mel saw it on the way inside with

Tessa and Nathan. They'd left Preston and Ruby waiting with their animals in the car.

"What are you all doing for dinner?" Mel asked. Tessa shrugged and reached up to wipe her bangs out of her face with one of the plastic bags she was clutching. It was full of hay for lining the rabbit cage. "Let me take that," Mel said and took the bag from her.

"Thanks," Tessa said. "Well, I hadn't thought about it yet, but I guess it is getting close to dinnertime, ain't it? I could whip up some mac and cheese, and we've got some hot dogs to cut up and add to it. That sound good?"

"How about some pizza?" Mel said, tilting her chin in the direction of Shakey's.

"Yes!" Nathan cheered. "I love pizza!"

"I bet you do, big guy. I'll run in and get a couple pizzas to take back with us."

"Oh, that'd be nice. You sure, though? I don't mind fixing us something back at my place. You already done so much for us today." Tessa reached out and touched Mel's arm, then quickly drew her hand away. "I mean, pizza would be great, but—"

"Me and the big guy want some pizza. Isn't that right, big guy?"

"Yup," Nathan said.

"Can you carry this stuff to the car with Tessa while I run in and get us our pizza?" Mel said. Nathan nodded and took ahold of all the bags Mel had in her arms. "Got 'em?"

"Yup," Nathan said.

"What kind of pizza you like, big guy?"

"Pepperoni and sausage," he said. "No mushrooms or black rings." Mel looked to Tessa.

"No olives," Tessa said.

"Got it. And the other one?" Mel said.

"How about just cheese for the other one?" Tessa said and pulled the side of her mouth into a sweet little half smile.

"You bet," Mel said. She could feel a warmness spreading in her chest. She knew it was trouble, but there was nothing she could do. She'd known she was in for it from the moment she saw Tessa waiting by the road with her popped-out belly and that milk crate resting on her hip. She knew it would be that way, and that was why she hadn't told Tessa she was back in town, and that was why she hadn't tried to see her, even though she had wanted to from the moment she got back. She'd done her best to keep a cool distance at their breakfast, but even then, Mel knew.

It was going to be trouble no matter how she played things. Mel shook her head walking into Shakey's and tried to rattle that little half smile out of her mind. She'd have some pizza and hang those feeders. Then she'd leave and that would be that.

When Mel got back to her Toyota, Tessa was in the back seat between Ruby and Preston, and Nathan was sitting up front. All four windows were down, and there was a tension hanging inside the car that no amount of crosswind could clear out.

"You playing musical chairs?" Mel said.

"These two can't seem to behave none. Puts me in the mind to go straight back to the pound and give their new pets right back so some other kids that know how to behave can have them."

"No, Mama," Ruby cried. "Patty's mine."

"Nathan's up front with me for the ride home, then?" Mel said.

"Looks like it," Tessa said.

"Alright, then. You get to hold the pizzas, big guy." Mel handed

Nathan the pizzas, and he gleefully held the boxes in place. He had something to be happy about sitting in his lap now too.

"Preston said he was going to let his puppy eat Ruby's bunny when it's big enough," Nathan reported in a cheerful tone.

"She said her rabbit was smart and that my dog was dumb," Preston said.

"Not one more word from either of you. I mean it," Tessa said. "I'm embarrassed by the way you two are acting after getting exactly what you wanted today. You should be ashamed of yourselves." Preston started sniffling and wiping at the tears on his cheeks. The car was quiet until Mel put the key in the ignition.

"Ruby said Preston was a farthead, and Preston called her a spoiled, whiny baby," Nathan said. Ruby started up a low, mournful cry. "That's when Ruby kicked Preston in the arm, and the puppy came out of the crate and jumped out the window. Tessa said two bad words. Then she got out and caught the puppy, and then she told me to get in the front seat."

"Alright, Nathan, honey. Mel gets the picture," Tessa said. Mel met Tessa's eyes in the rearview. Tessa's mouth was twitching, like she was trying hard not to laugh. She shook her head and threw her palms up, then let them land on her lap.

By the time they were pulling up to the trailer, Nathan had given a detailed scene-by-scene retelling of *Teenage Mutant Ninja Turtles* and was about to spring right into *Teenage Mutant Ninja Turtles II: The Secret of the Ooze* when Tessa stopped him.

"Nate, honey, we're home. How about you and Mel see about hanging your feeders while I figure out what to do with these two and their pets? Okay?"

"Let's get to it, big guy," Mel said.

"I'll put the pizzas in the oven to keep warm. Nate, you show

Mel where your daddy's old toolbox is. Use whatever you need for hanging, and meet back here in twenty for dinner."

Nathan wanted to hang all four feeders right outside his window, where he could watch them from his bed. They found a stepladder and the toolbox in the garage easy enough. Nathan held the ladder steady while Mel put up the hooks. Then, one by one, he handed up the feeders filled with red sugar water. Mel came down off the ladder after placing the last one and stood looking up at them next to Nathan.

"What do you think, big guy?" Mel said.

"I like them very good," he said.

"They look nice up there, don't they? It won't take more than a day or two before the hummingbirds catch wind of them. Then you can practice sitting still while you watch them out the window."

"When will you come to show me how to feed them by hand?" Nathan said.

"We'll have to see about that. Could be that I'll need to tell you how to do it over the phone. Why don't you run and get a pen and paper so I can write my number down for you to call when you think you're ready to try." Nathan ran back into the garage. Mel watched the road up the way from the trailer. She wanted to split before Henry got home but hadn't worked up the nerve to ask when that would be. Nathan came back with a pencil and an empty old packet of flower seeds.

"That'll work," Mel said. She went over each number twice so that they were dark and clear enough to read. "Put that in your pocket so you don't lose it, and let's get this other stuff put away. I think it's just about time for pizza."

Tessa had the table set and ready when Mel and Nathan came back. Ruby and Preston were sitting quiet at the fold-down table.

Patty the rabbit was sleeping in her cage on the counter next to the sink, the puppy was whimpering from behind the closed bathroom door, and Tessa was leaning up against the oven with her hands resting on her hips. She lit up when Mel and Nathan stepped inside. It made Mel's stomach kick up and then drop flat.

"Well, come on in and have a seat, you two." Tessa opened the oven and pulled out the pizza boxes. "Hand me up your-all's plates and tell me which kind you want. And you've got your pick of Kool-Aid or lemonade to drink." Tessa dished out the pizza and took the seat at the end of the table that wasn't connected to the wall. Mel had slid in next to Nathan. Tessa tore off a paper towel and put it on her lap. She looked up from her lap to Ruby and then to Preston. "You two have something to say?"

"Thank you for driving us to get my puppy and Ruby's bunny, and thank you for stopping to buy puppy food and pizza," Preston said.

"Thank you," Ruby said.

"And?" Tessa said.

"And we're sorry we misbehaved," Preston said. Tessa nodded and looked to Ruby.

"Sorry," she said quietly.

"That's alright," Mel said. "I was glad to help out."

"And I bet Nathan is awful appreciative of the pizza and you buying and hanging those feeders. Ain't you, Nate?" Tessa said. Nathan had his mouth full. He was already halfway through his first slice, but he took the time to nod, set down the pizza, and give Mel a side hug. Mel thought she saw tears forming at the corners of Tessa's eyes, but it could have just been the way the light was hitting them.

"Well, that's settled. Let's eat," Tessa said. Tessa picked up her slice of cheese pizza. "Cheers," she said. Ruby, Preston, and Nathan all lifted their slices to meet Tessa's at the end of her stretched-out arm. They all watched and waited on Mel to lift hers.

"Cheers," Mel finally said and bumped the end of her pizza into each one of theirs.

They were close to having eaten all but a few slices of the pizzas and Preston was in the middle of telling a volley of improvised knock-knock jokes when the phone rang. Tessa threw her used-up paper towel down by her paper plate and pushed away from the table. She picked up the cordless by the door. She answered in the middle of laughing. Then she lowered her voice and turned her back, so Mel could just barely hear her over the ruckus at the table around her.

"My cell is in the bedroom. I didn't hear it ringing." Tessa turned back and looked over at the table then and saw that Mel was watching. She walked back into her bedroom. A few minutes later, she came out and put the phone back up on the wall.

She took her seat back at the table. "Pres, your daddy is going to be home in an hour. He's stopping to pick up fencing for you and him to put up tonight. Finish eating so you can wash up and be ready to help when he gets home."

"Okay, Mama," Preston said. Then he promptly put his hand back into his shirt and under his armpit to continue with the fart noises he had been producing there. He had Ruby and Nathan going. The whites of their teeth showing in their open giggling mouths looked bright next to their red, Kool-Aid-stained tongues and lips. Mel chewed and swallowed her last bite of crust.

"I'll help you clean up," she said.

"Ain't much to clean up, really," Tessa said. "Just have to toss the plates and napkins in the trash. I'll keep what's left on a plate in the oven for Hen."

"Well, I'll help with the trash, then." Mel slid out from behind the table and stood up.

"Can we go play outside until Dad gets home?" Preston said.

"Sure, but wash your hands before you go touching everything with greasy fingers, and take your sister with you," Tessa said. Preston made a face at her last point but must have thought better than to argue it. All three of them squeezed in front of the kitchen sink to rinse their hands. Then they ran out the door flinging soapy sprinkles from their fingertips. "Stay away from the road," Tessa called after them as the screen door slammed shut.

Mel pressed the trash down and closed the lid. Tessa was wiping off the table. "Well, you were right about it being an easy cleanup," Mel said.

"Thanks to you," Tessa said. "We haven't had take-out pizza like that in a long time. That was real nice of you, Mel."

"It's nothing. Besides, it's good to have dinner with someone other than Doreen every once in a while, and she doesn't care for pizza much."

"Well, I sure appreciated your company and everything you done for me and the kids today," Tessa said. Her voice wavered toward the end of the sentence, like she was maybe going to cry. Mel bent to pick at the linoleum where a bit of pepperoni and tomato sauce had landed. When she stood back up, Tessa was just standing there, like she didn't know what to do with herself either. Mel flicked the pepperoni into the sink and wiped her hand off on her jeans.

"Hope we left enough for Henry," she said.

"There's plenty for him. He's going to be real happy to have pizza for dinner."

"Good," Mel said. She put her hands in her pockets, leaned up against the wall behind her, stared down at her boots, and hoped for the right words to come. After a while like that, she looked up to see that Tessa had an aching look on her face, like maybe she was trying to come up with the right words too. Since Mel didn't know what the right words were, she said the truth of what she was feeling just then.

"Today was awful hard on me, Tessa." She felt the honesty of the words stinging her eyes, and she had to concentrate to make her mouth form the shapes of the words instead of letting the hurt and longing behind them spill out instead. Tessa took two steps toward her and stopped. Her lips pressed together and gathered to the side where she was sucking in her cheek. Tessa looked to where her fingers rested on the table and then back up again. She let out a little puff of air, and with it her eyes filled with tears.

"It was hard on me too," she said.

"It was hard enough that I don't know if I can do it again," Mel said. Tessa dropped her chin to her chest. She drew the sleeve of her dress down over her hand so it pulled off her shoulder some, and wiped at her face.

"I understand," she said. Mel went to her then because she couldn't stand not to. She put her arms around her waist, and Tessa rested her head on Mel's shoulder, where Mel could hear her sniffling and feel her breath. Mel started to sway her from side to side like there was music they were dancing to. Tessa let out an airy little laugh and sucked in snot. She pulled her head back to look at Mel. Mel felt the ache that she'd pressed down and carried with her for years come rushing to the surface when she saw the tears caught in Tessa's eyelashes and the freckles on her cheeks up close. She gave Tessa a warm smile, took Tessa's hand in hers, and swayed even more so that they were both taking little steps side to side to the music that wasn't playing. Tessa rested her head back down on Mel's shoulder, and they went on dancing like that. Mel leaned her lips close to Tessa's ear and whispered.

"In another life?" she said. A couple of warm tears escaped and went sliding down the sides of Mel's face. Tessa took a deep, shaky inhale and held it.

"You bet," she said. She sobbed then with her cheek pressing into Mel's collarbone. They went on swaying, and after a while Tessa's breath became regular. She sniffed and rocked her head against Mel a little. "Dumber than doornails," she said.

Mel hugged her closer. "You and me both."

1991

Mel

Tessa's head was resting on Mel's bare stomach. The subtle after-noon breeze shifted the fluttering white curtains in Mel's bedroom window so that the sun dashed and receded in waves across Tessa's face. Tessa squinted up into the waxing light and smiled at Mel. It was late summer, and the days they spent together felt damn near perfect. Doreen worked most of those days, and some nights, too, as a checker at the Save-A-Lot. Without the restrictions of school or Doreen hovering over them, they were left to do as they pleased.

Tessa reached up and rested a hand on Mel's chest. Mel liked the weight of Tessa's hand being there. She liked the feeling of her heart beating up into it. She closed her eyes and faded in and out of snippets of pleasant late-afternoon dreams. When she opened her eyes next, the purple marks that wrapped around Tessa's upper arm stuck out against her pale skin and made Mel wince.

"Those are pretty good bruises you've got there," she said as she grazed the marks with her own fingertips. Tessa took her hand away and tucked her elbow to her side. "Wayne do that?" Mel asked.

"Yup," Tessa said, then sighed and moved away on the bed so that her body was curled up in direct sunlight.

Mel knew to tread lightly. These weren't the first bruises she had noticed. She'd seen plenty of them on Tessa before. Some real nasty ones, like the one right up under her jawline that was only now fading after weeks into a yellowy brown smattering. Things weren't right, Mel knew that. And she wanted to do something about it, but any time she pointed them out or asked about the marks, Tessa would get defensive and angry, as if Mel were the one putting them on her. Tessa would go back home and disappear for days at a time as punishment. It would make Mel sick with worry. Today, though, Tessa hadn't reacted so sharply. Maybe it was the easy feeling they both had from napping in the cool breeze after being out in the sun all day, or maybe it was the weed they'd smoked before coming inside to lie together. Mel was quiet while she thought about how she might take advantage of the opening. She didn't want to ruin things, but she knew she'd regret it later if she said nothing at all.

"Doreen uses the belt on me sometimes. It's never too bad, though. Most of the time, I've done something to deserve it. Sometimes I just need the sense knocked into me, I guess." Mel shifted onto her side so that she was talking to Tessa's back. "Is it that way with Wayne?"

"No, Mel," Tessa said. "It ain't like that with Wayne. And I expect you know that. There's nothing to be done for it. And I would just as soon prefer you not bring it up again. I spend plenty of time thinking about it as it is." Tessa pushed herself up and turned to Mel. "Understand?"

Mel nodded, although she knew she didn't, not really.

"Good," Tessa said. "Let's talk about something else." She lay back down on the pillow next to Mel.

"Okay. What should we talk about?"

"You and me moving away from here."

"Sure," Mel said.

"I mean it," Tessa said.

"Where should we go?"

"Anywhere, just as long as we could live there together in peace."

"Sounds like a plan to me," Mel said and hugged in close to her. Tessa twirled a strand of Mel's hair around her finger and gazed toward the upper corner of the room, leaving Mel for her private thoughts, as she often would. Right before Mel drifted off to sleep, she heard Tessa whisper.

"I sure would like to move away," she said.

Mel woke to a loud cracking noise and a stinging on her thigh. She didn't have time to put what was happening together in her mind before the next lash landed across her back. Tessa yelped and jumped out of bed. Doreen chased her into the corner of the room, where Tessa crouched and tried to cover her head with her hands. Doreen brought the belt down hard and fast. She got four good licks in before Mel could make it over to her.

"Stop it!" Mel yelled. Doreen spun around and came after Mel again.

"Stupid, ungrateful bitch," Doreen said. Mel let her land another two lashes before she caught Doreen by the wrist.

"I said stop it." Mel felt a throb at the outer edge of her right eyebrow and the warmth of blood coming down the side of her face. Tessa remained still and crouched in the corner. Mel squeezed her mother's wrist hard and pushed her back into the wall behind her with a hand on her chest. The hand that was holding her mother's wrist became shaky, and Mel felt herself crumbling. "What's wrong with you?" Mel said. Her bottom lip began to tremble. Doreen was unfazed. Mel felt hot tears on her cheeks. She let Doreen go and dropped to her knees in front of her. She bent her head and sobbed at Doreen's feet.

"Mel," Tessa whispered.

"Leave," Doreen said. There was a long, quiet pause followed by the rustling of Tessa's clothes as she got dressed. Mel heard Tessa move toward the window, whereby she would often come and go. Then she heard her stop.

"Come with me," Tessa said. Mel didn't move. "Mel?"

"Out!" Doreen shouted. Mel lifted her chin from the carpet. Doreen reached for the snow globe on the dresser beside her and whipped it at Tessa's head. It missed, just barely, and smashed through the drywall to the left of Tessa's ear.

"Crazy bitch," Tessa said. Tessa took a half step toward Mel. Mel met eyes with her, and then she turned back to face Doreen's feet. A moment later, she heard Tessa's boots land on the ground outside the window.

EIGHT

1999

Henry

Metal fencing rattled in the back of Henry's truck when he turned at the mailboxes and made his way up the driveway. The fencing was simple, a few posts and some chain link. It was just enough to build a small and sturdy enclosure for the time being. Even still, it cost more than they had to be spending on things they didn't need. Especially now that Tessa had it in her head that she needed a car and another place for them to live. He couldn't imagine how she figured he'd be able to pull that off. She knew what he was bringing home every month, and yet the way he heard it, she was giving him an ultimatum. An ultimatum after everything they'd been through together. It picked at the scab of the feeling that he didn't actually know her at all.

Preston, Nathan, and Ruby came running up to the truck from the field behind the trailer. Ruby got there first. "Daddy!" she yelled. "I got a pet rabbit today." Henry left the windows down and opened his door.

"Is that right?" he said.

"Yes! It was at the pound, and Mama said I could have it," Ruby said. Henry looked up to see Tessa standing in the trailer's doorway watching. He lifted his toolbox out the back of the truck and made his way to the trailer with the three of them in tow. Tessa stepped back and held the screen door open to let them inside.

"Well," Henry said, taking the two steps up and into the trailer, "a puppy and a rabbit."

"Hen, I'd've called and checked with you about the rabbit," Tessa said. "It's just that," she stammered, "it's just—it was a setup. They had the thing sitting on the counter as we come in, right after I told Ruby there wasn't rabbits at the pound." Henry walked up to the cage and bent down to have a look. It had its backside to him, so he stuck his fingers in the cage and poked at it to try and get it to stir, but the thing was sleeping and didn't seem to want to wake up.

"Do you like her, Daddy?" Ruby said.

"What's her name?"

"Patty," Ruby said.

"Didn't have to pay for it. And they gave food for it that should last at least a month. And the cage was free," Tessa said. Henry stood up and took off his hat.

"That's a good rabbit, Rube. I like her laid-back style." Henry turned to Tessa and leaned in to give her a kiss. "How was your day?" he asked and put a soft hand on her belly. Tessa seemed to relax then.

"It was a good day. Got the puppy and the rabbit. Got Nathan some hummingbird feeders. Got pizza for dinner," Tessa said. "Let me get you a couple slices."

"Yes, please. I'm hungry. Need to eat something before me and Preston put up the fence."

"Can I show you the puppy, Dad?" Preston said.

"Let's see it," Henry said. Preston took off toward the bathroom and came back a moment later with the pup squirming in his arms and licking at his face. It looked like it had some Australian shepherd in it, maybe. Henry couldn't quite tell what else it might be.

"Is it a boy or girl?" Henry asked.

"Boy," Preston said.

"What's his name?"

"Winslow Sharp Fang," Preston said. "Winslow for short." Henry looked to Tessa and raised his eyebrows as he nodded his head.

"That's quite a name. How'd you come up with that?"

"I don't know. TV, I guess," Preston said and went to shut the puppy back up in the bathroom. Tessa pulled a plate full of pizza from the oven and walked it over to the microwave.

"That's alright. I don't need it heated up," Henry said.

"You sure?" Tessa said.

"I don't like the way the microwave makes the cheese all oily. It's good as it is. Give it here," Henry said and smiled. Tessa sat the plate and a paper towel down in front of him. "What have we got here? Pepperoni and sausage. You must've picked this one out, huh, Nate?"

"Yup," Nathan said.

"And plain old boring cheese. I know who picked that one." Henry put an arm around Tessa's waist.

"Where'd you scrounge up the money for pizza and humming-bird feeders and that big bag of dog food over there?" Henry pointed the slice of pizza in his hand at the bag of puppy chow sitting in the corner of the room. "Mama give you some money?"

"Mel bought it," Nathan said.

"Mel?" Henry said.

"Mama's friend," Preston said. "She drove us to get Winslow." Henry chewed.

"Angie took the truck for the day." Tessa stepped to the window and parted the curtains to look. "She still ain't back. I had to call my old friend, the one I told you about the other day."

"It's too bad she couldn't have stuck around," Henry said. "I'd've liked to meet her."

"Well, we took up enough of her day as it was with all the stops."

"Next time, then," Henry said.

"Sure," Tessa said.

"She at least eat dinner here?"

"She did, but she had to be going to get home to her mama, who she looks after."

"I see," Henry said. "Well, nice of her to do all that. We'll pay her back when we have the money."

"Of course," Tessa said. Henry shoved the last of the pizza crust into his mouth and wiped his hands.

"You about ready to help me with the fence, Pres?" Henry said.

"Yup," Preston said.

"What about you, Nate? You want to help?"

"Yeah, okay," Nathan said.

"Ruby?"

"I want to stay with Patty," Ruby said and hugged both arms around the cage with the unmoving rabbit inside. Preston rolled his eyes at Nathan. The puppy was crying loud from inside the bathroom. Tessa was keeping busy tidying up and moving things around, trying to act like the high-pitched whining wasn't bothering her, like she wasn't regretting bringing the thing home.

"Grab your pup and some rope from under the kitchen sink. We'll tie him up outside with us while we put his fence together," Henry said.

Nathan was strong and good at working the post-hole digger. He had almost every one of the holes that Henry had marked in the dirt for him to dig finished before Henry and Preston had the quick-set cement mixed and ready and the posts laid out. It was easy to forget that Nathan was his big brother and a grown man. Henry had always looked out for him, as far back as he could remember. It was Henry who had gotten into fistfights with the boys that would tease Nathan on the playground and Henry who had taught him how to fish.

Henry had always felt Nathan was too gentle and good-natured a person for where they lived, maybe for anywhere. People considered him simple. Part of what they dismissed as simplicity, Henry thought, was the fact that Nathan was above the greed and fear and distrust that had everyone else all screwed up and scrambling and at each other's throats. Maybe Nathan was like a big brother in that respect. He set that example to aspire to, anyway.

"We're going to need to build Winslow a doghouse this weekend," Henry said. "We can't keep him in the bathroom every night."

"Okay, Dad," Preston said.

"And you're going to have to get up and keep him quiet every time you hear him whining in the night, understand?" Preston nodded. "Your mama and sister need their sleep, and keeping him quiet at night is part of showing that you're grown enough to have a dog."

"I won't let him whine, Dad. I promise."

"I know you won't. I'm proud of you. You're a good boy, and you're on your way to growing into a man I'll be real proud of too." Henry felt his throat constrict and his eyes threatening to well up with the words he spoke. He had to stand up from the squatted position he was in for a moment.

"You okay, Dad?" Preston said.

"Yeah, I'm okay, son." Henry let a breath out and looked back at the trailer. "I just got lost in thought there for a minute."

"What were you thinking?"

"Well, I was thinking how proud I am of you, like I said. And then I was thinking of how it might have felt to hear my dad say something like that to me at your age, or at any age, for that matter."

"Grandpa Buck was never proud of you?"

"No, I think he was proud of me and my brothers. Especially you, Nate. He was always proud of you." Nathan was sitting cross-legged, swiping at the dirt with a tree branch, and didn't seem to be listening, but Henry said it just in case he was. "I think my father had a hard time showing or saying it. Guys of his generation just didn't go around saying things like that. Truth is, he didn't say much at all to me or my brothers. He wasn't one for words, except for telling stories and jokes. He was good at that, and he was good at charming strangers." Other times, Henry thought, when he or his brothers had gotten caught making trouble, Buck had a more corporal way of letting them know how he felt about things.

"What about to Grandma? He speak to her?" Preston said.

"Grandpa Buck and Grandma liked being quiet together. That was their thing. They knew each other so well they didn't feel the need to talk, I guess. They'd sit out on the porch for what seemed like hours at a time without sharing a word." Henry looked back at the trailer again. He could see Tessa folding laundry through the window. Ruby was bouncing around her, talking excitedly. About what, Henry could only guess.

"Preston?" Henry said.

"Yeah, Dad."

"I don't want you teasing your sister about her rabbit or about anything, for that matter. Like I said, you're getting older now, and part of that means looking out for your little sister. You got to be the bigger person and not get into fights with her anymore, not even when she's getting under your skin."

"Okay."

"You're about to have another little sister to look out for in just about a month from now. And you're going to have to grow even bigger. It may be that we are moving off Grandma's property not too long from now, and I'll need you to take care of your mama and sisters when I'm working and not around to look after them. You think you can manage that?"

"I'll look after them, Dad."

"You're moving away?" Nathan said. He sounded so wounded and betrayed that it just about yanked the heart from Henry's chest. He hadn't meant for him to find out like that. Henry cursed himself for being so stupid and bigmouthed with Nathan sitting right there.

"Well, it's a possibility, Nate. But nothing is for sure. It's just a thought right now. We ain't got a place to move to yet or anything."

"Why are you thinking of moving away from me and Mama?" The hurt behind the question made Henry sick, but he couldn't think of what to say to fix things. To tell him that it was Tessa who was wanting them to move away would crush him. Nathan threw down the tree branch in his hands, pushed up to stand, and went running for the trailer.

"Nate, hold on a second. Wait!" Henry called after him, but it was no use—he was already swinging the trailer door open to find Tess. Henry wondered what she'd say to him. He wondered if she would think he had made Nathan upset like that on purpose to try and get Nathan to make her stay or to make her feel bad for wanting to leave. At least Tessa would be able to calm Nathan down. She'd always been able to put him at ease, better than anyone else ever could. Nathan was the only other person in the world that Henry was sure loved Tessa as much as he did.

"Should I go and try and bring him back here, Dad?"

"No, let him go. Your mama will set him right. We need to finish up this fence before dark."

A few minutes later, Tessa came walking out the trailer with Nathan leading her by the hand and Ruby following after. "How's it coming along?" Tessa said.

"Should be ready to wrap the fencing around the posts in a minute here," Henry said. He stood, lifted his cap, and wiped the sweat at his hairline. "What are you all up to?"

"Nathan is going to show me and Ruby the feeders he put up earlier today. Ain't you, Nate?"

"Uh-huh," Nathan said. He pulled Tessa up the way toward the house, and Tessa gave a little wave goodbye as they went. Maybe she hadn't thought he'd spilled the beans on purpose. Maybe she knew him to be better than that.

"You help Nate hang those feeders?" Henry said.

"Nope," Preston said.

"He did it by himself?"

"Mel helped him."

"I see," Henry said.

"She's nice, Dad. You'd like her."

"I'm sure I would."

"Mama really likes her."

"That so?"

"Yeah, Mel makes her laugh. She says stuff and does stuff Mama thinks is funny."

"Well, that's good. It's good that your mama has a friend that makes her laugh."

"Yeah," Preston said. "Except I think she made her sad too."

"Oh?"

"Or maybe Mama was crying from laughing so much because they were being silly. I couldn't really tell."

"What do you mean?"

"I saw Mama crying on Mel's shoulder. Except, like I said, maybe it was that she was crying from laughing because they were being silly."

"How were they being silly?"

"They were slow-dancing like you and Mama do sometimes, but they were being silly because they're both girls and there wasn't any music."

"You all were with them when they were being silly like that?"

"No, me and Nate and Ruby were playing up by Grandma's house. I got thirsty and come back for water, but saw through the window that Mama was crying, and I couldn't tell how come—I mean, whether she was happy or sad—so I thought I should stay outside."

"That was probably a good idea. I wouldn't worry about it, though. I bet she was crying from laughing because they were being silly, like you thought."

"Yeah," Preston said. "Probably."

Henry looked up the way toward the house, where he saw Tessa pointing up at the feeders and making a big fuss over them. Ruby was sitting on the front step with her chin resting in her hands, expressing much less enthusiasm.

Right then, Henry heard familiar music coming from up the road behind him, and he knew that it was Angie kicking up dust, driving too fast like she always did. She was playing Hank Williams with the windows down, which meant she was in a sentimental mood, which meant she was thinking about Buck. She tooted the horn and turned down the music when she rolled up next to Henry and Preston.

"What are you building a fence for?" she said. Preston pointed to Winslow, who was napping next to the scrub oak they had him tied to.

"A puppy! Ain't that a surprise," Angie said. She waited for an explanation that Henry didn't have or feel like trying to give.

"His name is Winslow Sharp Fang," Preston said.

"Wow, sugar. That's some name," Angie said.

"Come meet him," Preston said.

"I can't just now. I've got groceries in the back I need to stick in the fridge. I will though, honey, and I'm looking forward to it."

"Okay," Preston said.

"Your chin ain't no better, huh?" Angie said. Preston shook his head. "Don't worry, we'll get it fixed up." Angie waited again for

Henry to say something more, and again he didn't. "Gonna head up to the house, then."

"See you later, Mama," Henry said.

"See you, honey," she said. Angie looked both Henry and Preston over one more time. Then she turned her head straight and drove on up to the house. Henry watched as she got out of her truck and walked over to where Nathan and Tessa were standing. Tessa shifted on her feet as they exchanged what looked like cordial greetings. Then Tessa pointed back at the trailer, and Ruby jumped up from where she was sitting and went bouncing over to her. Ruby gave Angie a hug, and then she and Tessa came walking back down Henry's way while Nathan started helping Angie unload the truck.

After Tessa and Henry tucked the kids in bed, Henry stepped outside to see the night sky. It was clear and cool and dark out. Just the way he liked it. Henry put the tailgate down, climbed into the bed of his truck, and leaned himself up against the cab window with his legs stretched out in front of him. He looked up at the stars and thought about his wife and her friend and wondered if that friend was the cause of Tessa's recent demands. He wondered if he should be worried about Mel. He'd acted like he hadn't heard of Mel when Tessa admitted to having breakfast with her after first lying about it, but Henry knew exactly who she was talking about when Tessa had said the woman's name, and it had caused a sick feeling to wake deep inside his belly.

Henry had heard the speculation around Mel and Tessa's friendship, back when he'd first started to take an interest in Tessa. He gave his buddy a fat lip after he got finished telling Henry what he'd heard about the two of them being together like that. The more Tessa came around the house to check in with his mama back then, and the more he started to fall for her, the less he gave credence to the rumors, the less he cared. The girl, Mel, had skipped town anyhow. In his mind back then, it was a moot point. Nonetheless, when the thought crept in and he was honest with himself, the idea of the two of them together in a romantic fashion bothered and confused him more than he was willing to admit or try and deal with. So he chose to forget about it, which had served him well all these years. They'd had their bumps in the road, and there was the constant push and pull between Tessa and his mama, but there was never really a question of loyalty between him and Tessa. They'd stood by each other through the best and worst of their years together. Henry knew Tessa had her own interior world and that there were parts of herself she wouldn't share with him, but he'd made peace with that years ago, and he knew she appreciated and respected him for it.

Henry saw the kitchen light go out and the bedroom light turn on, and figured Tessa was done working her crosswords at the kitchen table and was getting ready for bed. She'd given him a questioning look when he said he was going to step outside for some fresh air, but she'd said nothing.

Henry felt a gentle breeze on his bare arms and heard coyotes yipping off in the distance. He leaned his head back against the window behind him and felt the long workday and the wear of all the worry catching up to him. He closed his eyes and started to think about the work he had to do the next day. Before he knew it, he was slipping into sleep.

"Henry?" Tessa's voice startled him from the half-dream haze he'd drifted into. He sat up and blinked into the dark until he could see Tessa standing at the edge of the truck bed in her nightgown and sweater.

"It's getting late," Tessa said. "Thought I'd come check on how you was getting along with the fresh air."

"I nodded off a bit. What time is it?"

"Ten thirty," Tessa said. Henry was feeling groggy and not too quick to move or speak. "You coming to bed?"

"Yeah, I'm coming." Henry pushed himself up to stand, walked to the end of the truck bed, and jumped down next to where Tessa was standing.

"You okay?" Tessa asked.

"Just tired from the week," Henry said.

"We'll get you caught up on rest this weekend," Tessa said. She put an arm around his waist. He put his arm around her shoulder and kissed the top of her head, and they walked to the trailer.

Tessa was standing across the bed from him, pulling back the blanket and sheets, when he came out with it. He hadn't planned on saying anything, but something about the tenderness he felt watching her in that moment and the ache of not knowing where they stood pressed it out of him.

"Do you love her?" Henry said. Tessa froze, then stood up straight with the sheet and blanket still in her hand.

"What?" Tessa said.

"Preston said he saw you slow-dancing and crying on Mel's shoulder today, and I know what people said about you two back before I knew you. So, give me an answer, Tess. Do you love her?" Tessa stayed frozen. She seemed to be deciding what she was going to say or not say. Henry was tired of calculated responses. "Please just tell me the truth of it, Tess," he said. Tessa let the sheet and blanket fall to the bed and met eyes with him.

"Yes," Tessa said. His stomach dropped. Her mouth twitched at one corner, and she pressed her lips together. Tears filled her eyes and started rolling down her cheeks. "I love her in a way that I'll never love you." Henry wished to God then that he'd never asked the question. He felt his insides and life being ripped apart. He didn't want to stand there with her and the words she'd just spoken, so he went to the chair for his coat.

"But I love us—you, me, and the kids—more. It's you and the kids for me," she said. Henry stopped at the chair and listened with his back to her. He heard her come closer. "You have to understand, Henry. She come along in my life back when things were so awful and so dark. She was just this bright, bright magnetizing light, you know? She made me happy and hopeful despite all the ugliness. I loved her for that. And I loved her for who she was. I'm not ashamed of what we had. Her and me together meant something. She's important to who I come to be." Tessa paused. "I loved her then, and I love her now. And I don't think that love will ever go away. And I'll never stop being grateful with all my heart for her showing up in my life like she did, or for the time we had together. I thought we might be able to be friends now after all these years, but that's not the way her and I fit together. I know that now. She knows it now too. That's why I was crying on her shoulder earlier today. I was saying goodbye." Henry let his hand drop down to the back of the chair to help sturdy himself so he could keep standing there while he took in all of what Tessa was saying.

"Henry?" Tessa said. He couldn't respond, not yet. Time was moving too fast, or maybe it was that it was going too slow. Either way, he couldn't figure things; he couldn't put his feelings into thoughts. "I didn't—" Tessa said. "Nothing has happened between us since she came back to town. I mean, we just went to breakfast the one time, and then we had the day together today. We slow-danced like Preston said, and I cried on her shoulder. That was the extent of things." Henry bit at the inside of his cheek and took a breath in and out of his nose.

"Okay," he said.

"Okay?" Tessa said.

"If that's the truth of it and you swear it's the kids . . ." Henry paused. Having to speak these words stirred up such a deep sorrow in him that he thought his heart might quit. He closed his eyes a moment to steady himself. "The kids and me you are choosing to-day and every day to come, even when things is hard—"

"It's the truth, I swear it," Tessa said before he could finish. She stepped forward and put her arms around Henry. She clasped her hands at his stomach and rested her cheek on his back. "I'm sorry," Tessa said, "for making you worry, and thank you for un-derstanding." Henry put a hand over hers. He didn't understand, not completely. He knew enough and accepted not knowing what he didn't. He wanted to put the struggle of the last couple of months behind them. It seemed like that was what Tessa was offer-ing. It didn't put his stomach at ease. He was still tasting bile at the back of his throat, but he was grateful for what she'd said.

"Let's get some sleep," Henry said.

"Sounds good." She let her hands drop, and they made their way to bed. Tessa curled in close to him like she hadn't done in months, and Henry hoped it was real and not just for show. He wasn't wondering over it for long. He was dead asleep about a min-ute after his head hit the pillow.

Next thing he knew, he was struck awake by the sound of Tessa shouting. His eyes flew open in time to see her shoot up to sit and take in a huge and terrifying gasp of breath that sounded like wind ripping through a cave. Henry pressed up next to her. He put a hand on her back. Her nightgown was soaked with sweat and stuck to her skin. She was breathing heavy and curled forward with her head in her hands.

"You okay?" Henry whispered in the dark.

"Yeah," Tessa said. "Just a dream. I'm alright." She straightened up and wiped her dampened bangs to the side. "Just a dream," she said again and touched the side of Henry's face. "Sorry I woke you." With that, she lay back down like nothing had happened and fell right back asleep. Henry watched her for a second, then lay back down too.

It was only when he closed his eyes to try and fall asleep again that he registered the words she'd screamed: *I'll kill you.* The hate in her voice echoed in his head and left his skin crawling. He got up out of bed and went to the kitchen for a glass of water. Winslow Sharp Fang started up crying at the sound of the cupboard door opening. Henry took a sip of the cool tap water, sat his glass down, and went to get the pup. He opened the bathroom door a crack, and the puppy tried to squeeze out right away. Henry bent down, opened the door wide, and picked little Winslow up. He stopped crying and licked at Henry's chin. Henry made his way back to the kitchen table with Winslow cradled in the bend of his arm. He sat down with the puppy in his lap. Henry took another drink of water and thought he could use something stronger. He looked at the microwave to check the time. It was after one, and he figured anything stronger at that point would make it harder to get up for work than the lack of sleep would. He looked out the kitchen window. The porch light was on up at his mama's place. She was probably out there thinking and worrying over the same person he was.

Tessa had night terrors now and then. They came on more frequently for a bit after Ruby was born, but in time, they went back to the every-once-in-a-while occasion they were before. He couldn't remember her ever yelling something like that, though. He wanted to chalk it up to the pregnancy and hormones and recent stress, but he couldn't ignore the way it made him feel. A deep cold was coming from within him, like his bones were made of solid ice, and he couldn't make the spit in his mouth he needed to swallow and soothe the dry of his throat. Her words wouldn't let go of him. They held him in place and went on repeating themselves over and over, like a busted siren in his head.

NINE

1999

Tessa

Tessa woke to the alarm buzzing on the nightstand on Henry's side of the bed. She rolled over to shake him, but he wasn't there. She stretched across the bed and turned the noise off. Then she pressed up to sit, slid her feet into her slippers, and went to check the kitchen. She flipped on the light and found Henry slumped over on the table, fast asleep. Winslow was curled up sleeping right next to him. The pup must have had a cold, or maybe it was just the way he breathed. Every exhale had a little whistle and swish to it, like the sound of a thin tree branch whipping through the air.

Tessa reached up into the cupboard and pulled down a coffee filter. She placed it in the maker and added four heaping scoops from the big red coffee tin, figuring Henry would need the extra lift. Then she went and laid his clothes out on the bed for him. The coffee machine was gurgling and sputtering its last bit of water through the filter by the time she came back. Henry went on sleeping through it. She pulled down his favorite coffee cup—big, blue, stained all the way on the inside—and filled it to the brim.

"Rise and shine, sugar," she said and brushed the hair on the top of his head. Henry blinked his eyes open, and she kissed his cheek. He yawned as he sat up, and she put his coffee cup down in front of him.

"Thank you," he said and took his first sip. "I sure need it."

"It's mighty strong this morning."

"I'm ever grateful for that."

"The puppy wake you?"

"No," Henry said. He paused and gave her a look like he was trying to figure something out. Wondering over the look and the hint of irritation in his voice caused Tessa to remember a snippet of the bad dream she'd had. She had startled him awake. Before she could apologize, he continued. "I got up to get some water and woke him. Figured I'd sit with him until he settled. Next thing I knew, you was handing me this coffee."

Tessa filled herself a cup and sat down across from him. "I wonder if I'm gonna have Nathan again today. You know what your mama's been up to?" Tessa said.

"I rarely do," he said. Tessa clicked her tongue.

"You gonna make it through the workday?" she asked. "You're looking a little rough, pal."

"I don't have much of a choice."

"You could call in. You never call in like all those guys you work with do."

"We've got bills to pay," Henry said. He looked at her, then down at his coffee. "And other, bigger expenses we ain't yet got the money to cover." She'd walked herself right into that one. Tessa reached across the table and rested a hand on his wrist.

"Hey," she said, "I know things haven't been going so smooth for us. I know I haven't been making things easy. But me wanting to move off your mama's property and get a car—that part of it is because I know it will make things better for us in the long run. Knowing you are on board and working to make it happen will help keep me sane in the short." Henry let out a long breath.

"I know that's how you feel," he said. "I'm working on it." Henry looked at the clock on the microwave. "I'm gonna be late." He got up and headed to the bedroom. Tessa waited a minute before she pressed up to stand. She pulled down a couple packets of instant oatmeal for the kids and herself and put toast on for Henry to take for the road. She'd just finished filling his thermos with coffee when he came in from dressing in the bedroom. She screwed on the lid and handed it to him along with two pieces of peanut-butter-and-honey toast wrapped in a paper towel.

"Thank you," he said.

"I'd've made you a sandwich for lunch, but that's the last of the bread. I had to give you the heel as it was."

"I'll get something from the food truck." Henry took a bite of the toast, then set it down for a second to pick up and shove his phone and wallet into his pockets. Tessa slid his keys onto the stretched-out finger of his thermos-holding hand. He leaned down and gave her a flat kiss goodbye. "See you tonight," he said and walked out the door.

Tessa stood on the steps to the trailer watching him get into the truck. "Henry," she said before he could get all the way in. He stood up and looked at her over the hood. "We'll get you caught up on sleep this weekend."

"It's cold out," he said. "Get inside before you freeze those little feet." Then he smiled, climbed inside the truck, and backed down the driveway.

Tessa closed the door as quiet as she could to keep the kids from waking and jumped about a hundred feet when she turned to see Preston standing in the middle of the kitchen, watching her with Winslow in his arms.

"Oh Lord," she said, putting a hand to her chest, "you nearly gave me a heart attack sneaking up like that."

"Sorry, Mama. I wasn't sneaking. I saw you being careful with the door and thought maybe we were being quiet." Tessa dropped her hand and smiled.

"I was being quiet trying not to wake you, but here you are. Come here, honey. Give Mama a morning hug." Preston went to her, put his arms around her, and rested a cheek on her belly. She kissed the top of his head. "Let me see your chin. Is it still itching pretty good?"

"A little," he said.

Tessa took his face in her hands and bent to have a look. "Well, it ain't any worse, at least. We can put just a big Band-Aid on it today." Tessa sighed. "And we'll try some of Grandma's stuff."

"Okay." He squirmed away from her hold and put Winslow on the ground.

"You hungry?"

"Uh-huh," he said.

"I'll fix you some oatmeal." Preston frowned at this.

"Can't we have pancakes?"

"We're out of flour."

"Okay," Preston said gloomily.

"We can add some sprinkles to it. We still have some of them left. That sound better?"

"Yeah, I guess," Preston said. Ruby came walking down the hallway with a blanket hanging from her arm while she sleepily chewed on a chunk of the ends of her hair.

"Morning, baby," Tessa said. Ruby came up and leaned her body into Tessa's legs. Tessa bent and gave her a little squeeze and a rub on the back. Ruby lingered, pressing more of her weight into Tessa. Tessa bent down again and picked Ruby up to rest on her hip. When Tessa stood, she felt an electric shock run up and seize her back. It made her gasp, but the pain left as soon as it come on, so she went on holding and patting Ruby on the back.

"You want some sprinkled oatmeal, Rube?" Tessa asked.

"What's that?"

"Just what it sounds like. Oatmeal with a bit of sprinkles on top."

"Can I still add sugar?" Ruby said.

"A pinch," Tessa said.

"Okay," Ruby said. She squirmed down off Tessa's hip and went over to check on Patty.

They were just sitting down to eat when Tessa heard Nathan's heavy footsteps outside followed by his thump, thump, thump on the door.

"Hey, Nathan," she said, opening the door wide and standing aside for him.

"Hi," he said and came tromping on in. He set the dish towel–covered pan he was carrying on the kitchen table along with a carton of chocolate milk. Preston reached over and lifted the dish towel away. It was cinnamon pull-apart bread, still warm from the oven. He looked at his lumpy, sparsely sprinkled oatmeal and then up at Tessa. Ruby had already pushed her bowl aside and was reaching for the bread.

"Pass your bowls down this way, and wait a second until I get plates." She went for the plates and got cups for milk. Nathan was at the counter, crouching down and talking quietly to Patty through the cage.

"You hungry for monkey bread, Nate?"

"Yup," he said. Tessa added some of Ruby's extra-sweet oatmeal to her own and finished the bowl. She'd eat the rest of Ruby's and Preston's for lunch.

"Nathan, honey, Angie say where she was going today?" Nathan had his mouth full and shook his head no. "She say when she'd be back?" Nathan shrugged his shoulders. "Okey dokey," Tessa said. She stood from the table and placed her bowl in the sink.

"Mama, can me and Nate go play outside awhile?" Preston said.

"As long as you stay in shouting distance. Ruby, you want to go play outside with Uncle Nate and Preston?"

"No, I'm gonna give Patty a bath." Tessa saw a wave of relief wash over Preston's face and figured she'd wait until he left to negotiate the terms of the bath with Ruby.

"Alright, Pres, put on play jeans and long sleeves and take Winslow with you. Keep an eye on him."

"Okay," Preston said.

"And we need the shovels," Nathan said. Preston elbowed him in the ribs. Tessa remembered just then that she'd seen two shovels leaning up against the side of Angie's garage when she was up there admiring Nathan's hummingbird feeders the day before.

"You two better not be digging holes for people to fall into," Tessa said.

"We aren't, Mama."

"Uh-huh. Well, I'm gonna check and see what it is you been up to before the end of playtime today. Don't go digging up more than can be put back easy, understand?"

"Yes, Mama," Preston said.

"Shouting distance, no farther."

"Yes, Mama." Preston popped up to go change.

"You making trouble out there?" Tessa said to Nathan with a smile.

"No," he said, shy and excited. "We're making a surprise."

"Okay, honey, you go and have some fun with that surprise, but let me get you one of Henry's flannels to wear over that shirt first. It's chilly out." Tessa went into the bedroom and came back out with a stiff old green flannel. The kitchen had gone quiet and empty. She had to run out front to catch Nathan. She threw the flannel to him. "Button it up all the way."

"Okay," he said. As he swung his arms into the shirt, he turned and took off running to catch up to Preston, who was already halfway up to Angie's place. Tessa hugged her sweater around her waist and went back inside. Ruby came skipping out of the bathroom with a bucket, a bar of soap, and one of the good towels Tessa kept under the sink.

"Wait a second there, honey," Tessa said.

"I'm going to give Patty a bath," she said.

"So I heard. You can give Patty a bath, but you have to give her a rabbit bath."

"What's that?"

"I'm going to give you a towel with a little water on it to clean her with. Rabbits don't like to sit in water. You've got to clean her the rabbit way."

"But I want to give her a real bath." Ruby's lip started to turn out.

"After you give her a rabbit bath, I'll find a brush you can use on her. I bet she'll like that. You can make her look all pretty."

"Can we put a ribbon on her?"

"Yes."

"And a bracelet?"

"I'm not sure I have a bracelet that would fit, but I'll give a look for one."

"Okay, Mama," Ruby said. Tessa took the soap, towel, and bucket from her and wet an old dishrag for her to use instead. Tessa lifted the cage and set it down on the kitchen floor.

"Be gentle with her now," Tessa said.

"I will," Ruby said. "Can you watch me, Mama?"

"I've got a box of things to sort through. I'll bring it in here so I can watch. How's that sound?"

"Okay," Ruby said. "But can you sit right there?" Ruby pointed to the corner of the kitchen where an extra wooden chair sat. She wanted her mama far enough away that her mama wouldn't bother her, or maybe she just wanted to give Tessa a little sting by telling her she didn't want her too near.

"Sure, hon," Tessa said. She stood up and bent to comb Ruby's soft, fine hair through her fingers. "Hey, Rube, I'm starting to get things out and ready for when your little sister comes along. You getting excited to be a big sister?"

Ruby acted as if she hadn't heard her. She opened the cage, reached inside with the towel, and started in on Patty's backside with it. Tessa waited a minute to see if Ruby would respond. When it was clear she wasn't going to, Tessa went back into the bedroom, where she lifted the mattress to get to the storage space beneath it.

She opened the tops of two boxes before she found the one she was looking for. She lifted it out and set it to the side a minute while she poked around in some linens for the soft yellow baby blanket that she liked to line the cradle with. The little wooden cradle she'd used for both Preston and Ruby was up in the attic at Angie's place. She'd have Henry get it down that weekend or the next. When she didn't find the blanket in with the sheets, she went on sifting through things and moving them aside. Her hand paused when her fingers grazed the top of the old shoebox full of pictures and letters from her and Mel's days together. She picked it up and felt the weight of it tugging on the muscles of her arm. Tessa tried hard not to think of Mel. It hurt and mixed her up too much.

She had her hand on the lid when Ruby started calling for her to come back. Tessa bent and tucked the box in under the pile of sheets and gave one more glance over things for the blanket. When Ruby called again, she decided the blanket must be up at Angie's with the cradle. She let the mattress fall back into place and slid the box she wanted down the hall, pushing it along with her foot.

Tessa set the box on the kitchen table and turned to see that Ruby had moved a chair over to the sink to get more water and left the faucet running. The trail of splashes on the floor led to Ruby and her fur-soaked rabbit quaking in its cage.

"I said just a bit of water. You've got the floor all wet, and that poor rabbit is shivering cold." Tessa stepped around the puddles on the floor to get to the sink and shut the running water off. "Give me that towel, and go sit your bottom down at the table until I clean this mess up."

"But, Mama—"

"Scoot!" Tessa went to the kitchen drawer and grabbed a couple dish towels out, then threw them down on the ground to drag around with her feet. "Why can't you never listen to your mama, huh?" Tessa said. Right then Patty the rabbit made a move out of her open cage and hopped right past Tessa's mopping feet down the hallway toward Preston and Ruby's bunks. "Lord have mercy," Tessa said. She went to the drawer again and picked out another towel to swoop the rabbit up in. Then she went following Patty down the hallway until she caught up with her; fortunately, Patty wasn't all too quick. Tessa wrapped her up like a baby and held her in her arms like one too. Ruby had her arms crossed and her chin buried in her chest when Tessa came walking back into the kitchen. Ruby kept her chin down but moved her eyes up to glare at Tessa under her wrinkled-up forehead.

"Don't you give me that sourpuss look." Tessa crouched to set Patty down. She shooed her back into her cage and closed its little gate. Then she grabbed the edge of the kitchen table to help pull herself up. "Sit here at the table, and I'll get you a coloring book. If you behave, I'll still let you brush Patty's hair out after it's had a chance to dry some. Ruby dropped her forehead to the table.

"Fine," she said down to her feet.

"Wonderful," Tessa said and went to find some crayons, a coloring book, and the small space heater they had so she could plug it in somewhere near enough to warm the rabbit. The last thing she needed was for the damn thing to get sick.

Tessa got Ruby coloring at the table and stretched the cord of the heater so she could place it just a few feet from the cage. Then she rummaged around in the refrigerator and turned up a partway-limp carrot to shove between the little metal bars toward Patty's sniffing nose. She went back to the table, where she had placed the box, and began to pull from it things she might want when the baby came along. She lifted the manual breast pump out in an act of wishful thinking. It was still in its plastic case. Never opened, never used, even though she'd bought it before Preston was born. She was never away from either Ruby or Preston long enough when they were nursing to have needed to use it. Now that she was pushing to move away from Angie's, there'd probably be even less of a chance she'd need it. Maybe she could get Carly to come out and help some. It would be good for the both of them.

"What's that, Mama?" Ruby said. Tessa's mind had been traveling so swiftly into the future she nearly forgot Ruby was sitting at the table with her. She lifted the packaged breast pump.

"This helps get milk out of Mama for the baby."

"Doesn't the baby supposed to do that?"

"Well, she does—she will—but if I want to get some milk out to save in a bottle in the fridge for her, I'll have to use this." Ruby sat quiet, staring at the pump that Tessa had now placed on the table.

"How, though?"

"Huh?" Tessa said.

"How does it get milk from you?" Ruby said.

"Well," Tessa said, working at prying the plastic open. A slip of folded paper printed with directions splashed onto the table when Tessa pulled the pump out of the case. "You know where the milk mamas make for their babies comes from?" To this, Ruby nodded and aimed her fingers like guns at Tessa's breasts. "Right. Well, this"—Tessa held up the pump—"goes where the milk comes from, instead of the baby, and it pulls the milk out of the mama and into a bottle you connect to this." Tessa held up the tube. Ruby's face was blank. "See here?" Tessa unfolded the paper. "That's the mama's breast, and she puts it there, then squeezes this to help get the milk out." Ruby's eyebrows tightened together.

"Does it hurt the mama?"

"Not really, no."

"Does the baby hurt the mama?"

"Not really. A little bit, sometimes, but not bad."

"I don't want to ever do that."

"You don't have to."

"Not even have to have a baby?"

"Nope. Not if you don't want."

"What, then?"

"What do you mean?"

"What would I do?"

"Anything."

"Live with you and Daddy forever?"

"If you wanted."

"Maybe," she said. That seemed to settle things for the time being. She picked up an orange crayon and started rubbing it on the paper until she paused again. "Mama, how long until I'm going to be a big sister?"

"About a month. Not too long from now."

"Will she have to listen to me?"

"If I ever put you in charge, she will."

"Will you?"

"Probably. When you and her are a bit older, I will."

"Until then, you will be in charge of her and me?"

"Yup."

"Okay," Ruby said and went back to the coloring book. Tessa went back to the box. She started with the clothes and searched through Ruby's infant-size onesies and little stretch pants. She lifted out and set aside a pair of tiny overalls that were unpractical, but very cute. The buttons ran up the inseam to the crotch.

They were next to impossible to line up, let alone snap, when a baby was fussing. She turned to the stack of baby clothes in the box again. The little peach-colored knit leg warmers Angie had made sat waiting for her, crossed one over the other in the shape of a small X. Tessa remembered pulling them up over Ruby's doughy little baby thighs. She could hardly hold in the love and tenderness she felt for Ruby just then, and the tremendous guilt she had for being so lost and numb for a while there after Ruby come along. She wondered if Ruby had ever felt the emptiness in her touch back then. She wondered what kind of aftereffect it had on Ruby today.

Tessa had to believe that she had loved Ruby just as fierce and deep back when she was born as she did now. It was just that it was buried under the rest of things. Her body and heart had felt so heavy and impossible to move and carry back then. It had taken all her strength to keep them both working during those first few months after Ruby was born. She felt like if she hadn't been vigilant in her effort to keep her heart beating, if she hadn't continually reminded herself to try, the functions of her body that were supposed to be automatic would have just quit and given up and left her to die.

Tessa had thought those feelings happening to her back then were caused by whatever it was that had affected her mama, the thing in her mama that had made her lie in bed for days on end. Tessa had believed it was some of that coming through in her, and maybe that was partly right, but now she understood the whole of things better. What had really done it to her was the terrible truth that comes with having a daughter. Tessa knew she could never completely protect Ruby from the kind of world she was born into, and the deep knowledge of that truth had swallowed her up and broke her brain for a while. It wasn't until she found out that she was having another baby girl this time around and felt those familiar feelings that had tried to scramble her thoughts and stamp out her breath that she had fully understood.

Tessa looked across the table at her Ruby, who was getting to be so big and smart and willful. She scooched the box up against the wall and went to rummage through the kitchen junk drawer. She found the ruler-length piece of thin purple ribbon that she'd kept from the bunch of flowers Henry had brought home for her last Mother's Day and a lone fuzzy green pipe cleaner left over from one of Preston's school projects. She went back into her bedroom, where she carefully picked up the small, delicate jewelry box that sat on top of her dresser.

She'd found the porcelain jewelry box with wispy, pastel-colored flowers painted on the lid years ago. It had seemed out of place sitting on the nightstand in the fluorescent lit motel room where her mother's body had been discovered two days before. It had smelled like Pine-Sol, piss, and cigarettes in that room. She'd driven twelve hours straight to get to the few personal belongings her mother had left there, hoping to find some answers to the questions she had about her mother's life and death. In the end, the motel room hadn't offered Tessa any new understanding of her mother. She'd left the room with just the jewelry box and a stomachache.

The jewelry box was missing one of its gold-plated hinges. Tessa gently opened the lid and fingered through its contents until she found the single turquoise clip-on earring she was looking for. She closed the lid, put the earring in her pocket, and swooped up a hairbrush on her way out of the room.

"You know what, sugar?" she said as she came back into the kitchen.

"What?" Ruby said, not looking up from her coloring book.

"I think Patty's had enough time to dry. I bet she's ready for you to brush her hair out for her."

"Really?"

"Uh-huh. And I found ribbon and a special rabbit bracelet to put together for her too."

"Yeah!" Ruby slipped out of her seat and clapped her hands together.

By the time Ruby had Patty brushed out and decorated with the ribbon and clip-on earring bracelet, she was wanting to put a little blush on her too. Tessa let her do it. She watched as Ruby highlighted the fur on Patty's cheekbones with her pink blush. Tessa drew the line at adding lip gloss, thinking that whatever made up the gooey shine could make the rabbit sick. Besides, the rabbit didn't really have no lips to speak of.

Tessa was just putting the kettle on for the tea party Ruby wanted the three of them to have when she heard a faint, high-pitched scream. She was confused at first, thinking that the scream was coming from the teakettle she'd just put on the stove's glowing burner. It didn't take a second more for her to recognize that it was Preston desperately shrieking for her from outside. She felt a sick flush through her that dampened her skin. She flicked the burner off, flung the door open, and ran outside for him.

She saw his shape frantically running for her from the top of a hill not more than three hundred yards away. He kept on screaming for her.

"Mama!" he cried. He stumbled, fell, and picked himself up. "Help, Mama!" Tessa held an arm around her belly and ran for him as fast as she could. As she got closer, Tessa saw that his face was covered in dirt and his forehead and cheeks were wet with sweat and tears. Tessa dropped to her knees in front of him. He was howling. She grabbed his shoulders and looked him in the face.

"Baby, what's happened?" Tessa said. He tried to speak, but he was out of breath, and his crying was keeping him from getting words out. Tessa wiped his face with her sleeve. "It's okay, baby. Take a deep breath and tell mama what's the matter. Where's Uncle Nate?" Preston pushed away and sucked in air.

"He's buried!" he screamed. "I can't dig him out. The tunnel collapsed too deep. Hurry! Please, Mama!" He pulled her by the arm and started running with her up over the hill in the direction he'd come from. They came down the hill and through a patch of sagebrush to a clearing. They passed several huge piles of dirt and a turned-over wheelbarrow. Preston ran her over to the spot where he'd last been digging. The top dirt was loose from the collapse and about two, two and a half feet lower than the firm, undisturbed dirt around it. "He's down there!"

Preston picked up a shovel and handed it to Tessa. Then he went to fetch the other one that was lying not far away. Tessa thrust the shovel down, then hauled up dirt and pitched it to the side.

"How deep down is he?" Tessa said as she scooped up and flung away another shovelful.

"Deep, Mama," Preston said through sobs. He was back at her side, digging now with his own shovel. Tessa was swinging out another pile of dirt when she saw the opening of a hole a couple yards away and the top of a ladder angled down into it. It must have been the start of the tunnel. She kept the shovel in her hand and ran the few steps it took to see the depth of it. The hole, not wider than a metal trash-can lid, was deep enough to be a clear foot over Nathan's head if he were standing up straight inside it. He must have been lying belly down at that depth back where she and Preston were digging.

"Oh God," Tessa whispered. She ran back over next to Preston and got to shoveling with all that she had. "Hold on, Nate!" she screamed. "I'm here, baby. You hear me, Nathan? Tessa's here. Just hold on!" She and Preston were moving as fast as they could. She kept calling out to Nathan, repeating the same phrases: "Tessa's here, Nate! I'm coming to get you. You're alright now." She needed him to know that he wasn't alone. She needed him to hear her words and breathe them like air until she could get to him.

Preston was slowing down. He was hardly making headway. He was weak from all the running and digging he'd already done. Tessa twisted, flung, and felt her back seize up and electrify the muscles there like it had before in the kitchen. This time, the shock was followed by a familiar tightening and ache in her thighs and lower belly. It ripped the wind from her lungs and squeezed. She thought it might make her drop the shovel, but it let up, and she kept digging.

"Mama," she heard Ruby call from not far away. Ruby must have seen which way Tessa and Preston had run and come after them. Tessa didn't stop to answer her. She kept her head down and focused on moving dirt.

"Grab your sister and run as fast as you can back to the house," she said to Preston as she forced the shovel down with her foot and hauled another load up. "Call nine-one-one and then call your daddy. Tell them what's happened. Tell them we need help. Stay there until someone comes." Preston continued his weak shoveling.

"I got to get him out," he said, whimpering.

"Now, Preston!" Her voice came vicious and hoarse.

He dropped the shovel and ran. She heard him shout for Ruby

to come with him. She listened to the faint crackling of legs and feet moving quickly away through sagebrush until the sound was gone and all she could hear was her shovel working the dirt.

Ten minutes, maybe fifteen, had gone by since Preston had left. Her shoulders ached. Her arms were heavy. The rounds of contractions kept coming, gripping her violently, then letting her go. Her palms were wet with sweat and the fluid that had sprung from the blisters and torn skin on her hands. None of it mattered. She could think only of Nathan underneath all that dirt, counting on her to save him. She made herself believe that the dirt might be loose enough for him to be getting air somehow. She made herself think of all the stories about miracles she'd heard. Stories like them had been told all over the world since the beginning of time. She had to believe that if even just one of them was true, if there was a God or good force of any kind out there looking to give away such a thing, Nathan had earned it. If there was anyone ever deserving of a miracle, it was tender- and purehearted Nate. She had to believe that she could save him still. She ran the shovel into the dirt. Her hands burned as they slipped down the wooden handle. She pulled up and slung away. She called to him. She begged him to please stay.

She'd lost track of things and didn't know how much time had passed when she heard the sirens coming. The edges of the hole she was standing in were just up above her waist. Her mouth was dry. Her arms and shoulders had stopped hurting and gone numb. "Here they come, Nate." She forced out the words that were catching in her throat. "It won't be long now." She heard voices and car doors slamming. She rammed the shovel down. "Hear them, baby?" She went to pitch the dirt, but her arms quit and would no longer lift. She let the shovel fall and dropped to her knees and began to scrape dirt away with her hands. "We'll get you out now, honey."

The voices were right above her then, but she couldn't make out what they were saying. She felt the thump of boots land on the ground next to her. The voices got louder. One was speaking next to her ear, but still she couldn't understand what was being said. She clawed at the dirt. Next thing she knew, she was being lifted from under her arms. She was passed up to hands reaching for her from aboveground. Legs were running under her that weren't her own. The back doors of the ambulance were swung open wide. The person whose arms had been holding her now spoke right over her face. Someone next to him covered her mouth and nose with a hollow plastic mask that fogged up right away.

"To help you breathe," she heard.

"Wait," Tessa said. She saw someone jump from the back of the ambulance and reach to close its swung-open doors. "Wait!" She sat up and pulled the oxygen mask off her face, her senses coming back to her. She felt a hand pressing on her chest, trying to lay her back down.

"Just relax," the man said.

"Don't," she said and threw the man's arm away from her. She swung her legs over the side of the gurney. Her feet hit the metal ground beneath her, and she shot up to stand. Her legs felt shaky. She focused on the bright light above her to keep steady. A gust of wind blew in through the ambulance's opened doors. She felt it hit the wet of her jeans from where her water had broke.

"There's a boy trapped under the dirt out there," she said. She moved quickly toward the open doors and took a big step down and out of the ambulance before anyone could stop her. She saw a flurry of people in uniform moving around the place where she had been digging moments before, but she couldn't tell if anyone was in the hole working to get Nathan out.

"Let us help you," the man said.

"*He* needs help!" Tessa yelled.

"Ma'am, you're in labor. We need to get you to the hospital." He walked up slowly and put an arm around her to try and guide her back to the ambulance. Just then, she saw Henry's blue truck come bouncing up over the hill and flying down toward them.

"Henry!" Tessa cried. He hit the brakes, and dust flew up around the truck. She felt the man's arms forcing her to turn around, and she shoved him away hard so that he stumbled and nearly fell back.

"Ma'am," the man said in a stern voice.

"Henry!" Tessa yelled, ignoring the man who was grasping at her wrist. "Henry!" She felt a tug on her arm and turned back to yank her hand away. "Get the fuck off me!"

Henry was over to her and had the man by the collar in three quick strides. "What're you doing?" he shouted into the man's face.

"I'm helping," the man said, pushing away from Henry's grip. "She's in labor, dehydrated, and all scratched up. She's not thinking clearly." Henry turned to Tessa and looked her over. She nodded.

"I'm in labor," she said, "but I'm fine. The baby's not coming yet." The relief of seeing Henry, knowing he would help, it let the sadness and desperation surface. She started to cry.

"Nathan is buried in the dirt over there. I couldn't get to him. He's down there all alone." She felt her legs wanting to buckle and bent to brace her hands on her thighs. Henry went to her, and she took ahold of his forearm and held it tight. She gathered herself and spoke direct and clear. "He needs help. No one's listening. Please,

Henry, save him." Henry looked to where people were scrambling and then to the man standing next to Tessa.

"Take her to the hospital," he said. Tessa started to speak, but he wouldn't let her. "I'll be there soon. Don't worry, I'll get Nate." Henry turned and ran toward the crowd of people. The man stepped forward and draped a blanket over her shoulders.

"I'm sorry, ma'am," he said.

"I'm not leaving until they get him out."

"You need to think of your baby," he said. More tears came then. She couldn't swallow.

"I'm. Not. Leaving," she said through gritted teeth.

"Okay," the man said. "Okay. At least let's get you sitting down. I want to take your vitals. Can we do that while we wait?" She let him walk her to the ambulance, where she sat on the bumper while he put a blood pressure cuff around her arm. A moment later, a short, spiky-haired woman in a blue jumper was stretching the elastic band of the oxygen mask around the back of her head again. Tessa felt the cool air of it on her nose and lips. She felt herself catching her breath. The small woman put a gentle hand on her shoulder and then sat down beside her.

Tears ran down over the plastic mask as Tessa watched shovelful after shovelful of dirt flying out of the hole she'd just been inside. The rescue workers were taking turns, jumping in and out, relieving one another. She didn't see Henry jumping in and out with them and knew he was down there, not taking breaks. He wasn't getting out of that hole until he brought Nathan out with him.

The woman took ahold of Tessa's hand, and they both stared ahead. "They'll get him out now," the woman said in a soft, kind voice.

"He's already gone," Tessa said, flat and certain. She felt another contraction coming on and scooched back into the ambulance enough to lie down on her side. She curled up, hugged her belly, and watched for Nathan's too-late rescue to come.

Four and a half hours later, Tessa was sitting up in a hospital bed with a newborn baby in her arms. The baby had come early, but the doctors said that she was strong and healthy and would be just fine. Henry was sitting in a chair pulled up close to the bed. They were both quiet, both exhausted. Nothing could be said. Every once in a while, Tessa saw Henry reach up and wipe at his cheek.

Their assigned nurse came in for the third time in half an hour to check on them and ask if they had a name to give for the birth certificate. Again, Tessa said that they didn't. This seemed to annoy the nurse. She was probably nearing the end of her shift and needed to tie up loose ends. She let out a sigh as she wrote down numbers from the beeping machine next to Tessa's bed. She clicked the top of the pen and slid the chart back into its cubby by the door.

"Keep thinking on that name, you two. She'll need one," the nurse said with a wink in a fake, cutesy voice. "I'll be back to see what you come up with in just a few." Tessa looked to Henry, who was lost to the moment and staring out the hospital window.

"Tell you what," Tessa said. "We'll let one of you all know when we have a name for her. In the meantime, why don't you leave, shut the door behind you, and give us some goddamn peace?" The nurse clicked her tongue and stood there a moment. Then she brushed the front of her smock off, though there was nothing on it, and cleared her throat.

"Sure thing," she said, then walked out and closed the door behind her. Time passed, and Tessa figured she ought to try and get the baby to nurse. Tessa woke her by gently brushing her cheek with the back of her fingers. The baby blinked her eyes open and stared up at Tessa.

She latched on right away and started feeding without a fuss. She hadn't made any trouble since the moment she was born. The doctor had to work at making her cry when she first come out, and she went straight back to pin-drop quiet the second they handed her to Tessa. It was like she knew she'd come at a bad time and was trying not to cause any more grief.

Henry turned from staring out the window. He took ahold of Tessa's free hand that was resting on the bed beside her, and held it between both of his. He cleared his throat.

"You need anything? Some water?"

"No, thank you," she said.

"How you feeling?" Tessa shrugged, and he nodded.

"Hen?"

"Yeah?"

Slow, heavy tears wet her cheeks then. "I tried."

"I know you did." Tessa leaned into Henry's shoulder, and he pulled her into his chest.

"I couldn't save him."

"It wasn't your fault," he said. Tessa nodded and let her mouth fall open with the sobs that were coming. All the while, the baby stayed quiet, still nursing in her bent arm. She pulled away after a while and wiped her nose with the back of her hand.

"I think you better go see how Angie and the kids are doing. I'm awful worried about them."

"I don't like leaving you here alone," Henry said. Just as he spoke, the door opened again. Tessa was ready to let the nurse have it, but she didn't have to. It was Carly who peeked her head inside.

"It alright for me to come in for a bit?" she asked.

"Of course," Tessa said. Carly walked slowly up to the side of the bed opposite Henry. She put a hand on Tessa's shoulder and leaned in to have a look at the baby.

"Oh, honey," she said, "isn't she just precious? Look at that. She's got Henry's nose." Carly looked up and grinned at Henry, who gave her a warm, tired smile. She started up crying then. "I'm . . ." Her voice wavered. She closed her eyes, and tears black with mascara dripped down onto the pink blanket the baby was wrapped in. She took in a breath and opened her eyes. "I'm so sorry we lost Nathan."

"Thank you, Carly," Henry said.

"If there's anything I can do to help, you just let me know. Anything."

Tessa lifted her chin from looking down at the baby. "Might need some help settling in with this one, and Angie might need some help arranging the funeral," Tessa said. "You think you could spare to stay a few days at our place?"

"Honey, I'd love to," Carly said.

"Carly," Tessa started. She'd thought to ask Carly if she wanted to hold the baby but changed her mind. Even though her arms and back hurt like hell, she wasn't yet ready to give her over for someone else to hold. "Will you stay here with me? Henry's got to go check on Angie and the kids."

"'Course I will."

Tessa turned to Henry. "Will you leave the car seat so Carly can drive us home when it's time?"

"Okay," he said.

"And Hen?"

"Yes?"

"What do you think about naming her Natalie after her uncle Nate?" Tessa said. Henry's eyes welled up. He bit the inside of his cheek and nodded.

"I'd like that," he said.

"I want her middle name to be Jean. That okay with you?" Henry blinked and lifted his eyebrows like a puff of cold air had hit him. Then he made a serious face, like he was giving it a think.

"Natalie Jean's a beautiful name," he said after a moment. Tessa considered the sound of it.

"What about Natalie Angie Jean Jenson?" Tessa said.

"Four names?" Henry said.

"Too many?"

"No," Henry said. "I think it's the right amount." He stood and bent to kiss Tessa on the forehead. Then he leaned down close to the baby and kissed her too. "See you at home," he said.

"See you then," Tessa said. Henry shut the door softly behind him, and Tessa let an exhale drain slowly out over her bottom lip. Then she stared blankly at the slightly crooked painting of a beach hanging on the wall in front of her. She and Carly let the room be quiet for a while like that. Tessa searched the setting sun far out on the choppy ocean's horizon for some kind of meaning or reason. She found neither. Instead, she thought of Nathan's fear of drowning and wondered if that wasn't exactly what it felt like to him when his lungs were filling up with dirt. Instead, she felt the dull ache and repeated shock of the ocean's icy waves lapping up against her chest.

"I'm gonna need help," Tessa said finally.

"Sugar," Carly said. She gently lifted the hospital gown that had slid down off Tessa's shoulder back up into place and touched her palm to Tessa's cheek. "You've got it."

Henry

Henry sat inside his truck out front of Angie's place, telling himself he needed to be strong. Part of him knew that seeing his mama just then might be the thing that finally made him break, and he didn't want that. His mama had been nothing but strong for him and his father and brothers and Tessa and every other person who'd ever come to her in need. It was his turn to be strong for his mama. She had suffered loss and heartache in her life, but nothing, Henry knew, could compare with how she must be feeling now that Nathan had been taken from her in such an awful way. After all the saving she'd done in her fifty-nine years, no one had been able to return the favor and save Nathan for her.

Henry wrung the steering wheel between his hands and ground his teeth to try and stop the tears from coming. It was all too much. How could he balance it in his head? His baby girl was born the same day he'd sunk a shovel into his brother's thigh while trying to dig him up. After getting to Nathan, he'd climbed out, dropped to his knees, and sobbed with Nathan hanging limp in his arms. How could he hold the image of his baby girl looking up at him for the first time and not also think of Nathan's dirt-filled nose and mouth and crusted-open eyes staring up at the clear spring sky above them?

Henry put his head to the steering wheel and let himself bawl and shake until he had nothing left to empty out. He lifted away from the wheel and pushed the truck's cigarette lighter in to heat. Then he grabbed his handkerchief out of the glove compartment.

He blew his nose and wiped at his face and took some deep breaths. The cigarette lighter popped ready. Henry rolled the sleeve of his shirt up to his left bicep. Then he took the lighter's glowing red circle and pressed it into the soft inner flesh of his arm just above his elbow. He held it there for a three count, then lifted it away. The red glow pulled some of his gooey burned flesh away with it. Henry hoped the raw sting of it would keep him both present and distracted enough to stay put together. He rolled his sleeve, still dusty with the dirt that had buried his brother, back down his arm, ran his hand through his hair, and got out of the truck.

Henry didn't knock or ring the bell. He just came on inside through the unlocked front door, not wanting to make Angie get up. "Hello?" he said. The kitchen and dining room were empty. He heard the faint noise of the TV going and found Ruby sitting about a foot away from the screen that was lit up by the brightly colored characters of *Sesame Street*. Preston was asleep on the couch with his arms hugging Winslow to him. Henry pulled the throw blanket off the back of the couch and covered Preston with it. The puppy woke but didn't stir. Henry patted the top of its head and whispered, "Good dog." Then he walked over to Ruby.

"Hey, honey," he said, placing a soft hand on her shoulder.

"Hi, Daddy," Ruby said, not moving her gaze from the screen.

"You okay here?" Henry said. "You need anything?"

"No," Ruby said. Henry took a knee next to her.

"Let's scooch you back a bit."

"Then I can't hear it good. Grandma said to keep it low so Preston could sleep."

Henry looked back at Preston. He was sleeping heavy. "We'll

turn it up a bit. Scooch." Henry turned the volume knob some and patted the carpet with his hand a couple feet behind Ruby.

"Move back here a bit." Ruby crawled to where Henry gestured, hugged her knees into her chest, and resumed watching. "You hungry?" Henry asked. Ruby shook her head. "Alright. Sit tight here with Big Bird and his buddies. Daddy will be back."

Henry knew where he'd find Angie. He let the screen door close softly behind him and heard the familiar groan of the old wooden planks he and his father had laid beneath his feet as he stepped outside. Angie was sitting in her rocking chair with her back to him. Wisps of smoke from the cigarette in her hand floated gracefully off the porch toward the pink horizon and yolk-like glow of the setting sun. The cigarette went out of view as she brought it to her mouth. Then she leaned forward to ash it in the coffee can sitting by her feet. She settled back into the chair, exhaled a cloud of smoke, and said without turning, "Pull up a seat."

Henry took a chair from the wicker table by the door and set it down beside her. "How's Tessa?" Angie said.

"She's alright," Henry said. Angie nodded.

"And the baby?"

"Healthy," Henry said. "And so sweet, Mama."

"Good," Angie said. "That's good." She didn't look at him. She kept smoking and staring out in front of her.

"Carly said she has my nose," Henry said.

"That right?"

"Tessa said so too, but I think her nose is too small to look like anything other than a baby's nose." Angie didn't respond. Henry wasn't sure she was hearing him. "You'll have to tell me what you think when you see her."

"Carly made it down to the hospital, then?" Angie said.

"Yeah, she's with Tessa and the baby now."

"I'm surprised she could pull her lips from the bottle long enough to make the trip."

"Mama," Henry said softly, "she's a good woman."

"I know." Angie let out a sigh. "Don't pay me mind. I'm one to talk, anyhow." Angie gestured with her cigarette hand down at the tumbler by her feet with just a couple cubes left melting inside.

"I don't think anyone would begrudge you a drink today, Mama."

"Could be," Angie said. Henry had never seen his mother like this. Cool and empty and smoking out in the open where the kids could easily come out and see her.

"Is there anything I can do?" Henry said. "To help?"

Angie patted Henry's thigh then. "I'm afraid there's nothing to be done, which is the real ugly of the whole thing." Angie leaned forward to ash and then settled back in again. "Of Nathan being buried alive, I mean." The way she said it, plain and matter-of-fact like that, stung. "Nothing we can do to change that."

Henry didn't know what he could say. She was right. Nathan died the way he did. It was pure ugly, and no one was able to keep him from it. It was an innocent thing to be doing, digging those tunnels. You couldn't blame Nathan or Preston for not seeing the risk. *Tragedy* was the word people kept throwing around, but that word didn't begin to describe what had happened. It didn't come close to capturing the horror and heartbreak of it.

"I saw that they'd left the shovels out, you know," Angie continued. "For a couple days, I saw that. Didn't think nothing of it. Figured it was just the kids playing. Thought maybe they were making ramps for their bikes, like they do. That was part of the trouble, I guess." Angie paused. "Thinking of Nathan as just a kid. Not remembering he had a grown man's strength. A kid would never have been able to dig a hole so deep in just two days. It would have took a couple kids Preston's age at least a week, if not more, and by then some adult would have noticed or the kids'd've given up."

Angie shook her head and sucked her teeth. She blinked, and tears streamed down her face. "I saw him at the hospital. I know." Angie took a shaky breath and let it go. "I know he's dead. I saw him, touched his cheek, held his hand, but I just can't hardly believe it." Angie put her face in her palms, and Henry's guts wilted inside of him.

"I'm so sorry, Mama." He placed a gentle hand between her shoulder blades and kept it there. A breeze kicked up. Leaves blew across the yard in front of them, and Henry noticed the abundance of white streaks in Angie's wiry, rustling hair. He wondered when it was that she'd begun to grow old. Henry had never seen her as anything other than lasting and sturdy. He wondered if she'd crossed some invisible threshold that very day. Maybe it was that he never paid her the attention needed to see something as gradual as aging, or maybe he somehow stupidly believed that she never would.

Angie stayed leaned over and spoke through her hands. "I know you must be hurting awful bad too. He was your brother. You and me raised him together. Buck hardly gave him—or any of you, for that matter—much fatherly attention. And your other brothers, God bless them, have always been more self-interested and solitary, like Buck was." Angie wiped her nose with the back of her cigarette hand, then stretched down and snuffed the cigarette out on the ground before tossing it into the metal coffee can at her feet. She sat up, brushed her lap of ashes, and took sight of

Henry with a seriousness that grabbed at his chest and made him fear the truth of what she was about to say.

"You take after your mama. And I'm afraid it hasn't made your life much easier for it. I'll tell you what, though. Nathan sure loved you, honey. He loved you. He thought you were just—" Angie shook her head and blinked tears. "He wanted to be just like you. Told me all the time. You're a good, good man, Henry. Nathan knew that, and I'm"—Angie pursed her lips a moment and gathered herself enough to continue speaking—"I'm sure proud and grateful for it." Henry hugged his arms across his chest, pressed his thumb into the stinging skin of the cigarette-lighter burn, and clenched his jaw against the pressure swelling in his throat.

Angie used a finger to brush away a stray tear on the side of Henry's face. Then she reached out and held him at his shoulder. "Now's the time for us to be there for the family like we know how to be. That boy of yours hasn't said a word since I picked him up from the hospital's waiting room with his sister. I don't think Ruby understands what's happened, and then there's Tessa and your new little baby girl. They all need every bit of love you have to give. That's how we're going to survive this. We're going to love them so much that it carries us all through." Angie left her hand on his shoulder for a moment more. Then she let it drop to the arm of her chair. "You take a few minutes out here to really wallow, Henry. Feel the full weight and darkness of it. You let yourself feel damn cheated and heartsick. When you're ready, leave all those feelings to scatter in the wind, and come inside the house.

"When you come inside, it ain't about you or all that rightful pain losing your sweet and gentle brother earned you." Angie pressed up to stand, put her hands to her lower back, and pushed her hips forward to stretch. "I'll go fix us coffee." She dropped her arms, turned, and took a couple steps toward the house. She put a hand on Henry's shoulder as she passed. "Before you get up from that chair, you get your mind right, and think of your wife and children. When you come back inside the house, you're strong as steel and going on that way for them."

TEN

1999

Angie

The days between Nathan's death and the funeral were a blur of casserole dishes, phone calls, and check writing. It seemed like anyone who'd ever met him had heard about what happened to Nathan, and of course, anyone who'd ever known Nathan, even just a bit, wanted to be at his funeral to pay their respects. He was that kind of light. The kind that drew a person in and brought a moment of ease and simple grace to anybody within shining distance. He did that for the shy, middle-aged man with a missing canine tooth at the Circle K. That man always worked the register and liked to show Nathan magic tricks behind three inches of bulletproof glass.

Four days after the tunnel collapsed, that man broke down blubbering at the sight of Angie. It was the first time she had braved going into town since they'd lost Nathan. The door hardly had a chance to chime before he was a snotty mess. Angie was there to pick up a carton of cigarettes and a liter of Diet Shasta Cola, the two things she had been able to stomach since Nathan's passing.

All Angie could think about while looking at that man, whose big tears were now winding through his patchy orange beard and cratered cheeks down to his wobbling chin, was the way he had smiled so big the last time she and Nathan had stopped in. That day, he'd forgotten to press his lips together like he normally would to hide the hole in his teeth. He had pulled an unwrapped Twinkie out of his own ear and folded it up in a napkin to pass under the window for Nathan. Nathan cheered and clapped and bit into the Twinkie and the man's lips pulled away from his teeth and stretched way up toward the wrinkles at the corners of his eyes. She saw then that it wasn't just the one canine that was missing. There was empty gumline where two back molars were supposed to be as well.

The day she'd come for cigarettes and cola, the man wouldn't take the ten-dollar bill she slid under the glass. He kept sliding it back and shaking his head. When he mouthed "I'm so sorry" and pushed the bill back for a third time, Angie slipped him a couple of tissues from her purse under the glass instead.

Angie didn't want to have Nathan's funeral in a church. After what happened to Nathan, she wasn't willing to sit there and listen to some man of God try and give a sermon about how the Lord worked in mysterious ways. The memorial service would be grave-side. Old Rick Munson from the Perris Community Center, where Nathan had spent most every Tuesday and Thursday afternoon of his life making arts and crafts, offered to lead it.

Angie would hold the reception at her place. The six picnic tables she'd rented were being delivered that morning. She, Carly, and Henry would have things set up and ready for everyone to come back to before they left for the service. Everyone had either brought or was bringing something to contribute to the gathering at the house after. Angie's refrigerator was packed with all sorts of Jell-O dishes and potato and chicken salads and other containers that she hadn't bothered to open.

Everything was just about all set up and ready by ten, which left Angie some time to freshen up in her room before heading over to the cemetery. She'd told Henry she wanted to drive herself. Everyone had been very supportive since she'd gotten back from the hospital and word had gotten out about what had happened. There was always someone stopping by to check in on her and keep her company. It was kind of them, but what Angie really wanted was to be alone. That's the way she had felt after Buck died too. A person needs privacy and quiet to grieve—she felt she did, at least. No one had given her that when she lost Buck. She was too polite to say anything then. This time, with Nathan, she told people to leave and asked for the space she needed, because she knew she wouldn't be able to keep herself from crumbling if she didn't.

Henry and the team of helpers that had come to set up that morning had all left, and the house was finally empty. Angie stood in front of the bathroom mirror. She smoothed and flattened out the round collar of her simple black dress. Her hands shook as she lifted the pearl brooch that had once belonged to her mother and pinned it into place just above her heart. She tried to practice a brave smile in the mirror, but the muscles in her cheeks didn't respond. Instead, it seemed like the loose skin of her face was being pulled down by some invisible weight, and she thought she could see what the hollowed-out nothing she'd been feeling looked like in her tired, puffy eyes. When she could no longer stand to see herself in the mirror that way, she went and sat on Buck's side of the bed. For years she hadn't touched his side, except to make the bed. She hadn't been thinking when she sat there, but when she realized she had, she didn't get up.

Somehow, sitting there made her feel like Buck was closer to her, like she wasn't having to go through things alone. She imagined him sitting there with her and reached her hand out to touch the soft of the comforter beside her, as if placing a hand on his knee. She shook her bowed head and swallowed. "Buck, honey," she said, "how can this be?" She blinked, and tears dripped from her eyelashes and trailed down the tip of her nose. She felt like her lungs were tied shut with fishing wire and had to open her mouth to breathe. "How on earth can this be?"

She turned her chin to look at the place where her hand was resting. She sniffed and let out a sigh. "Quiet as ever, you," she said with a weak laugh. She saw from the watch on her wrist then that it was a quarter till. "Let's just sit here awhile longer until we feel ready."

Angie pulled up five minutes late. She didn't rush to get out of the truck. She knew they wouldn't start without her. Her cell phone had started up chiming the moment she'd gotten into her truck and went on going like that right up until she had powered the damn thing off. She parked on the far side of the cemetery so that she could have a little more time without everyone being so damn supportive, without everyone needing to be reassured she was okay. She walked around the long way from there.

As she got closer to where all the chairs were set up and all the people were standing, she could see that they were all looking in the other direction, waiting on her to come walking up from that way. She was glad for that. This way, she could arrive without an audience. With any luck, she could find her seat up front next to her three remaining boys before the bulk of the crowd noticed she was there.

A few hundred yards away, Angie felt her feet stop moving. Her legs wouldn't budge. They refused to walk her body over to her boy's funeral. She needed to stand there a minute. She wasn't ready. Angie reached out a hand to sturdy herself against the trunk of the magnolia tree beside her. She was trying to talk herself out of turning back for her truck when she heard someone walking up slowly from behind her. She felt that someone gently thread their fingers between the fingers of her own hanging hand. She turned and saw Tessa lift the back of Angie's hand to her lips. Tessa kissed Angie there and then she let their connected hands drop back to hang in the space between them. They stood there silent, looking out toward the odd mix of people Nathan had brought together. Most of them were dressed in black, but a few wore bright colors. Angie figured they thought Nathan might have liked it better that way, or maybe it was that they were just damn fools who didn't know better.

"I thought you might take the long way here," Tessa said. "We can stand here as long as you'd like." She gave Angie's hand a little squeeze. Angie felt the warmth of Tessa's palm and started to get some feeling back in her legs.

"Thank you," Angie said finally. It was then she noticed that Tessa's other arm was bent and cradling her sleeping newborn. Angie could just see its little bulb-shaped nose, definitely Henry's, and pursed lips. The rest of her was covered in a fuzzy yellow blanket.

"Well, look at that," Angie said. Tessa followed Angie's eyes to the baby in her arms. She flushed and beamed proud. Angie guessed by the reaction and the life she saw in Tessa's eyes that it wasn't going to be like it'd been for Tessa after Ruby come along with this one, and Angie felt a release in her chest that allowed her to take in the first full breath she'd had all week. "I'm sorry I didn't come to see you in the hospital or since you two come home."

"You got nothing to be sorry for," Tessa said.

"No, I should have," Angie said. "That wasn't right. I just . . ."

"I know," Tessa said. The baby started to stir, and Tessa bounced her arm a little. She squeezed Angie's hand again. "I know."

Angie reached her free hand over and tucked a bit of the blanket under the baby's fleshy little chin and smiled. "She's beautiful like her mama," Angie said. "What's her name?"

"Natalie," Tessa said, "after her uncle."

Angie felt her throat tighten. She hadn't let Henry talk to her about the baby. Not even enough to find out its name. She'd cut him off every time he'd tried over the past week. A little part of her, a part she wasn't proud of, felt like she wanted to keep that baby from getting into her heart, the way she knew it would if she saw it. Another part—she was ashamed of this part more than the first—wanted to blame Tessa for what had happened to Nathan, and not going to see her or the baby had been a kind of nasty punishment. Angie gave a little nod. "She got a middle name?"

"Angie Jean," Tessa said. She waited a moment before she continued. "For both of my mothers."

Angie clucked her tongue and shook her head. "There's parts of you I'll never understand."

"You've always seen who I was best, though, better than anyone. You know that."

Angie let out an easy breath. "I guess I do," she said. She put her loose hand on her hip and turned her head away from Tessa to look out over the row of graves by her side. "I found you and Henry a place," Angie said. She felt Tessa's eyes on her then but kept looking over that row, knowing that if she looked Tessa's way just then, she wouldn't be able to get the rest of it out. "Not too far away but far enough that you'll feel like you have your own space." Angie felt her heart not wanting to beat saying those words.

"Angie," Tessa started, but Angie forced herself to continue.

"I think it's everything you two were looking for, from what Henry told me. There's a yard and three bedrooms. They're small rooms, about the same size each, but having a wall between you makes all the difference. It's a home."

"Angie," Tessa said again, softly.

"And I found you a car too," she continued. "It's a little nothing. All beat up on the outside, but I had the mechanic look it over twice, and he swore to me it was safe and had lots of miles left in it before I went ahead and bought it off Betty's nephew." Angie looked down at her feet and sniffed. Then she looked back up again. "That's where I was gone to those days I had you watching Nathan. I was getting all that sorted." She heard Tessa try and swallow a sob.

"Angie, I need you to know how sorry I am for what happened to Nathan. I should have checked on what those boys were up to sooner." Tessa shook her head and pressed her lips together tight until she could speak. "I'll live with that mistake for the rest of my life."

"It wasn't your fault." Angie reached in her purse for a cigarette and put it in her mouth. She left the lighter where it was, remembering the newborn sleeping in Tessa's arms. She took the cigarette from her lips and rolled it between her fingers. "I don't want you thinking like that. I knew they were up to something and didn't check what it was neither. It was a terrible accident. No one to blame. We have to leave it at that. There's no going on if we let ourselves think any different."

Angie saw Tessa lift her shoulder and bow her cheek to wipe at the tears there. "I don't know if now is the time for Henry and me to be moving. Maybe we ought to wait some."

"It's past time for you and Henry to have your own place. We both know that. I just wasn't ready to see you go, is all." Angie took her hand from her hip and used it to shade her eyes while she studied the light above them. First there was the clean light coming through between the thick branches and broad leaves, and then there was the secondary light that glowed off the leaves' polished surface. "But you're ready," Angie continued. "I know it. And it's time I figure out who I am when I'm not busy trying to manage the lives of the people I love best." Angie squinted and let the different lights blur together for a moment, then dropped her chin level again. She slipped the cigarette back into her pocket for later. "Besides, I sold a piece of my property, including the land your trailer is sitting on, to buy you the new place. You've got till the end of next month to be moved."

"Angie," Tessa breathed.

"You don't have to say anything. You deserve it, and I trust you. I trust that you're wise enough to see the good things you've got, even when you get that antsy feeling you sometimes get. I hope giving you this space helps with that. I hope it eases whatever it is in you that gets you thinking you need to run away or be something different." Angie looked at Tessa then. She wanted so badly for the house and the car to be enough for Tessa to stay and be happy. She tucked a loose strand of Tessa's hair behind her ear. "You've come a long way, Jacky Rabbit. It's been a privilege watching you grow into the woman you are today."

"I wouldn't have made it without you," Tessa said.

"Sure you would have, honey. You'd have made it. I'm glad it was my field you decided to come running through, though. Your coming along made my life a whole world sweeter. You're a stubborn little creature, and you make me crazy sometimes trying to figure you out, but I love you through and through. Nothing is ever changing that." Tessa dipped her cheek to her shoulder again. Her lip was turned out, and her forehead was all crinkled up when she lifted her head. Tessa had made the same face all those years ago, when she and Angie were alone together in the living room the night Tessa had come running for help all bloodied and busted up. Angie didn't like to think about that night.

"You wanna hold her?" Tessa asked after she had cleared her throat and pulled herself together some. She stepped toward Angie to bring the baby closer to her.

"I think I better. You're gonna need both hands to clean up your face." Tessa dropped her chin and laughed. Angie kissed the top of Tessa's head and put her arm under Natalie for Tessa to pass her over.

"Ohhh, it's just like I said, isn't it? This is a big baby." Angie bounced the baby in her arms a couple times to feel the full weight of her. "And she come early too. Can you imagine if she had been in there another month?!"

Tessa blew her nose and shoved the tissue back inside her purse. "I don't want to imagine that, thank you very much. It was hard enough getting her out as it was. Things will never be the same down there."

Angie snorted.

"Lord, I mean it, Ang. You should've seen the hell this one put me through getting her out."

"She's an angel now, though, huh?"

"She is. Easiest baby so far since the delivery."

"Good," Angie said and smiled down at her new grandchild. "We're all about ready for some ease, aren't we?" Tessa finished wiping up her face and put her arm around Angie's waist.

"Should we go say goodbye to our Nate?" Tessa said. Angie nodded and sucked in her cheek.

"I think that's a goodbye I'll be working on for the rest of my life," she said, "but let's go anyhow." Angie closed her eyes then, just long enough to imagine Nathan and Buck laughing and drinking lemonade together someplace sunny and nice. "Alright," she said, blinking her teary eyes open. "It ain't going to get any easier by waiting."

They started walking, and Angie felt the threads that held her heart in place snapping as it tried to pull itself up and out to where she imagined Nathan and Buck might be. She thought to let it happen. Then she felt Tessa's arm around her waist, and she remembered Henry and Preston and Ruby, and she firmly shook the thought away. Angie kept her legs walking and let the weight of the baby in her arms ground her heart inside her chest, where, for at least a little while longer, it was meant to be.

EPILOGUE

1999

Tessa

Tessa was up before the sun. She sat quiet at the kitchen table with a cup of coffee and watched the first glow of light bloom from the top of the mountain range outside the east-facing kitchen window. That window and the Box Springs Mountains beyond it were a couple of the things she liked best about their place. She had spent almost a whole hour sitting there thinking and watching out that window before she heard the baby stirring back in her and Henry's bedroom. She was just getting ready to go check on her when Henry came walking in with Alie lying belly down on his forearm, her legs and arms dangling and her chubby cheek pressed against the crease of his elbow.

Ruby had shortened her baby sister's name. *Natalie* had been too much of a hassle to get out in her heat-of-the-moment complaints: "Alie's messing up my drawing! Alie scratched me! How come Alie gets to sleep with you and Daddy?" After a while, they all started calling her Alie without really noticing. The shortened version suited her better anyway.

"Morning." Tessa smiled and stood to take Alie from Henry's arm. "Coffee's ready." Tessa lifted Alie up onto her hip, and Henry kissed her cheek.

"How many times she wake you last night?" Henry asked.

"Three. I bet she'll be sleeping through the night pretty soon, though."

"I heard just the once." Henry poured himself a cup of coffee.

"I know. You were sawing logs throughout the other two."

Henry laughed. Tessa smiled and pushed him aside so she could turn the oven on to warm up some cinnamon rolls.

"I'm going to wake the kids," she said. "Enjoy your minute of peace."

Tessa went to Preston's room first. He was curled up around Winslow and hugging the dog to his chest. He and Winslow had been inseparable since they'd lost Nathan. Tessa worried how he'd manage with school starting back up again in just a couple weeks. He'd have to leave Winslow at home then. She figured they'd just have to cross that bridge when they got to it.

Tessa sat on his bed and rested her free hand on his shoulder. "Morning, baby," she said. Preston blinked his eyes open.

"Morning," he said. He lifted his arm to reach for Alie's hand, and Alie took ahold of his finger and tried to bring it to her mouth. Preston laughed and pulled his finger away, so Alie grabbed a fistful of Winslow's fur instead. Winslow lifted his head to see Alie tugging on him. Then he plopped his head back down, exhaled through his nose, and tried to continue sleeping.

"Take Winslow out, then get dressed. There's cinnamon rolls

for breakfast." Tessa stood and watched to make sure Preston had sat up and started moving before she left.

Tessa went across the hall and pushed the door to Ruby's little pink room open. Ruby had insisted on the Pepto Bismol–pink paint, and Angie had found her sheets and a blanket to match. Patty the rabbit was in her cage in the corner of the room, drinking water out of a hanging spout. Her cage was stinking up the room and overdue for a clean. Ruby rolled over to face Tessa.

"I'm awake," she said.

"I see that."

"I heard you wake Preston up, and I heard you and Daddy in the kitchen before that."

"How come you didn't come say hi?" Tessa said.

"Because I wanted to lay here some more."

"Well, are you ready to say hi now?"

Ruby nodded and sat up. "Did Daddy leave yet?"

"Not yet, but pretty quick here, I think." Tessa lifted Alie's hand and bobbed it up and down. "Good morning, Ruby."

"Morning, Alie," Ruby said flatly.

Tessa brushed the hair hanging in Ruby's face back over her shoulder. "Your hair is getting so long." Tessa held Ruby's cheek in her hand. "And you're getting so big." Ruby reached both arms up and stretched, leaning away from Tessa's hand.

"I know," Ruby said. She slid off the bed and went to crouch down by Patty's cage.

"You want me to pick out something for you to wear, or are you doing that today?"

"I'm picking. Long or short?"

"I think long pants and a short-sleeved shirt will be good for today."

"Okay," Ruby said.

"Cinnamon rolls in the kitchen after you're dressed. If you get dressed quick enough, you'll catch your daddy before he leaves."

They were all in the kitchen together a few minutes later. Henry was about ready to head out the door. Tessa handed him his thermos and lunch, and he shoved the last of his cinnamon roll into his cheek. Ruby popped up to give him a hug. Preston smiled, then put his fingers to his forehead and saluted in Henry's direction.

"Bye, Dad," he said.

"Will you pick up some sliced bread and milk on the way home?" Tessa asked.

"Sure," Henry said.

"Okay," Tessa said. Her heart was beating fast. She wanted the goodbye to last a little longer, but Henry was running late and already moving toward the door. She followed him and caught his hand. "Have a good day," she said. She pressed up onto her toes to give him a kiss. He leaned down to meet her lips and gave Alie a kiss too.

"Dinner just us two Friday," he said. "Don't forget."

"Sure won't," Tessa said, and then out the door he left.

Tessa went back to the kids in the kitchen. She put the rest of her cinnamon roll on a napkin to take with her to the bedroom. "You two wash your hands and brush your teeth after you finish," Tessa said. "Then you can watch cartoons for a few minutes while Mama and Alie get ready."

"Okay, Mama," Preston said.

Ruby took a drink of her milk and set it down. "Ahhh," she said.

Tessa handed Alie a little cotton butterfly with crinkly-sounding wings to play with while she buckled her into her small vibrating lounge chair and set it next to the shower so she could keep an eye on her. Every time Tessa pulled the curtain back to check on her, Alie was just sitting there with a wing in her mouth, kicking her legs around some while looking up at the bathroom light and waving her hands through the steam from the shower.

Tessa moved her chair to the bedroom while she got dressed. "What's Mama gonna wear today, hmm?" Tessa pulled her underwear, bra, a pair of jeans, and a T-shirt from her dresser drawers and threw them on the bed. Then she put some lotion on her arms and legs. She was standing near the closet rubbing her hands together when she thought to reach up and feel around for something on the shelf above her hanging dresses. She brushed her hand around until she felt the strap and pulled down her mama's old purse. She paused a moment with a hand resting on the dry brown leather. Then Tessa tossed it onto the bed too.

"And what about you, Miss Alie? What should you wear today?" Alie lit up and kicked her legs and arms when Tessa smiled at her. She always got excited like that when Tessa gave her even the littlest bit of attention. She'd squirm about that way at least a hundred times a day, as if it were the first time she was seeing Tessa in over a week. Tessa pulled out a little onesie Angie had bought that was patterned with ponies and pigtail-wearing cowgirls. She laid Alie down on the bed and buttoned her into that onesie. Then she put a pair of blue stretch pants on her over that. She pulled the pants up around her little round belly, kissed Alie's neck, and shook her hair in her face so that Alie let out a little gleeful giggle. When Tessa pulled away, her eyes were wet with tears. She stood there a minute looking at her baby's sweet face. Then she buckled her back into her vibrating chair.

Tessa swept her mother's jewelry box off the top of her dresser, wrapped it in a cotton T-shirt, and shoved it into the purse. She grabbed her wallet and keys and put them in too. Then she went to the nightstand on Henry's side of the bed. She pulled the drawer open and pushed Henry's things out of the way so she could get her fingernails into the crack at the inside edge to try and pry up the fake bottom Henry had installed. She tried that for a minute before she saw the butter knife among the things she'd swept aside. She used it to wedge the bottom up. Tessa lifted a metal box out from the secret compartment, opened the lid, and pulled out Henry's handgun along with a box of bullets. Tessa loaded the gun and made sure the safety was on. Then she carefully wrapped it in another shirt and put it into the purse as well.

She dressed and ran her fingers through her hair. Then she rested her hands on her hips and took a moment to look herself over in the mirror hanging on the bathroom door. She turned away and pulled her hair up into a tight bun. She grabbed a sweater and swung the purse over her shoulder. Then she unbuckled Alie, picked her up, and flipped the light switch off on her way out.

"Ready, Freddies?" Tessa said as she walked up to stand behind her two little towheads sitting in front of the TV screen. Preston popped to his feet.

"Ready, Freddy," he said.

Ruby crawled to the TV set and clicked it off, then stood up. "Ready."

It was about a fifteen-minute drive to Angie's from their new place. Ruby and Preston played I Spy the whole way. It was Ruby's turn, and she was changing what it was she was spying every time Preston got close to guessing it. Preston was starting to lose his patience and a fight was about to break out when Tessa pulled up to Angie's driveway.

"We're here," Tessa said, bright and cheerful in hopes of erasing the growing hostility in the back seat. Tessa put the car in park. Preston opened the door, and Winslow jumped from his lap to chase after Willie, who went zooming off the porch. Preston and Ruby came running out of the car next. Tessa went around to the other side of the back seat, where Alie was patiently waiting for her. She unbuckled the car seat and lifted Alie out and up onto her hip. Tessa shaded her eyes to look in the direction of the house and saw Carly leaning against the doorframe, giving her a pretty smile.

"Boy, isn't that a nice car you got there?" Carly said. "And you wearing those sunglasses like that with that tiny waist of yours? Shit, you look like a movie star that just drove out from Hollywood." Tessa lifted her sunglasses to the top of her head and rolled her eyes.

"Honey, I think movie stars got better cars, more style, and less kids than this." Tessa turned to see the dogs and kids still chasing themselves around in the yard and shut the car door. "You got coffee ready in there?"

"Sure do, sugar. Come on in." Tessa walked up the porch steps and brushed a gentle hand over Carly's little bit of belly on her way inside.

Carly was just three months pregnant. It turned out to be that Luke had been shooting blanks all those years they were together. He and Carly had an awful ugly breakup four months back, when Carly found out Luke had been seeing some barely legal waitress out in Temecula near his construction site. The cops had to be there to keep things civil when Carly packed up Willie and her belongings to bring over to Angie's.

Carly went out one night with her old cheerleader friends a couple weeks after moving into Angie's and got knocked up by some passing-through-town fella she met at the bar. She didn't even get the guy's last name. Tessa came in on her puking her guts out one morning about four weeks after that night. Carly looked up from the toilet bowl, grinning at her with a twinkle in her eye.

Carly didn't mind not knowing how to contact the father. From what she'd said she remembered of him, he wasn't the sharpest tool in the shed and didn't strike her as the fatherly type anyhow. "I think I'd be better off raising this one with you all instead," she'd said.

"Angie's out doing her shopping for the week," Carly said as she pulled a couple of mugs down from the cupboard. She went to the coffeepot to fill Tessa's and put some hot water in hers for tea.

"I knew it was today she was going but thought I'd catch her before she left," Tessa said.

"You'll see her when you come to pick the kids up."

"Yeah," Tessa said. "I'll see her then. Anyway, how you been feeling? Still queasy?"

"Hardly anymore," Carly said. "Just a bit when I first wake up. It's gone in time for breakfast."

"You getting plenty of rest?"

"Sure am. Angie sees to that. She don't hardly let me lift a finger around here."

"That's the way it should be. Trust me, you'll spend plenty of time hungry and tired after that little babe comes along." Tessa set her mug down on the counter. "You don't mind keeping an eye on the kids until Angie gets home, do you?"

"'Course not," Carly said. "What are you doing with your day off?"

"Well, I haven't quite decided yet. Might hit the library and coffee shop. Have some clothes in the car for running if I get to feeling like it." Carly reached over and patted Tessa's thigh.

"Sounds like a good day to me, except for the running part." She smiled. "Now how about you hand that little cutie over to me."

"You want to spend the day with your Auntie Carly?" Tessa said. She bounced Alie up and down a couple times to get her smiling and bubbling at the mouth. Then she passed her over to sit in Carly's lap. "Is it next week we have an appointment with Dr. Albertine?" Tessa said.

"Uh-huh," Carly said.

"Angie coming?"

"She is," Carly said.

"Good," Tessa said. She stood and walked her cup to the sink. "I think I'm gonna get going. I left the diaper bag in the living room, and I'm putting six bottles of breast milk in the fridge." Tessa unzipped the little nylon cooler bag on her shoulder and placed the bottles on the top shelf.

"That's a lot of bottles for just the day," Carly said.

"Well, I had them ready in the fridge at my place and grabbed what was there. Can't hurt to bring them back home later," Tessa said.

Tessa and Carly walked back outside to the porch. "Have a real nice time, whatever you end up doing."

"Thanks," Tessa said. "I will." She kissed Carly on the cheek, then leaned down to give Alie a kiss goodbye too. "Mama loves you, little girl," Tessa said and felt the words gumming up her throat. She stood up and slipped on her sunglasses. "Ruby, Preston," she called, "come give Mama a hug." Ruby and Preston came stomping up the steps panting, with the dogs jumping at their legs. "Come here."

Tessa got on her knees and hugged them both to her. She squeezed them tight and kissed the sides of their heads.

"You're hugging too much, Mama," Ruby said. Tessa let them go.

"Alright," Tessa said. "Go play." She stood and watched them run off. "Stay inside this yard, you hear? And listen to your aunt Carly and Grandma."

"Yes, Mama," Preston said and ran off dragging an old, sun-beaten garden hose behind him.

"Don't whip that around and hit no one. If you're going to carry it around like that, you make sure you keep it on the ground."

"Okay," Preston yelled.

"Inside the yard only." Tessa stood there watching the dogs and kids running in circles with worry in her gut.

"I'll keep a close eye on them," Carly said. "Me and Ang don't let them out of our sight when you drop them here."

"I know," Tessa said.

Tessa pulled off Highway 74 at the Circle K to buy a soda and Ding Dong to have on the road. She got back into her car after a few words with the kind, bashful man that worked the register there. She tossed the Ding Dong onto the seat beside her and put the soda in the cup holder for later. Tessa popped open the glove compartment and pulled out a map and a big white envelope. There was a sticker, a shiny little green hummingbird, keeping the envelope shut. There wasn't a return address, but it was postmarked from Eugene, Oregon. She sighed and let the map and envelope fall to her lap to rest a second while she tried to gather herself enough to open it. The sticker came off easy. It had been unstuck and re-stuck a dozen times since she'd found the letter in her mailbox. The first page was a handwritten letter on lined paper.

Dear Tessa,

I can't tell you how sorry I am for your loss. I can't imagine the suffering you and your family must be going through. I feel honored to have had the chance to have met such a kindhearted and special individual as Nathan was, and I am grateful to you for giving me that opportunity. I would have liked to have shown my support and paid my respects at Nathan's funeral in person, but thought maybe it was best for you and your family if I didn't.

I had my cousin look into those three names, like you asked after. Tessa, I don't know what it is you plan on doing with the information. I hope just knowing it will be enough. I'd ask you to let me help you in some way, but I don't figure you'd do that, and I don't figure my helping would give you what it might be you need to finally find peace anyhow.

I used to have this reoccurring dream for years after I left Perris. I would be lying on my belly in the weeds, watching you outrun a lightning storm. The lightning was so close and so bright, you'd disappear in the blinding flash every time it struck, and I'd lose my breath waiting to regain my sight to see if you'd been hit. I wanted to save you. But somehow I knew you running for your life that way was making you feel something better than any saving anyone could ever do for you.

I found this picture of us in my old dresser drawer not too long ago. I slipped it in with this letter because it made me smile and laugh and gave me a warm feeling in my heart. I hope it does the same for you. I like to think about us back then sometimes. Even after all the hurt that came with knowing you, and even after all this living I've done since, I still think meeting you was one of the best things that ever happened to me.

I owe you an apology for leaving all those years ago without saying goodbye or telling you where I was going.

I know that hurt. I guess I didn't want to say goodbye. I had to pretend it wasn't happening instead. I had lost Robby just a couple years before, and I just couldn't wrap my head around losing another person who meant so much to me. I didn't think I could survive that kind of sadness again. Of course, not saying goodbye didn't work. It didn't keep me from the heartbreak of losing you. I think that heartbreak and the one I have for Robby will be with me for the rest of my life.

I wish the very best for you, Tessa. Always will.

Mel

Tessa wiped at her cheeks and turned to the next page.

Wayne Crawford
  Deceased. Died June 3, 1994, at the age of sixty-two.
  Cause of death unspecified. Location: Clark County, NV.

Reggie Crawford
  Current profession: Car salesman in Sloan, NV.
  Current address:
  675 East Willow Street
  Sloan, NV 89054

Connor Jenkins
  Deceased. Died September 19, 1997, at the age of
  twenty-seven. Cause of death: Drug overdose.
  Location: Riverside, CA.

Tessa set the page on the seat beside her and took the picture in her hands. She and Mel were sitting on top of a big boulder they'd scrabbled up onto. Tessa remembered the day clearly. She'd lost her footing and scraped her elbow pretty bad at one point climbing that thing. She probably would have broke something if she'd fallen the whole way down, but Mel had caught her by the shirt just in time. Mel had taken the picture with a disposable camera by stretching her arm out in front of them. Because of that, her arm took up a third of the photo. The other two-thirds were made up of blue sky and their squinting, happy faces pressed in together cheek to cheek.

It was a three-hour drive to Sloan, Nevada. Tessa made just one stop on the side of the road to stretch her legs about thirty minutes out from Reggie's address. She pulled up to the curb in front of the house around eleven thirty. All the houses squeezed in together on that street had the same rectangles of grass bordering the same cement walkways leading to the same doors. Each one was painted the same burnt orange to match their terra-cotta roof tiles. Tessa grabbed her purse from the passenger seat. She stood and looked the street and houses over again before she swung the car door shut.

Tessa rang the doorbell twice and stood feeling lightheaded with her heart banging against her breastbone. Between the heat and her nerves, she was sweating through her shirt. She let her arms hang at her sides and hoped it wouldn't show. She couldn't do nothing about the trickle of sweat she felt inching down her back. Tessa took a breath, held it, and pressed the purse between her palm and thigh so she could feel the hard shape of the gun inside of it. That pressing and the weight of the purse on her shoulder settled her some.

A very tan blond woman opened the door, and Tessa let her breath out. The woman was pretty enough in that knockoff, California-bleached-blonde-living-in-Nevada kind of way. She was a couple inches taller and a couple sizes smaller than Tessa. Tessa guessed they were about the same age.

"Can I help you?" the woman said, kind and cheery-like.

"Hope so," Tessa said.

"Alrighty," the woman said. She waited a moment with an expectant stare. When Tessa didn't say anything, she tried again. "You have something you want to sell me?" Tessa swallowed.

"Is Reggie here?" she said. The woman stood a little taller and lost some of her smile.

"No," the woman said. "I'm his wife. Is there something I can do for you?"

Tessa wiped at the sweat on the back of her neck. "Hell," she whispered.

"Pardon?" the woman said.

"I'm an old friend of his from California. My name is Tessa. You ever heard of me?"

"Reggie doesn't keep in touch with the people he knew back then." The woman crossed her arms in front of her and pushed her hip out to the side.

"I'm sorry to bother. I was just passing through and was hoping to catch him, is all."

"How'd you get this address?"

"Like I said, I knew I was going to be passing through and looked him up."

"He won't be home for hours," the woman said. Tessa nodded.

"Well, could I get his work address?"

"I don't think that's a good idea. He doesn't like to be bothered there."

"Okay." Tessa kept standing there, not knowing what else to

do. The woman shifted on her feet and tapped her white-tipped fingernails on the door.

"Would you like to come in for a bit? It doesn't feel very Christian of me to keep you standing in the heat like this."

"Okay," Tessa said again. The woman opened the door wider.

"It's nice and cool in here," the woman said over her shoulder. Her heels tapped against the shiny white-tiled floor and echoed in the space of the tall-ceilinged entryway as she went. Tessa followed her down a hallway to the living room.

"Have a seat, if you'd like." The woman patted the back of the couch with her hand, which made the little charms on her gold bracelets jingle against each other. "Can I get you some water?"

"Sure," Tessa said. "Thanks." The woman left her sitting there on the hard white couch that didn't seem to be built for sitting on. There was a glass case over in one corner of the room with little porcelain figurines on each shelf, and an old, antique-looking Bible sat atop the coffee table in front of her. Tessa's eyes stopped scanning the room when they hit the family photo sitting in front of the lamp on the end table beside her. Sure enough, Reggie was standing there in a cheap car-salesman suit next to the blond woman and two little girls. He was as bony as he'd been when she'd known him, but he looked about fifty years older. He had these perfect extra-white teeth that seemed strange and phony next to his leathery, elastic-shot skin.

"Here you are," the woman said. She set a plastic coaster down on the coffee table in front of Tessa and then set the glass on top of it.

"My name is Kristen," she said. "I don't think I introduced myself earlier."

"Nice to meet you," Tessa said. The woman fidgeted where she stood a moment. Then she pulled a wooden chair over from the corner of the room to sit down across from Tessa.

"Did you have something specific you were wanting to talk with Reggie about? Maybe I can help?"

"I just wanted to stop in and see how he was living these days, is all."

"Well, I can just about guarantee you he's living much better than when you knew him in California. He fought off those demons that got him mixed up in drugs and let Jesus save him a couple of years before we met. Thank the Lord." Kristen closed her eyes for a moment, as if she were in prayer, then popped them open and continued talking, her words sped up like it was lighting her up to be telling his story.

"From what Reggie said, there was mainly the one big, old demon that sent him down the path of the wicked. His good-for-nothing father. He was just awful to Reggie growing up, you know. I mean, you probably do know. You said you knew him back then." Kristen didn't wait for Tessa to respond. "Some of the things Reggie has told me . . ." Kristen shook her head. "The suffering Reggie went through by that wicked man's hands—awful, awful, awful. He's the reason Reggie got into drugs in the first place. He didn't even want to try the stuff—he knew better—but that bad old man made him. Hooked on drugs by your own father, can you imagine?!" Kristen was nearly floating off the chair with the lift telling Reggie's story was giving her. Her eyes were all big and electrified in pure rapture. "And I'm sure you know about the incident that sent them both running out here for a fresh start." Tessa got the chills. The parts of her shirt still wet from her sweat felt ice-cold.

"You know, Reggie has had to live his life with an ileostomy bag since his father went crazy on him like that. Having to drag that bag around with him brings him so much shame." The woman made a frown and put a hand to her chest. "Oh, Reggie." She closed her eyes again, and then after a second, they sprang back open. "You know, even after his father stabbed him like that, he wouldn't turn him into the police. He told the hospital it was an accident. Reggie even pays for the old folks' home his father, that evil man, is living in now."

Tessa's stomach and throat tightened. She could hardly sit through the bullshit story that woman was telling and was just about ready to set her straight, but hearing that Wayne was still around sent a shock through her that made her brain turn to white noise and static. The blondie sitting across from her didn't seem to notice none. She kept blabbing on. "Reggie says that he is just following the good book and honoring his earthly father by paying for that place." She shook her head and threw her hands up like it was too much to know a man that good. "That's just the kind of man Reggie is," she said.

Tessa nodded a little to try and shake the stun off. She couldn't believe Wayne was alive or that she was sitting in Reggie's perfect, cookie-cutter house listening to his adoring wife tell a horseshit hero story about him. Tessa reached for the glass of water, took a sip, then set it back down. She cleared her throat and turned to the picture beside her again.

"These your girls?" she said.

"Yes, that's Lilly, and the younger one is Lisa," Kristen said, pointing.

"They're beautiful."

"Thank you. They're my angels, perfect in every way. You have kids?"

"I do. Two girls and a boy." Tessa leaned forward. "My youngest girl is turning six months old a week from today. My other daughter will be five this year. They're why I come here today." Tessa settled back into the hard couch and moved her purse to rest heavy in her lap. "You see, I've had this uneasy sort of sick feeling that won't quit. I haven't had a decent night's sleep in all my life, it seems like, but especially since the day I found out I was bringing a baby girl into the same world your Reggie and his father, Wayne, lived in. That's Reggie's father's name, by the way—Wayne. You know that?"

"Well, yes," Kristen said, looking a little agitated and deflated now that she wasn't high on telling Reggie's story or gloating over her angels anymore. "I just don't like saying his name in this house, is all."

"Wayne Lee Crawford," Tessa said. "That's his full name."

"What is it I can do for you?" Kristen said.

"You see, Kristen, that's the problem. I don't think there's anything you or anybody else can do to make things right. Believe me, others have tried." Tessa let out her breath and shook her head. "And where does that leave me, huh? Leaves me driving all the way here and still not sure what to do. You see, I'm not sure I can manage knowing Reggie is here living some kind of phony-ass suburban family life. I just don't know if I can live with that." Tessa leaned forward and rested her elbows on her knees, with the purse pressing into her stomach. Kristen looked like she was about to speak, but Tessa continued. "But I've got my three babies and a good husband at home. And doing anything I can think to do about Reggie—well, that would rob me of my life with them." Tessa folded her hands together and dropped her head a moment, then lifted it to look Kristen right in the eyes. "Your girls are beautiful. Really," she said. "They look just like you. I can hardly see a speck of Reggie in them." Tessa shook her head and clicked her tongue. "I'd be extra careful having those beautiful little girls around a guy like Reggie."

"I think you should leave," the woman said, but she didn't move, like maybe she was wanting to hear the rest of what Tessa had to say.

"And I think it's best you keep your distance from Wayne, like you've been doing. He had a thing for little girls too." Tessa started to stand. "You should know I filed a report with Reggie's name attached to it not too long ago. It don't match up with the good-man story you've been telling me. It tells the truth about how Reggie was in California and how he got that hole in his gut. The statute of limitations has run out on bringing him in on sexual assault charges against a minor, but it was pretty clear the sheriff of Perris, California, would be willing to make life unpleasant for him if he ever came back.

"You do what you will with the information I've shared with you today. If I were you, I'd divorce him, take all the money you can, and get you and your girls as far away from him as possible. That's up to you, though." Tessa was standing with her hands on her hips in front of the woman. "If it's not too much trouble, I'd like you to deliver a message for me." The woman looked up at her.

"What?" she said. The word came out quiet on her shaky lips.

"Tell Reggie that I've got eyes on him now and for the rest of his miserable life and that if he ever so much as steps a toe back into California, he won't have to wait for the authorities to catch up with him. I'll put another hole in his gut, and this time I'll stick around after I do so I can watch him take his last breath." Tessa lifted her purse strap higher up on her shoulder and put a hand under the woman's chin. "I'm sorry to have upset you, Kristen. You seem like a real nice woman. I just need one more thing from you. Then I'll be on my way, and I can promise you won't be seeing me again." Tessa took her hand from Kristen's chin and stood there waiting for a reply.

After a moment of blank staring, Kristen blinked, and tears spilled down her cheeks. "What do you want?" she said.

"I need you to write down the name and address of that old folks' home you said Reggie put his father in."

Tessa pulled into the Sloan Senior Care parking lot about ten minutes later. The place was just about seven miles away from Reggie's house. It was a long, single-story, faded beige building lined with mirrored windows. The harsh glare off those windows and the double doors she was walking up to made her pinch her eyes shut. She was hit by something different when she stepped inside. The air was thick with the smell of wet toilet paper, diarrhea, and beef stew. She tried breathing through her mouth, but that wasn't no good either. She could taste it then.

For a moment, she thought she might have to retch right there on the speckled brown carpet at her feet, but the sudden feeling that she was being watched distracted her enough to keep her from spewing. Tessa turned to see a small woman in a wheelchair staring at her through the plastic leaves of the little fake tree the woman was parked next to. She was missing one leg from the knee down. That pant leg flapped empty next to her other leg, and the rest of the skeletal woman's clothes hung off her bones like curtains off a rod. She couldn't have weighed more than seventy-five pounds soaking wet. Her stare cut into Tessa and fixed her in place. Then the woman's top lip started to curl back from her teeth like a growling dog. Tessa turned away. She stood up tall, tightened her stomach, and made her way toward the reception desk in front of her.

"First-time visitor?" the woman behind the counter asked.

"Yes," Tessa said.

"Sign in here." The woman at reception handed her a clipboard. "Who are you visiting today?"

Tessa cleared her throat. "His name is Wayne," she said. "Wayne Crawford."

"Alright. Put his name down here next to yours. And what's your relation?"

"He was a friend of my mother's."

"Okay, we'll just put *family member*." The woman winked. "That will make it easier." Tessa wrote "family member" next to the name she'd scribbled down, and the woman took the clipboard back from her. She moved some paper around and opened and closed a drawer or two. Then she came back over to where she'd left Tessa standing.

"Here you are, Sarah," she said and slipped Tessa a name tag. "Wayne is in room one-forty-five. He'll be in the first bed before the curtain, just as you walk inside. You're going to go straight down this hallway here. It's about halfway down on the left."

"Thank you," Tessa said. She peeled the sticker off and pressed it to her shirt just below her collarbone.

"Sarah?" the woman said.

"Yes?" Tessa said.

"I don't know how much you've kept in contact or know," the woman stammered. "It's just . . . Wayne isn't all there. He's not much there at all, really. I just wanted to let you know, in case you were expecting something different."

"Thank you," Tessa said. "This way, then?" Tessa pointed. "Right down there."

Tessa read the numbers by the doors as she passed them: one-forty-two, one-forty-three, one-forty-four. She paused just before she got to his door and thought about turning back, but she figured she'd better toughen up and find her spine right then, because it had been a long road getting there, and she was sure she wouldn't ever make the trip again.

Tessa lifted her mama's purse higher on her shoulder, held the strap tight between both hands, and walked right in. Sure enough, Wayne was in the first bed, like the woman had said. Tessa recognized him right away, but he was a sloppy, old, withered version of the man Tessa once knew. She quietly closed the door behind her.

Wayne was sitting up in a kind of slumped-over way. He was propped up by his lifted bed and the pillows shoved behind him, with his chin slightly bowed and his eyes closed. He was breathing all phlegmy and raspy sounding through his open mouth. Tessa could see the outline of his saggy chest through the thin, yellowing white cotton shirt he was wearing. It was caught and tucked up under the flesh of one of his breasts. He looked like a drooping old mountain, a mudslide, Tessa thought. He was nothing like the tough, solid, and sturdy man she'd known.

She wasn't sure what to do with herself then. She hadn't expected to find the Wayne from her memories, but she also hadn't expected to find this old lump of dough sleeping in front of her. What was she supposed to say or do to that lump that would solve a damn thing? Maybe seeing him in this pathetic state was something. Mostly, though, it felt gross and pointless being there. She was wishing she hadn't come at all when his eyes started to flutter. She was on her toes, fixing to slip out the door, when they opened.

346

Tessa saw the shadowy blue-green of them and finally found something of him that was just the same as she remembered.

"What do you want?" he said. Tessa stumbled back a couple steps and nearly fell into the chair behind her. She moved the pillow resting in that chair and sat down before her shaky legs collapsed under her. "Who are you?" he said. Tessa stared wide-eyed at him and put a hand to the sticker on her chest for a moment. Then she let that hand fall.

"I'm Tessa," she said. She took ahold of the arms of the chair, scooched a little closer, and leaned forward. "Do you remember me?" she said.

"Who are you?" Wayne said again. He put a hand to his forehead. "Why is it so bright in here?"

"I'm Tessa," she said. "Amber Jean's daughter. Do you remember me?" She thought she saw his face twitch, like he'd just bitten down on a cracked tooth.

"I'm so thirsty," he whined. There was a plastic cup with a straw sitting in it and a pitcher of water on the stand near his bed. She stood and filled the cup with water. Then she stopped herself and set the cup back down on the tray.

She leaned in close to his face. His lips were thin worms, and the corners of his mouth were gummy with pasty white gunk. His face was saggy and weak-looking, but his eyes, they were sharp. There wasn't no hiding who he was behind the old withering costume he was wearing. She was close enough to smell the cottage cheese on his breath. "Do you remember who I am?" she said. He looked away.

"I'm so thirsty," he moaned. "No one will give me a drink." He turned back to her and looked like he was about to cry. Tessa went for the water again. "Who are you?" he said as she put her hand around the plastic cup. She felt something in her snap. The cup slipped from her hand and spilled water out over the tray. Her jaw locked shut, and she reached for the pillow on the ground next to her chair.

"You know who I am," she said. "I can see straight through you, you lying sack of shit." Tessa pressed the pillow over his face and ground her teeth, forcing all her weight down. She hardly registered his hands feebly batting at her arms. She heard a kind of squeal come from under the pillow and pressed harder. Then his arms stopped stirring. His hands flopped down. One of them brushed her hip bone as it dropped to the bed. His touch jolted her, and she woke to what she was doing. She lifted the pillow away and stood in the horrifying silence of the room, watching the perfect stillness of his chest and face. Tessa saw in that stillness her life with her family fading away into a small, dark prison cell.

Wayne broke the silence when he took in a big, shuddering breath, put a hand to his face, and started to sob. Right then, there was a little knock on the door, and a woman in scrubs stepped inside the room.

"How we doing in here?" the woman said. Tessa couldn't move or speak. She was still holding the pillow tight in her first. "Are you crying again, Wayne?" the woman said, making a tutting sound and shaking her head. She walked up beside Tessa and put an arm around her shoulder. "Look, Wayne," she said. "You've got a visitor here." Wayne's sobbing got louder. The woman leaned in next to Tessa's ear. "You know, sometimes they just cry like this," she said, "for nothing. Don't let it upset you."

"Alright, Wayne," the woman said. "Let's get you put together now, dear. It's about time for lunch." The woman went to Wayne. She took his hand from his brow and wiped at his face with the used, balled-up tissue she'd pulled from the front pocket of the smock she was wearing over her scrubs. Tessa let the pillow drop from her hand and took a few steps back toward the door. Wayne let out a little sigh and sniffed.

"I'm thirsty," Wayne said.

"Alright, we'll get you a drink." The woman stood and saw Tessa moving backward.

"You leaving?" she said. Tessa nodded without taking her eyes off Wayne. "Okay, then. Say goodbye to your friend, Wayne." The woman looked at the sticker on Tessa's chest. "Tell Sarah goodbye, Wayne. She was nice enough to come visit."

"Bye-bye, Sarah," Wayne said, lifting his hand to wave. Tessa lifted her hand in reflex to wave back but let it fall to her side. She turned and went out the door instead.

She was almost to the double doors when she caught a figure moving toward her out of the corner of her eye. The woman in the wheelchair was using the heel of her foot to scoot quickly toward Tessa with the same nasty look on her face. "You wait, goddammit," the woman said. Tessa felt her stomach turn. She ran out the double doors into the dry heat and bent over in the dirt and bushes to empty her stomach.

Tessa drove dead quiet with the windows down and the taste of sick on her tongue for three hours before she stopped at a gas station. She paid inside and started the gas pump. Then she went around back to use the public restroom. Tessa locked the door behind her, turned the faucet on, and put her palms on the counter to hold herself up for a minute before she cupped her hands to splash water on her face and rinse out her mouth.

Tessa hung the gas nozzle up and got back into her car. A picture of Henry, the kids, Nathan, and Angie was taped to the dashboard. Tessa had taken the picture with the camera Nathan had brought to photograph birds that day by Lake Arrowhead. Next to that was a picture of little Alie in Tessa's arms on the day she was born.

"Give a smile, honey," Carly had said. "I know your heart is broken, but you're going to want to have a good first picture of you and that sweet baby of yours."

Tessa was staring at those pictures when a horn honked behind her. It startled her and made her jump out of her seat so that she nearly hit the roof. Tessa stuck her head out of her window and gestured to the pump across the way that was vacant on both sides. The guy in the truck behind her thought it was funny. He laughed and gave another honk. Tessa flipped him the bird and pulled up to park by the gas station mini-mart. She reached into the envelope Mel had sent her and took out the picture of them on the rock. Tessa slid that picture between the other two on the dashboard. At least they could all be together there, she thought. After a minute of looking over all their faces, Tessa felt for the can of warm Shasta Cola in the cup holder beside her. She popped the top, took a drink, and pulled back onto the road. She had just one more stop to make.

Tessa stepped outside her car. She looked around the empty little dirt parking lot of the cemetery where her mama was laid to rest. It would be summer for a while longer yet, but today it felt like the season was changing. The heat wave had finally broke earlier that week. It wasn't more than eighty-five degrees outside.

The sky was blue and marked with those Cool Whip–looking clouds Tessa loved and believed belonged to the sky above Perris alone. Tessa stood with her arms at her side, palms facing out. She closed her eyes a second and felt the sunshine and let the Santa Ana winds tangle up her hair and billow out her shirt. She'd always liked the wind. As a kid, she'd run up to meet the wind on the hill near Wayne's house. She'd close her eyes, put her arms out, and fall back. Tessa could swear she remembered that wind on the hill catching her. It would hold her suspended midfall like that in a gentle, soothing embrace.

Tessa opened her eyes and walked down the unkempt rows of headstones until she got to the one her mama was buried under. Tessa slipped her mama's purse off her shoulder and sat down on the pokey crabgrass in front of her mama's concrete plaque.

"Well, Mama, here we are," she said and brushed away the dead and dried weeds that had blown over and covered part of her mama's name. "I brought you something." She pulled the jewelry box wrapped in a T-shirt out of her purse and gently unfolded it. She held it in her hands a second and then put it on the concrete next to her mama's name. Tessa tucked her legs under her and sat back on her heels with her hands folded in her lap.

"Remember this? I don't know where you got it. I should have asked when I had the chance. I remember it seemed special to you somehow, though. It was always sitting there on your nightstand at Wayne's house. And you took it with you when you left, so it must have meant something to you." Tessa wiped the hair out of her face, put her nose in the direction of the sun, and closed her eyes again for a moment. She opened them slowly and turned back to her mama's grave.

"You know what, Mama? This weather, the sun feeling like it

does just now, reminds me of this perfect day we had together. I wonder if you remember it. I was maybe six or seven. It had been such a rainy winter that year there was a creek running through our property. You remember that creek that went through the drainpipe under Post Road and came out the other side in that little ravine in the backyard? I can't remember that creek ever running except for that year. That spring it did, though.

"This one day you were feeling good. You woke up like there was nothing weighing you down or giving you the jitters. You pulled a box of pancake mix that I didn't know we had from the back of the cupboard, and you made us pancakes for breakfast after never touching that stove once in all the years I had known you. It was like some fairy godmother had come in the night and connected the loose wires in your brain or undone whatever had happened to you that made you seem so nervous and beat down all the time.

"We went to that creek with a blanket and basket with fruit juice boxes and snacks inside. You were wearing your frayed jean shorts and this soft yellow shirt that I loved the feel of so much. I still think you must be the most beautiful woman who ever lived. I can see you standing there by the creek now with your long, toned legs, heart-shaped face, full lips, and perfectly freckled nose.

"We put bent blades of grass into the creek and watched them float away from us one after another. We said they were our little boats in our little stream. I stepped into the water and felt the refreshing cool of it on my feet and ankles. You walked right in and stood next to me with your hands on your hips, smiling like it was no big deal. You and me looked for arrowheads under the stream's glittering surface. When we had enough of the water, we went back to our blanket in the grass. I remember falling asleep in the sun with my head resting on your lap. Life had never felt so perfect.

"You woke up just as heartwrecked and scattered as ever the very next day. It wasn't too long after that you left for good. In the years since, I've often wondered if you knew you were leaving already and you were just pretending to be happy and feeling good. I've wondered if that perfect day was a kind of going-away gift. I hope it wasn't that, Mama. I hope you woke up feeling as light and beautiful as you looked that day. I hope the laughs we had and you letting me fall asleep on your lap in the grass like that was real and felt as sublime and natural for you as it did for me. I wouldn't say this to no one but you, Mama, but you know, in some ways I feel that just might have been the best day of my life. I hope it was like that for you."

Tessa chewed on her cheek some wondering over what she wanted to say next. She thought to talk about how she'd seen Reggie's wife and Wayne that day, but she realized it wasn't them she was needing to talk about with her mama. Reggie and Wayne had squandered enough of her and her mama's time together. There was something else she was needing to say. Tessa felt her throat grab and her eyes start to water.

"You and me, we didn't have it so easy, did we, Mama?" Tessa blinked, and tears rolled down her cheeks. She wiped at them with her sleeve and nodded some. "Now that I've come to understand how complicated and painful life can be, I don't hold nothing against you. Not even your leaving. I don't blame you one bit, because now I believe in my heart you must have been trying your best in your own way. I think mamas are mostly always trying their best. It just looks different depending on the cards they are dealt and the hurt they are holding."

Tessa took the purse up in her lap. "I was thinking of leaving this here with you too, but I've decided to hold on to it, Mama. I think I'd like a little something of yours to carry around with me." Tessa stood and brushed the dead grass from her pants.

Standing there, getting ready to leave, she thought of something Angie had told her the day after Nathan's funeral. They were in Angie's kitchen together cleaning up. The baby had started to cry in the other room. Tessa was just about to go check on her when Angie put a hand on Tessa's shoulder and said she'd do it.

"Angie, you must be dead tired," Tessa had said. "Let me get her."

Angie had turned to her then. "Honey, tired ain't something women like you and me get to be. Looking after is what I was built for. Friends, family, babies—they are given to us to love and care for. Yesterday, when that man was giving Nathan's eulogy, it come to me. I've always known it, I guess, but just never saw things so crystal clear before. People are always waiting on some God to reward or punish them for the good or bad they do in life, but there's no big guy upstairs keeping score. Each other is the whole of what we've got. People are there for us to love. It ain't the other way around. It's the greatest and most excruciating gift of life."

Tessa thought of the ones in her life that she had loved best. She had spent the darkest and brightest moments of her life asking God for help or begging God for the sweetness to last. She knew then that Angie was right, that those she'd loved had always been her saving grace. That there was no protector in the sky. There was no way to prevent heartbreak or change the things that had already happened. There was just the simple act of living, of finding those to love during the short and precious time you had on earth. That was the whole heaven and hell of it.

"I'll see you next time, Mama," Tessa said. She walked back down the row of concrete plaques and out the cemetery's old iron gate. She stopped at her car and turned her back to a gust of dust and dry air. She let her keys slip from her fingers and spread her arms out wide and thought to lean back to see if the winds of Perris, California, would catch her again, but she didn't let herself fall. Tessa figured there was someone out there that needed that wind to hold them up more than she did now. She didn't want to be greedy and take up any more of its grace. It had been there for her when she'd needed it most. Tessa opened her eyes and felt at her center the bittersweetness of parting with a dear friend. She would let the memory of that wind on the hill carry her home to her family instead.

ACKNOWLEDGMENTS

Profound thanks to the following:

My siblings—Rebecca, Laura, Tammy, Garren, Erik, and Guy. My mother, Shirley; father, Greg; stepmother, Cindy; nephews, Harold and Louvel; niece, Esmé; Grandma Roath; and my fairy godmother, Marilyn.

My agent, Stephanie Cabot, and editor, John Burnham Schwartz. Thank you for your guidance and for championing my work.

Helen Rouner, Juliana Kiyan, Lauren Lauzon, Nicole Celli, Lauren Morgan Whitticom, and the entire team at Penguin Random House.

Early readers, friends, and mentors who supported me and this book—Molly Moriarty, Mary Berner, Susan Straight, Salvador Plascencia, Jacinda Townsend, Matt Walsh, Alicia Carroll, Hannah Schwadron, Jorge Sanchez, Mario Ortiz, Jameelah Johnson, Ellen Moe, Naomi Williams, Greg Glazner, Kathleen Allen, Ryan Row, Julie Meiser, Franny Echeverria, Nathaniel D. Anderson, Jim Knous, Damian and Michelle Richardson, Sarah Lamb, Alysia and Dani Lewis, Scott Lamb, John Lawley, and Candice Woodard.